Sorcerer Hunters

Book 5

Sorcerer Hunters

Book 5

by Satoru Akahori & Ray Omishi

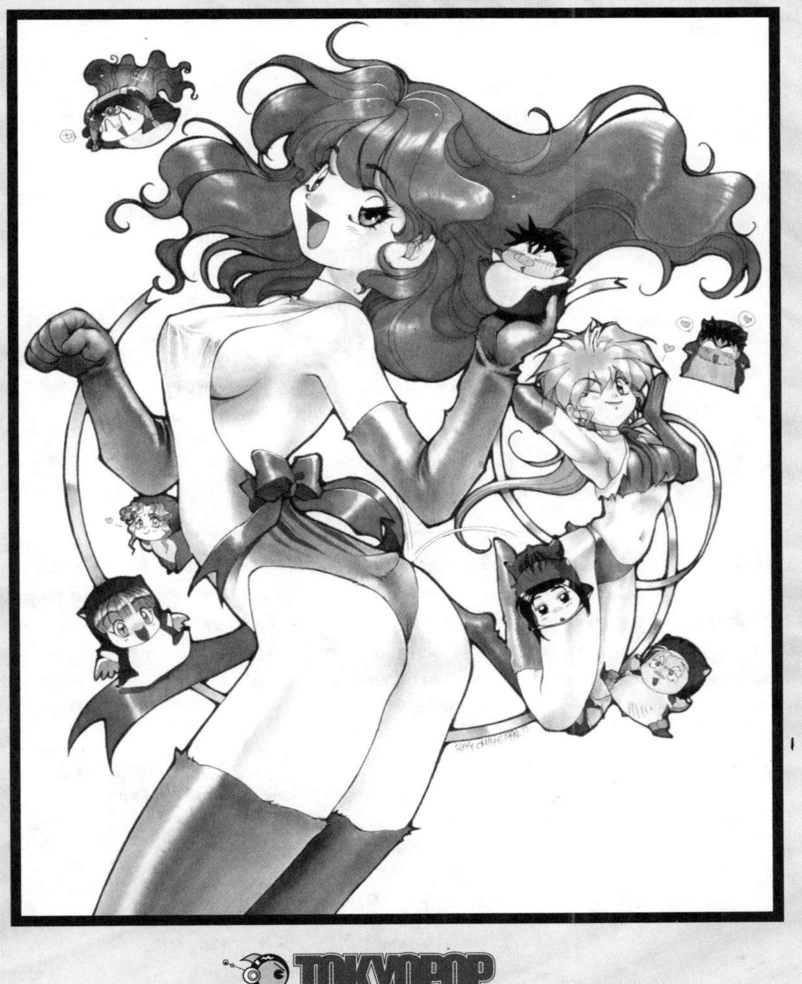

TOKYOPOP Manga

TOKYOPOP Presents
Sorcerer Hunters 5 by Satoru Akahori & Ray Omishi
TOKYOPOP is a registered trademark and
TOKYOPOP Manga is a trademark of Mixx Entertainment, Inc.
ISBN: 1-892213-92-3
First Printing August 2001

| 10 | 9 | 8 | 7 | 6 | 5 | 4 | 3 | 2 | 1 |

Translator - Anita Sengupta. Retouch Artists - Wilbert Lacuna, Romualdo Viray II.
Graphic Assistant - Dao Sirivisal, Graphic Designer - Akemi Imafuku.
Associate Editor - Katherine Kim. Editor - Michael Schuster. Senior Editor - Jake Forbes.
Production Manager - Fred Lui.

Email: editor@Press.TOKYOPOP.com
Come visit us at www.TOKYOPOP.com.

TOKYOPOP
Los Angeles - Tokyo

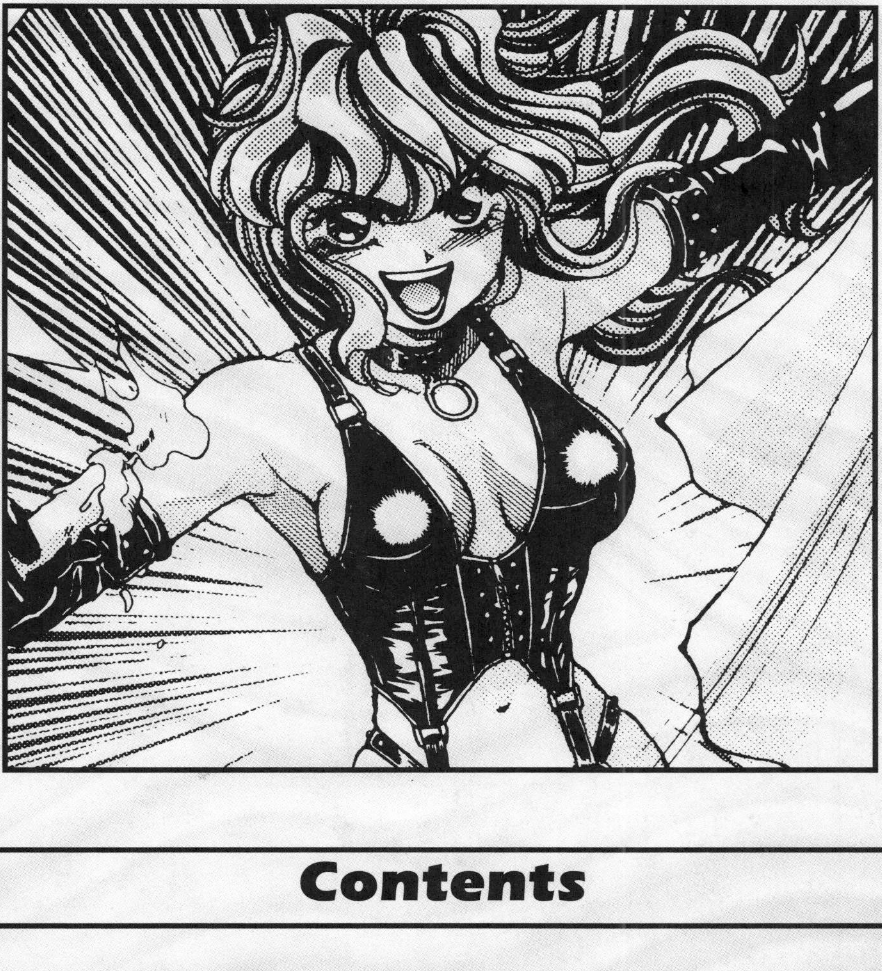

Contents

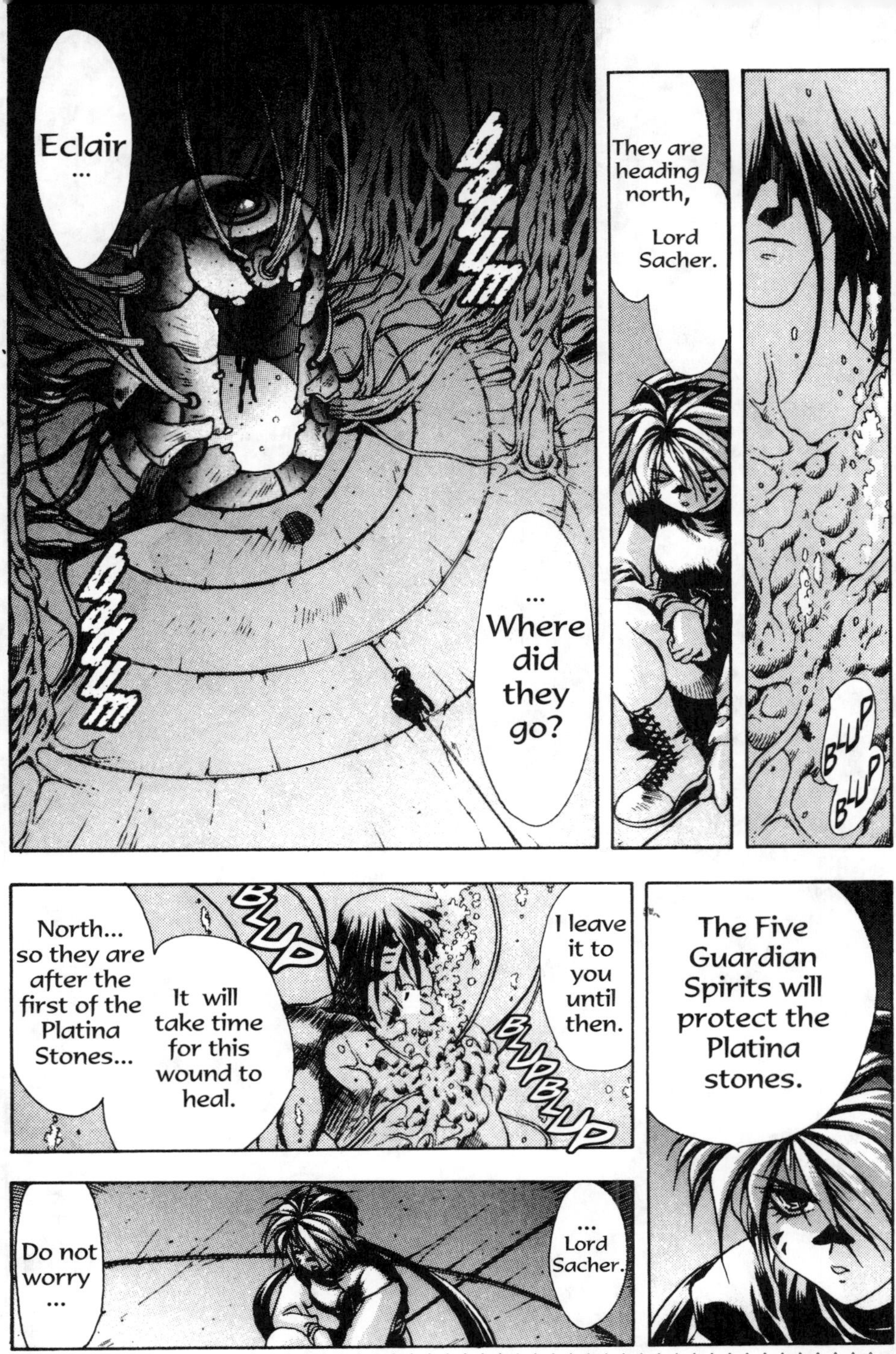
Eclair ...
badum
... Where did they go?
badum
They are heading north, Lord Sacher.
BLUP BLUP
North... so they are after the first of the Platina Stones...
BLUP
It will take time for this wound to heal.
I leave it to you until then.
BLUBLUP
The Five Guardian Spirits will protect the Platina stones.
Do not worry ...
... Lord Sacher.

The Zelkova House in the Autumn Rain (Part 1)

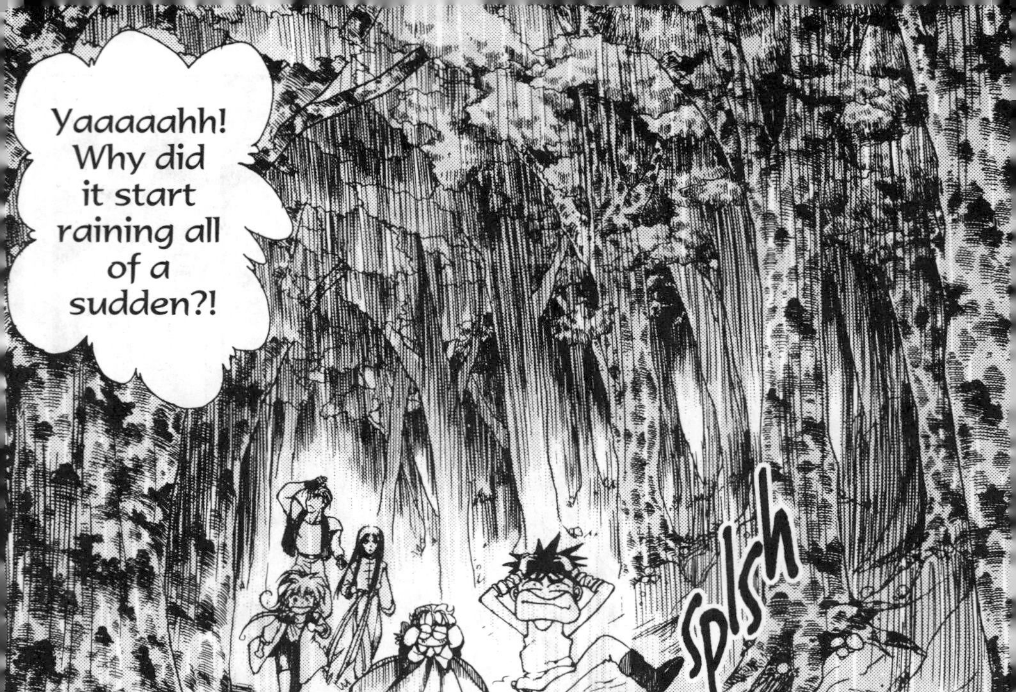
Yaaaaahh! Why did it start raining all of a sudden?!
splsh

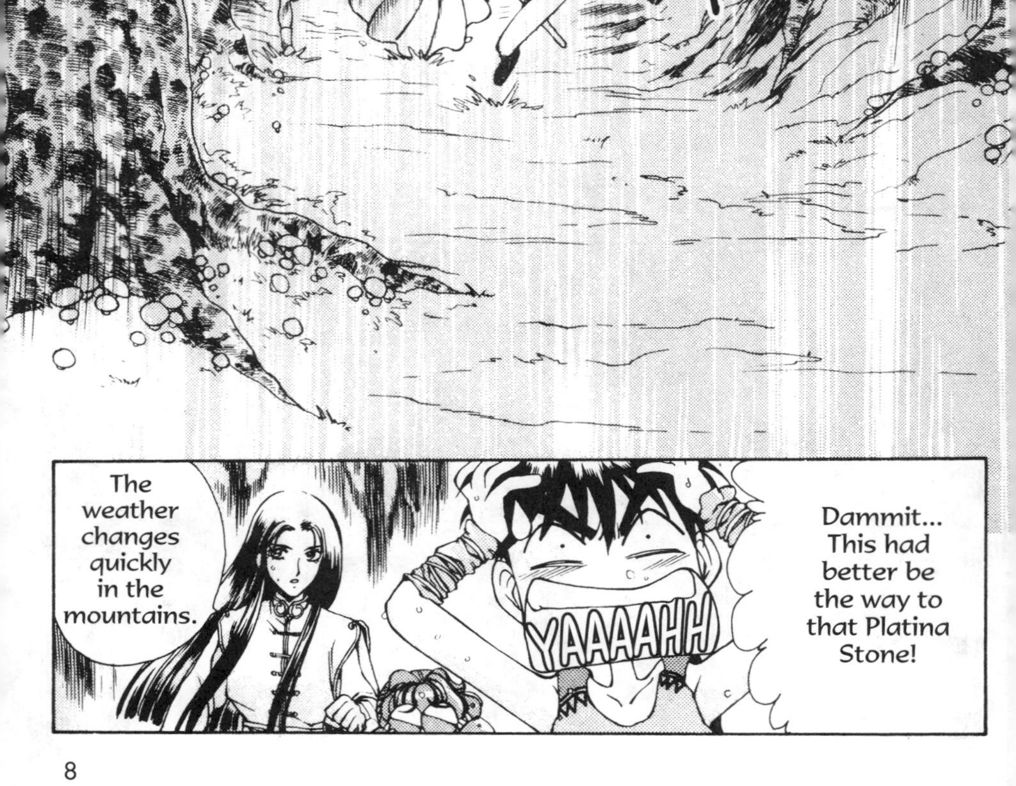
Dammit... This had better be the way to that Platina Stone!
YAAAAHH
The weather changes quickly in the mountains.

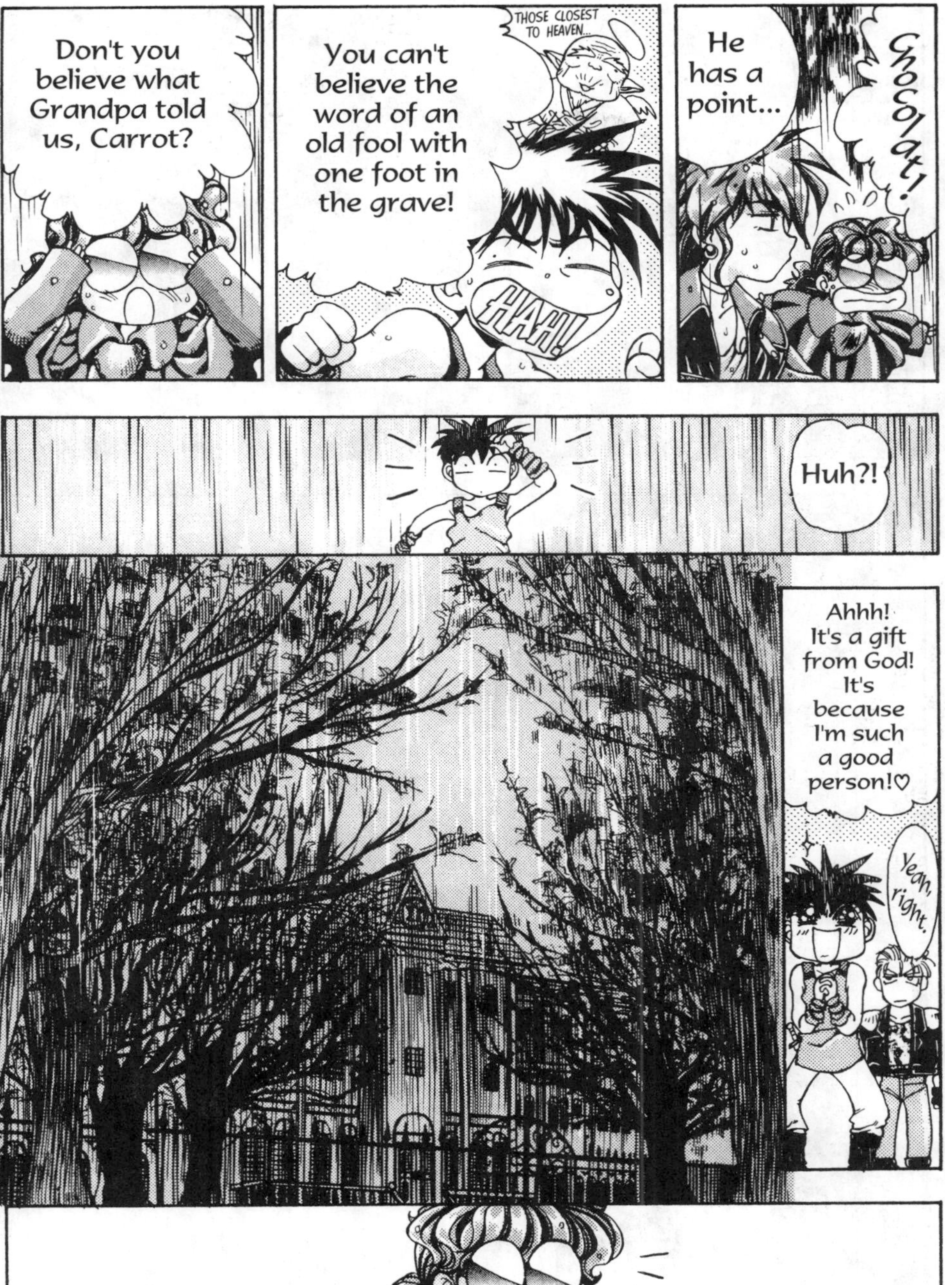

Don't you believe what Grandpa told us, Carrot?
You can't believe the word of an old fool with one foot in the grave!
HAH!
THOSE CLOSEST TO HEAVEN...
He has a point...
Chocolat!
Huh?!
Ahhh! It's a gift from God! It's because I'm such a good person!♡
Yeah, right.

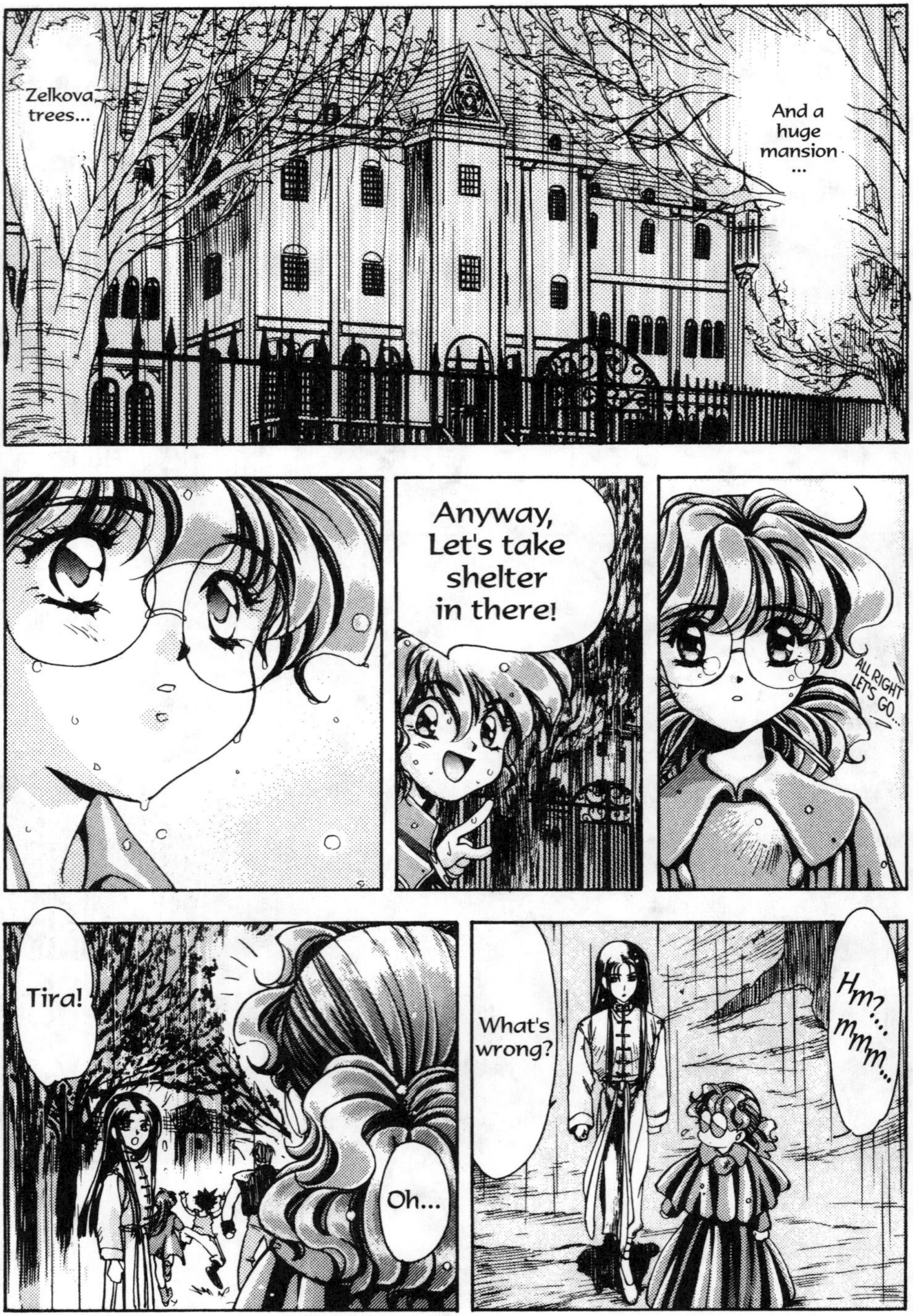
Zelkova trees...
And a huge mansion ...
Anyway, Let's take shelter in there!
ALL RIGHT LET'S GO...
Tira!
Oh...
What's wrong?
Hm?... mmm...

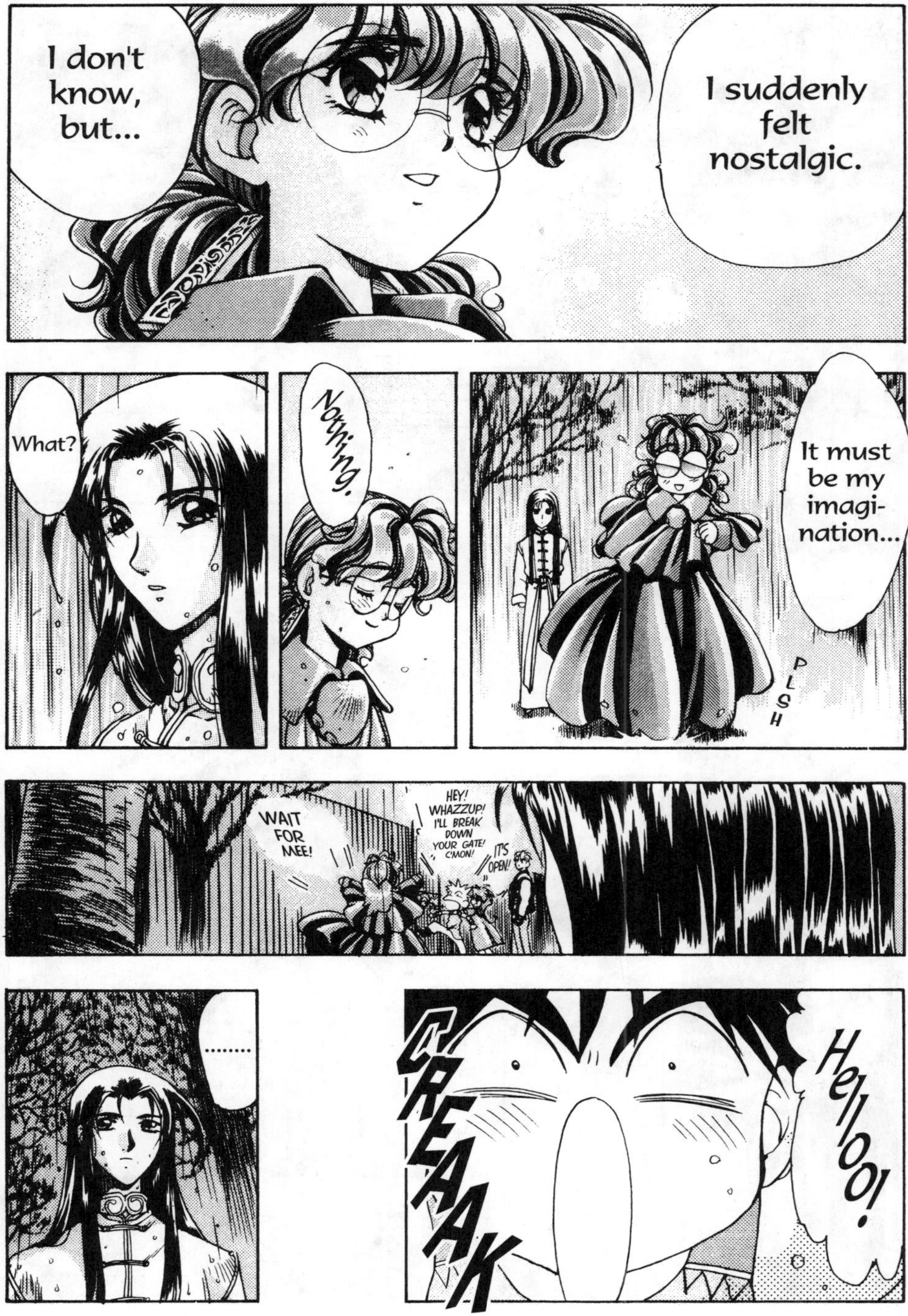
I don't know, but...
I suddenly felt nostalgic.
What?
Nothing.
It must be my imagination...
PLSH
WAIT FOR MEE!
HEY! WHAZZUP! I'LL BREAK DOWN YOUR GATE! C'MON!
IT'S OPEN!
....
CREAAAK
Helloo!

Anyone home?

STARE

What's wrong, Gateau?

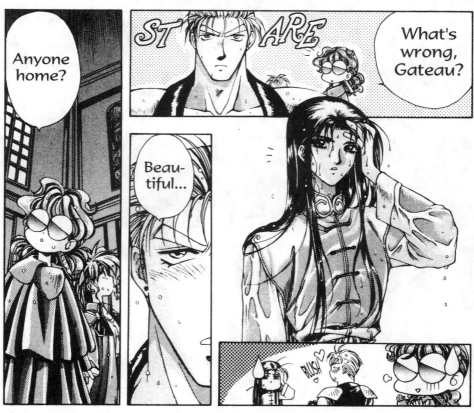

Beau-tiful...

BLUSH

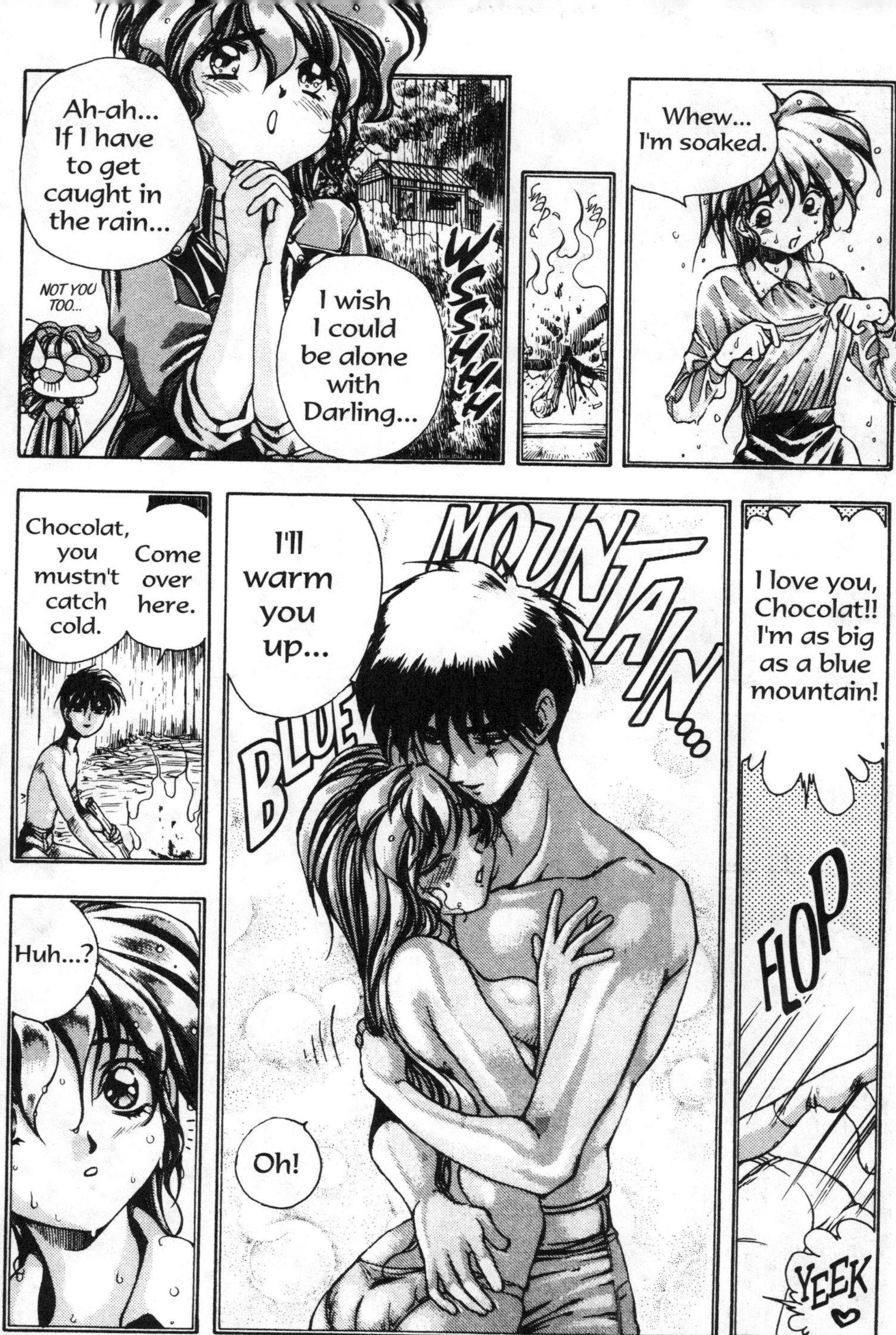
Ah-ah... If I have to get caught in the rain...
NOT YOU TOO...
I wish I could be alone with Darling...
WSSHHHH
snap~ snap
Whew... I'm soaked.
Chocolat, you mustn't catch cold.
Come over here.
Huh...?
I'll warm you up...
MOUNTAIN...
BLUE
Oh!
WHERE ARE YOUR CLOTHES...?
I love you, Chocolat!! I'm as big as a blue mountain!
FLOP
YEEK

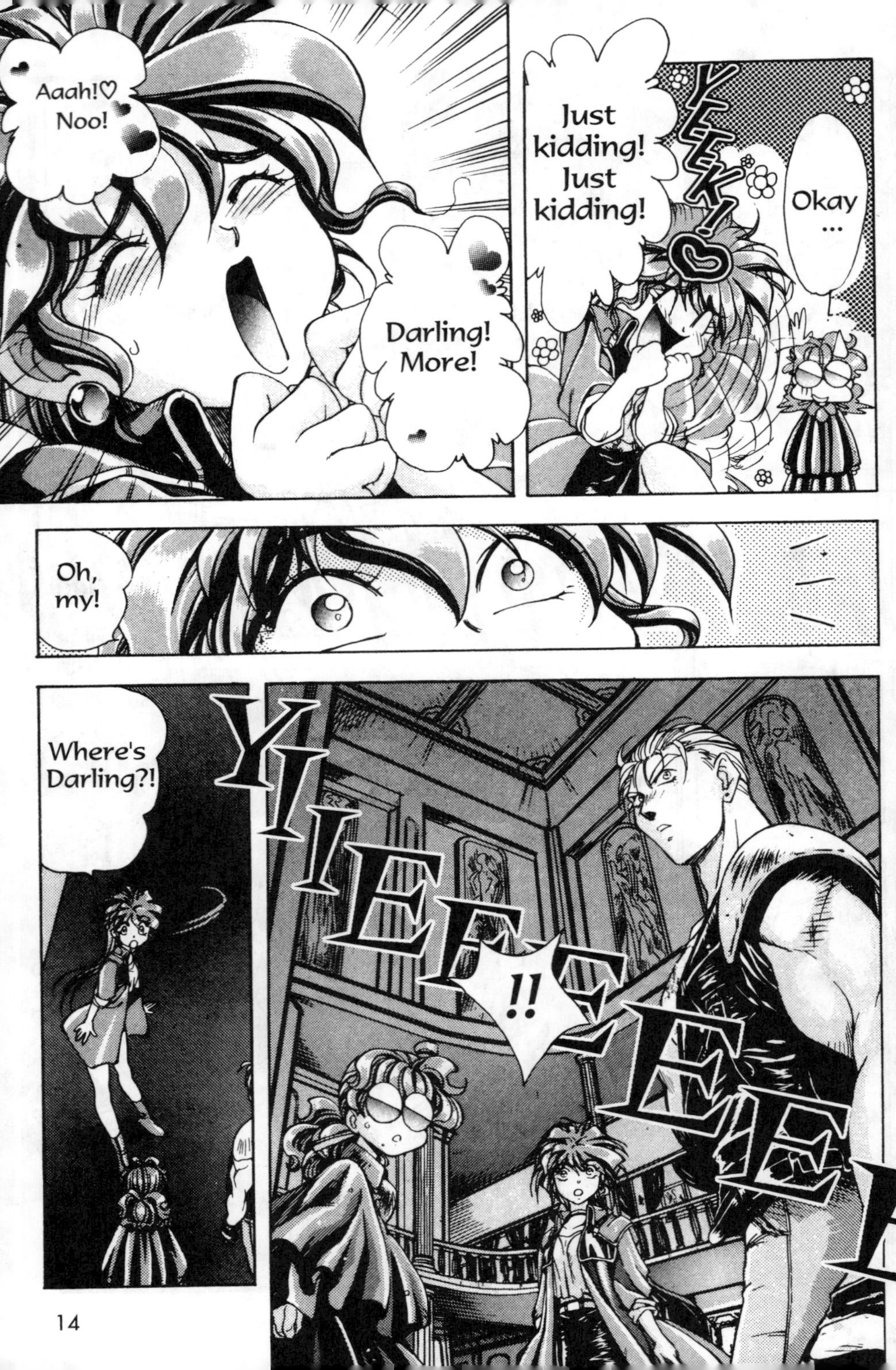
Aaah!♡ Noo!
Darling! More!
Just kidding! Just kidding!
YEEK!♡
Okay ...
Oh, my!
Where's Darling?!
YIEEEEE!
!!

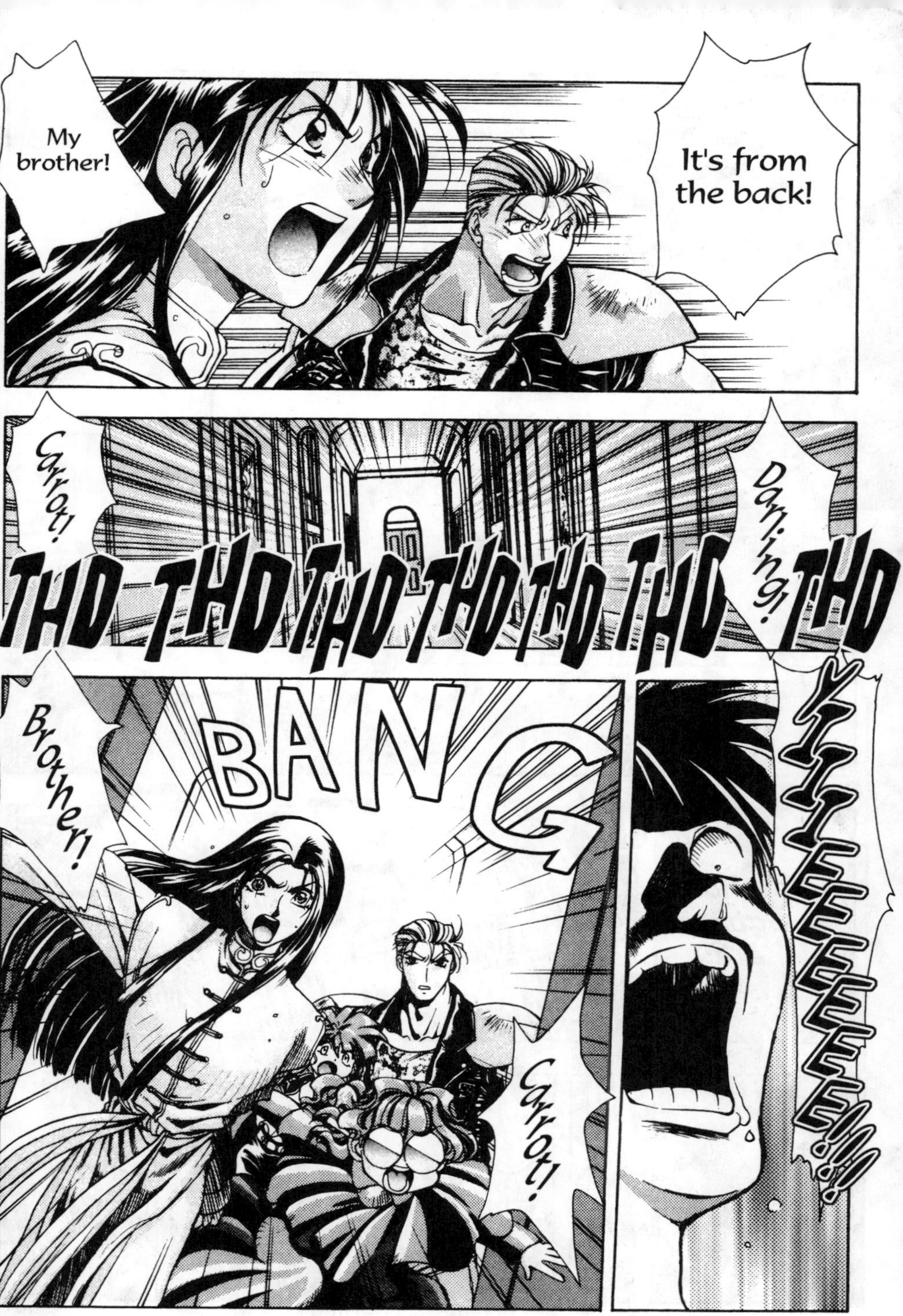
It's from the back!
My brother!
Darling!
Carrot!
THD THD THD THD THD THD THD
YIIIEEEEEEE!!!
Carrot!
BANG
Brother!

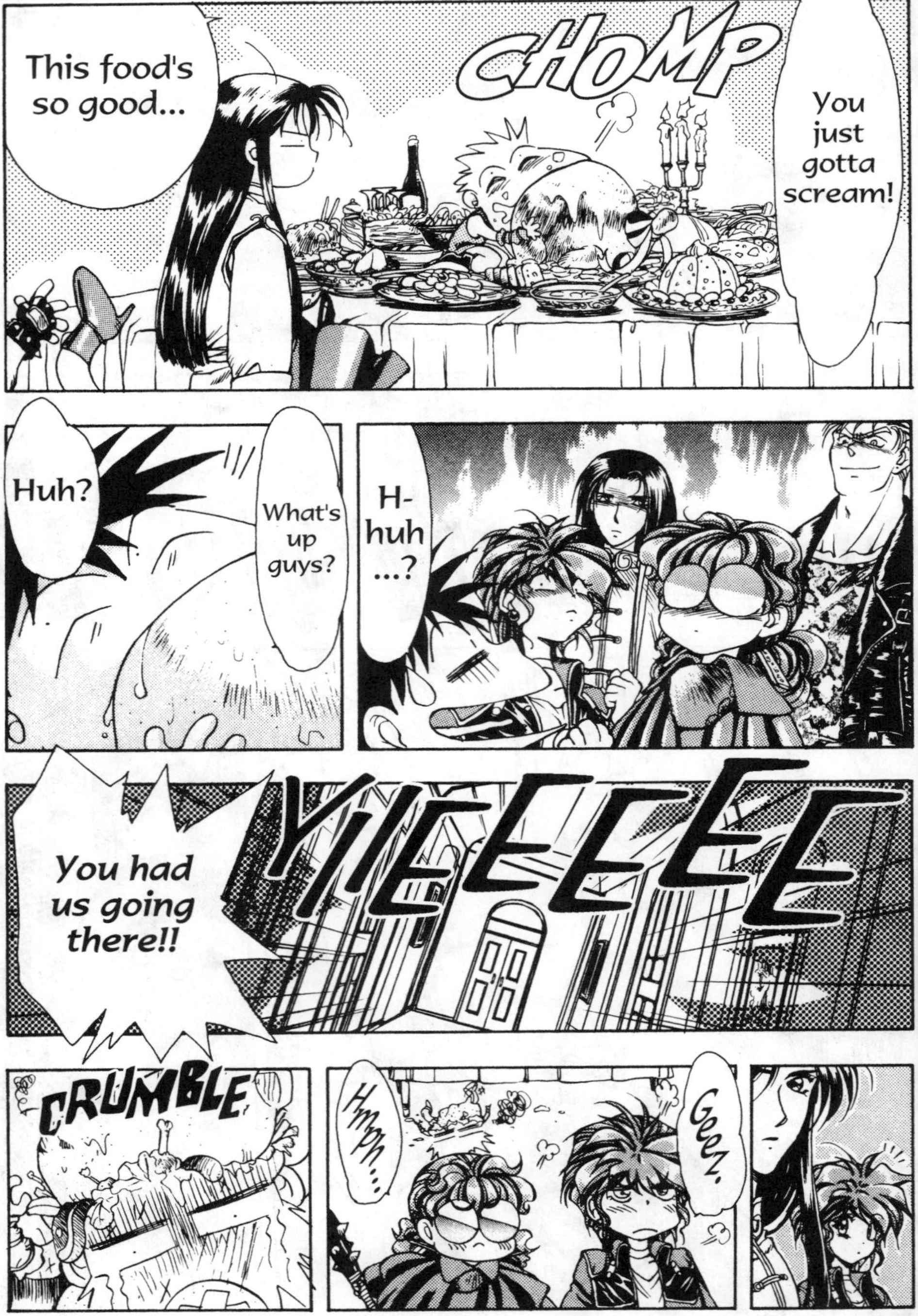
You just gotta scream!
CHOMP
This food's so good...
H-huh...?
What's up guys?
Huh?
YIEEEEE
You had us going there!!
Geez.
Hmph...
CRUMBLE

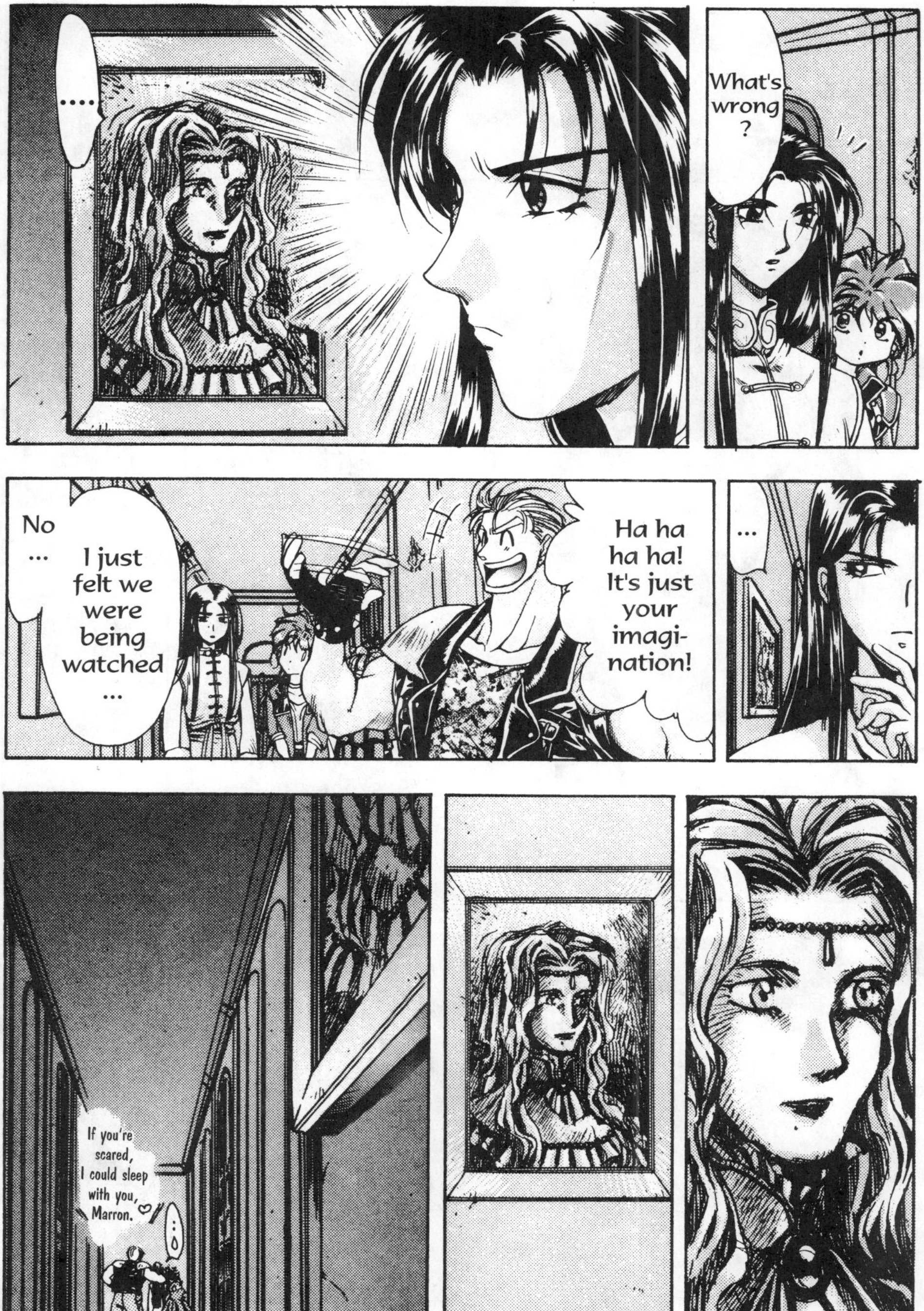
....
What's wrong?
No ... I just felt we were being watched ...
Ha ha ha ha! It's just your imagination!
...
If you're scared, I could sleep with you, Marron. ♡
...

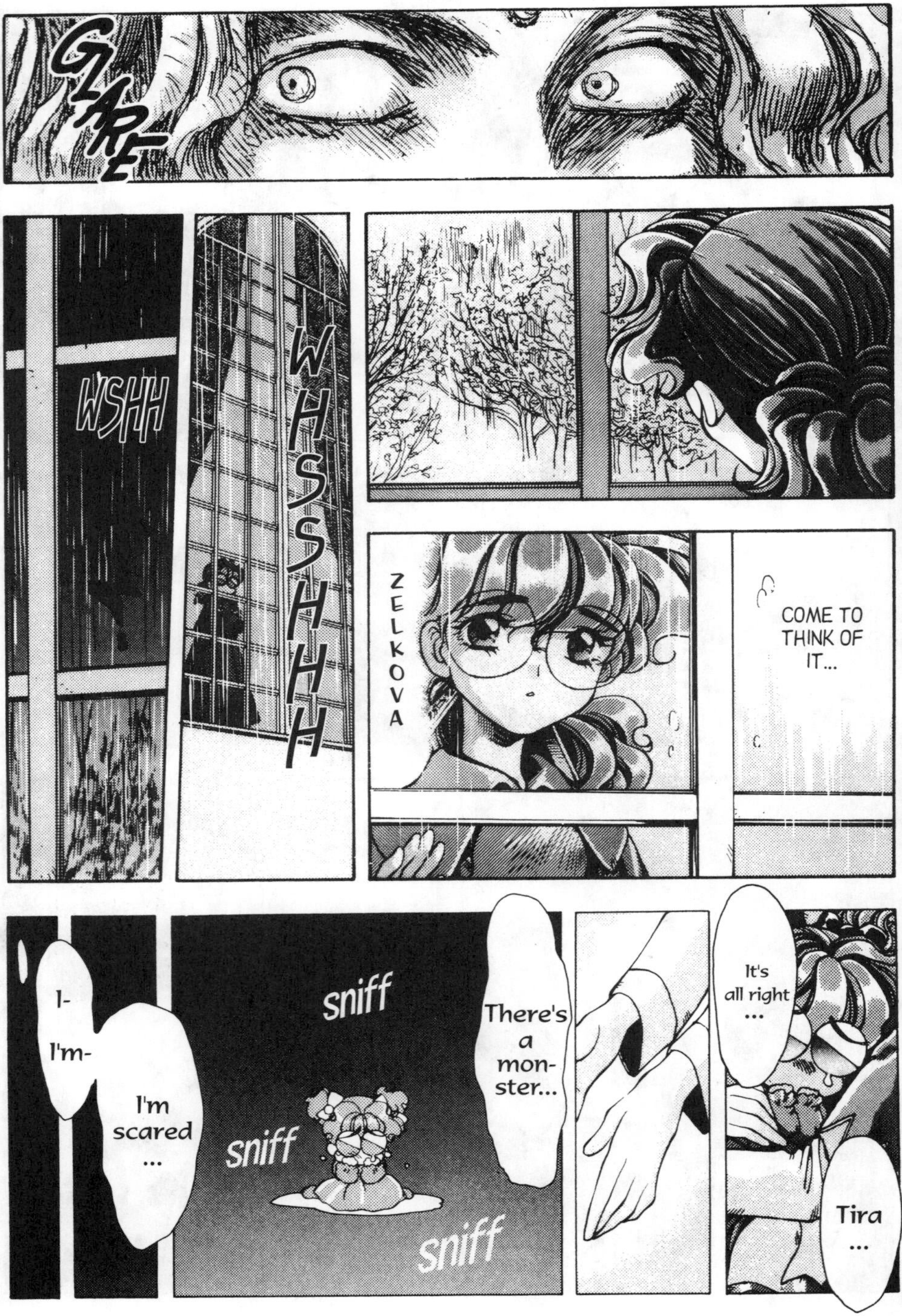
GLARE
COME TO THINK OF IT...
ZELKOVA
WHSSHHH
WSHH
It's all right ...
Tira ...
There's a monster...
sniff
sniff
sniff
I-
I'm-
I'm scared ...

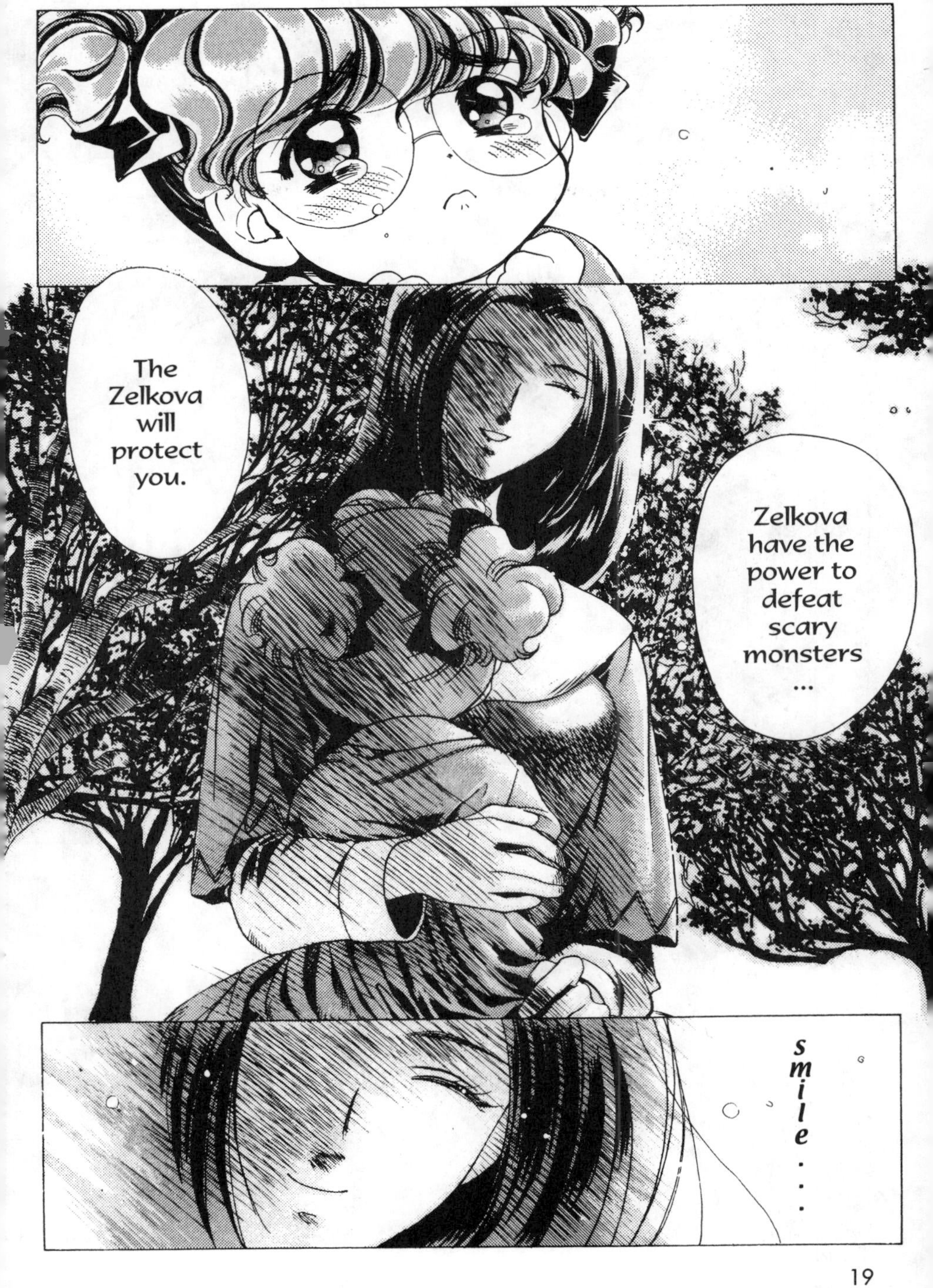
Zelkova have the power to defeat scary monsters ...
The Zelkova will protect you.
smile . . .

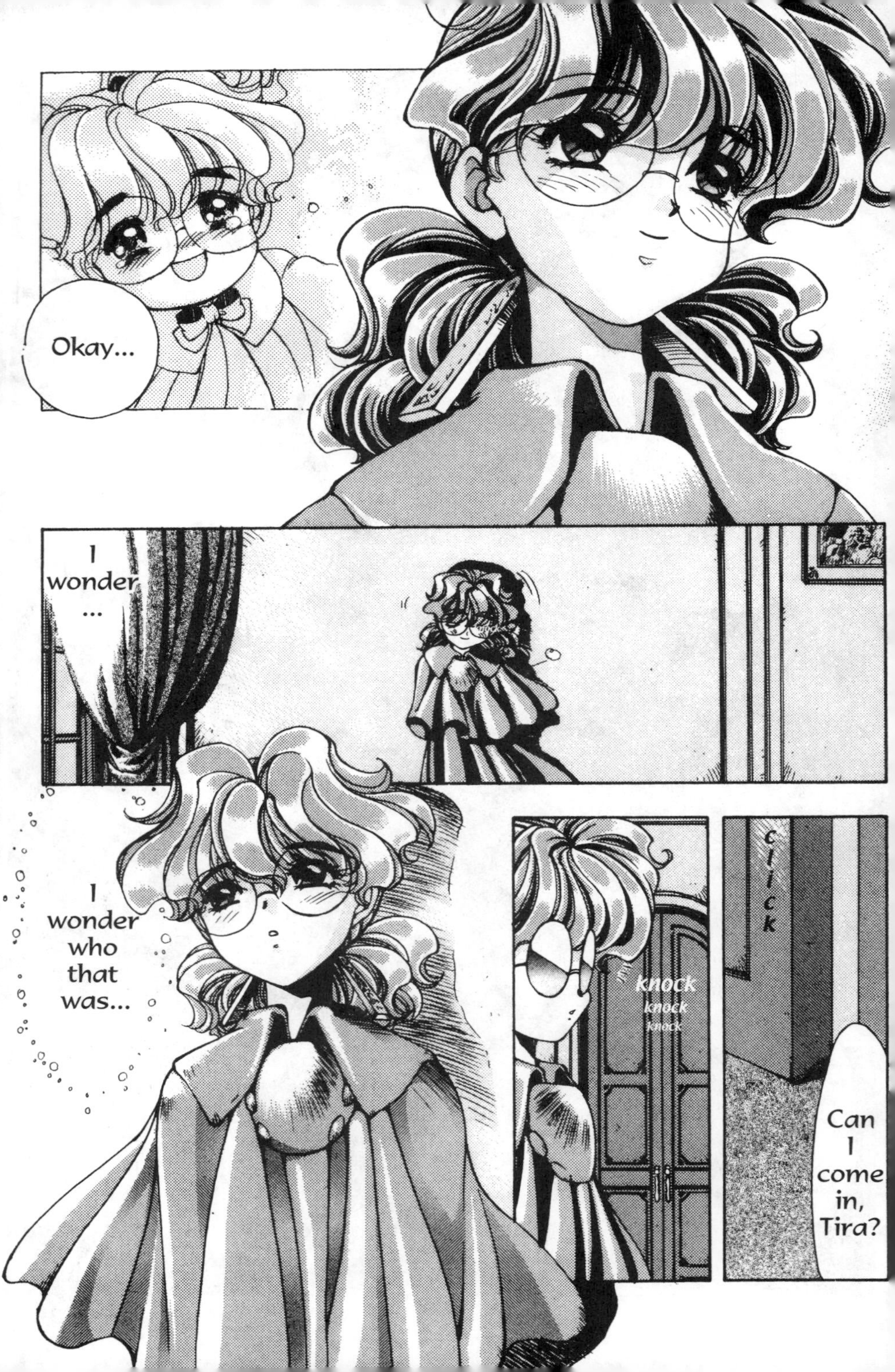
Okay...
I wonder ...
I wonder who that was...
knock knock knock
click
Can I come in, Tira?

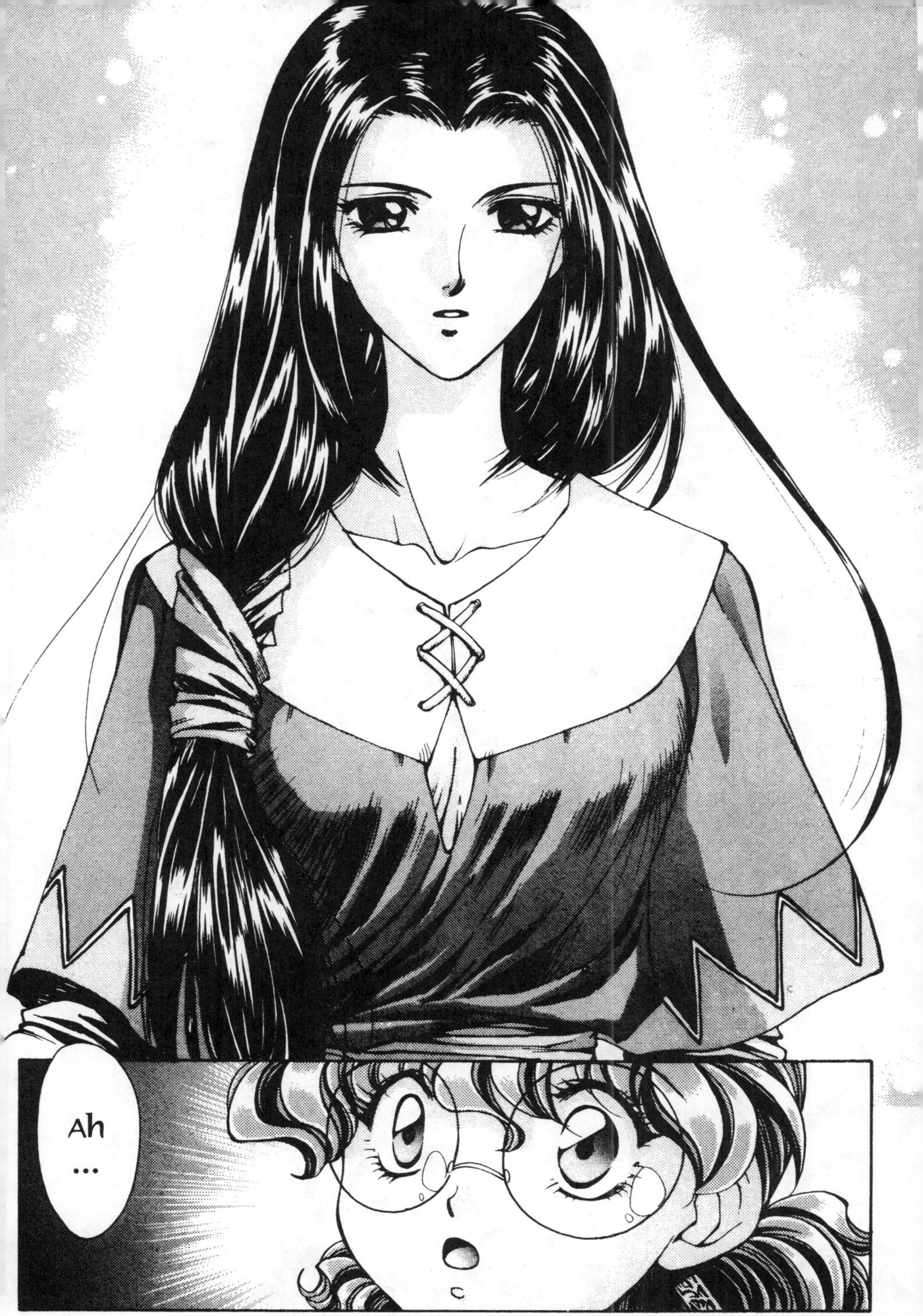
Ah
...

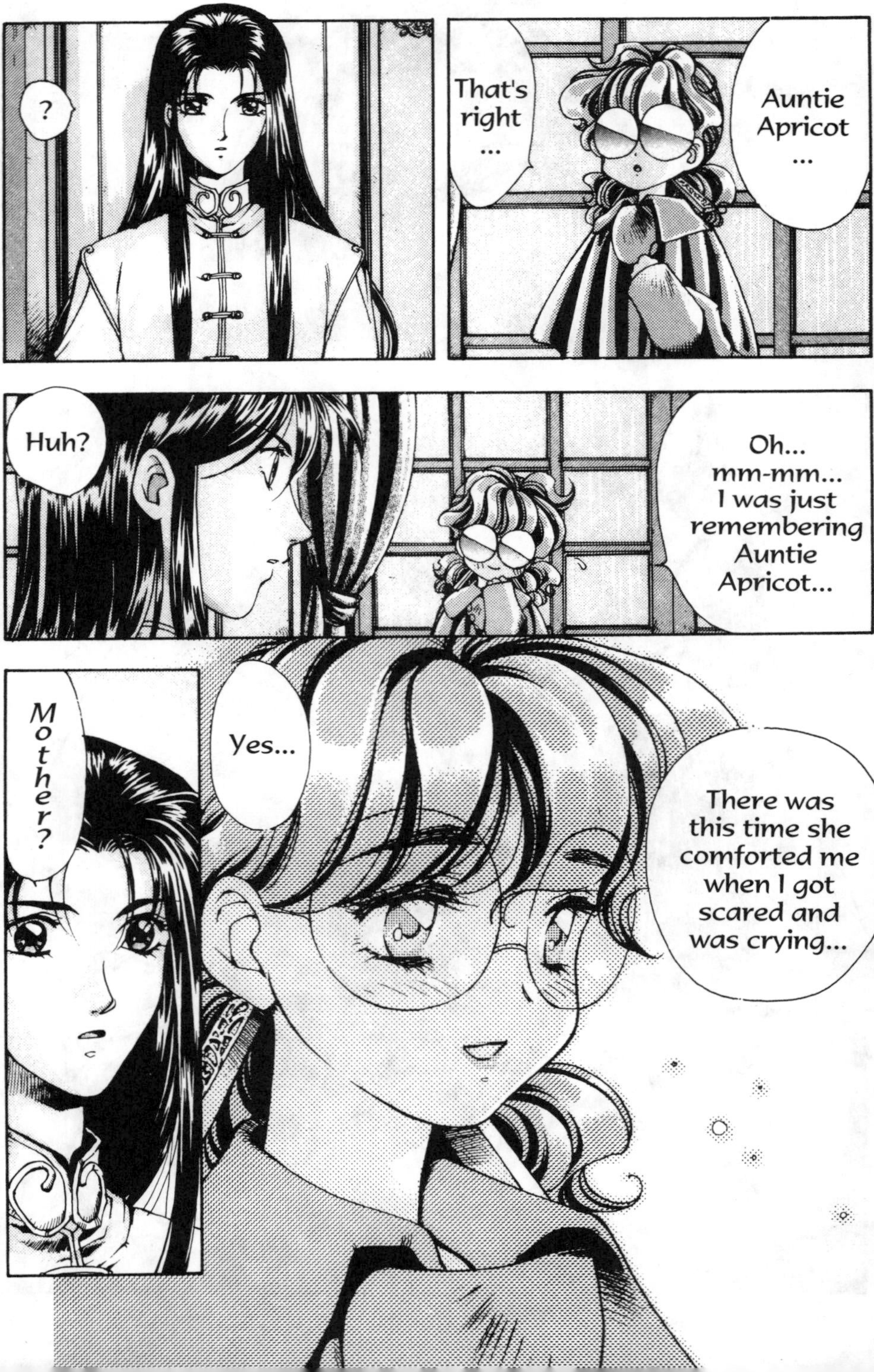
Auntie Apricot ...
That's right ...
?
Huh?
Oh... mm-mm... I was just remembering Auntie Apricot...
Mother?
Yes...
There was this time she comforted me when I got scared and was crying...

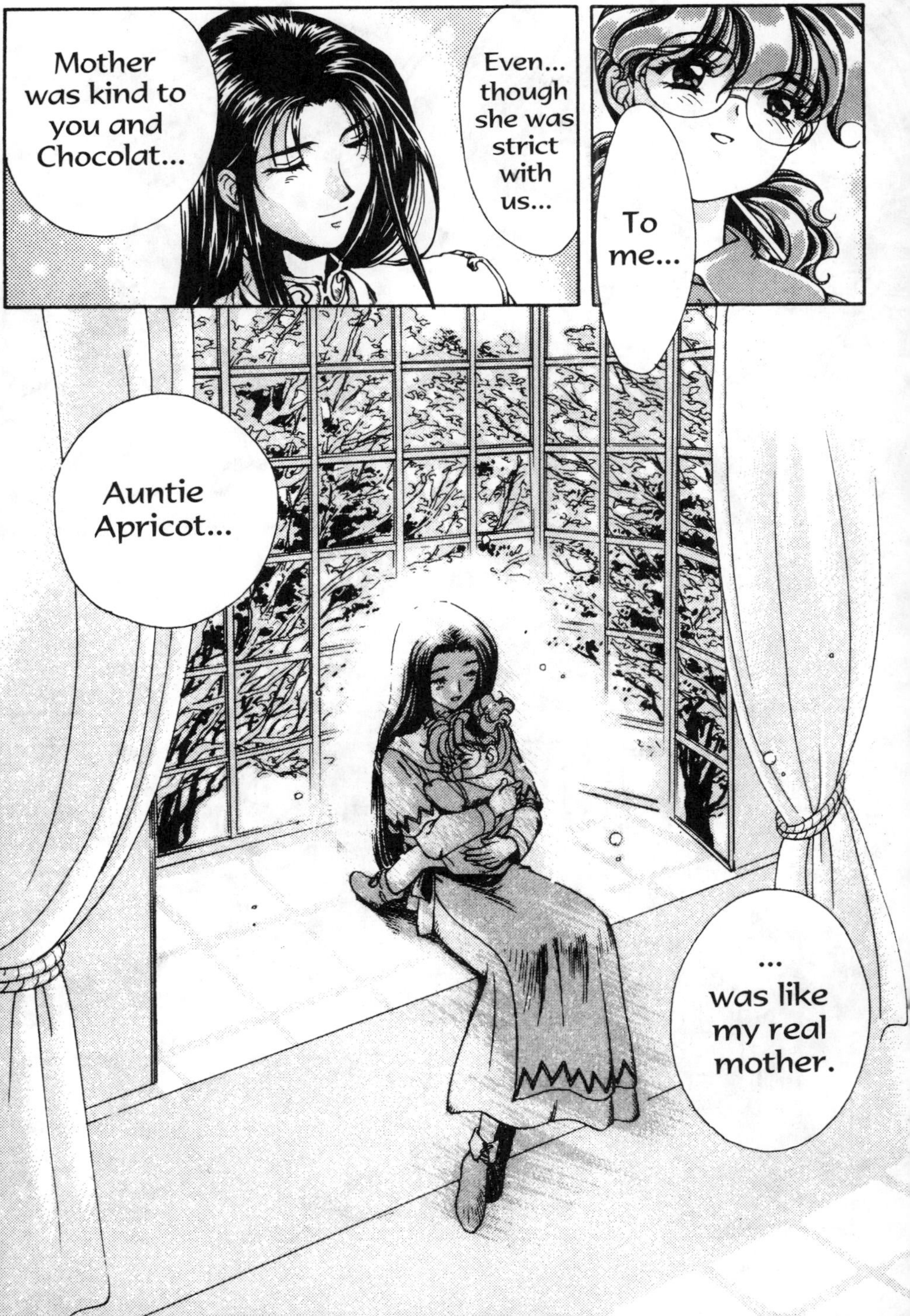
Mother was kind to you and Chocolat...
Even... though she was strict with us...
To me...
Auntie Apricot...
... was like my real mother.

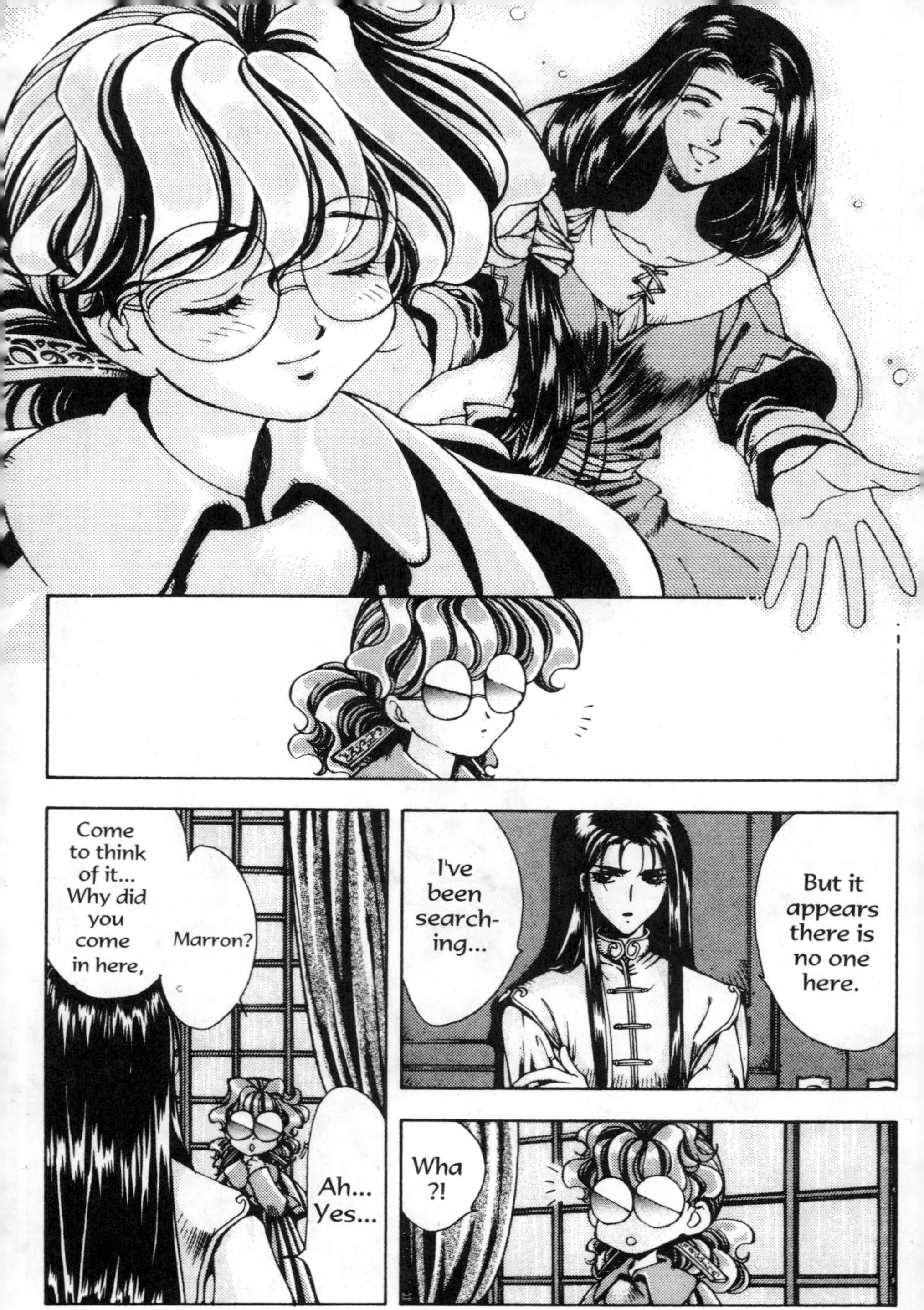
I've been search-ing...
But it appears there is no one here.
Wha ?!
Come to think of it... Why did you come in here,
Marron?
Ah... Yes...

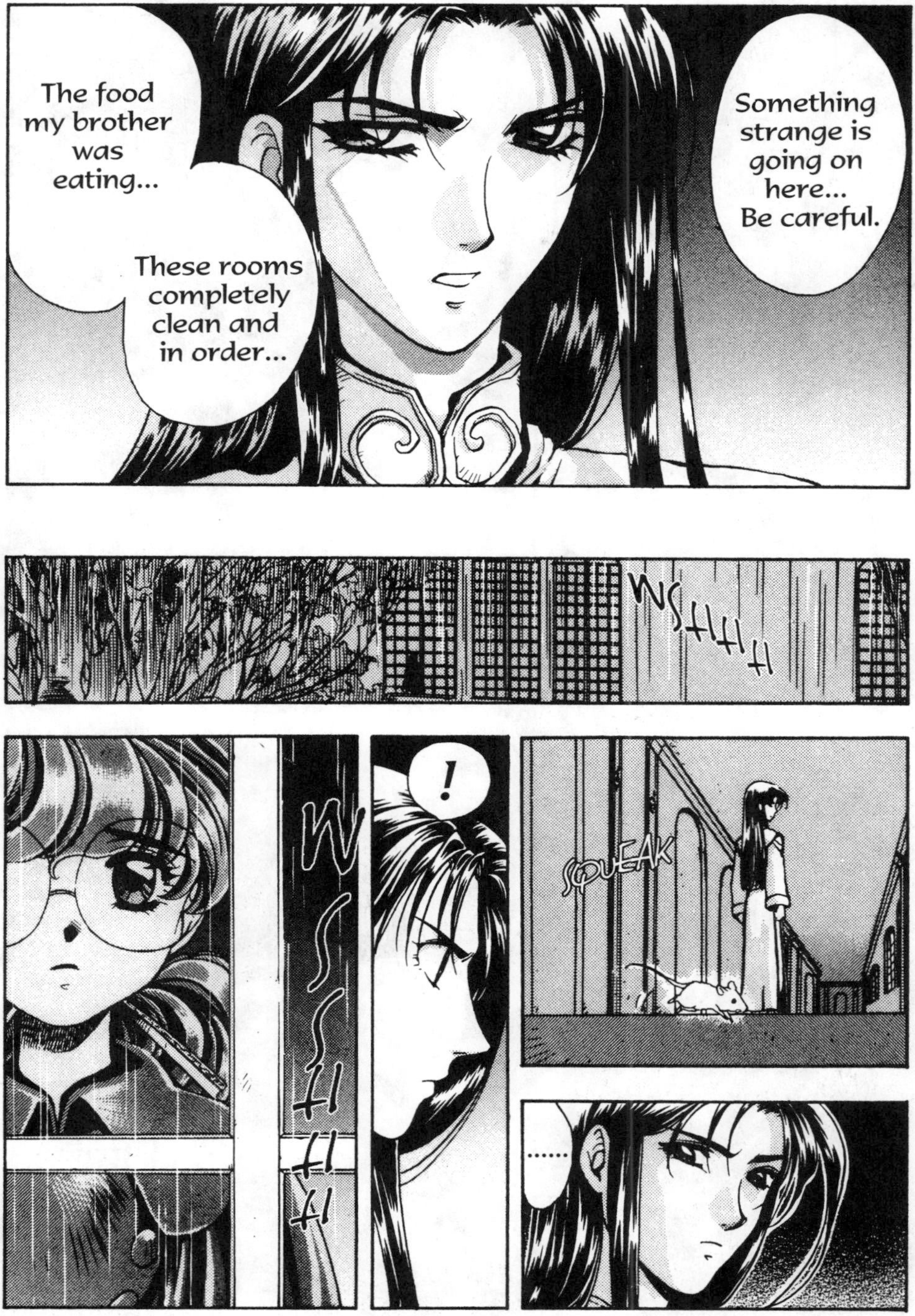
The food my brother was eating...
These rooms completely clean and in order...
Something strange is going on here... Be careful.
!
SQUEAK
......

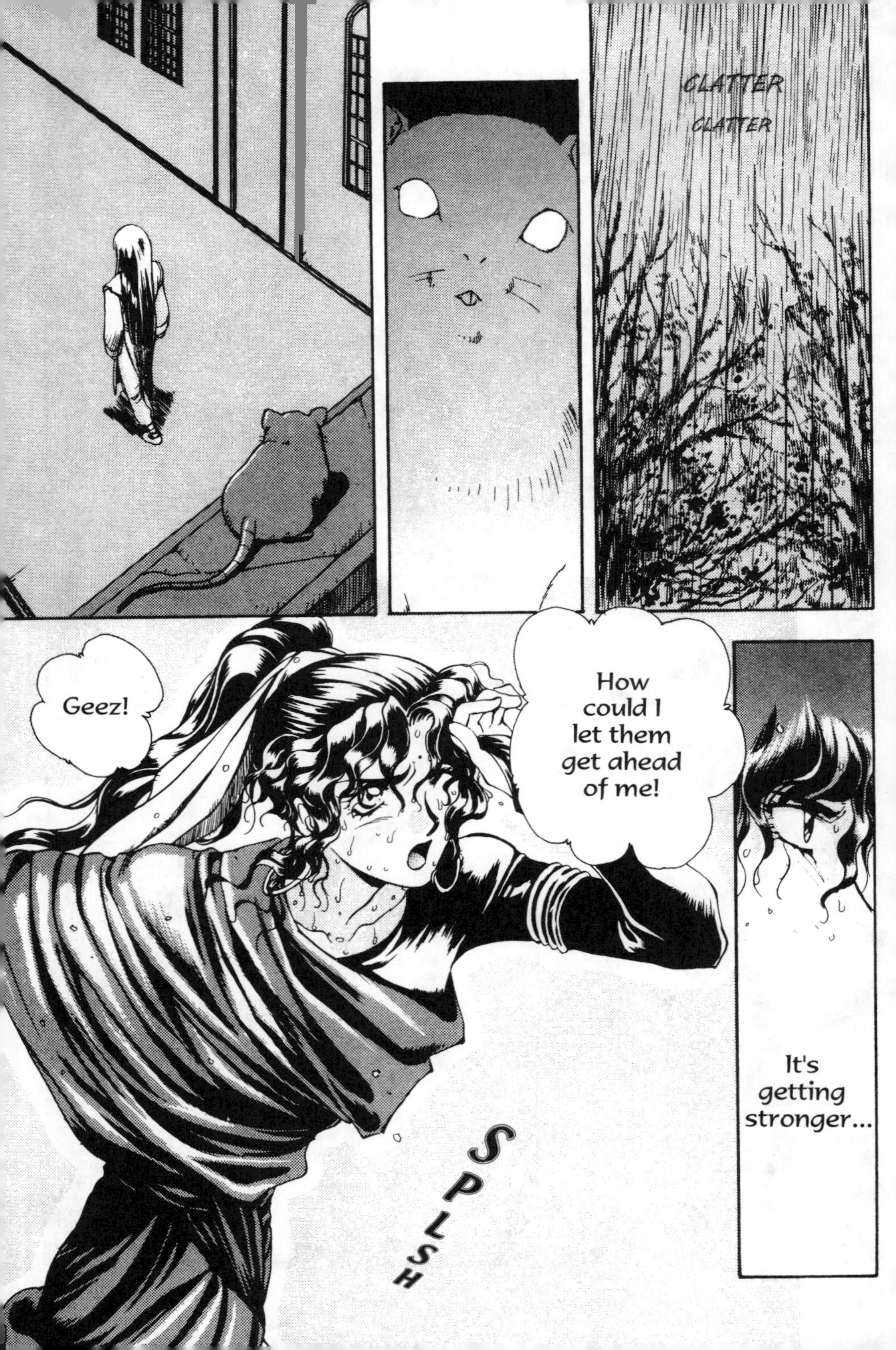
CLATTER
CLATTER
It's getting stronger...
How could I let them get ahead of me!
Geez!
SPLSH

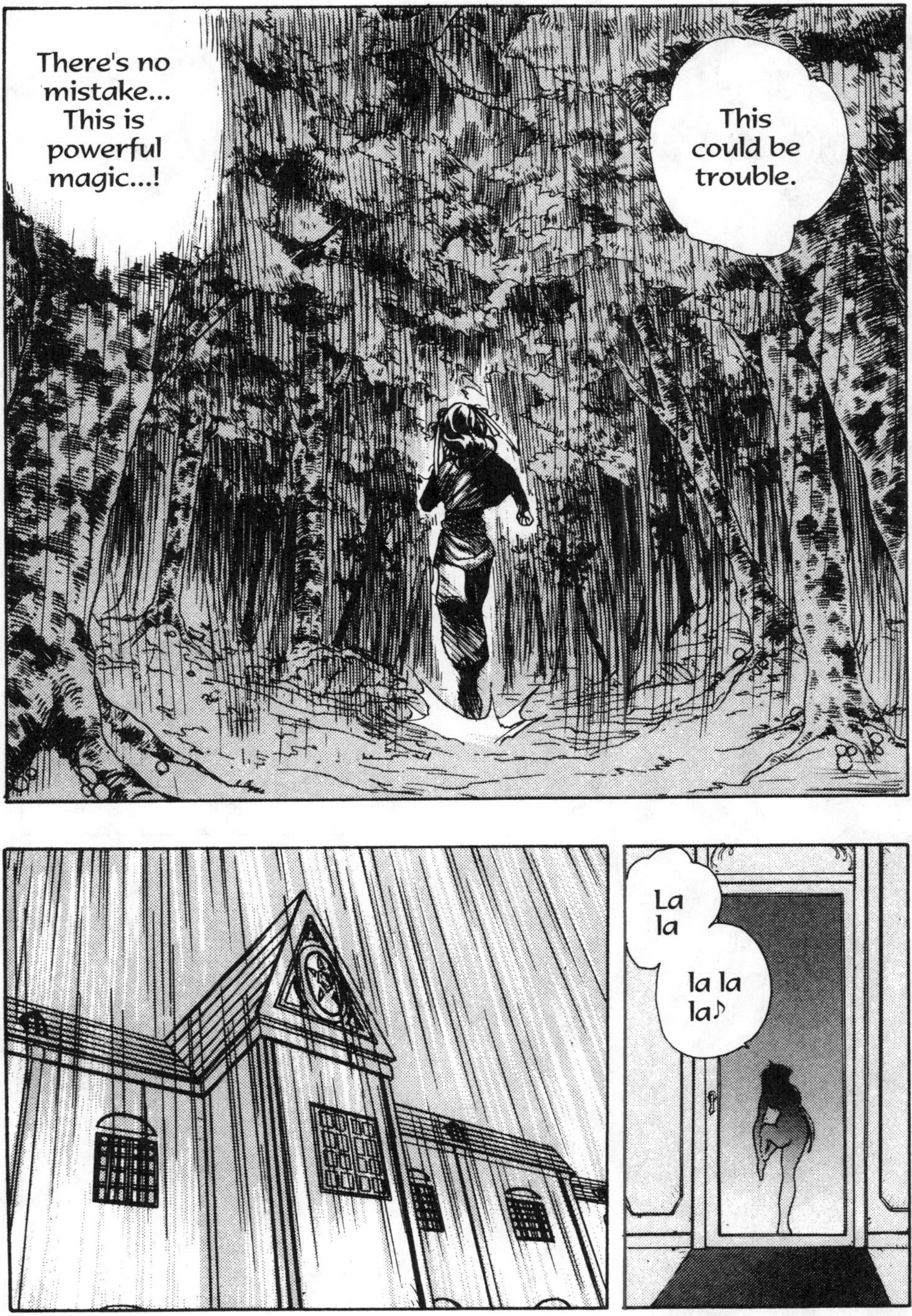
This could be trouble.
There's no mistake... This is powerful magic...!
La la la la la♪

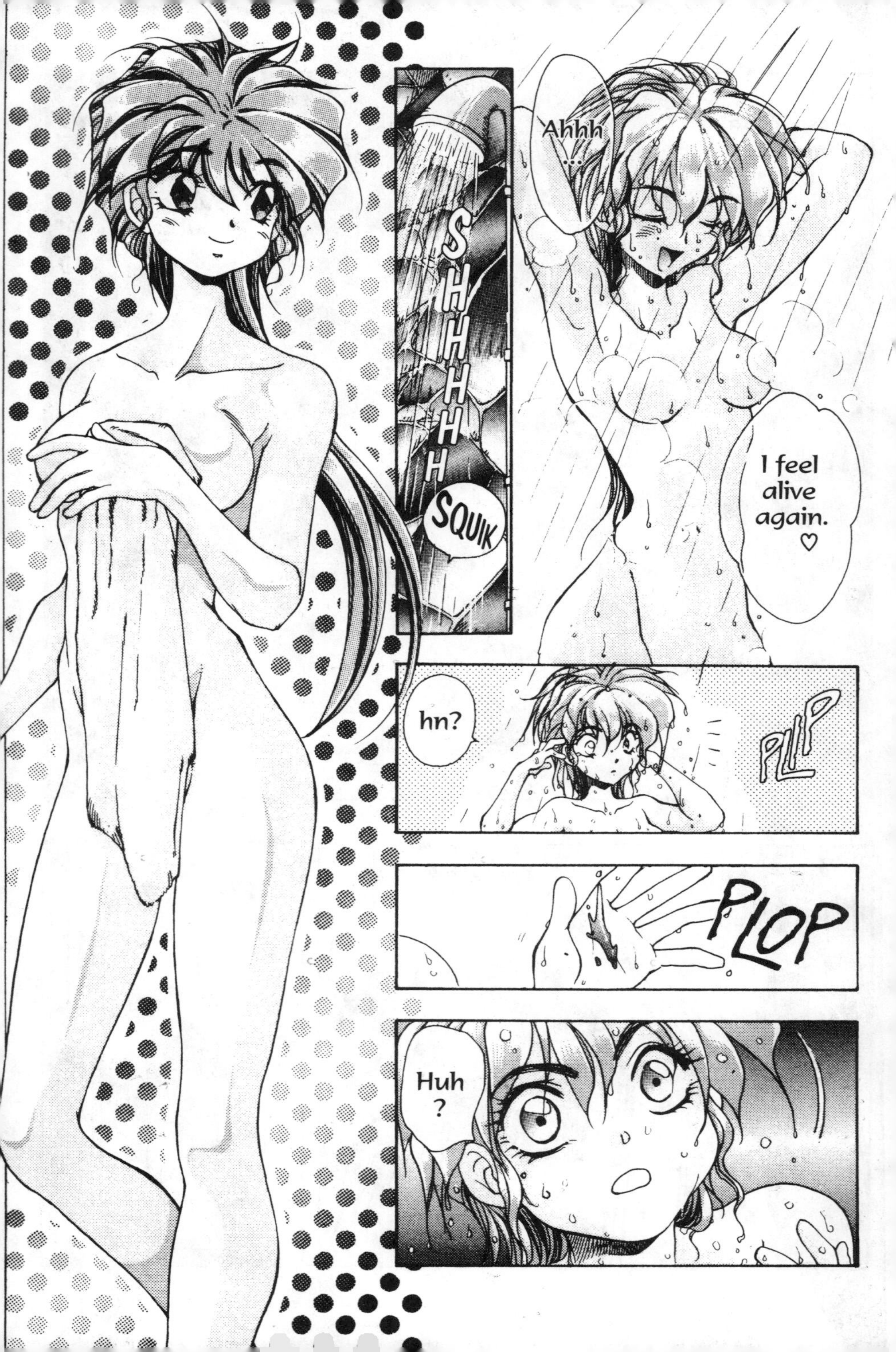
Ahhh ...
I feel alive again. ♡
SHHHHH
SQUIK
hn?
PLIP
PLOP
Huh ?

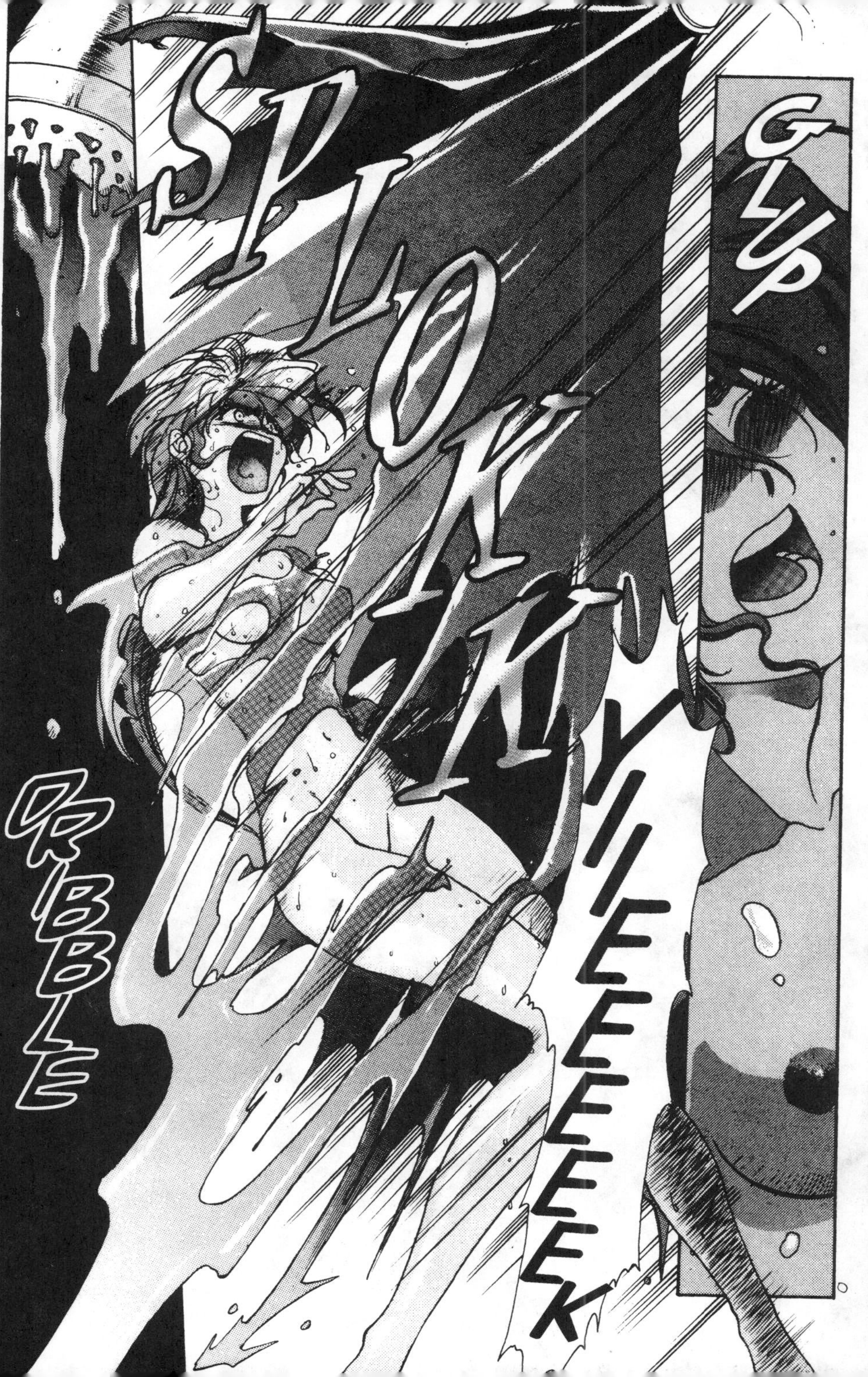
GLUP
SPLOKITY
WIIIEEEEEEEK
DRIBBLE

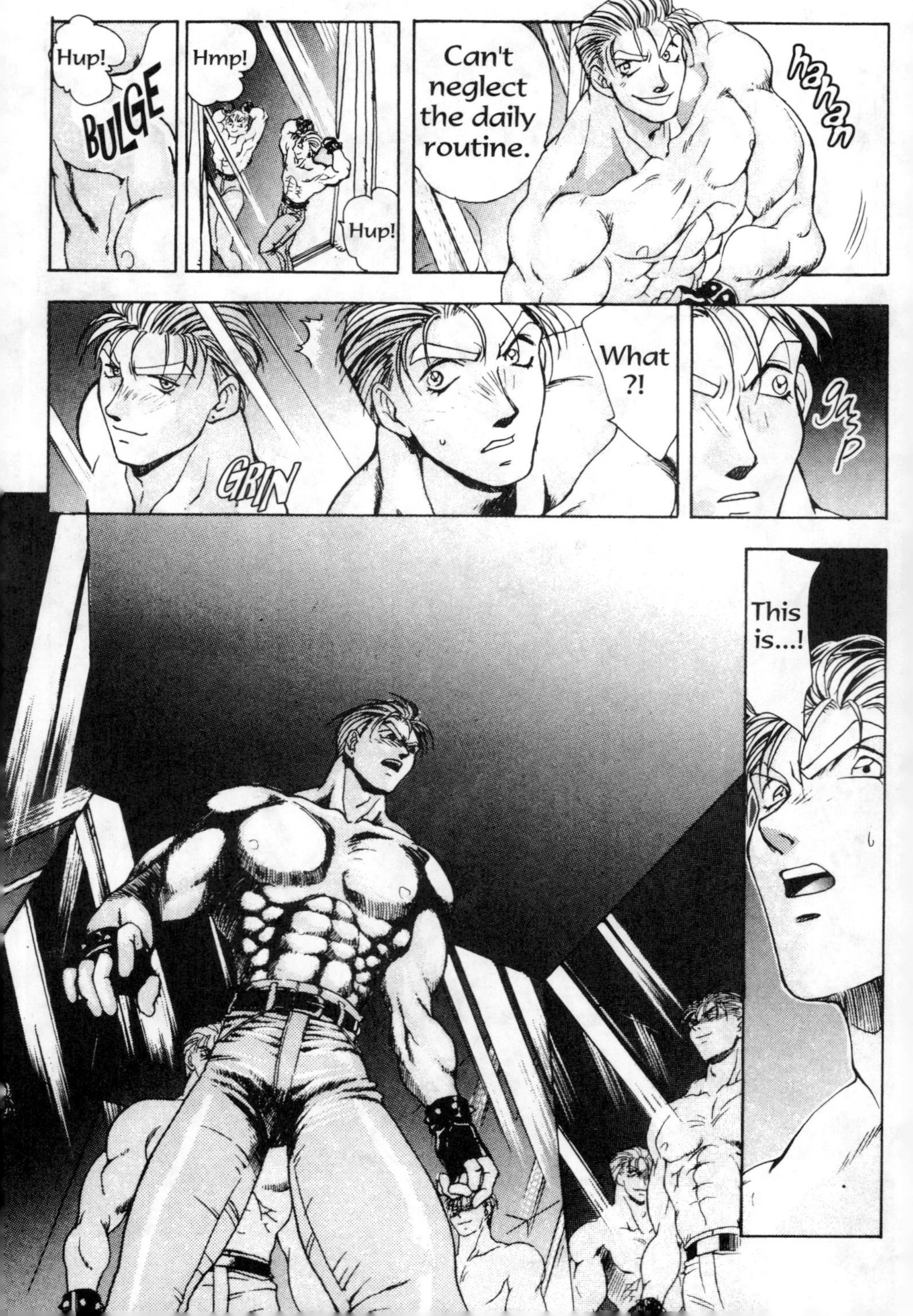
Hup!
BULGE
Hmp!
Hup!
Can't neglect the daily routine.
GRIN
What ?!
gasp
This is...!

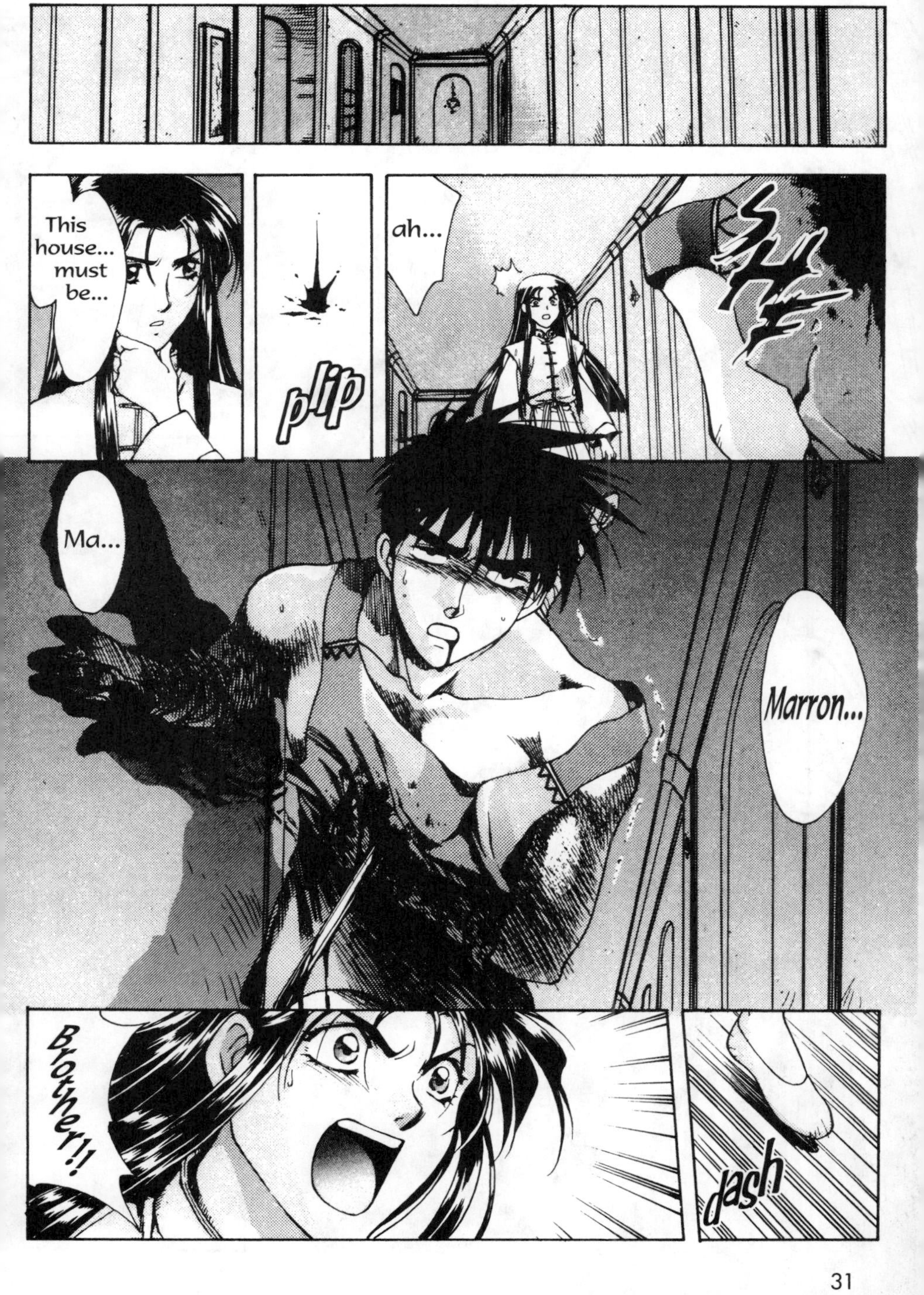
ah...
plip
This house... must be...
Marron...
Ma...
dash
Brother!!

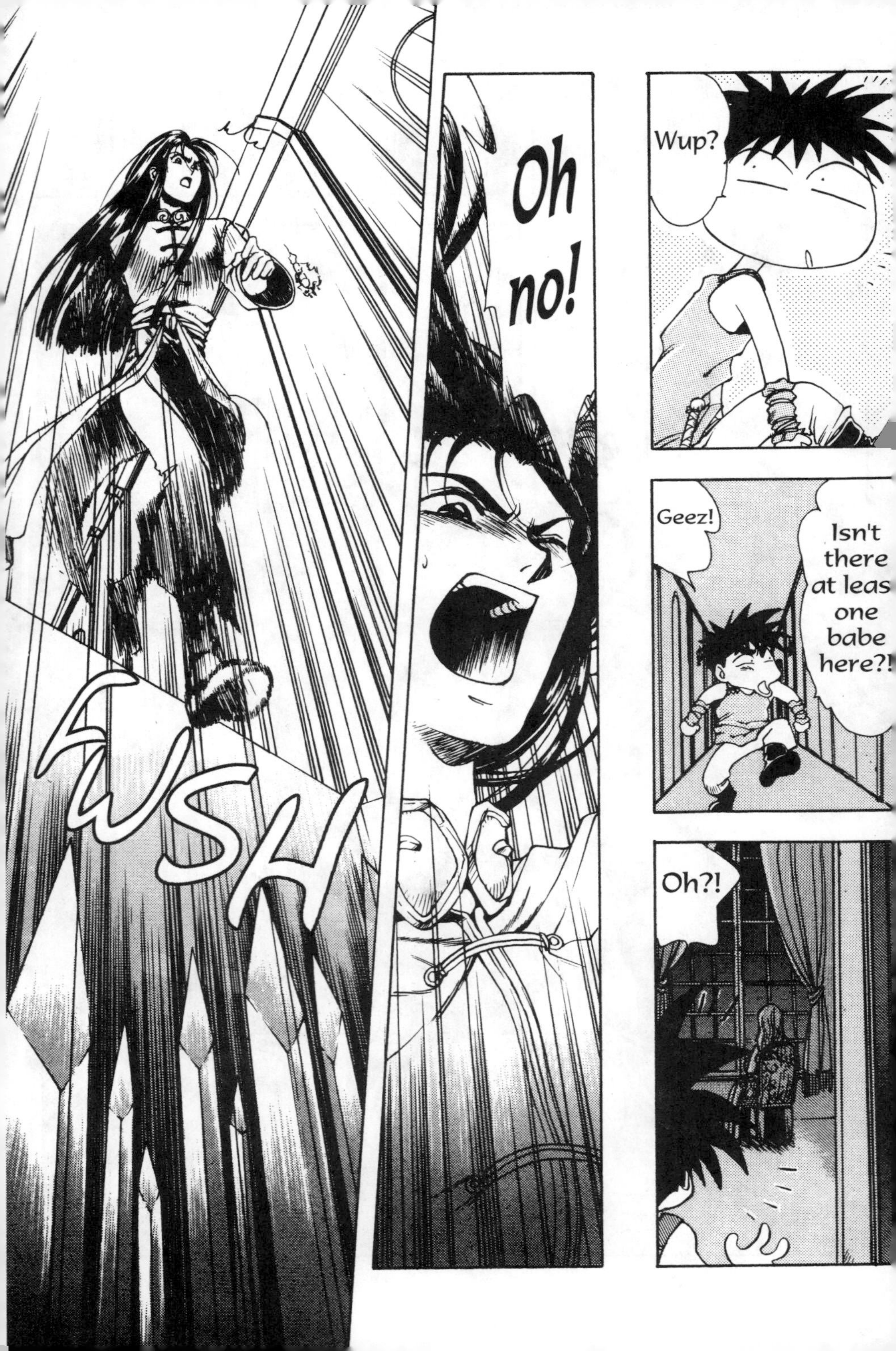
Wup?
Geez!
Isn't there at leas one babe here?!
Oh?!
Oh no!
FWSH

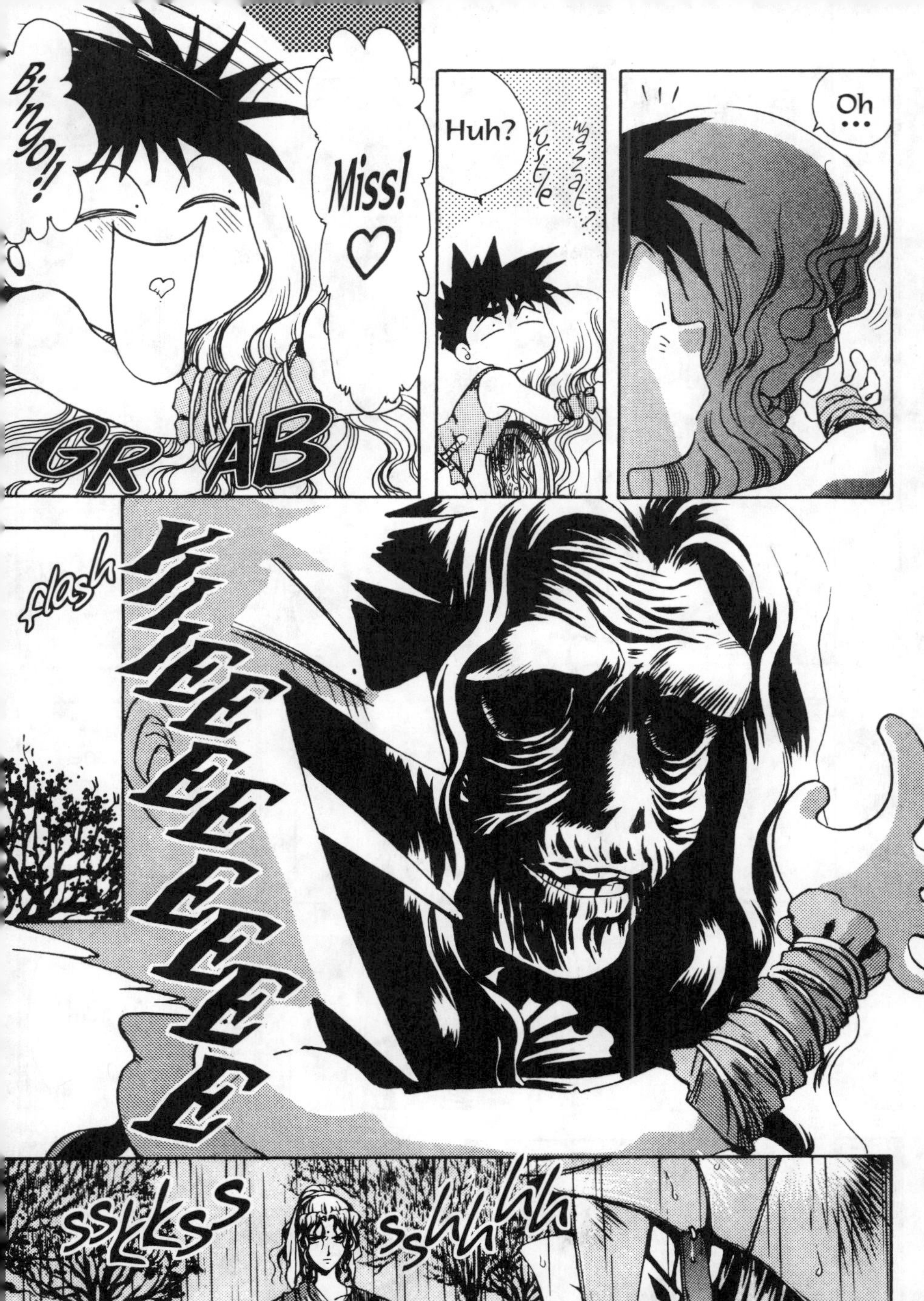
Bingo!!
Miss! ♥
GRAB
Huh?
wazzat?
rustle
Oh...
flash
YIIIEEEEEEEEEEE
sslkss
sshhhh

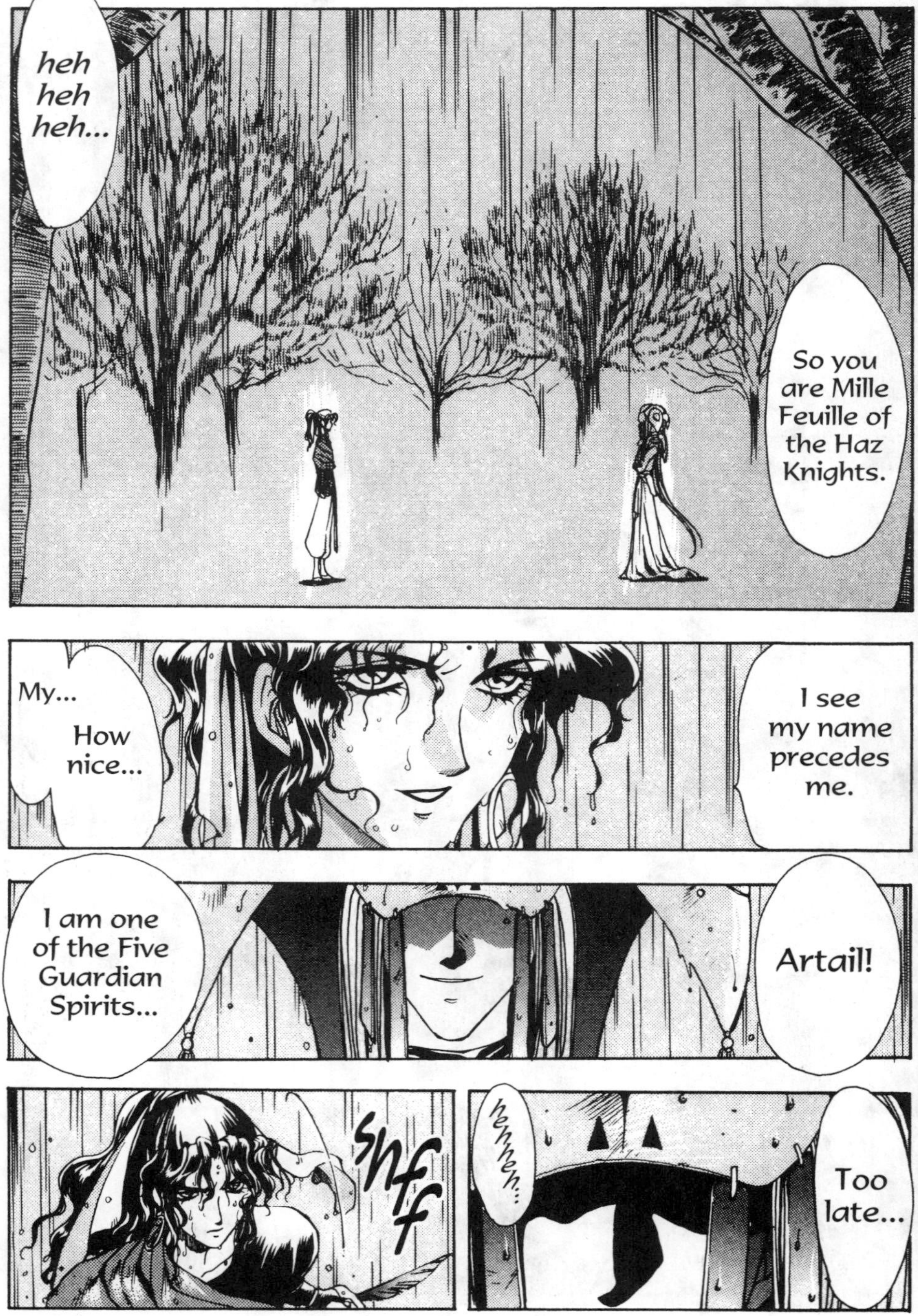
heh heh heh...
So you are Mille Feuille of the Haz Knights.
My... How nice...
I see my name precedes me.
I am one of the Five Guardian Spirits...
Artail!
snff
hehheh...
Too late...

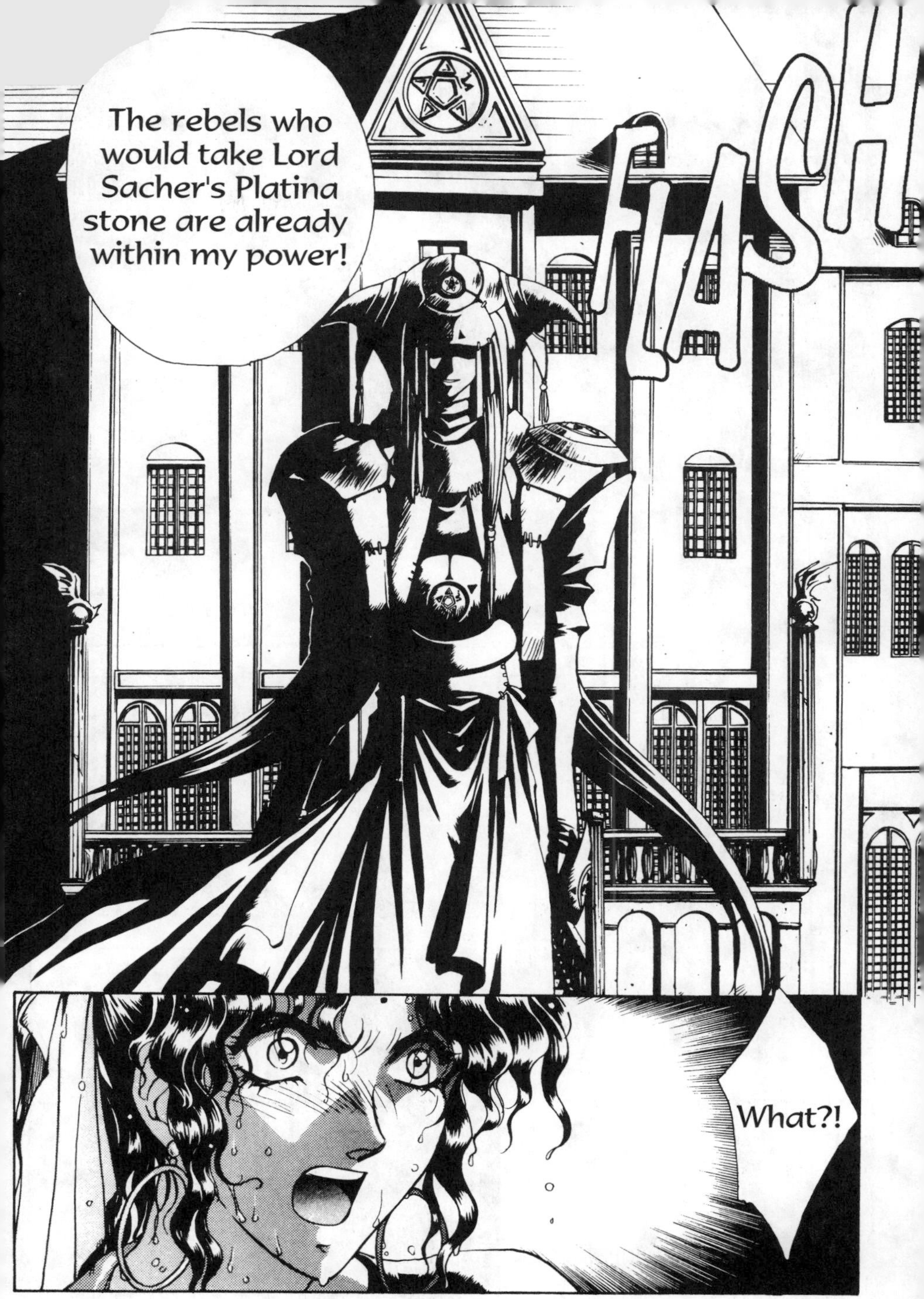
FLASH
The rebels who would take Lord Sacher's Platina stone are already within my power!
What?!

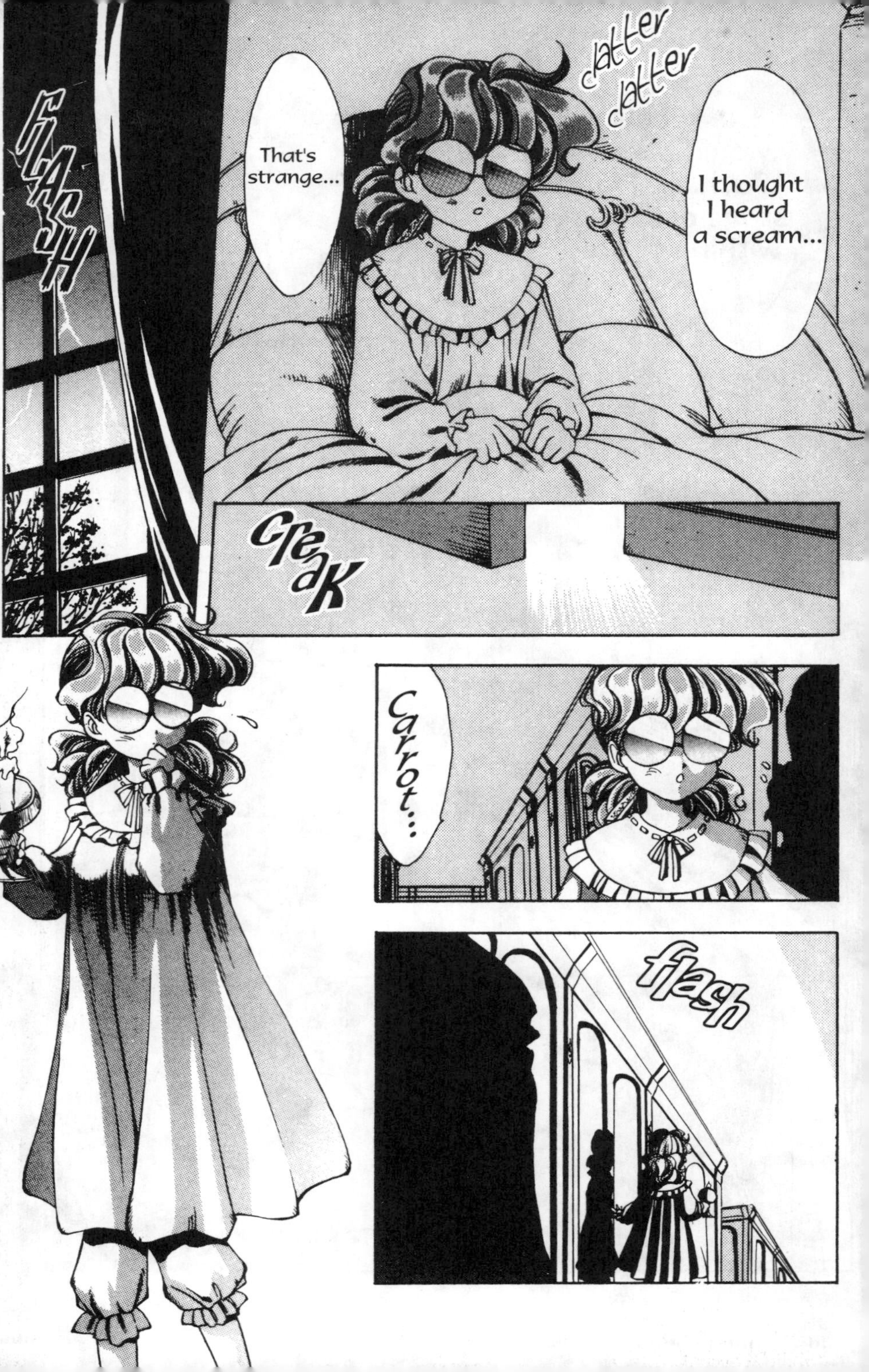
clatter clatter
I thought I heard a scream...
That's strange...
Creak
FLASH
Carrot...
flash

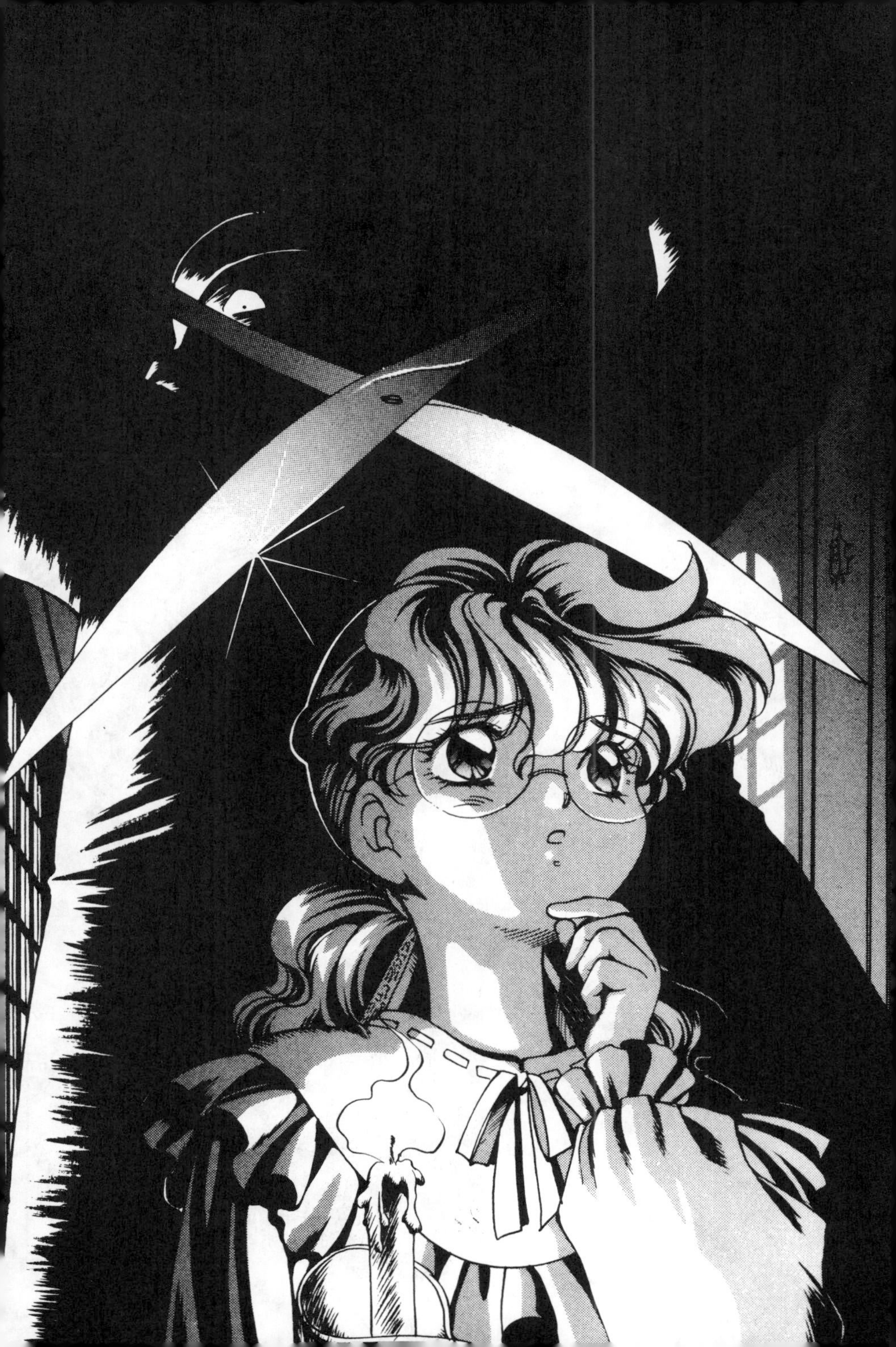

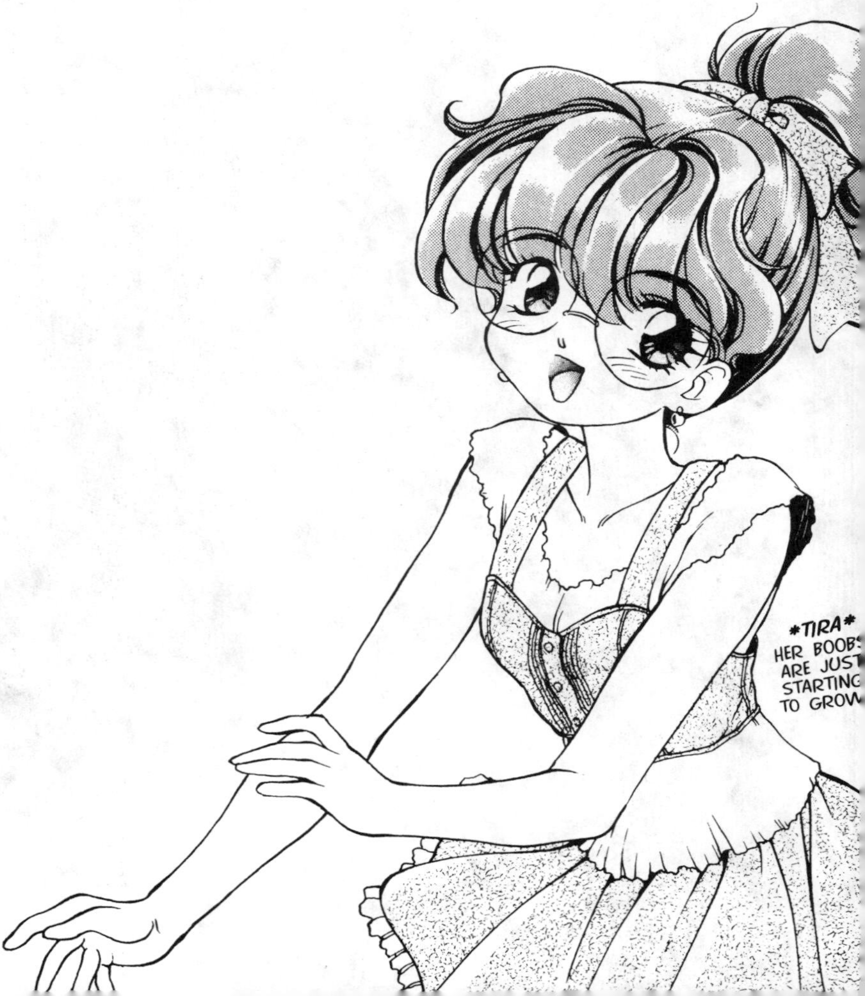
TIRA
HER BOOBS ARE JUST STARTING TO GROW

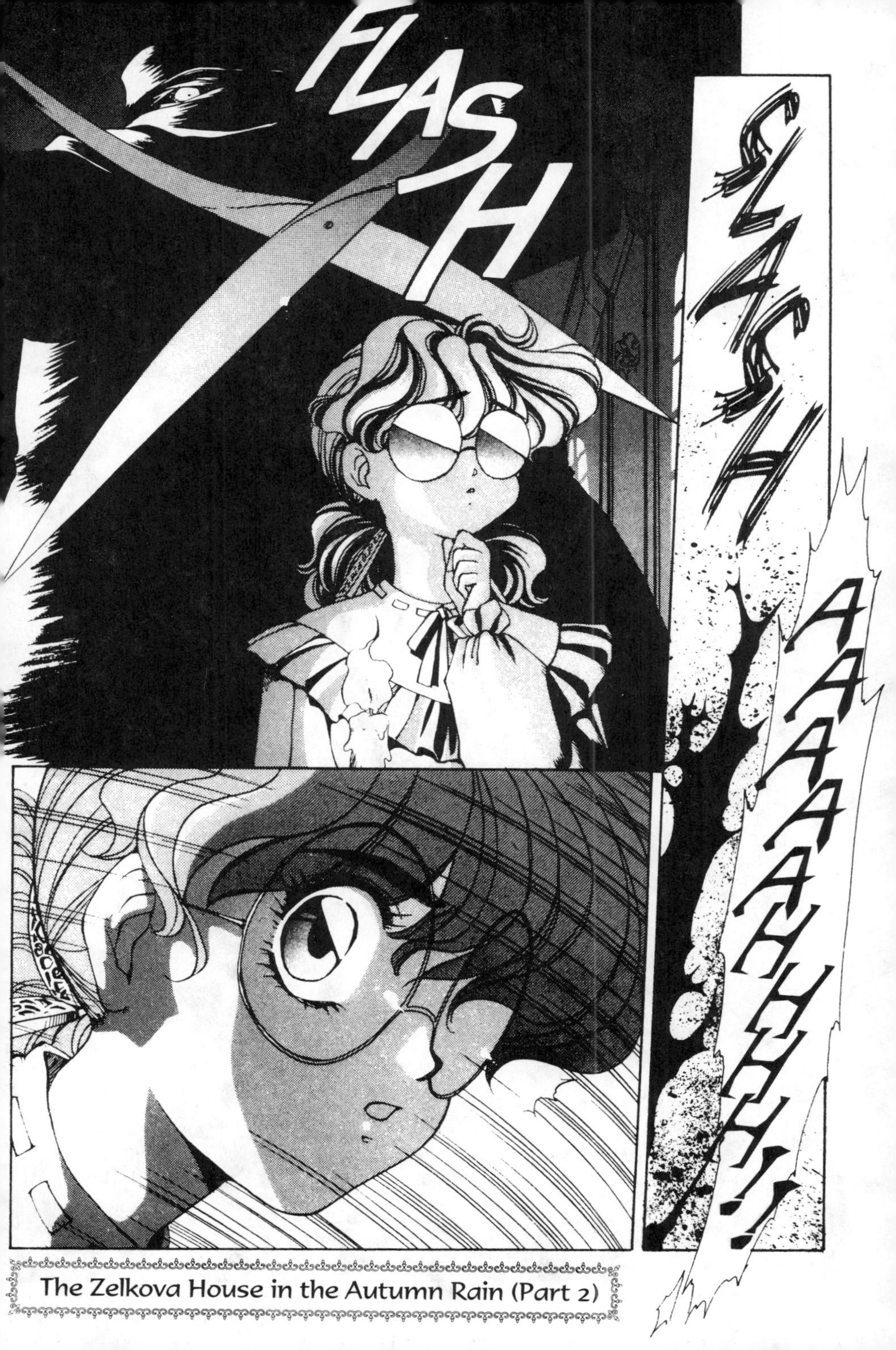
FLASH
SLASH
AAAAAHHHH!!

The Zelkova House in the Autumn Rain (Part 2)

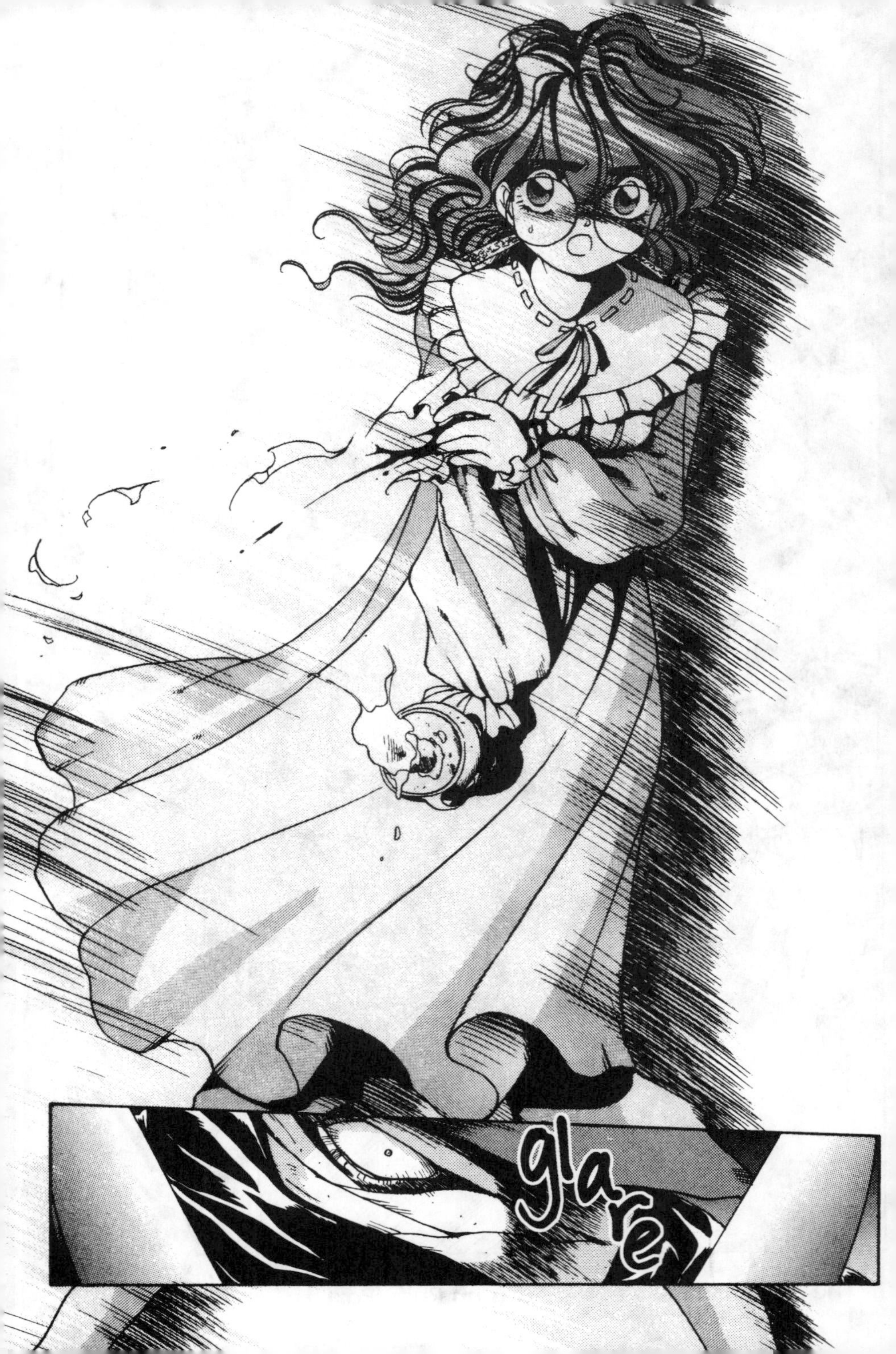
glare

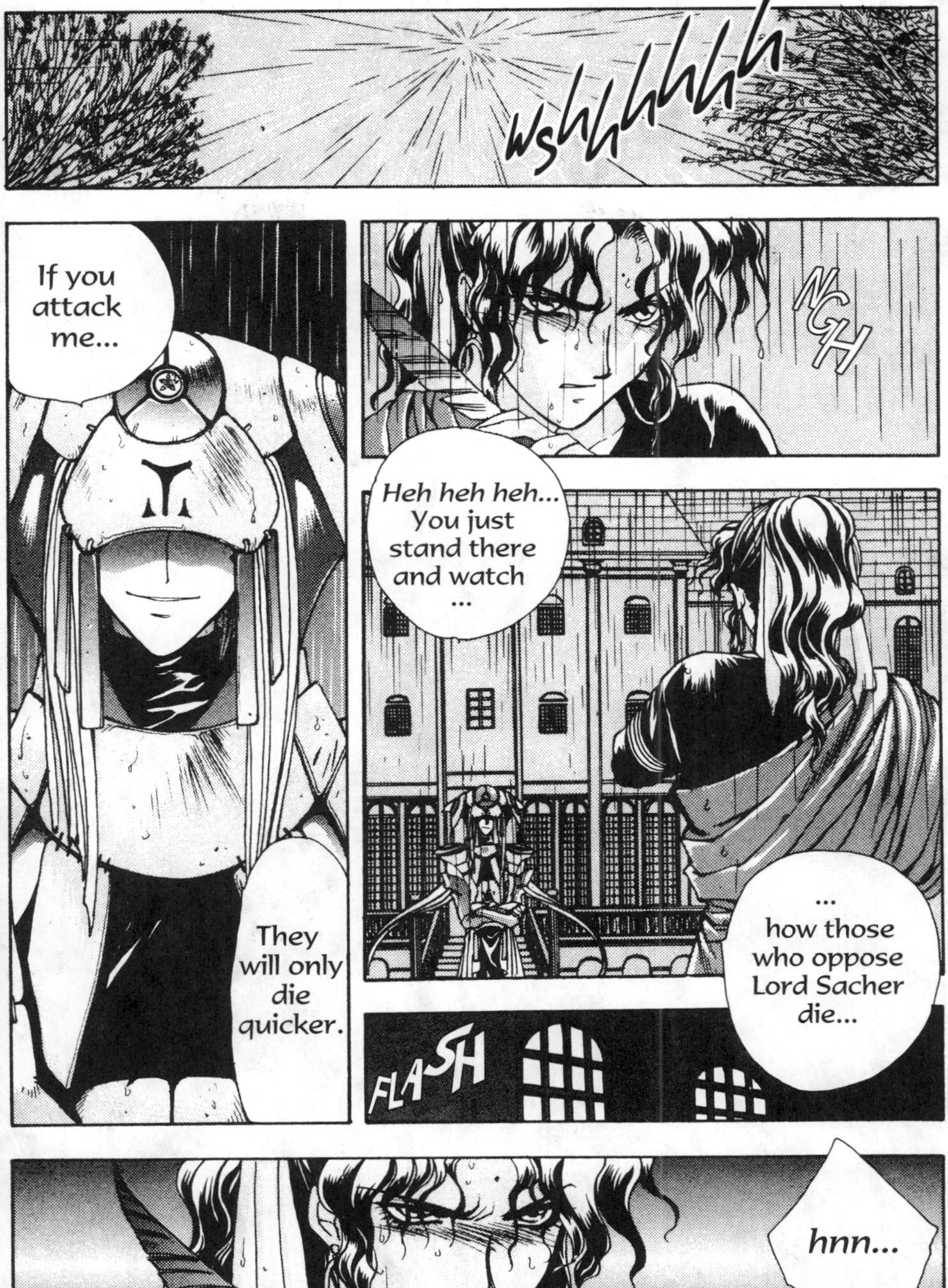
wshhhhhh
NGH
Heh heh heh... You just stand there and watch ...
... how those who oppose Lord Sacher die...
FLASH
If you attack me...
They will only die quicker.
hnn...

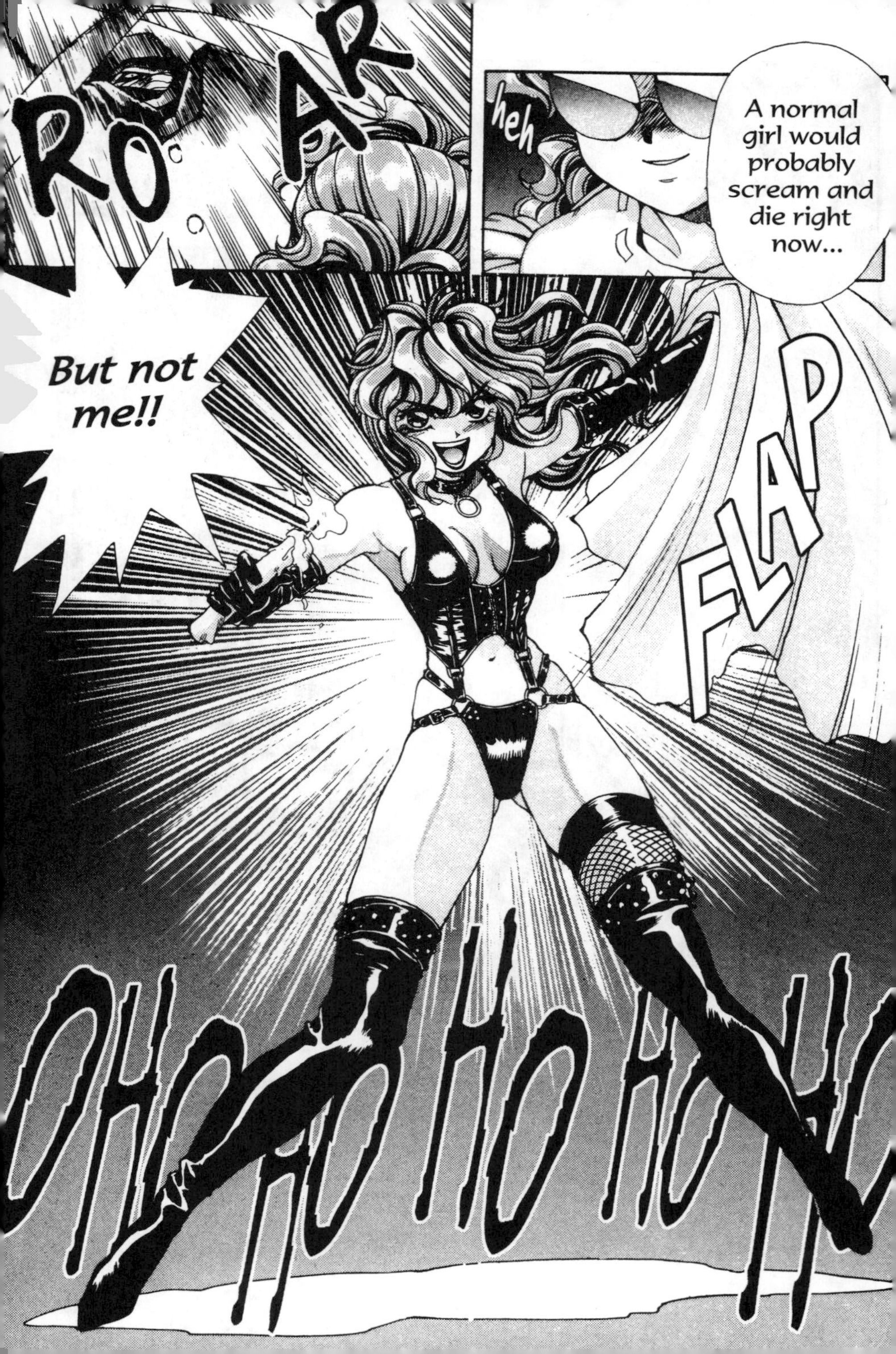
heh
A normal girl would probably scream and die right now...
ROAR
FLAP
But not me!!
OHO HO HO HO HO

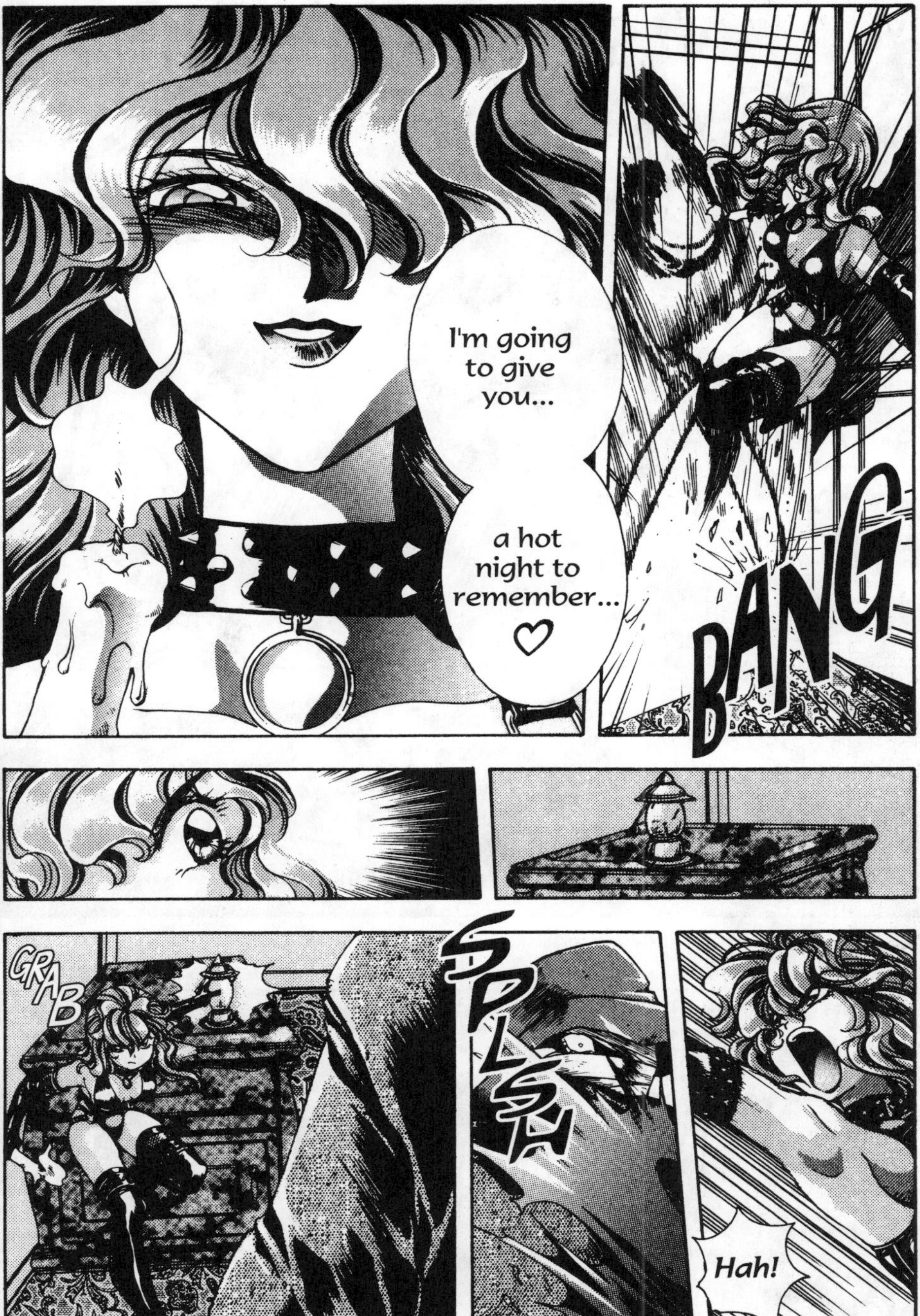
BANG
I'm going to give you...
a hot night to remember... ♡
Hah!
SPLSH
GRAB
THAT'S OIL...

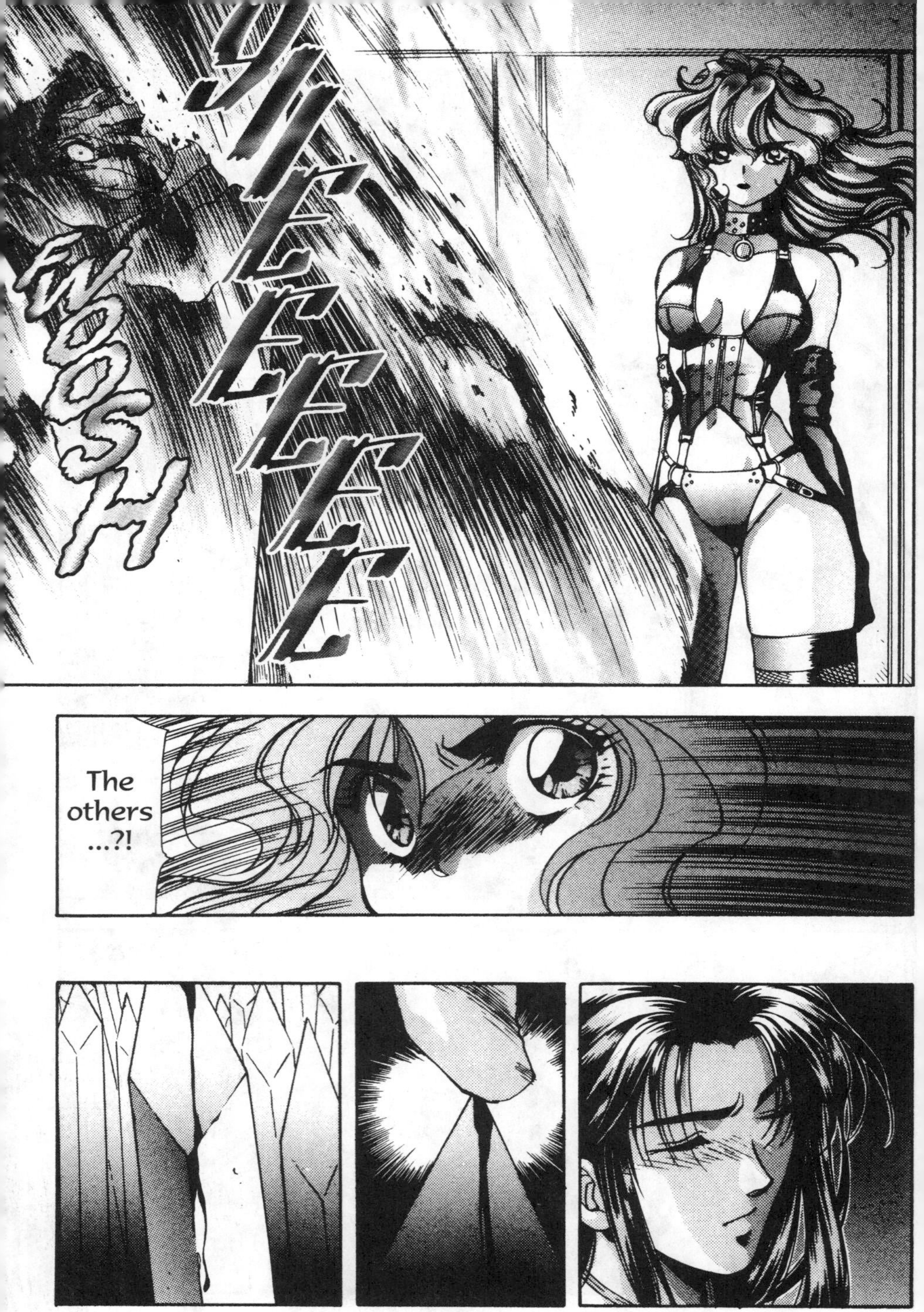
WOOSH
The others ...?!

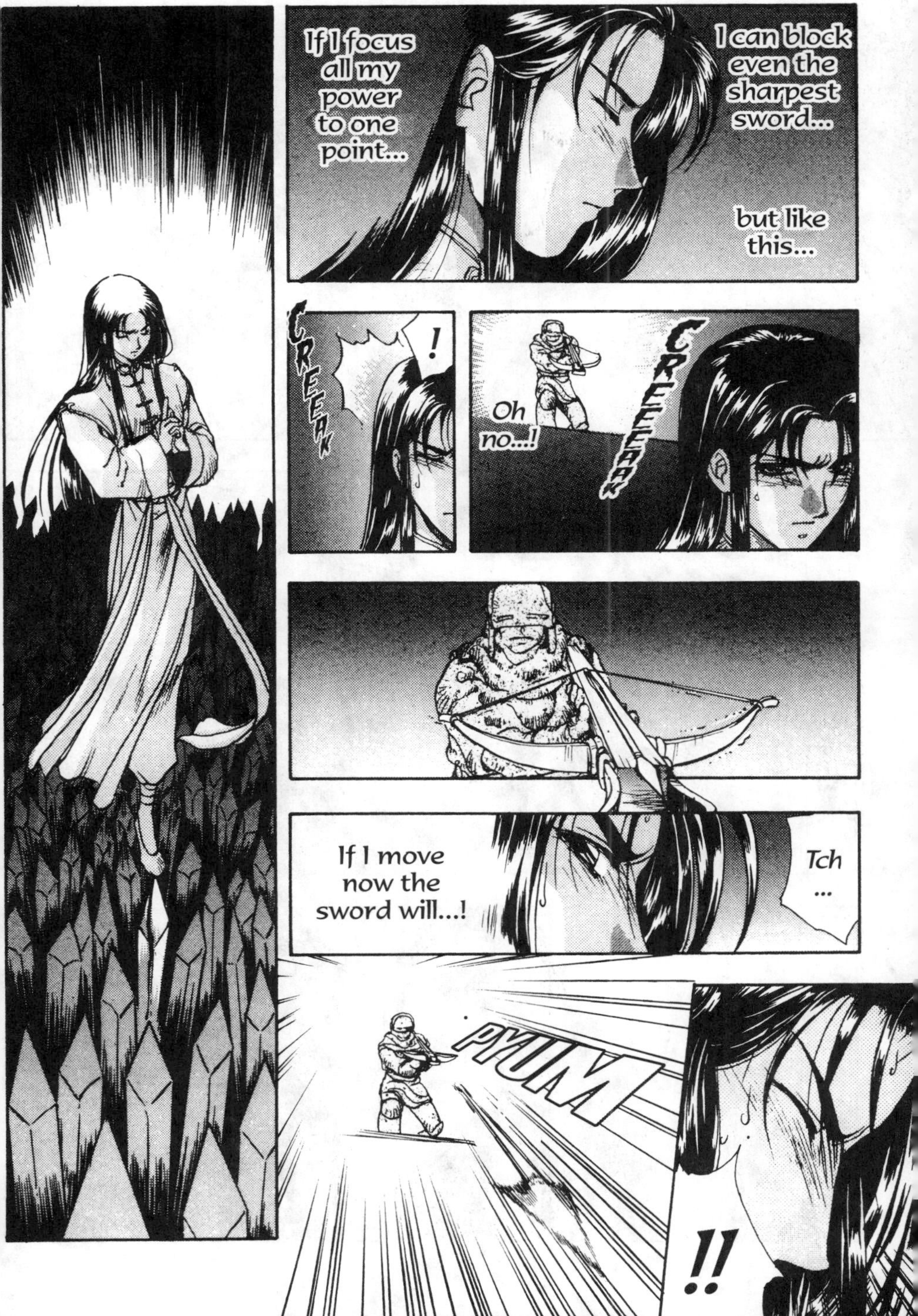

If I focus all my power to one point...
I can block even the sharpest sword...
but like this...
CREEAK
!
Oh no...!
CREEEAAK
If I move now the sword will...!
Tch ...
PYUM
!!

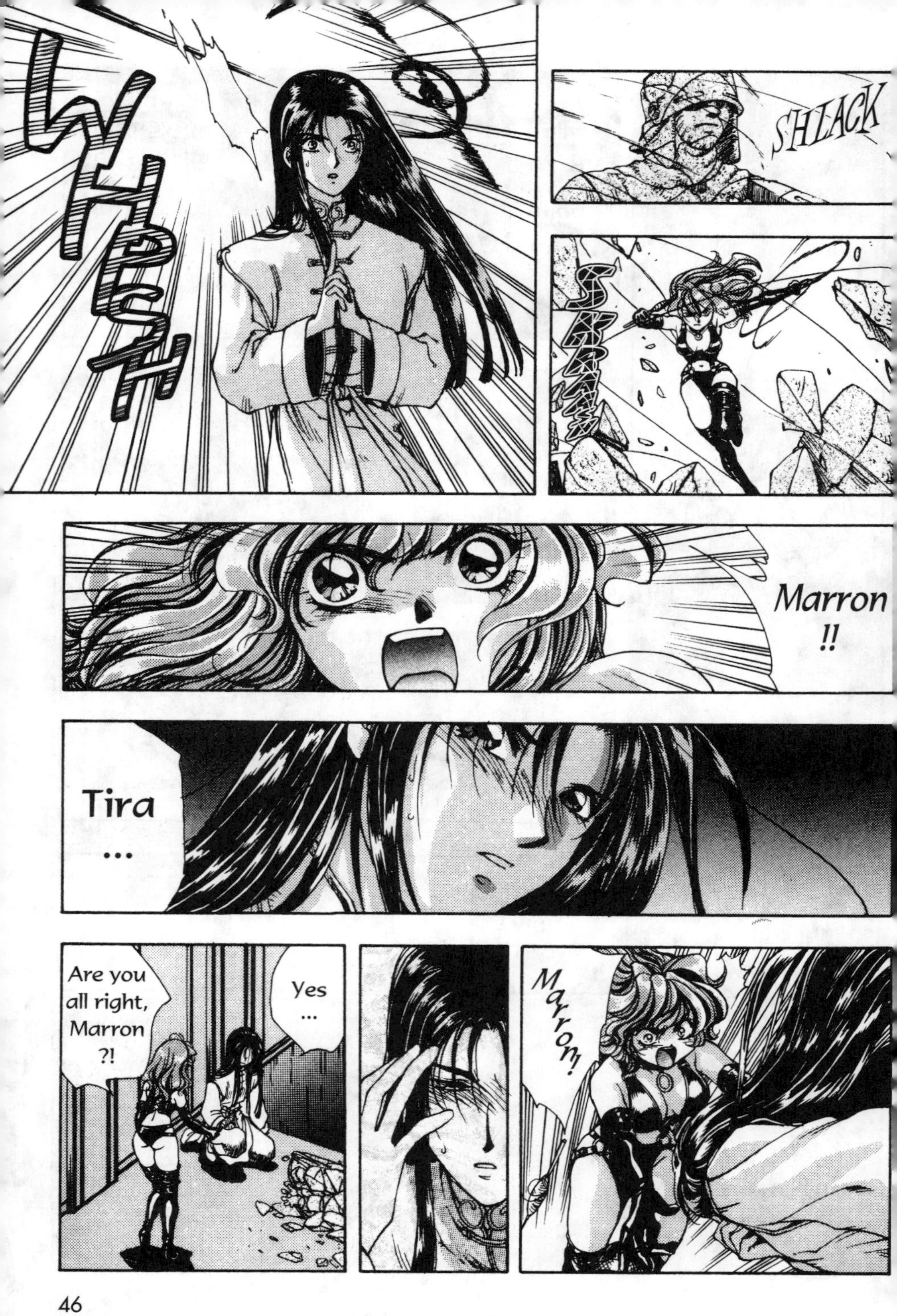
WHPSH
SHLACK
Marron !!
Tira ...
Are you all right, Marron ?!
Yes ...
Marron!

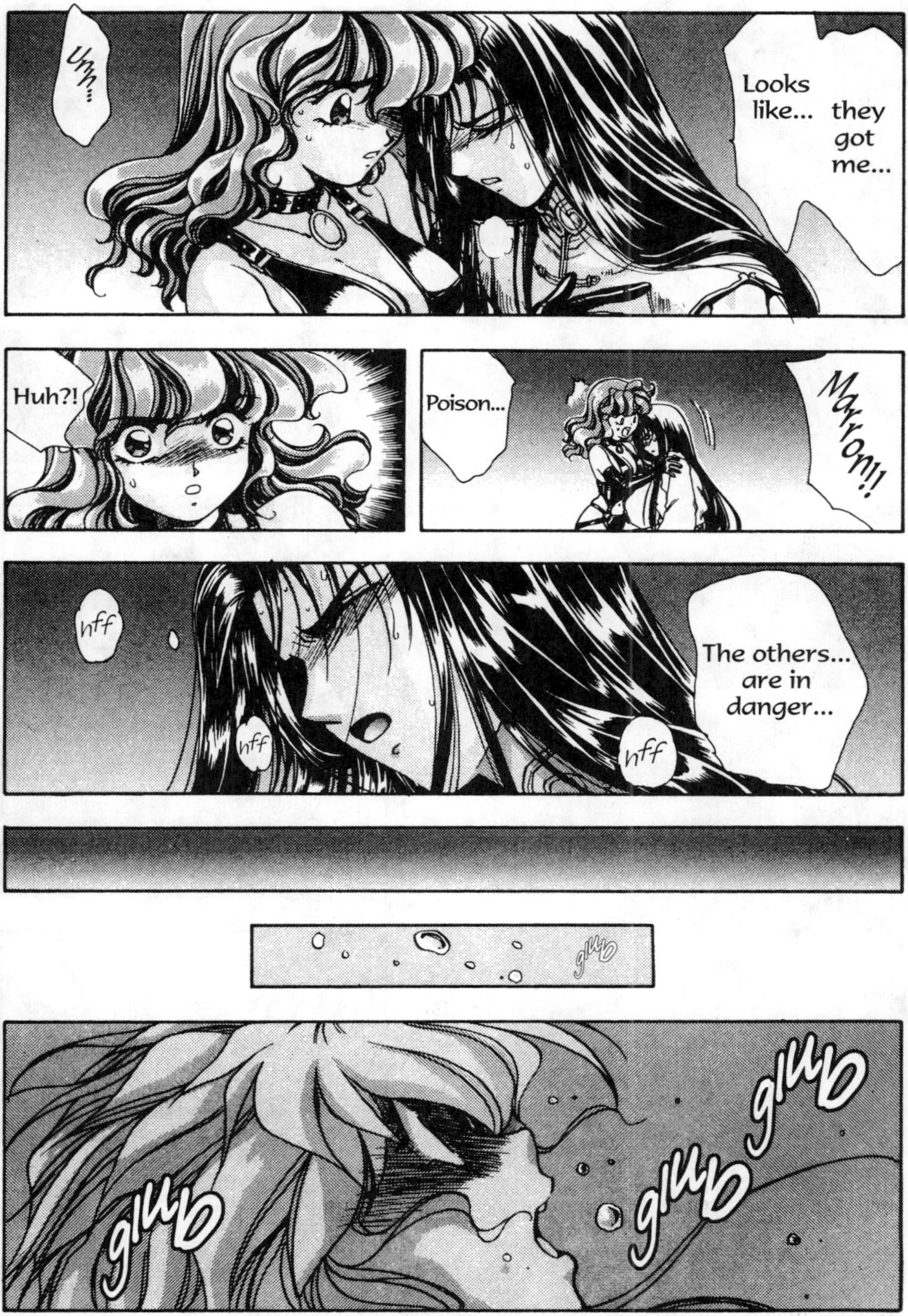
Looks like... they got me...
Umm...
Marron!!
Poison...
Huh?!
The others... are in danger...
hff
hff
hff
glub
glub
glub
glub

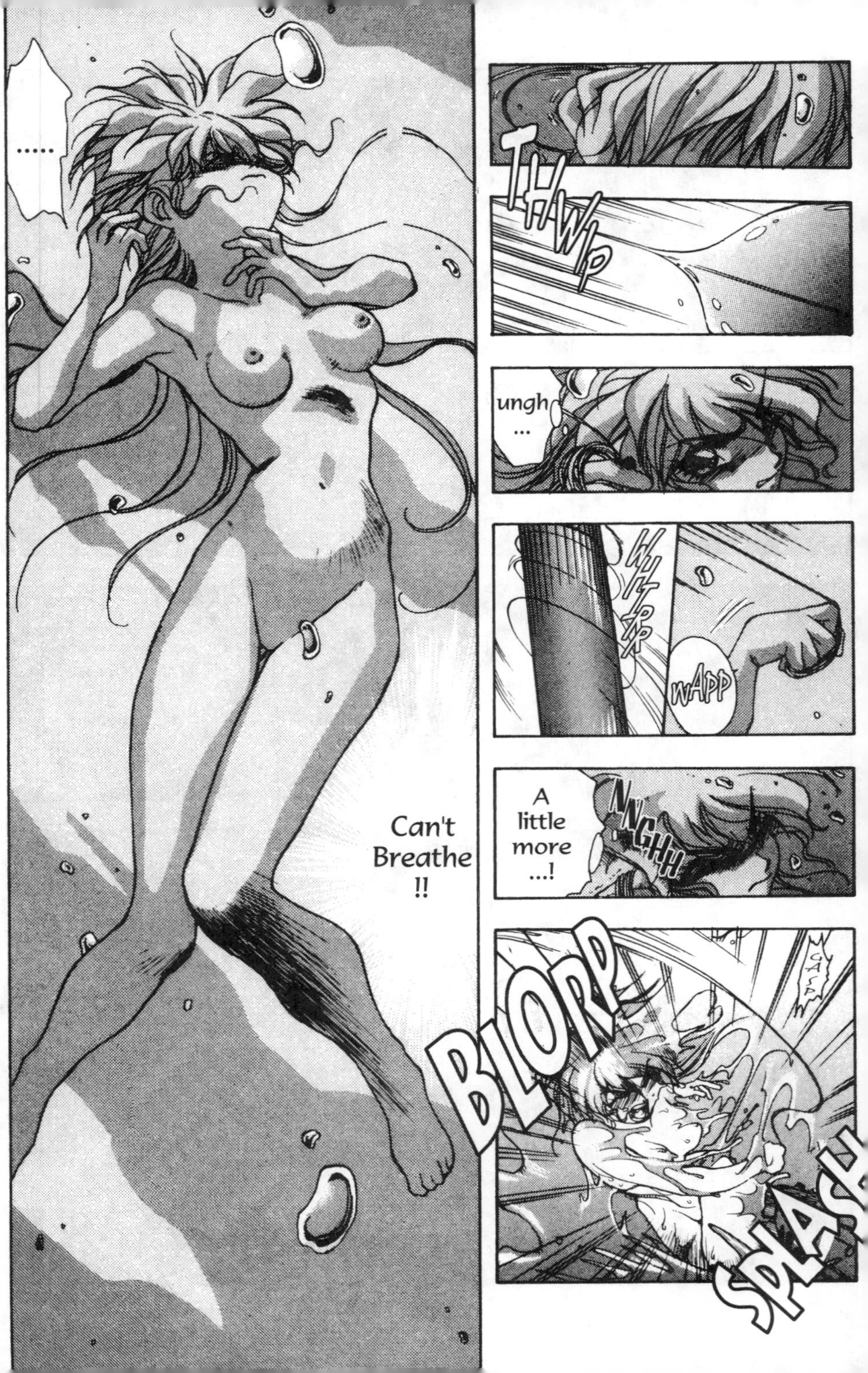

......
Can't Breathe !!
THWIP
ungh ...
WHIRR
WAPP
A little more ...!
NNGHH
BLORP
GASP
SPLASH

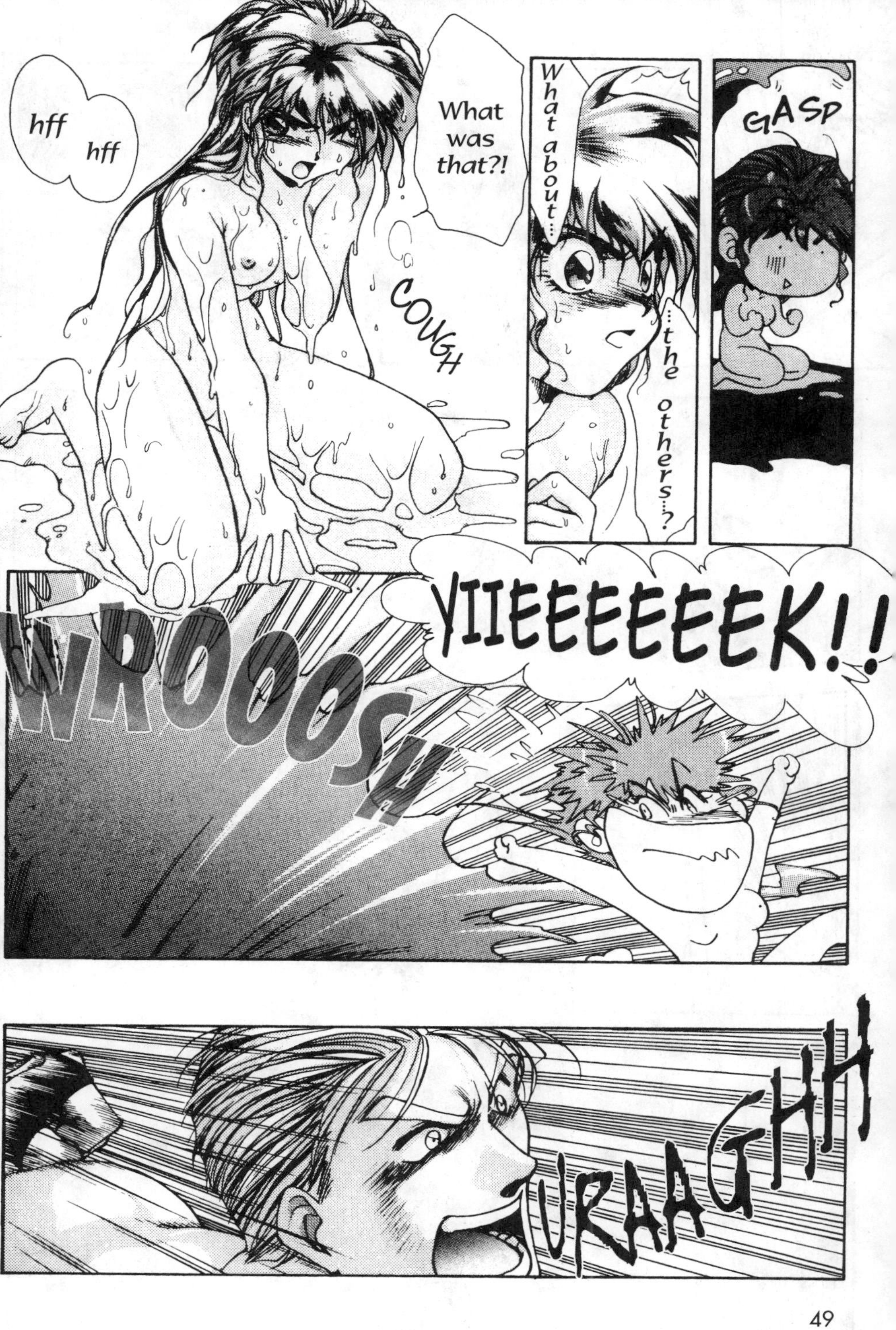
hff hff
What was that?!
COUGH
What about...
...the others...?
GASP
YIIEEEEEEEK!!
WROOOSH
URAAGHH

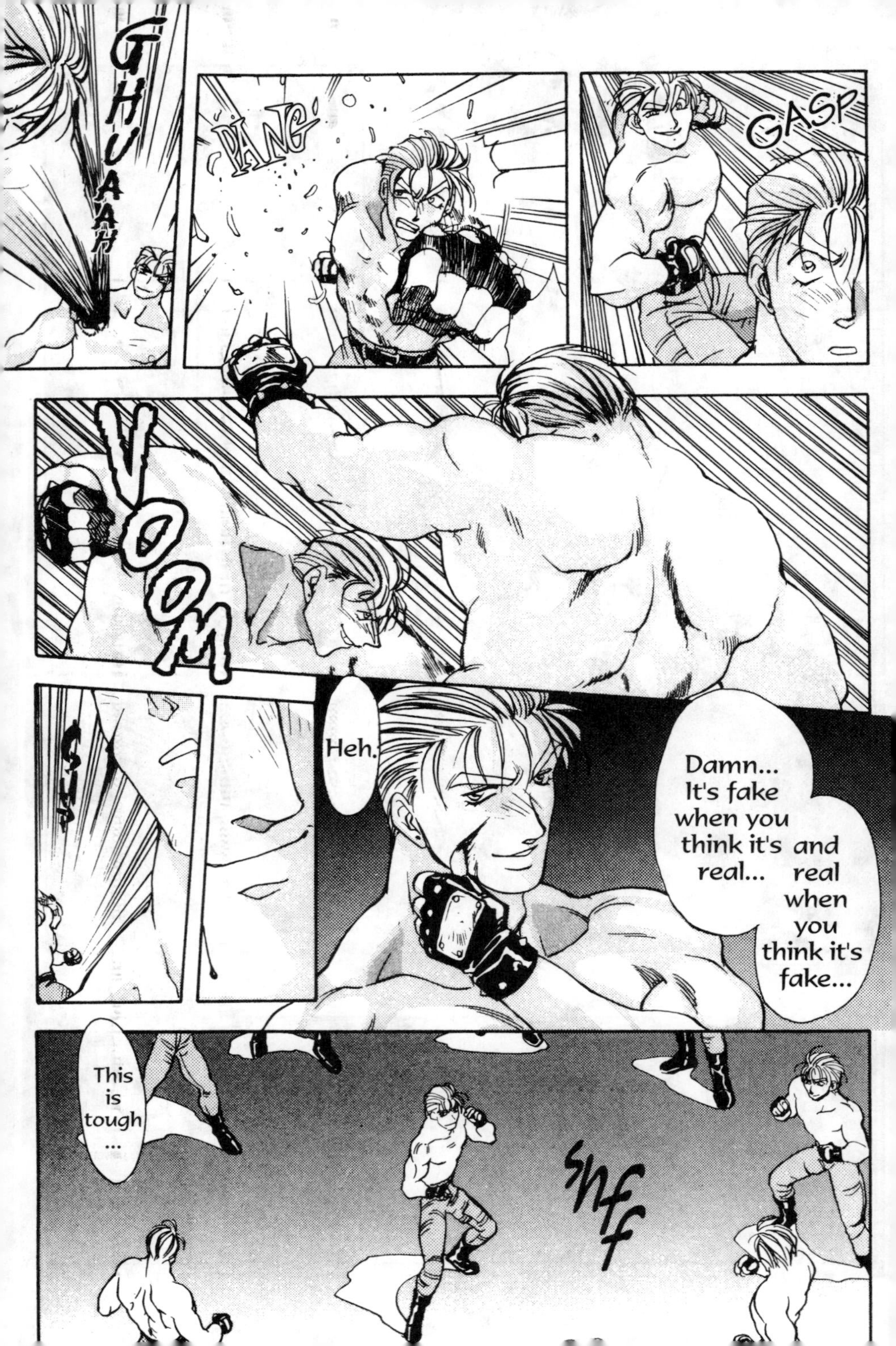
GASP
PANG
GHUAAAH
VOOM
Heh.
Damn... It's fake when you think it's real... and real when you think it's fake...
snff
This is tough ...

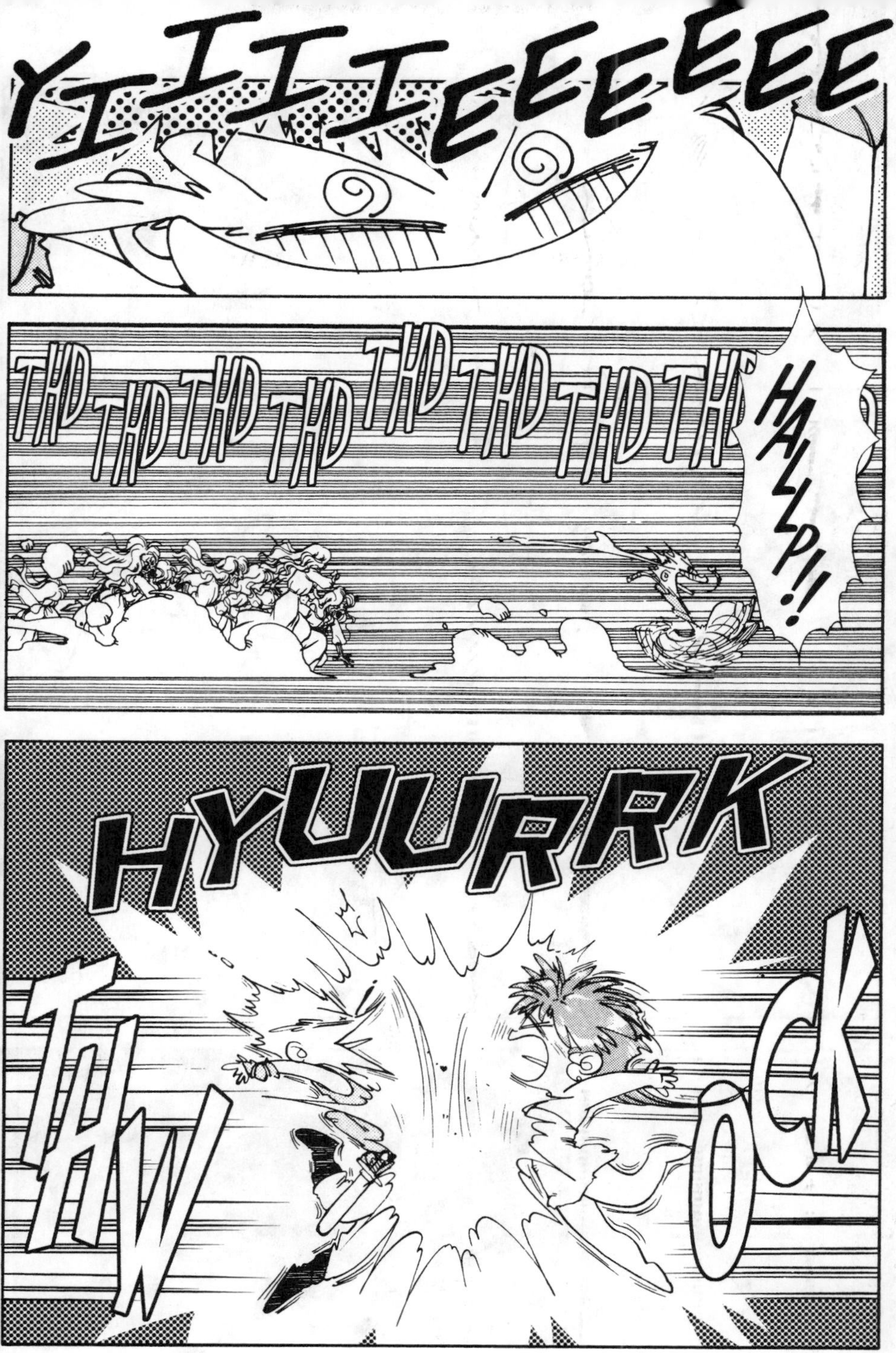
YIIIIEEEEEE
HALLP!!
THD THD THD THD THD THD THD THD TH
HYUURRK
THWOCK

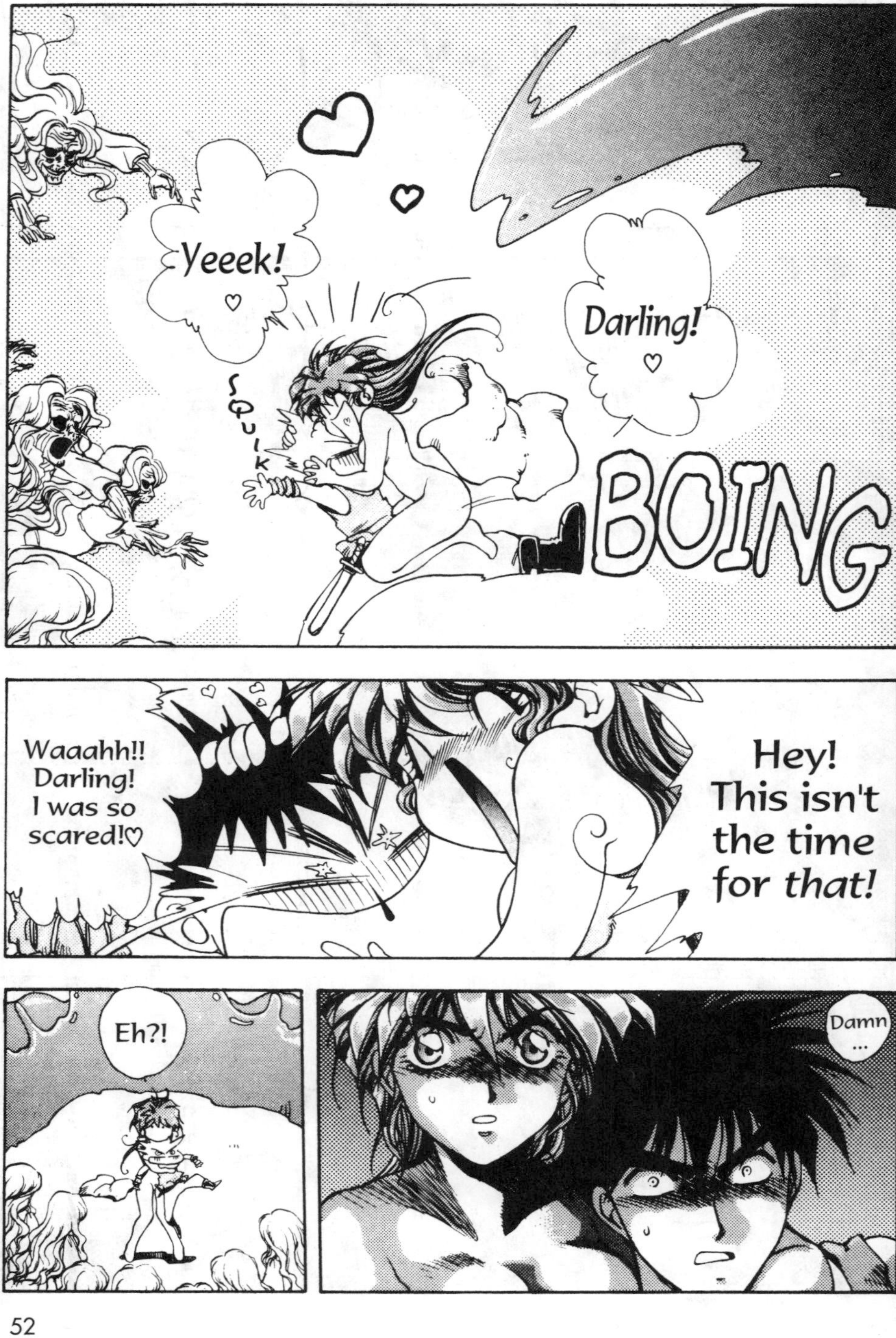
Yeeek! ♡
SQUIK
Darling! ♡
BOING
Waaahh!! Darling! I was so scared!♡
Hey! This isn't the time for *that!*
Eh?!
Damn ...

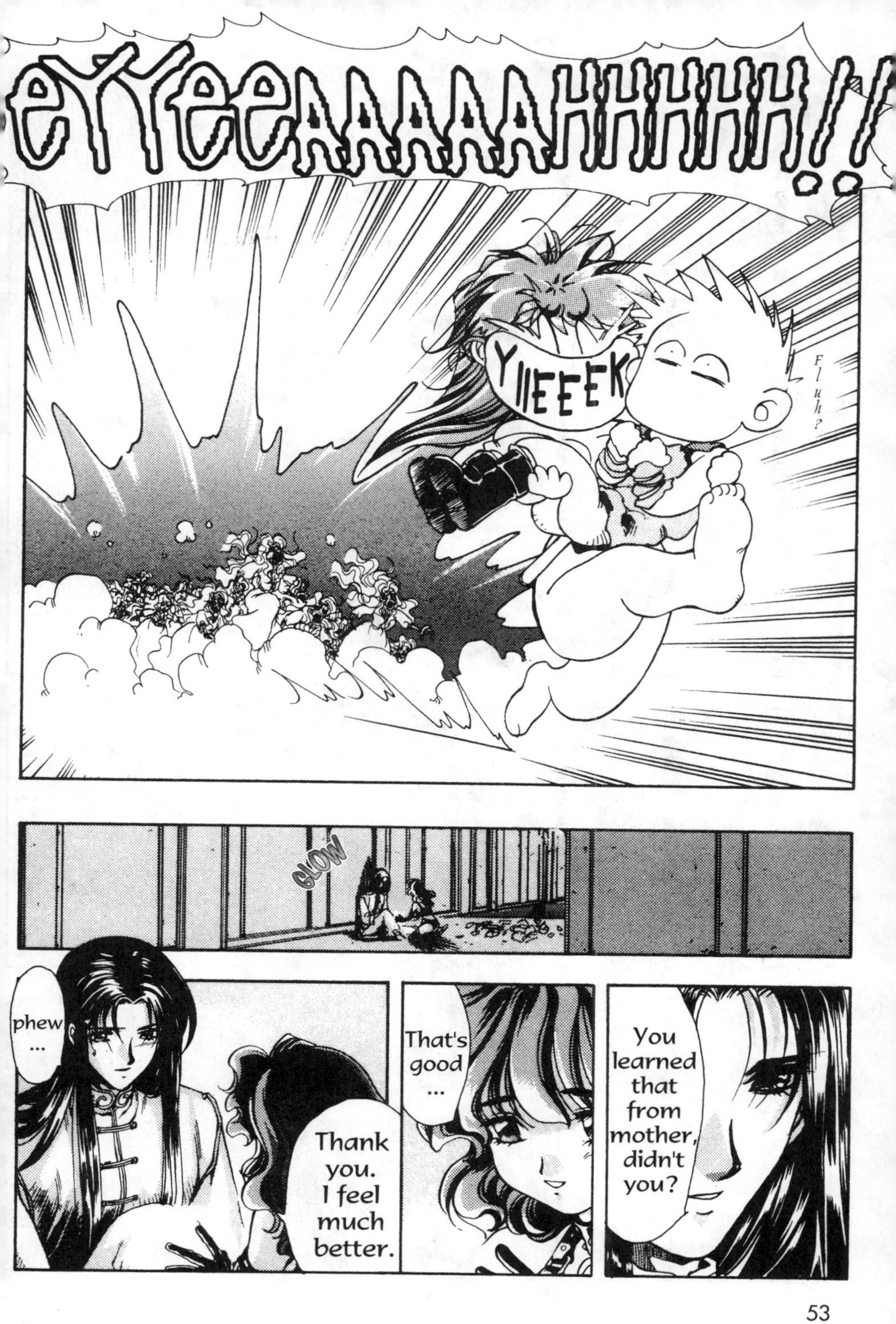
eYeeAAAAHHHHH!!
YIIEEEK
Fluh?
GLOW
phew ...
Thank you. I feel much better.
That's good ...
You learned that from mother, didn't you?

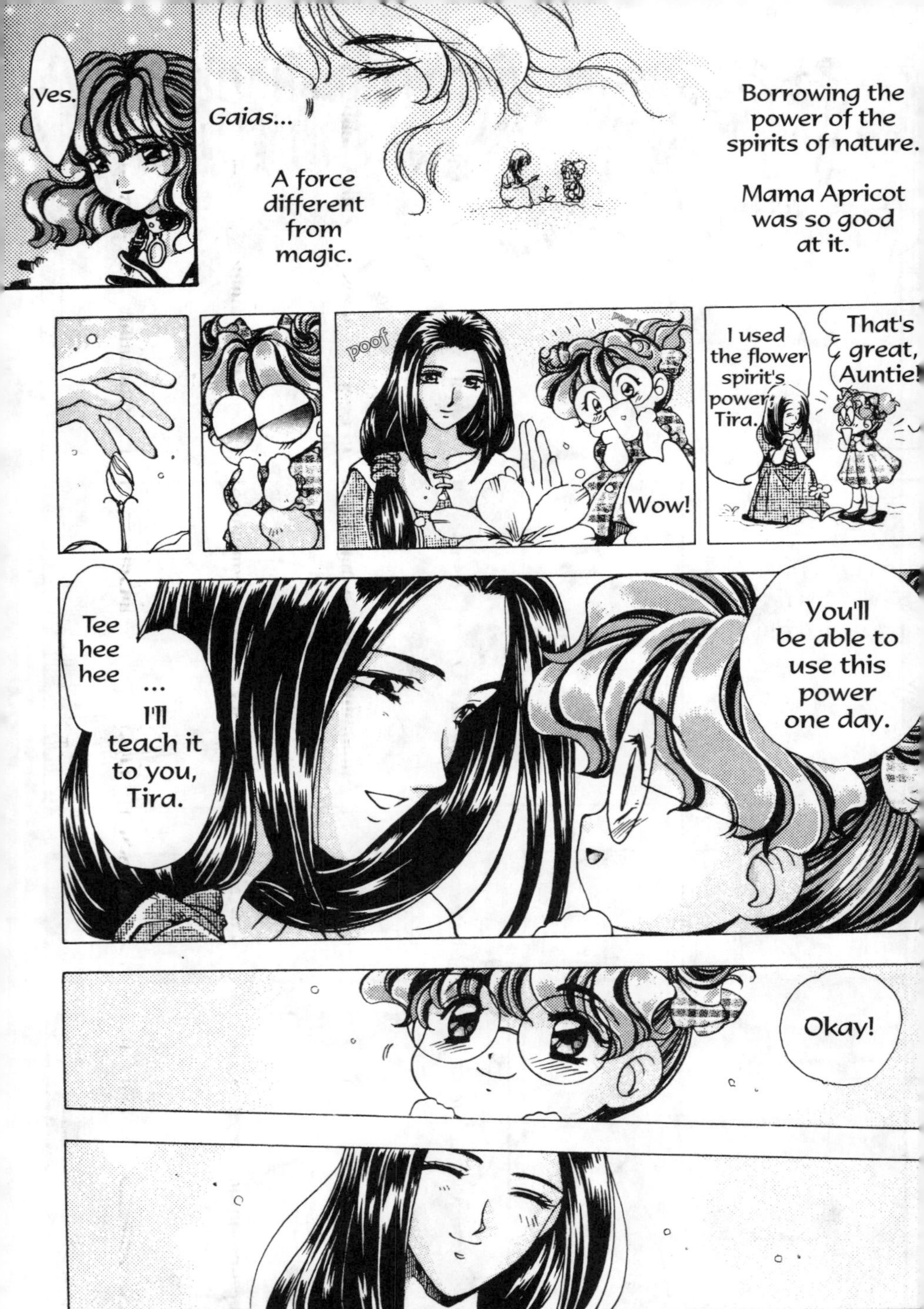
yes.
Gaias...
A force different from magic.
Borrowing the power of the spirits of nature.
Mama Apricot was so good at it.
poof
poof
Wow!
I used the flower spirit's power, Tira.
That's great, Auntie!
Tee hee hee ... I'll teach it to you, Tira.
You'll be able to use this power one day.
Okay!

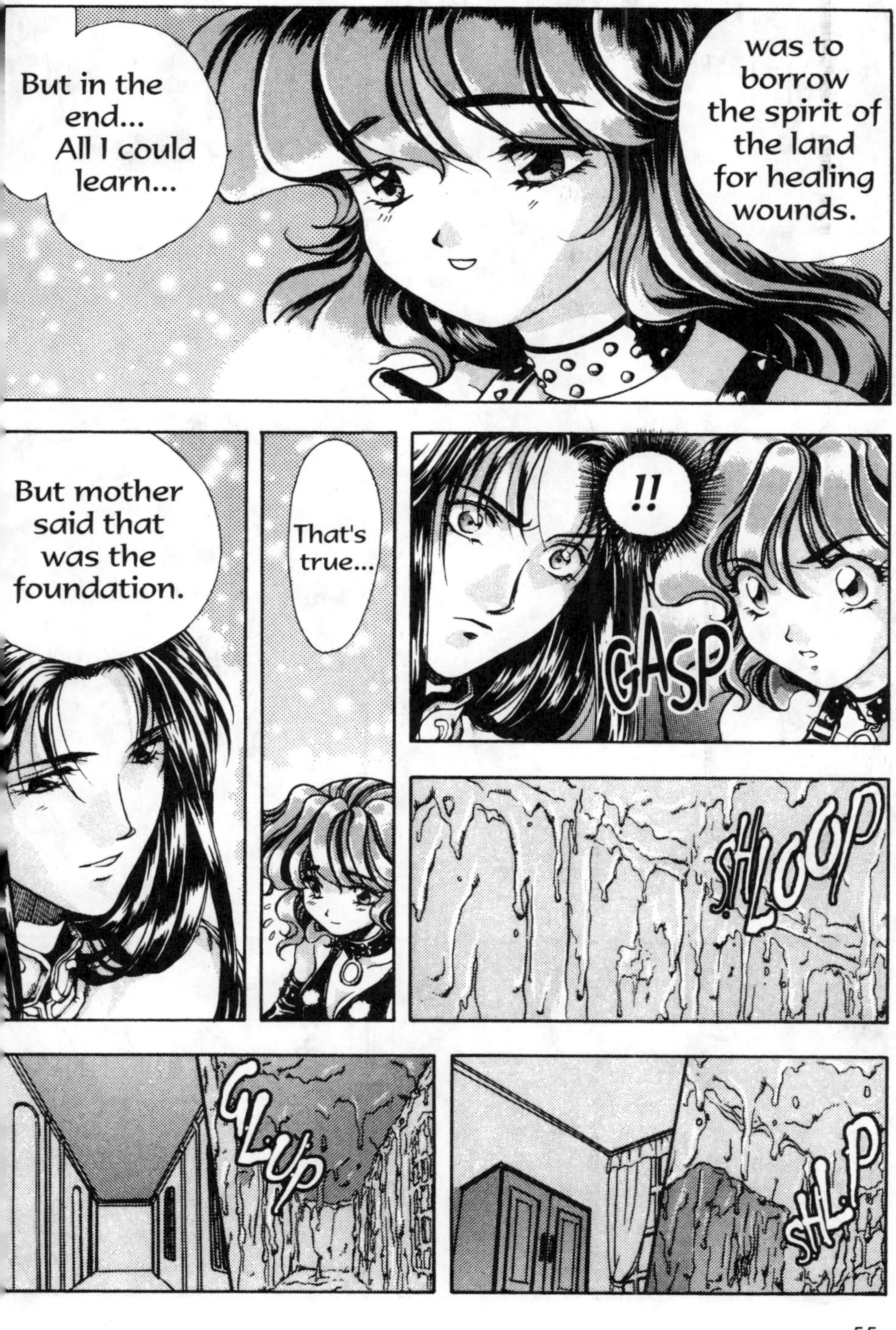
But in the end... All I could learn...
was to borrow the spirit of the land for healing wounds.
But mother said that was the foundation.
That's true...
!!
GASP
SHLOOP
GLUP
SHLP

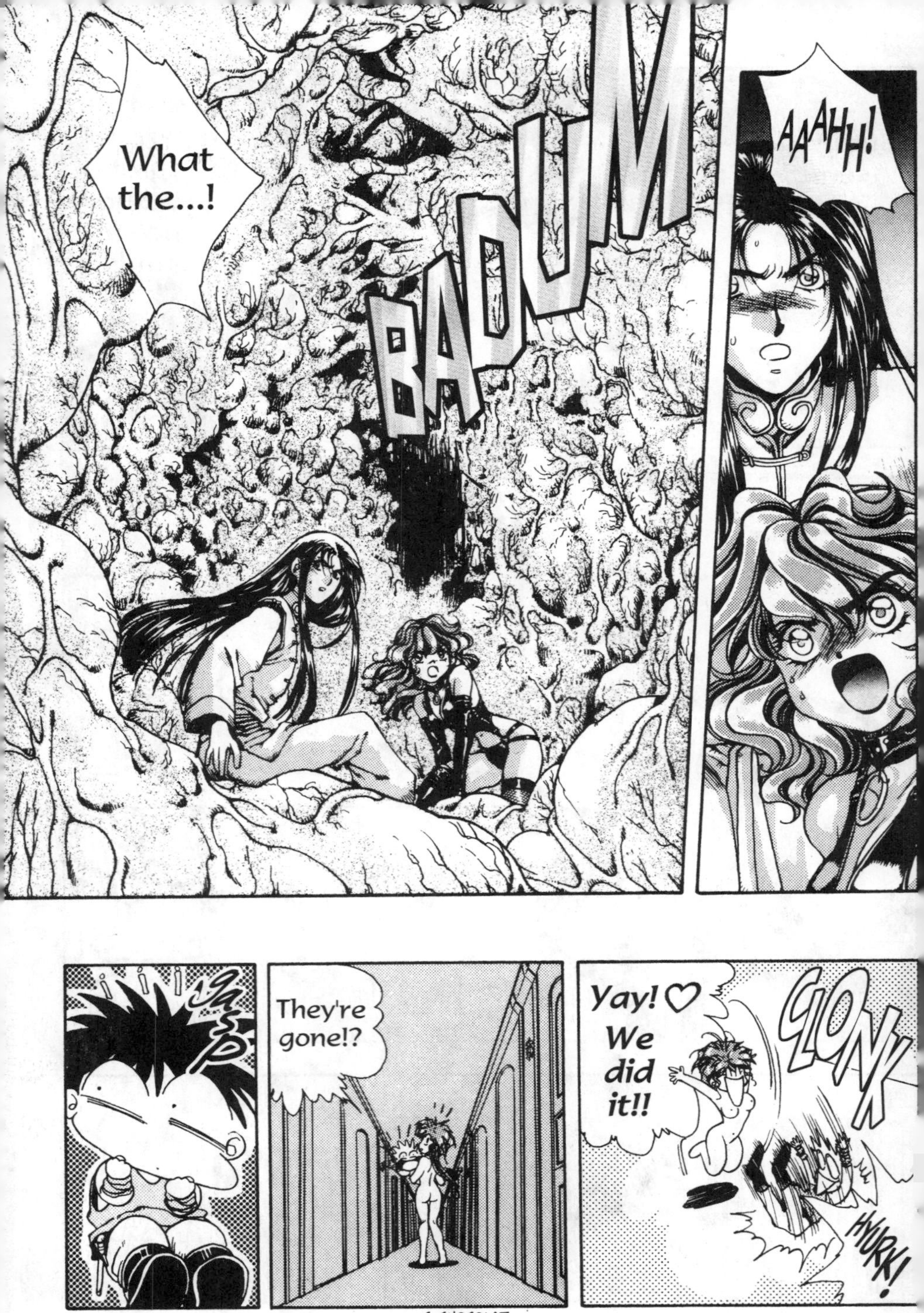
AAAHH!
BADUUM
What the...!
Yay! ♡ We did it!!
CLONK
HYURK!
They're gone!?
gasp
C-CHOCOLAT...

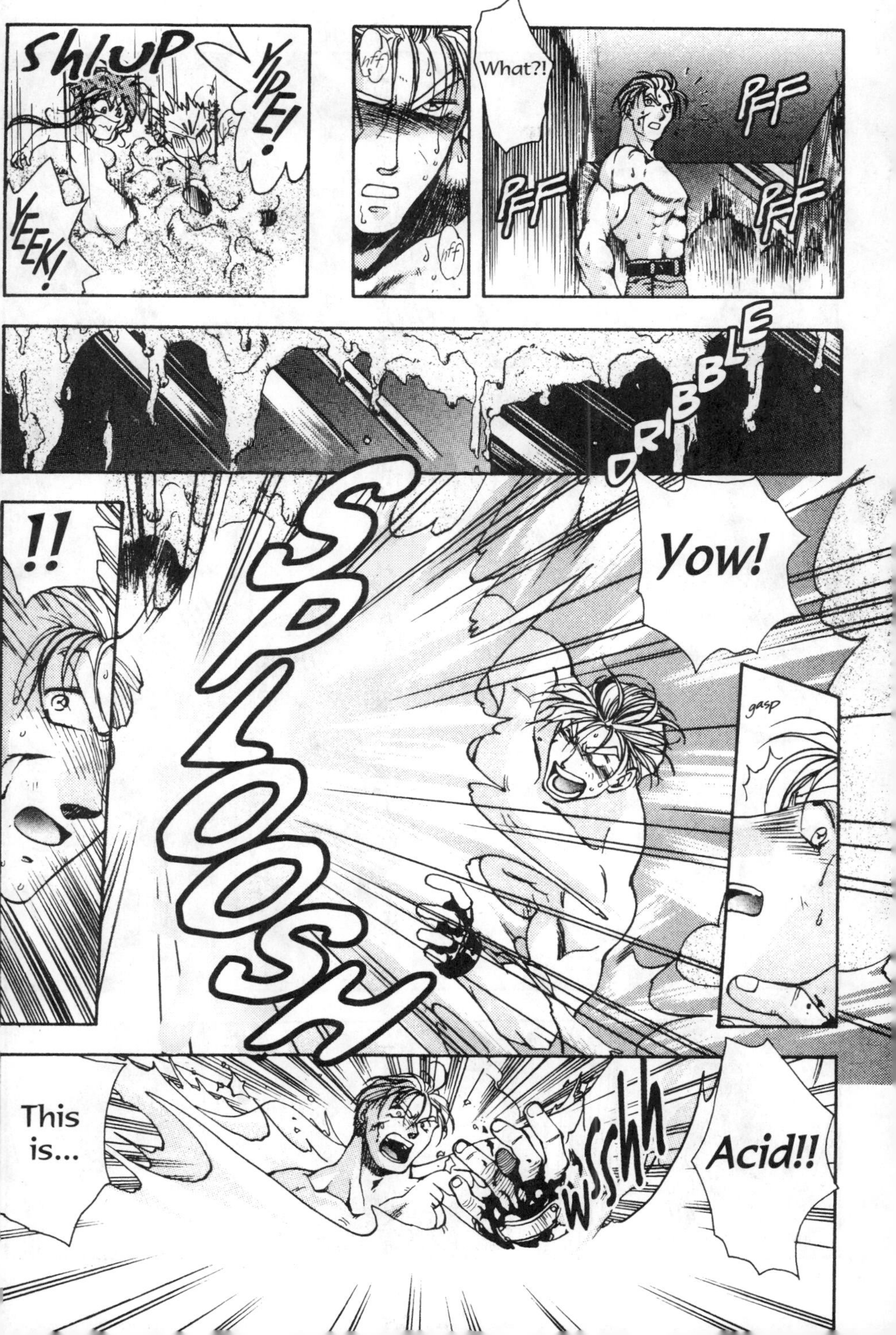

SHLUP
YIPE!
YEEEK!
hff
hff
What?!
PFF
PFF
PFF
DRIBBLE
!!
SPLOOSH
Yow!
gasp
This is...
WSSHH
Acid!!

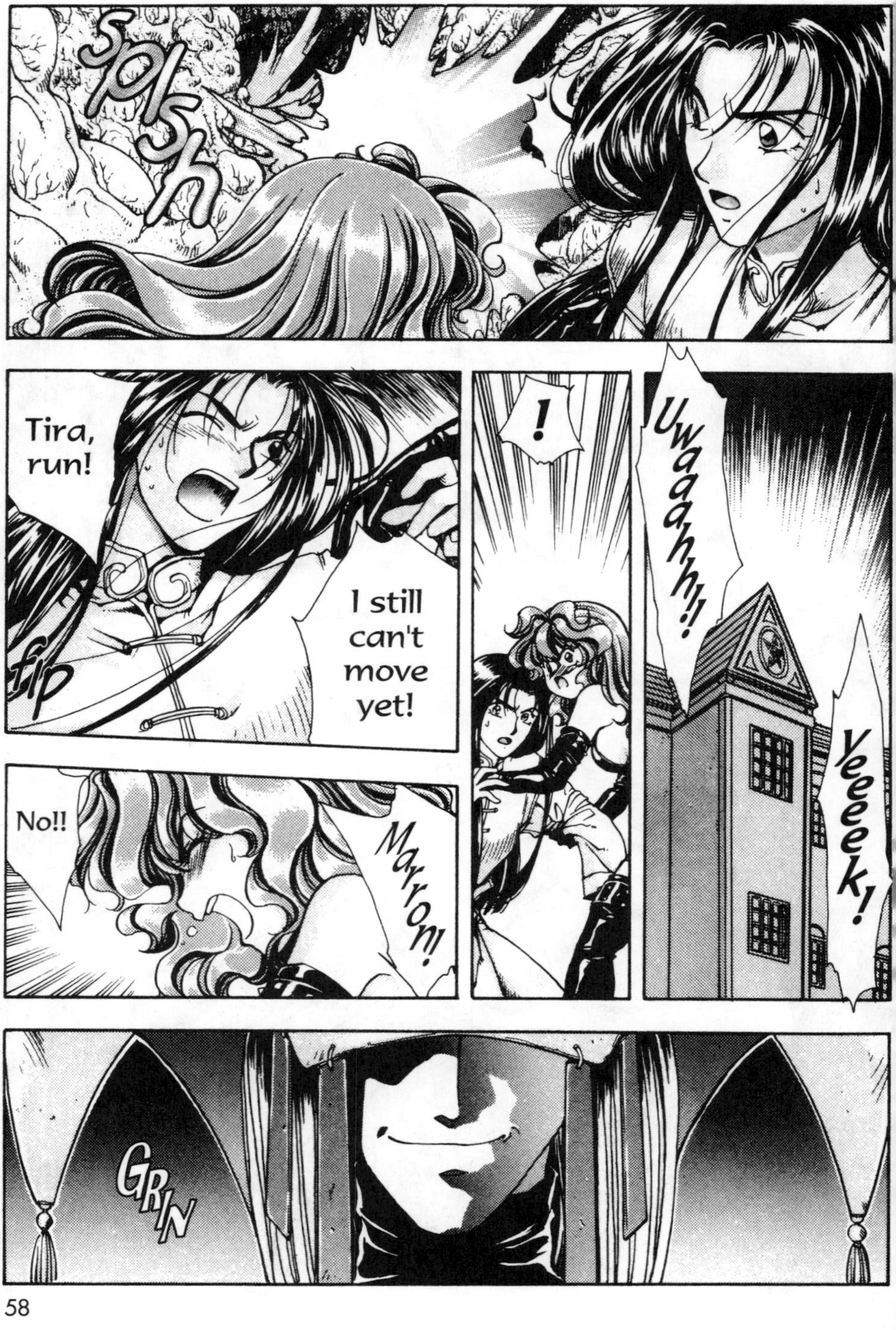
splsh
Uwaaahh!!
Yeeeek!
!
Tira, run!
I still can't move yet!
fip
No!!
Marron!
GRIN

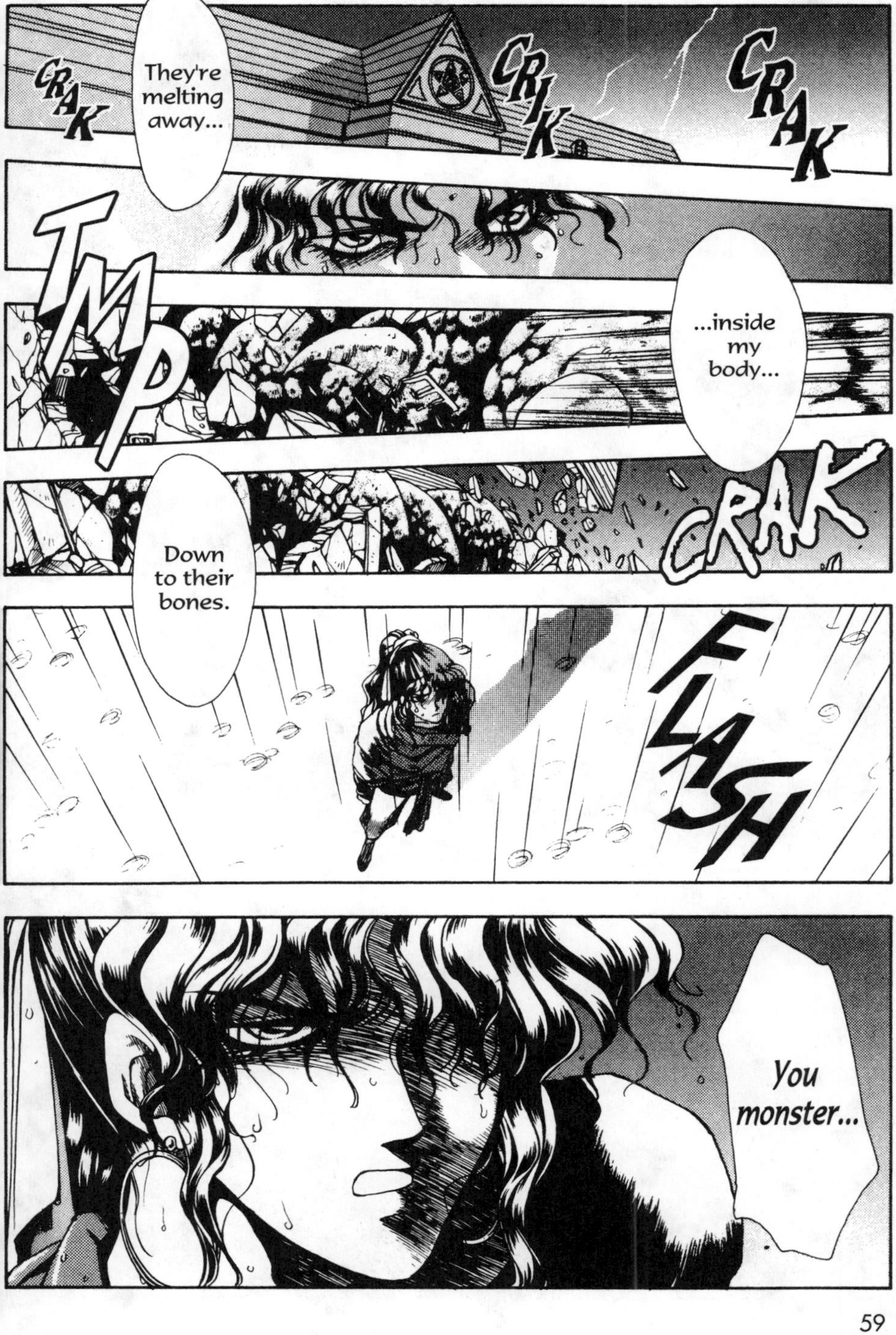
CRAK
CRIK
They're melting away...
CRAK
...inside my body...
TMP
CRAK
Down to their bones.
FLASH
You monster...

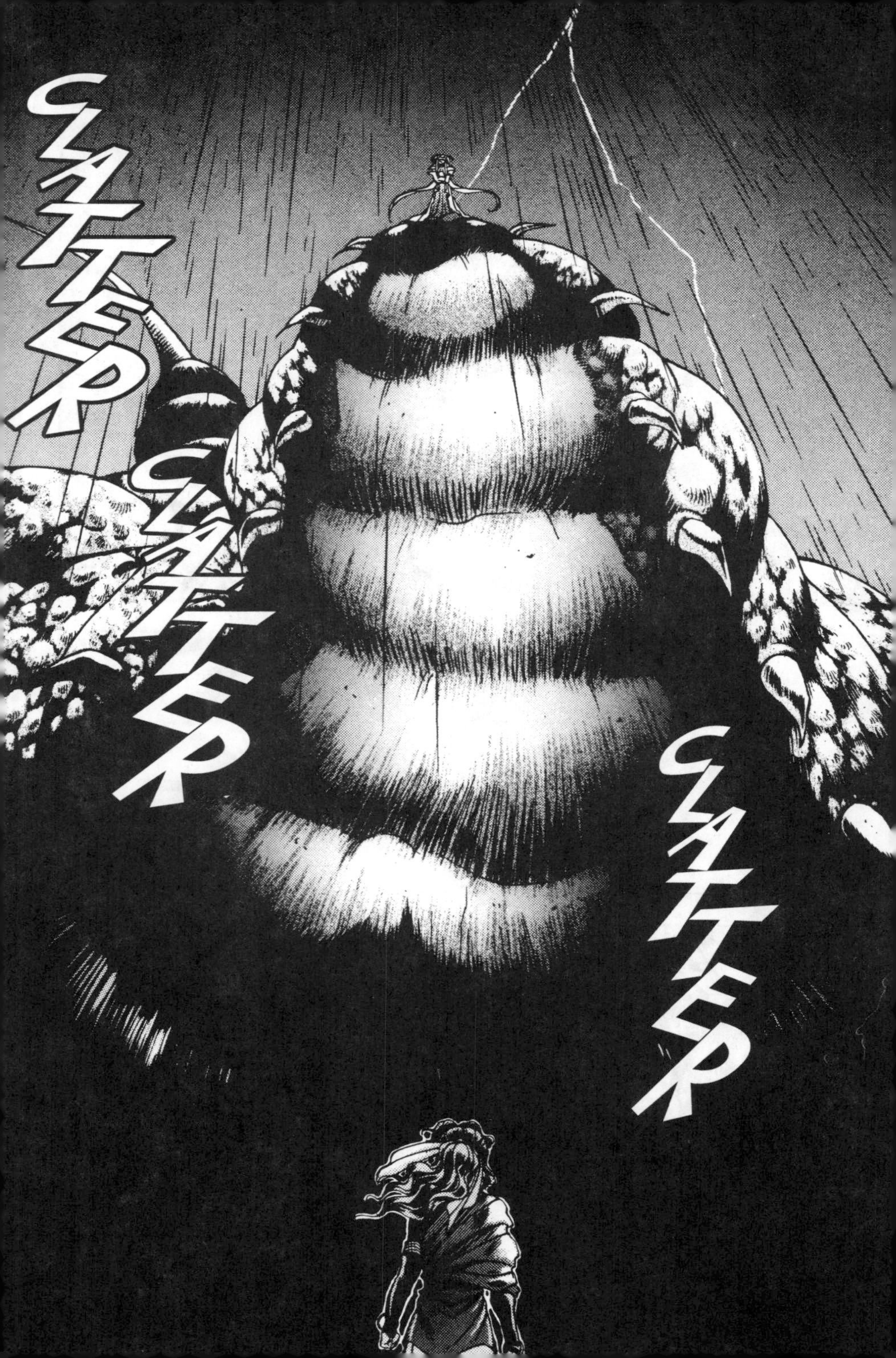
CLATTER
CLATTER
CLATTER

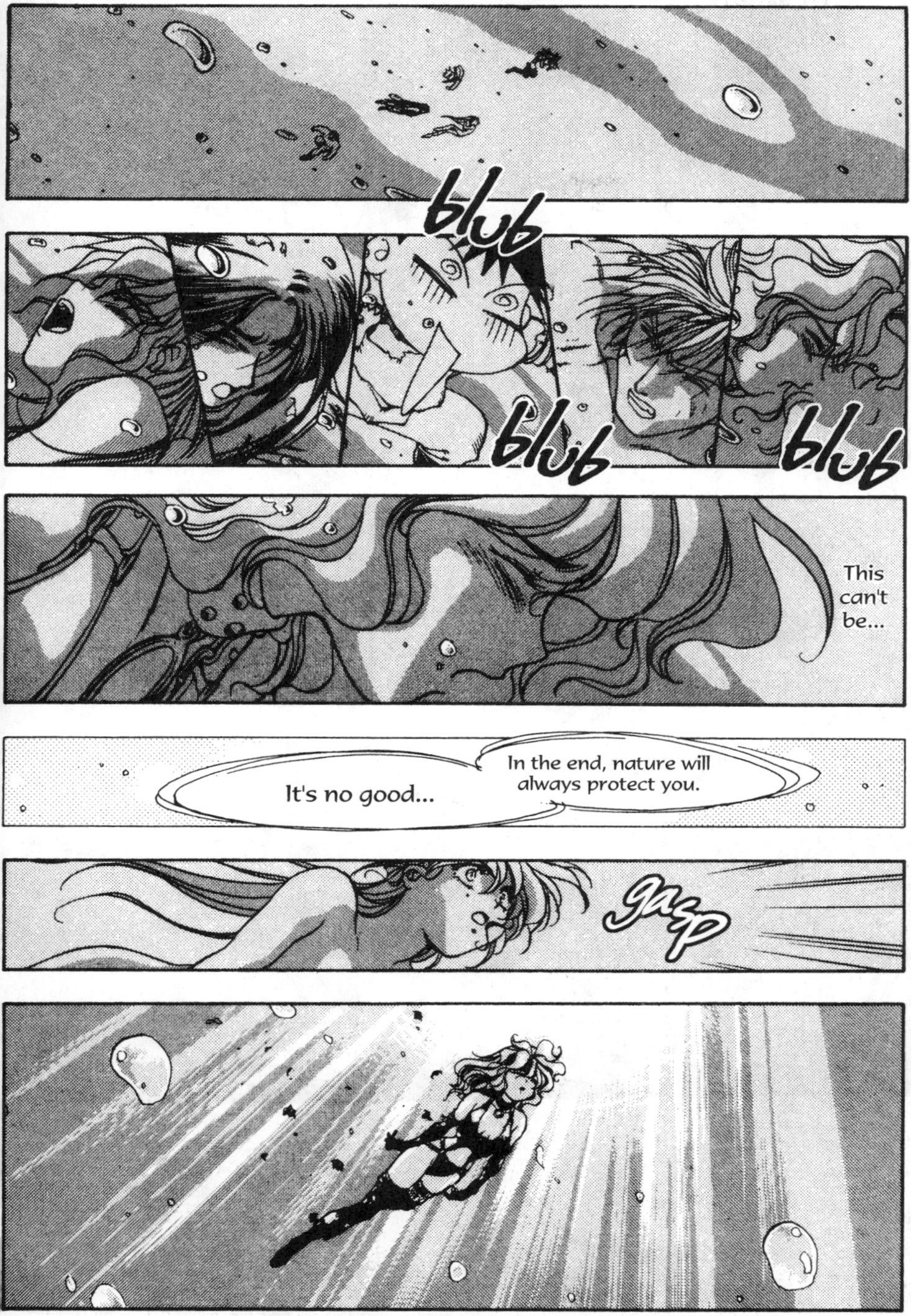
blub
blub
blub
This can't be...
In the end, nature will always protect you.
It's no good...
gasp

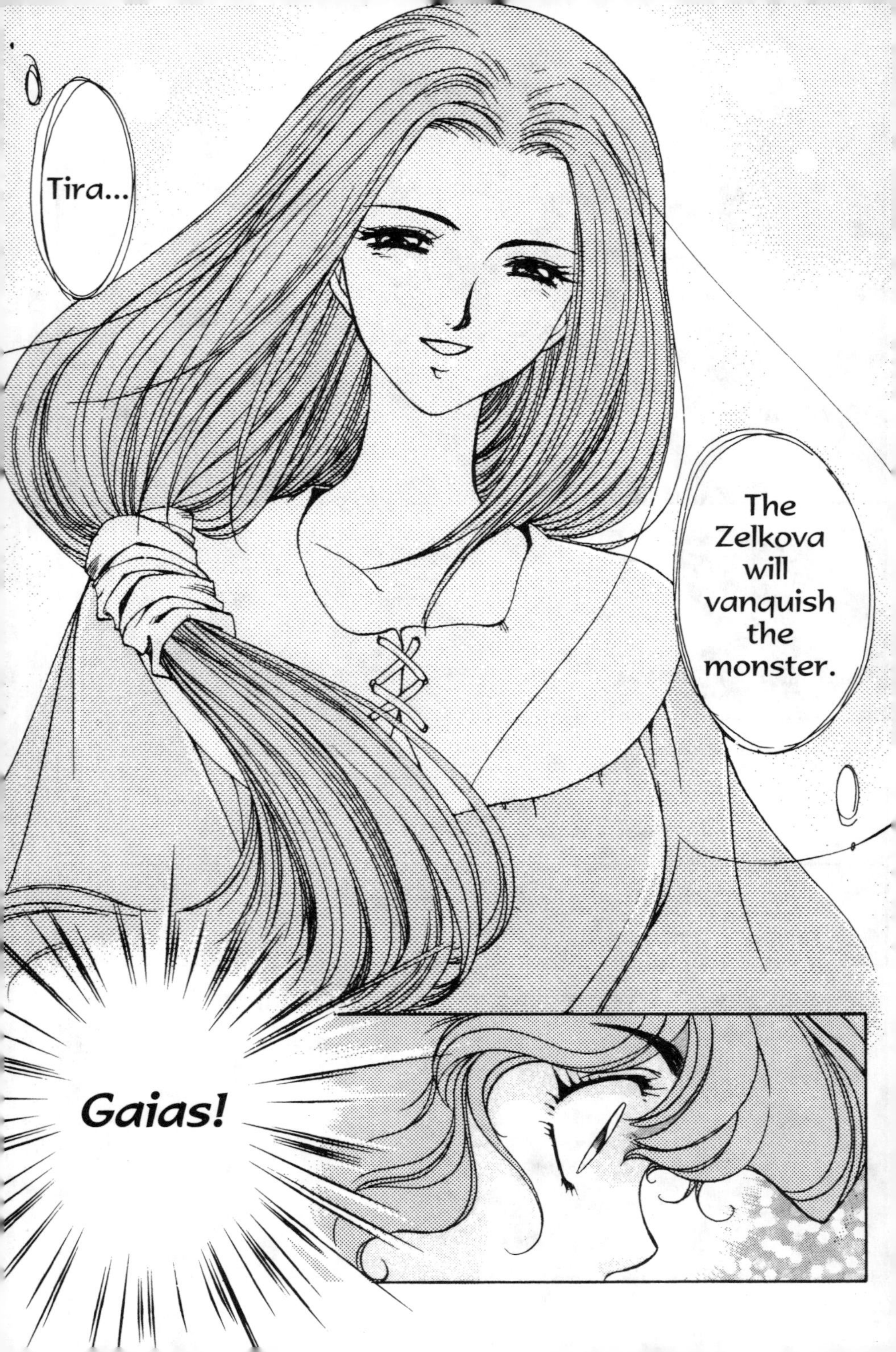
Tira...
The Zelkova will vanquish the monster.
Gaias!

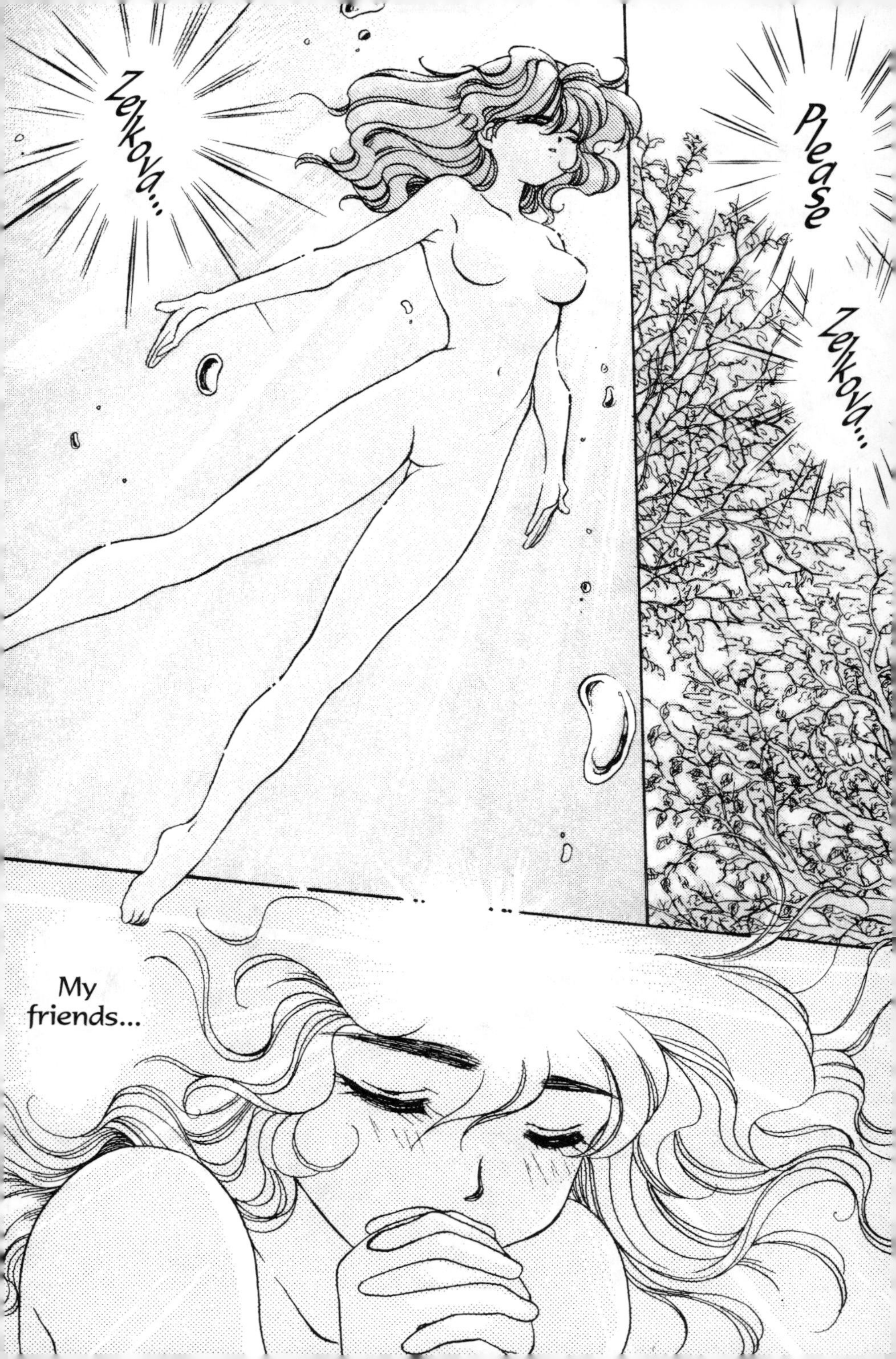
Please Zelkova...
Zelkova...
My friends...

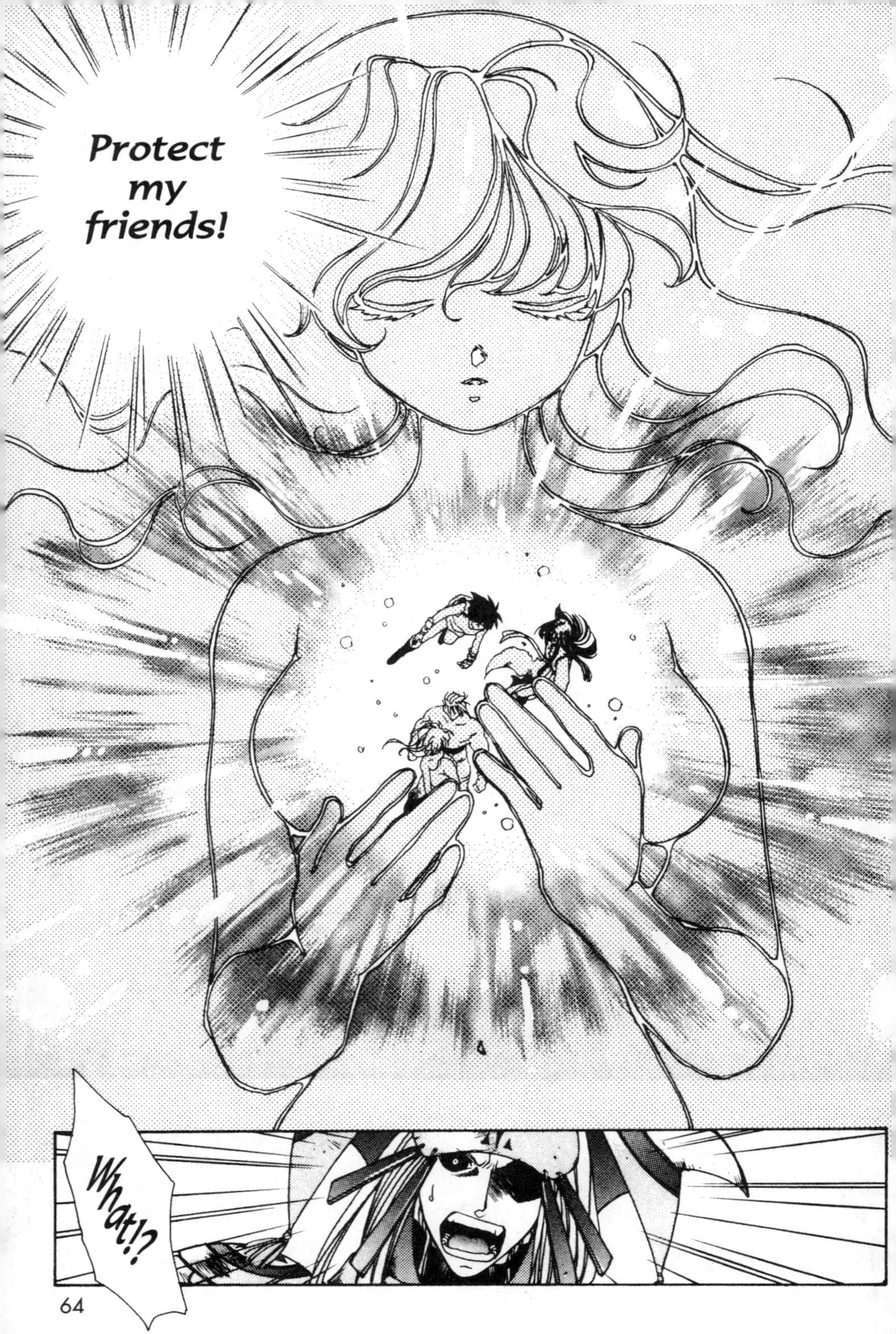
Protect my friends!
What!?

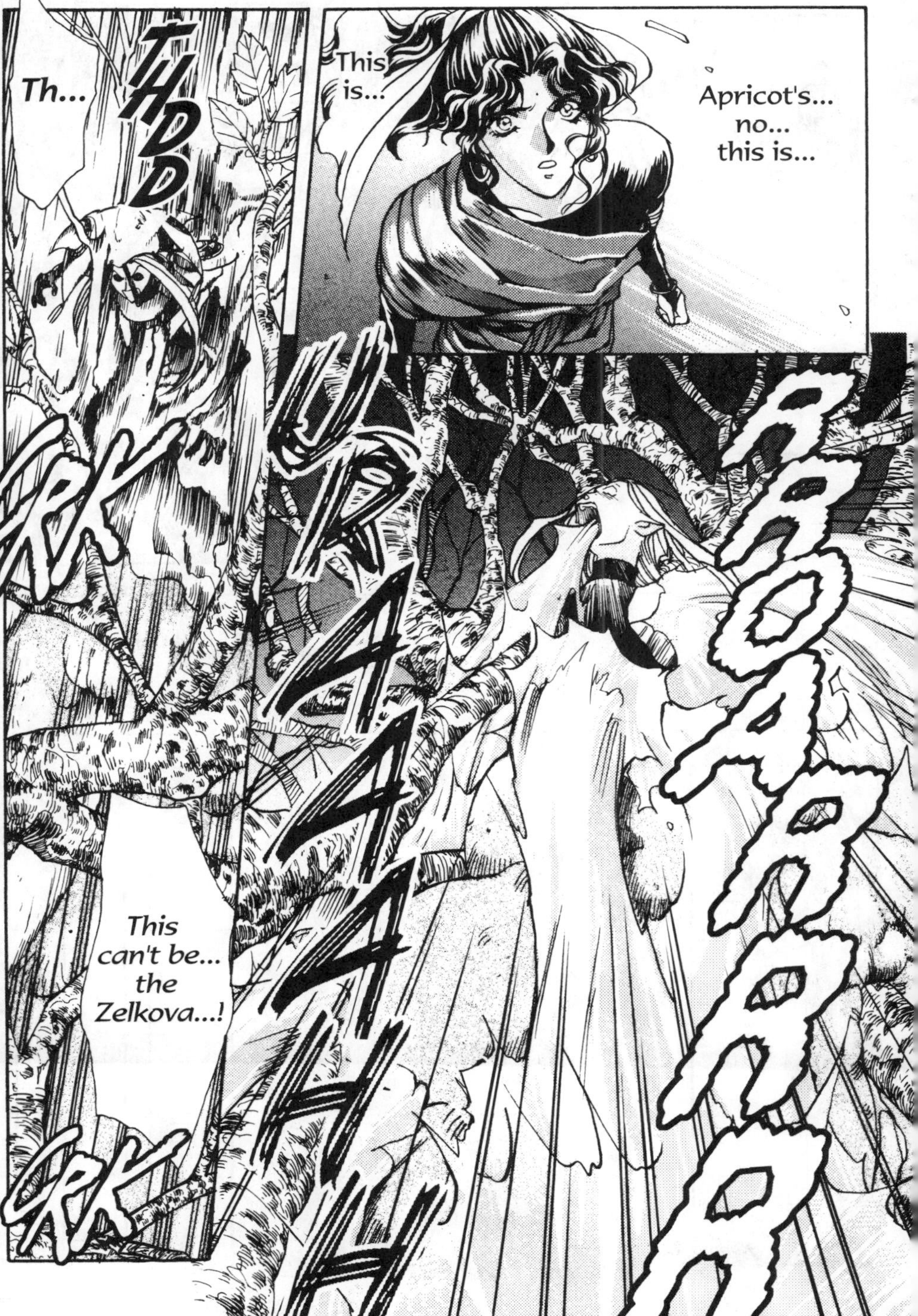
Apricot's... no... this is...
This is...
Th...
THDD
GRK
This can't be... the Zelkova...!
GRK

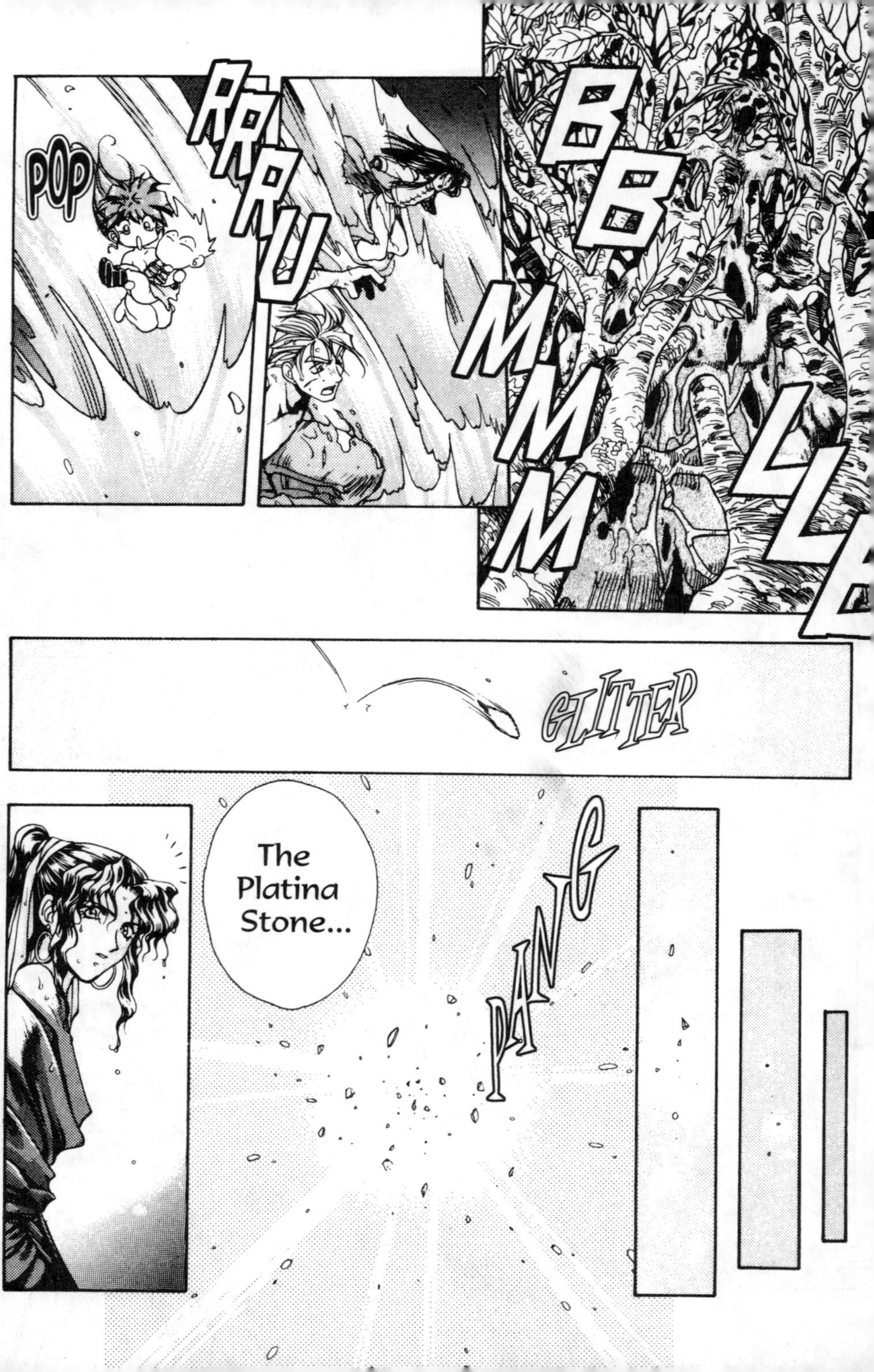
BBMMMLL
RRRRU
POP
GLITTER
PANG
The Platina Stone...

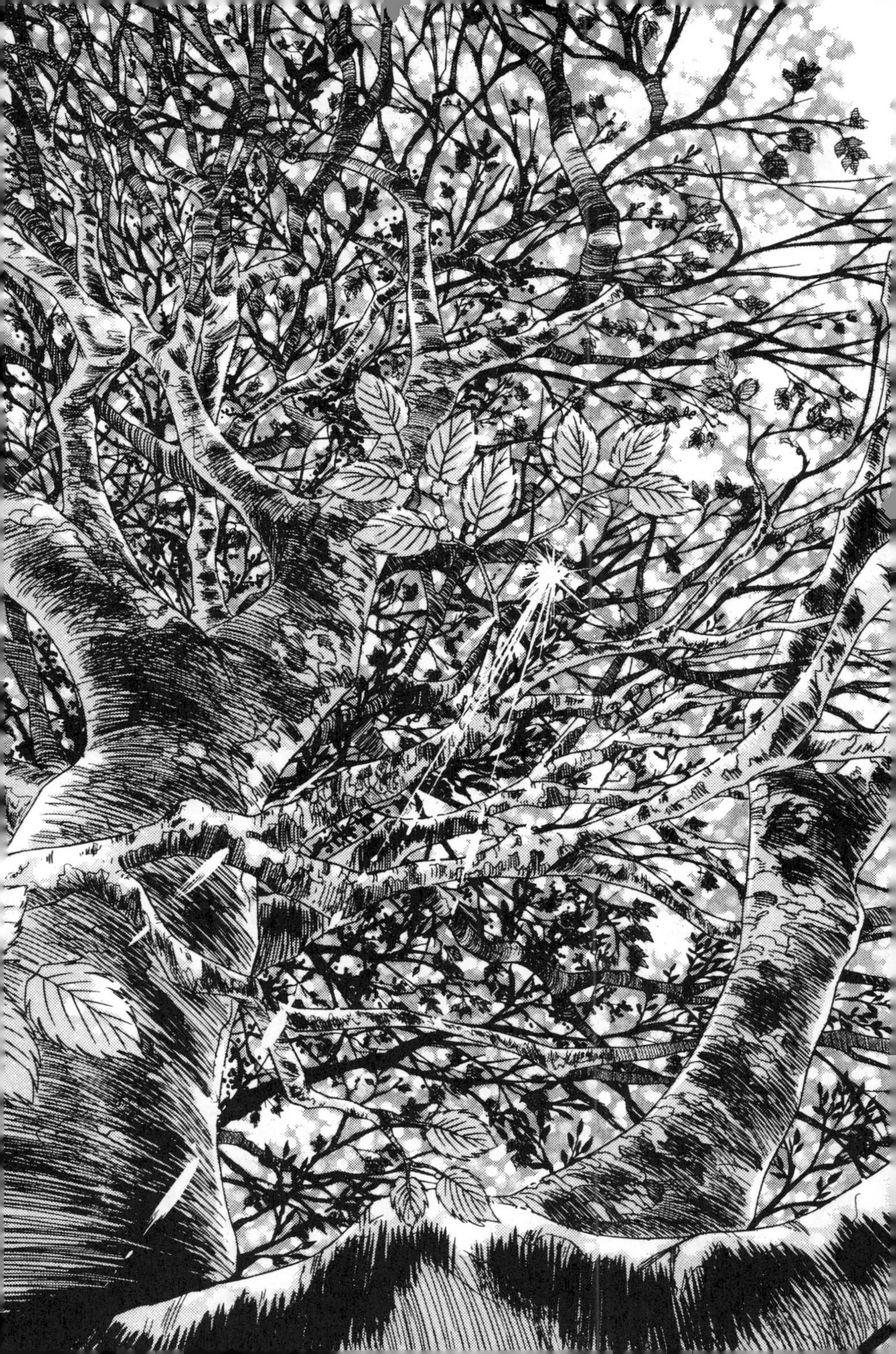

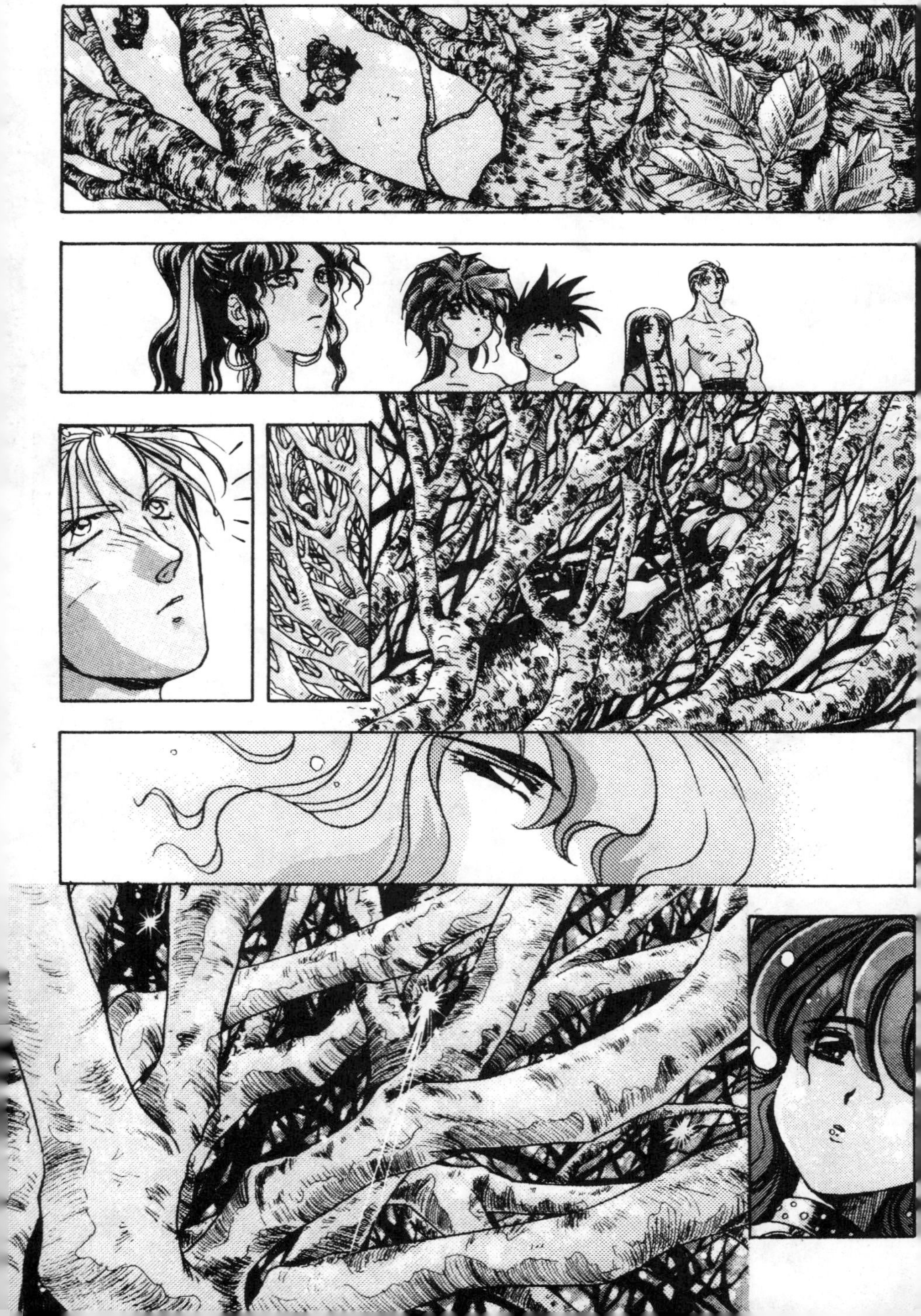

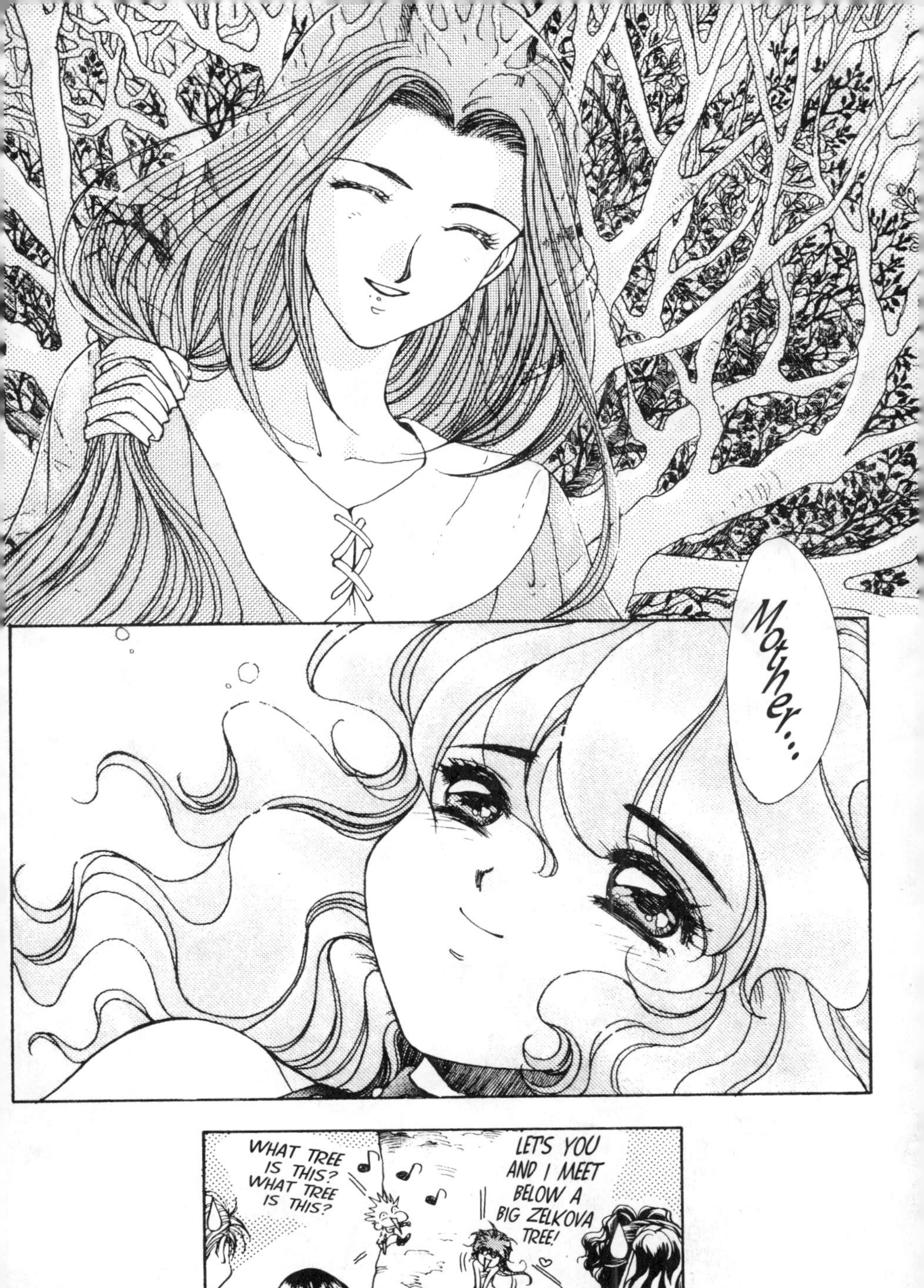
Mother...
LET'S YOU AND I MEET BELOW A BIG ZELKOVA TREE!
WHAT TREE IS THIS? WHAT TREE IS THIS?

CHOCOLAT
COME TO THINK
OF IT, WHEN
DID SHE START
WEARING
SKIRTS?

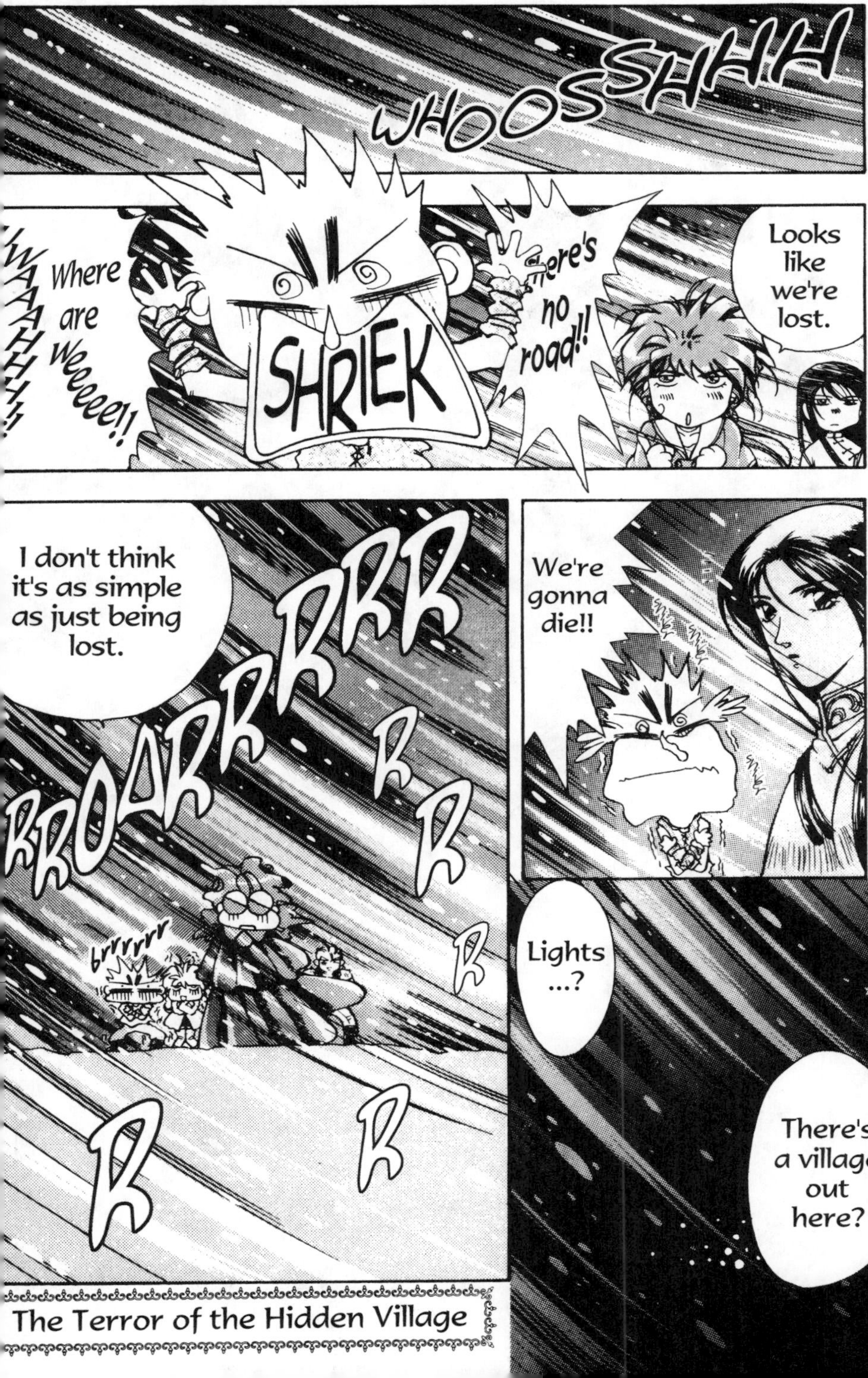
WHOOSSHHH
Looks like we're lost.
There's no road!!
SHRIEK
Where are weeeee!!
WAAAAHHHH!!!
We're gonna die!!
I don't think it's as simple as just being lost.
BROARRRRRRR
R
R
R
R
R
brrrrrr
Lights ...?
There's a village out here?

The Terror of the Hidden Village

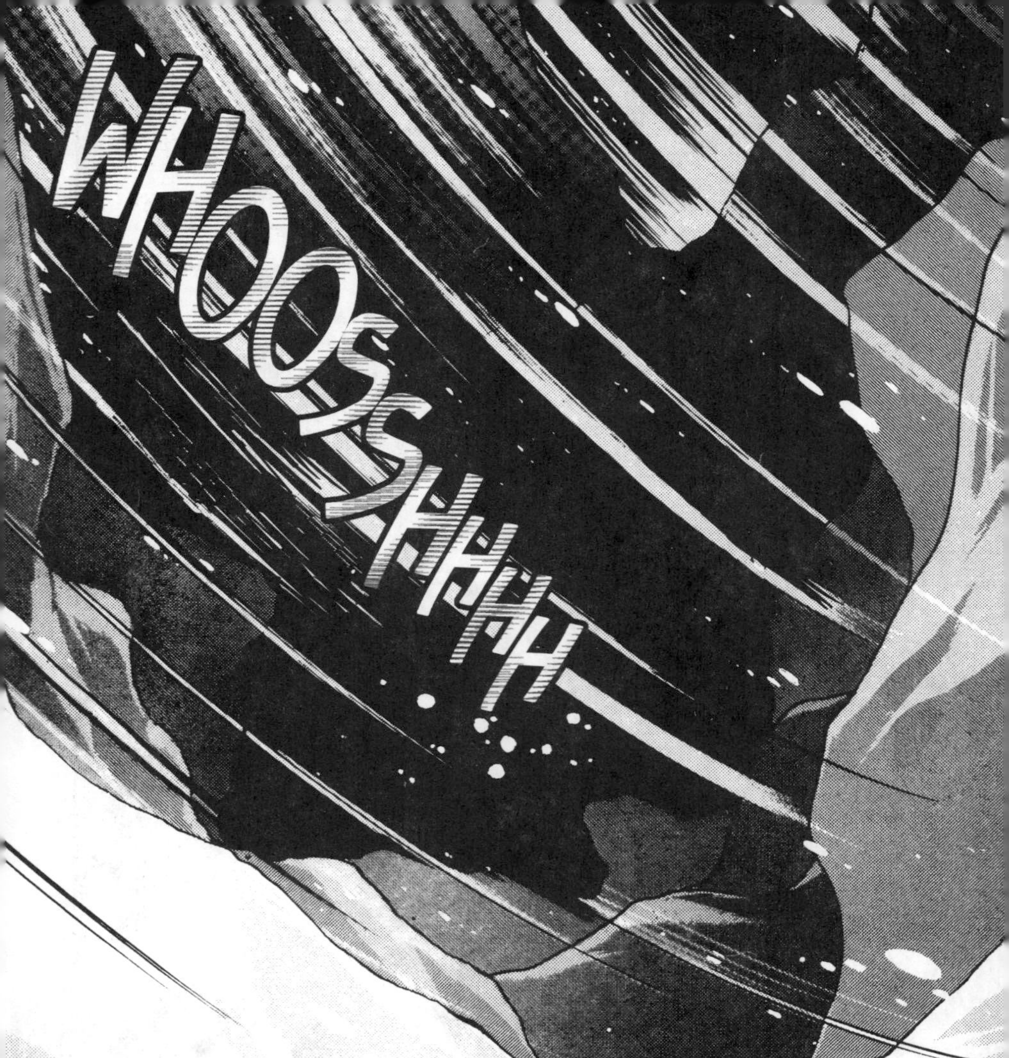
WHOOSHHHH

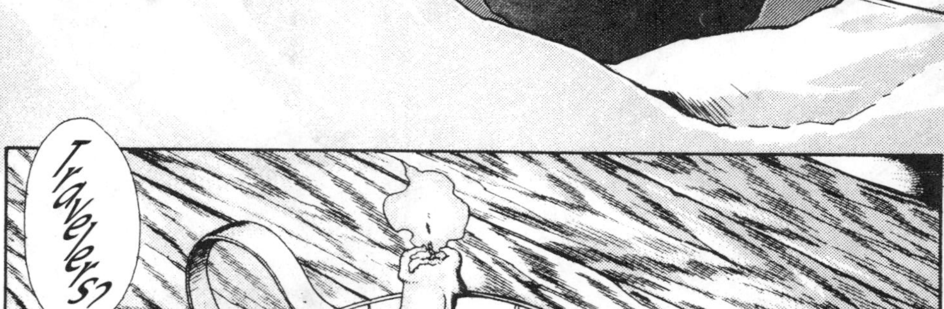
Travelers?

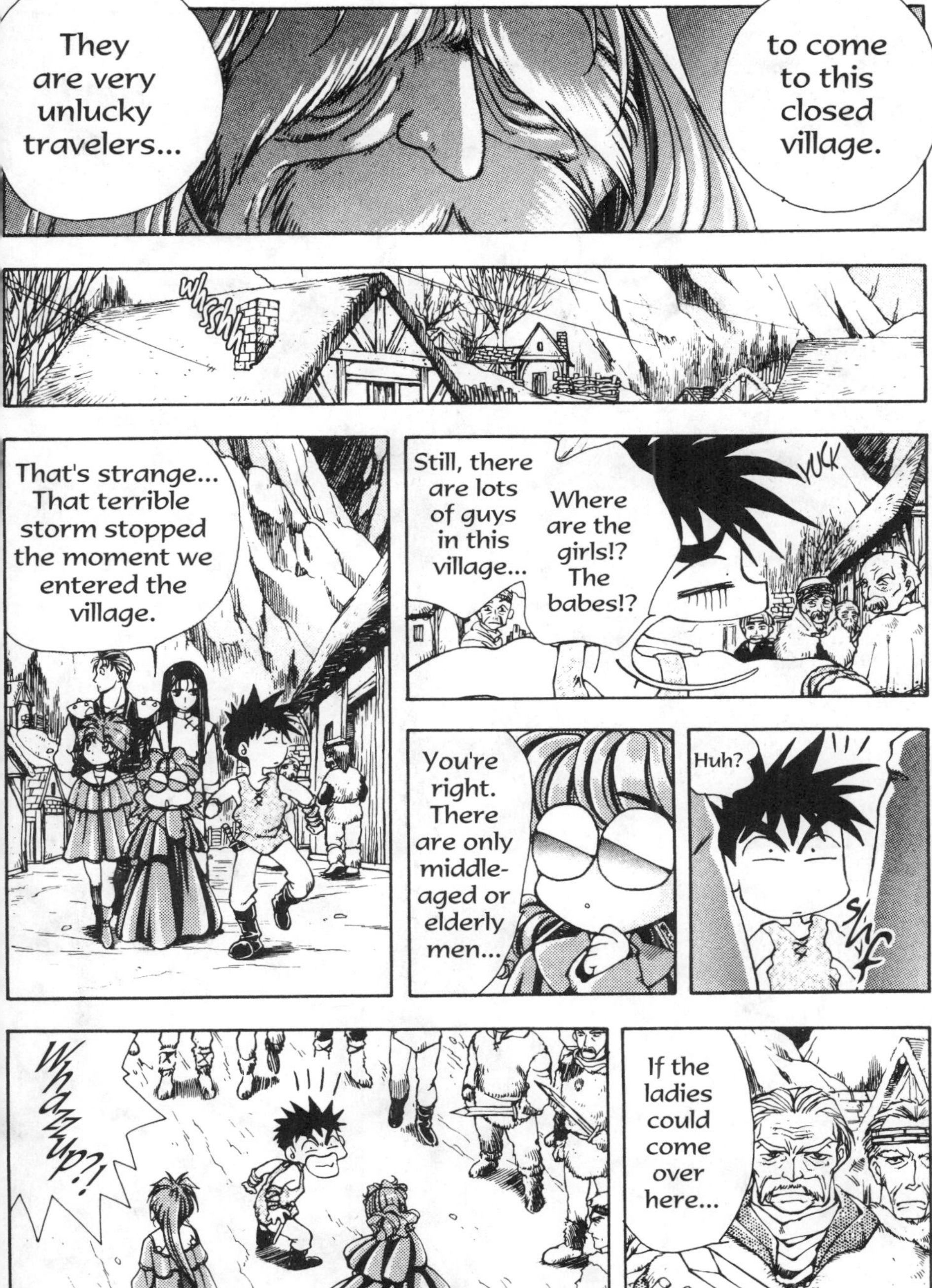
They are very unlucky travelers...
to come to this closed village.
whsshh
That's strange... That terrible storm stopped the moment we entered the village.
Still, there are lots of guys in this village...
Where are the girls!? The babes!?
YUCK
You're right. There are only middle-aged or elderly men...
Huh?
Whazzup?!
If the ladies could come over here...

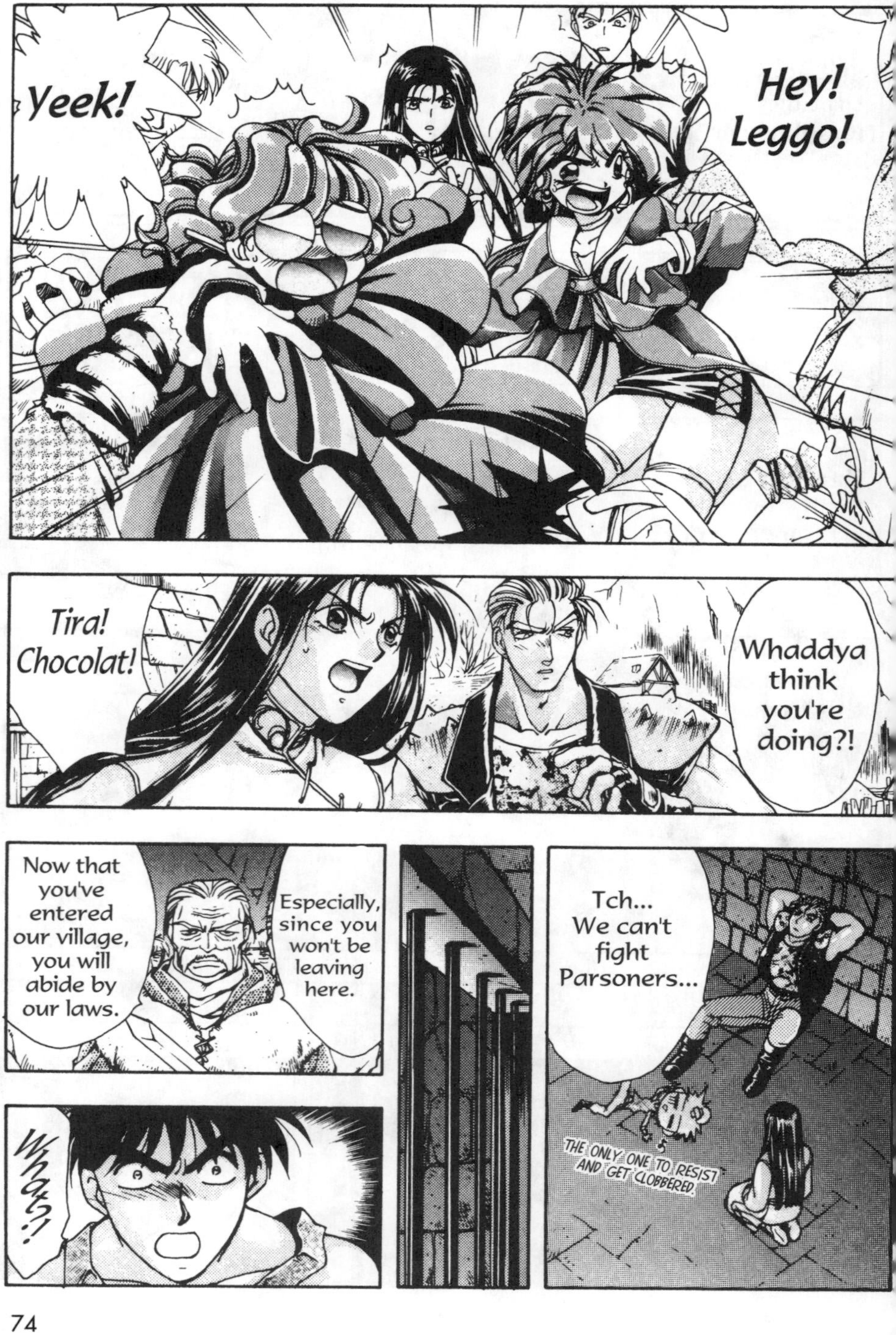
Yeek!
Hey! Leggo!
Tira! Chocolat!
Whaddya think you're doing?!
Now that you've entered our village, you will abide by our laws.
Especially, since you won't be leaving here.
What?!
Tch... We can't fight Parsoners...
THE ONLY ONE TO RESIST AND GET CLOBBERED.

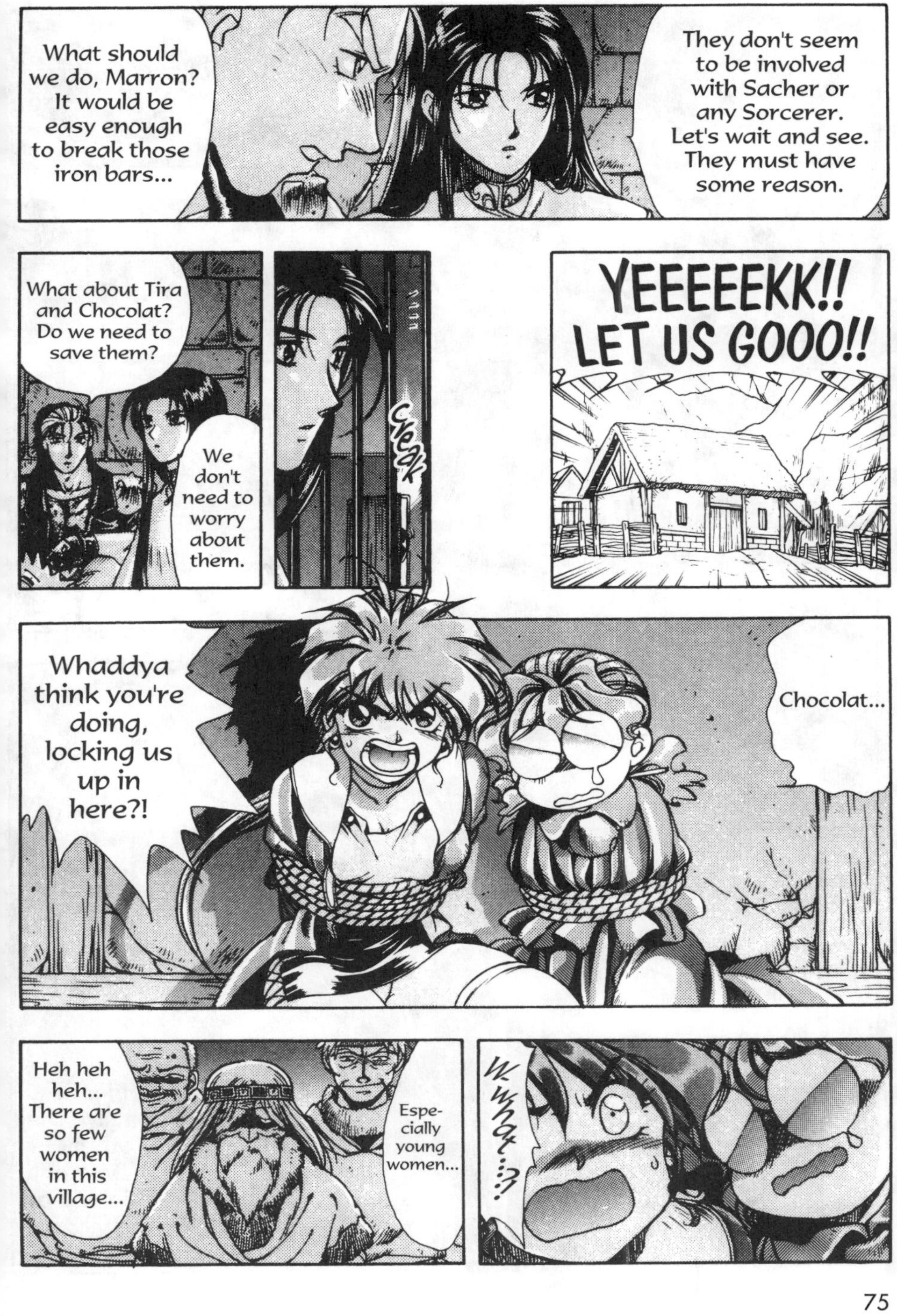
What should we do, Marron? It would be easy enough to break those iron bars...
They don't seem to be involved with Sacher or any Sorcerer. Let's wait and see. They must have some reason.
What about Tira and Chocolat? Do we need to save them?
We don't need to worry about them.
Creak
YEEEEEKK!! LET US GOOO!!
Whaddya think you're doing, locking us up in here?!
Chocolat...
Heh heh heh... There are so few women in this village...
Espe-cially young women...
W-what...?!

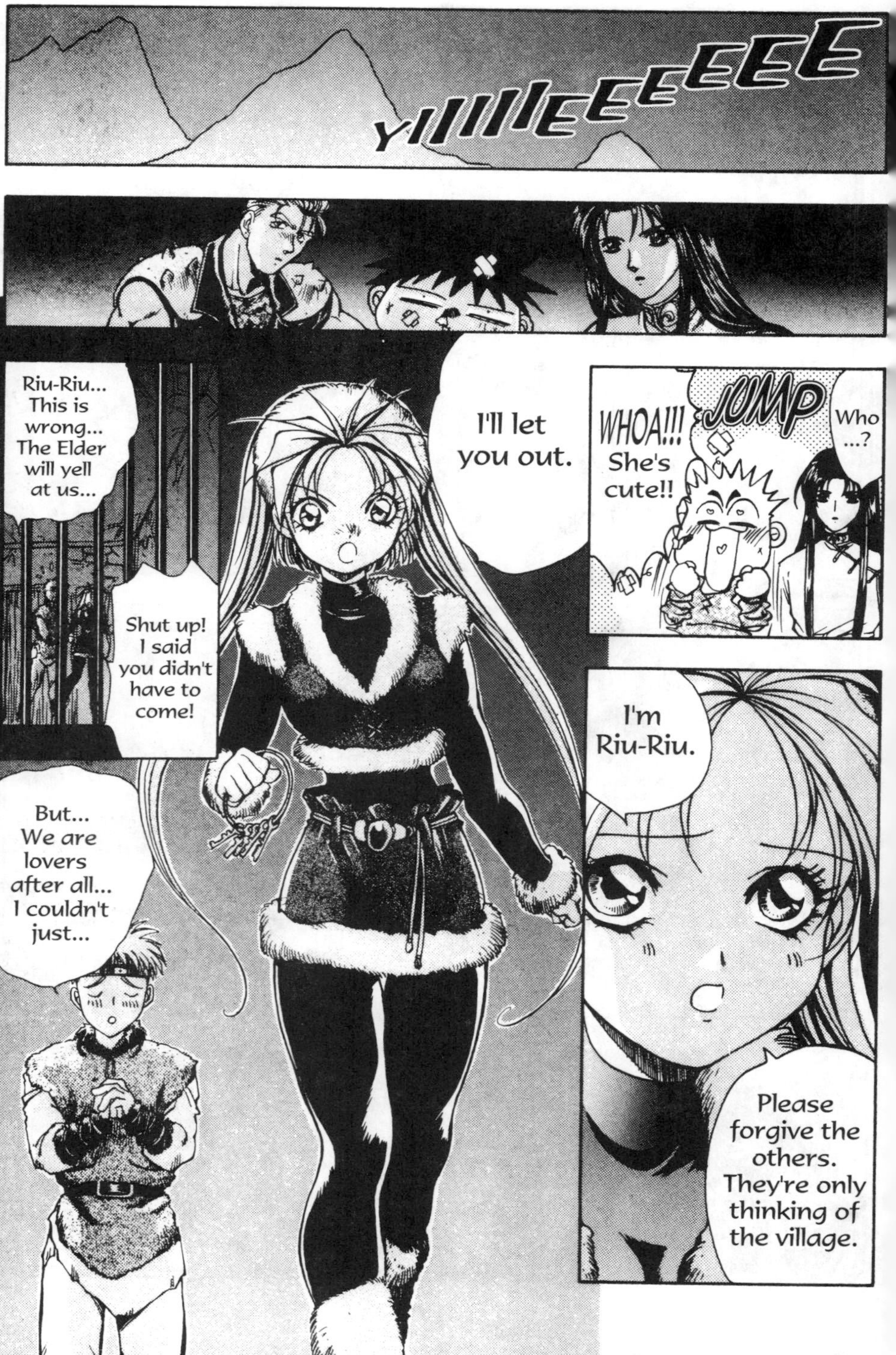
YIIIIEEEEEEE
Riu-Riu... This is wrong... The Elder will yell at us...
Shut up! I said you didn't have to come!
But... We are lovers after all... I couldn't just...
I'll let you out.
JUMP
WHOA!!! She's cute!!
Who ...?
I'm Riu-Riu.
Please forgive the others. They're only thinking of the village.

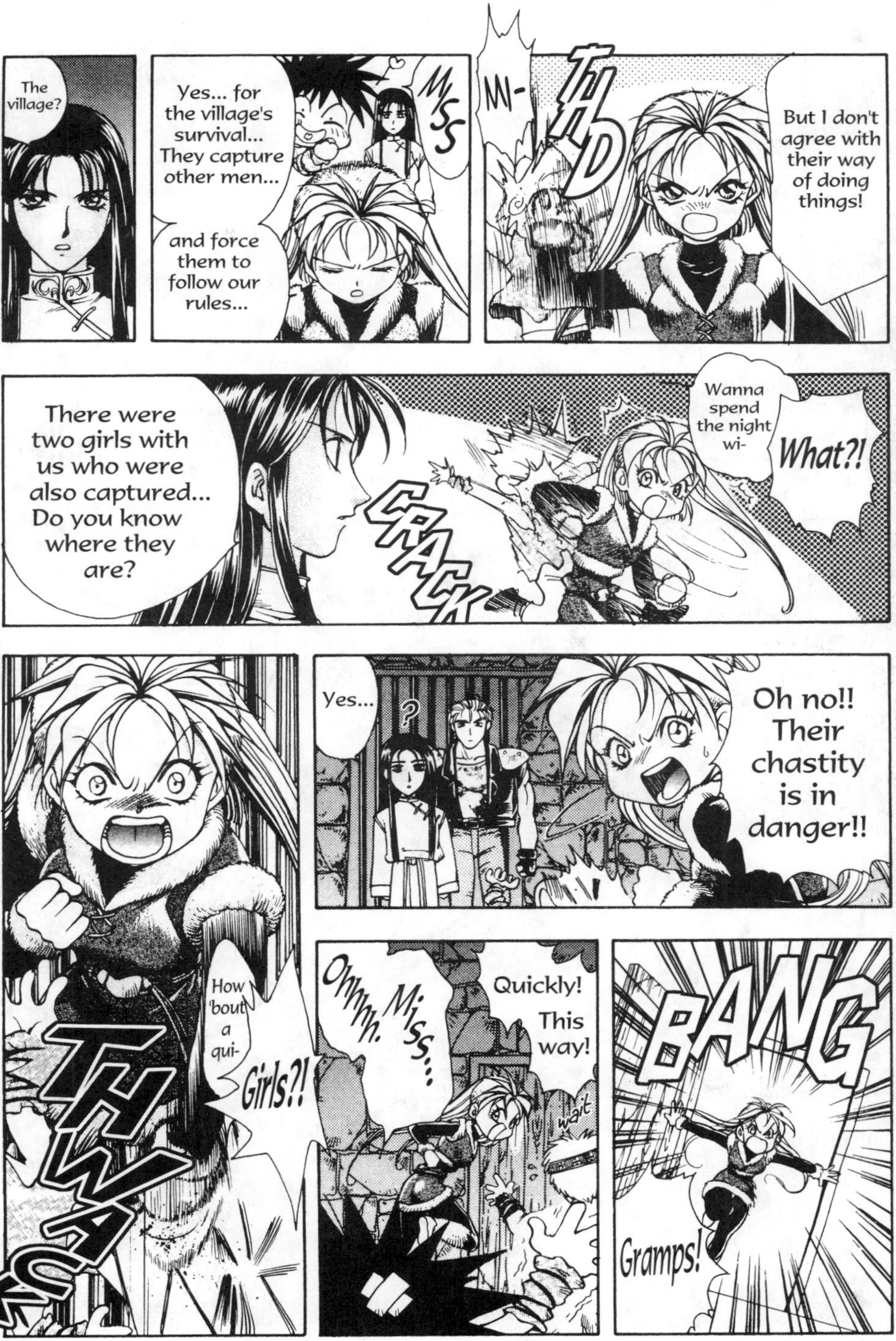
The village?
Yes... for the village's survival... They capture other men...
and force them to follow our rules...
MISS
MI-
THUD
But I don't agree with their way of doing things!
There were two girls with us who were also captured... Do you know where they are?
CRACK
Wanna spend the night wi-
What?!
How 'bout a qui-
THWACK
Girls?!
Yes...
?
Oh no!! Their chastity is in danger!!
Ohhhh.
Miss...
Quickly! This way!
wait
BANG
Gramps!

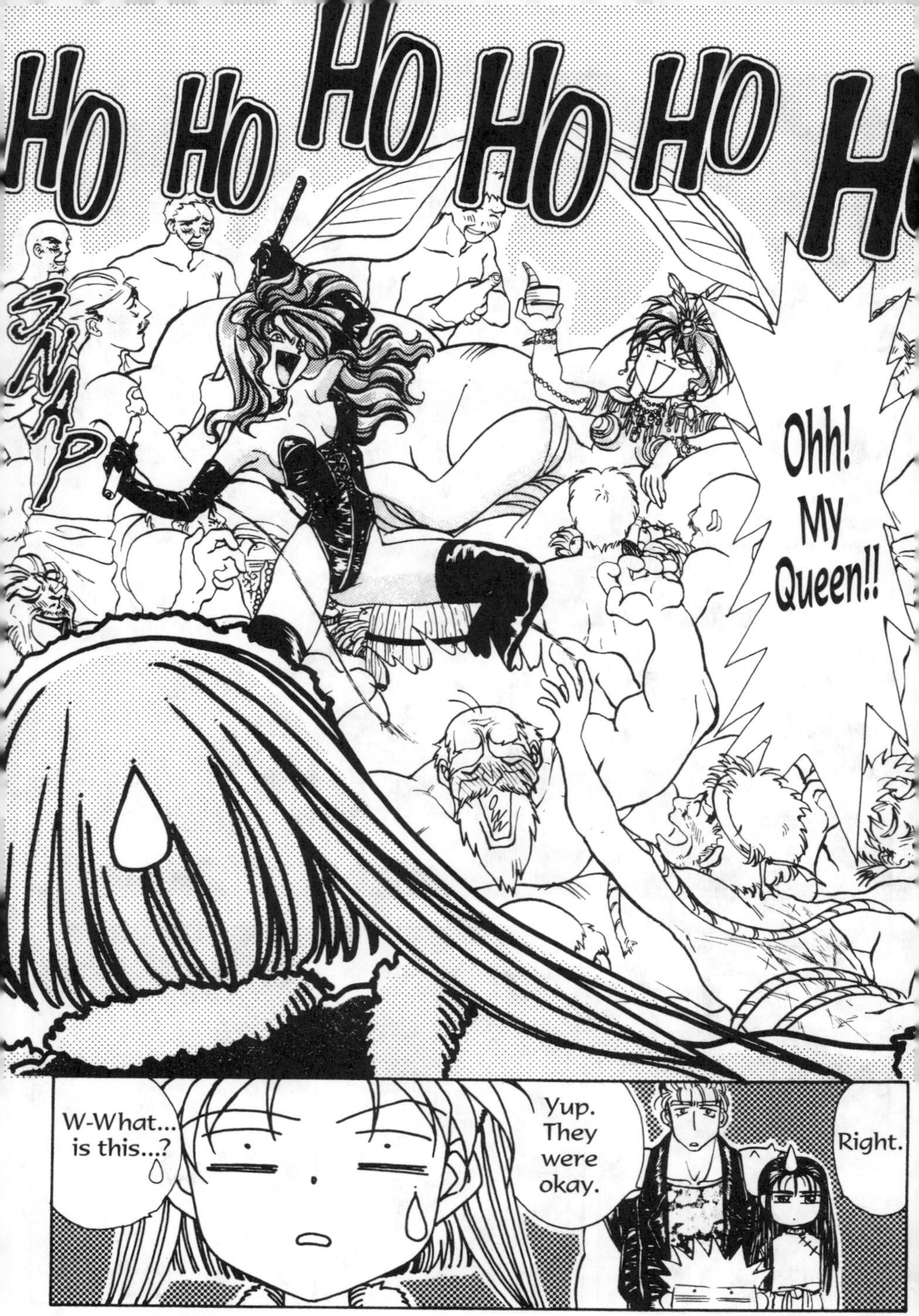
HO HO HO HO HO HO HO
Ohh! My Queen!!
SNAP
Right.
Yup. They were okay.
W-What... is this...?

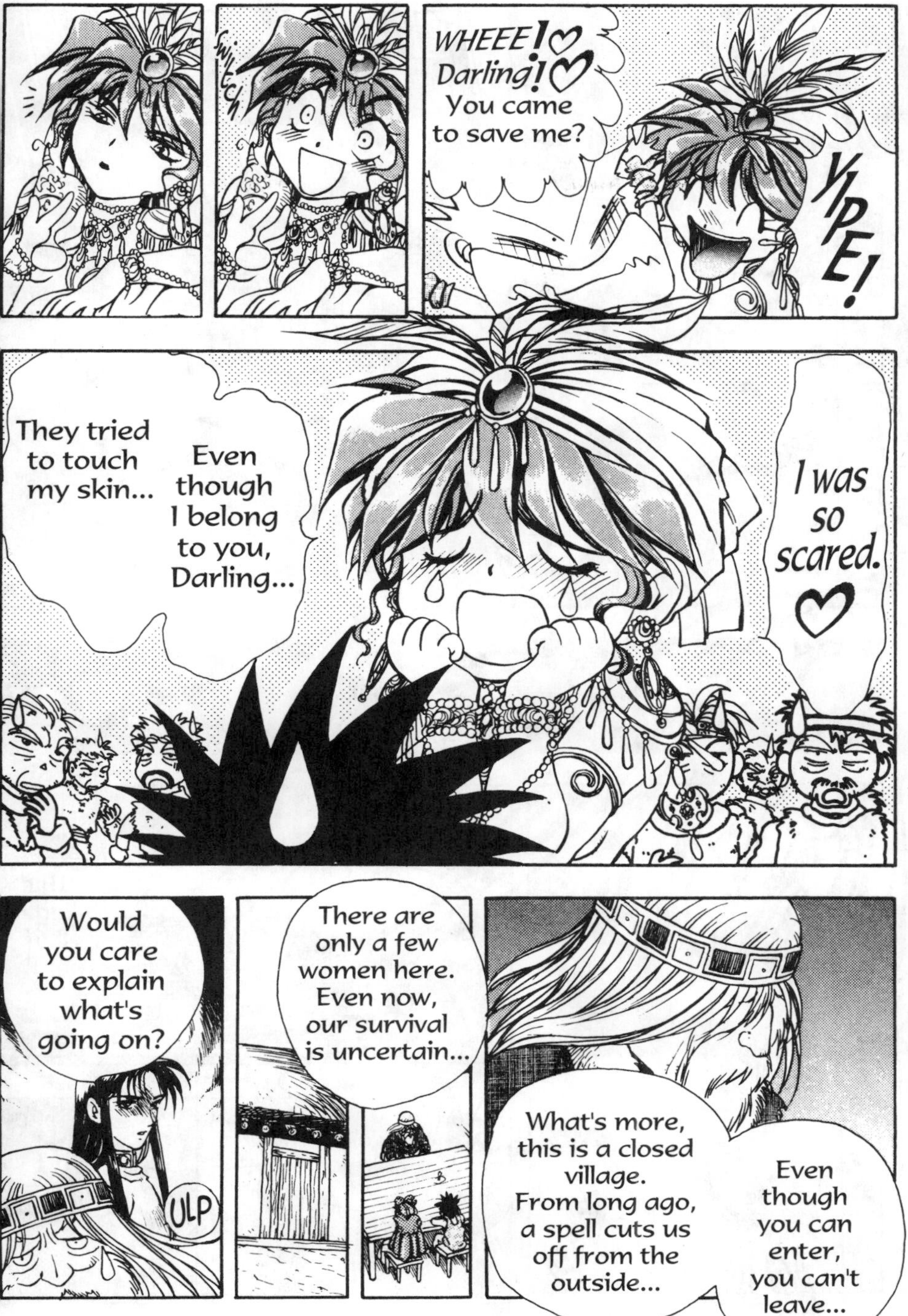
SWITCH
WHEEE!♡ Darling!♡ You came to save me?
YIPE!
They tried to touch my skin...
Even though I belong to you, Darling...
I was so scared. ♡
Would you care to explain what's going on?
ULP
There are only a few women here. Even now, our survival is uncertain...
What's more, this is a closed village. From long ago, a spell cuts us off from the outside...
Even though you can enter, you can't leave...

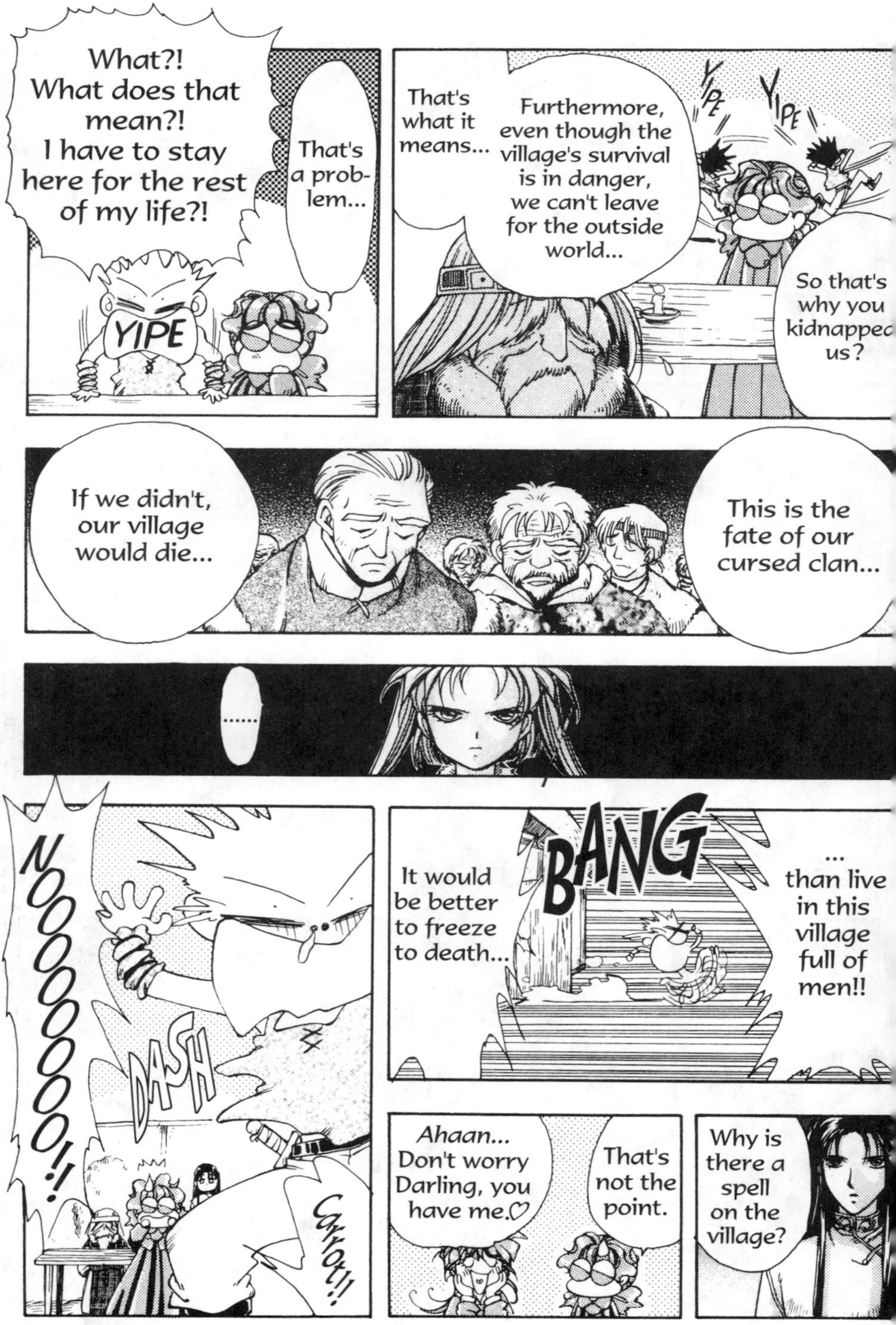

What?! What does that mean?! I have to stay here for the rest of my life?!
That's a problem...
YIPE
That's what it means...
Furthermore, even though the village's survival is in danger, we can't leave for the outside world...
YIPE YIPE
So that's why you kidnapped us?
If we didn't, our village would die...
This is the fate of our cursed clan...
......
It would be better to freeze to death...
BANG
... than live in this village full of men!!
NOOOOOOOOOOO!!
DASH
Carrot!!
Ahaan... Don't worry Darling, you have me.♡
That's not the point.
Why is there a spell on the village?

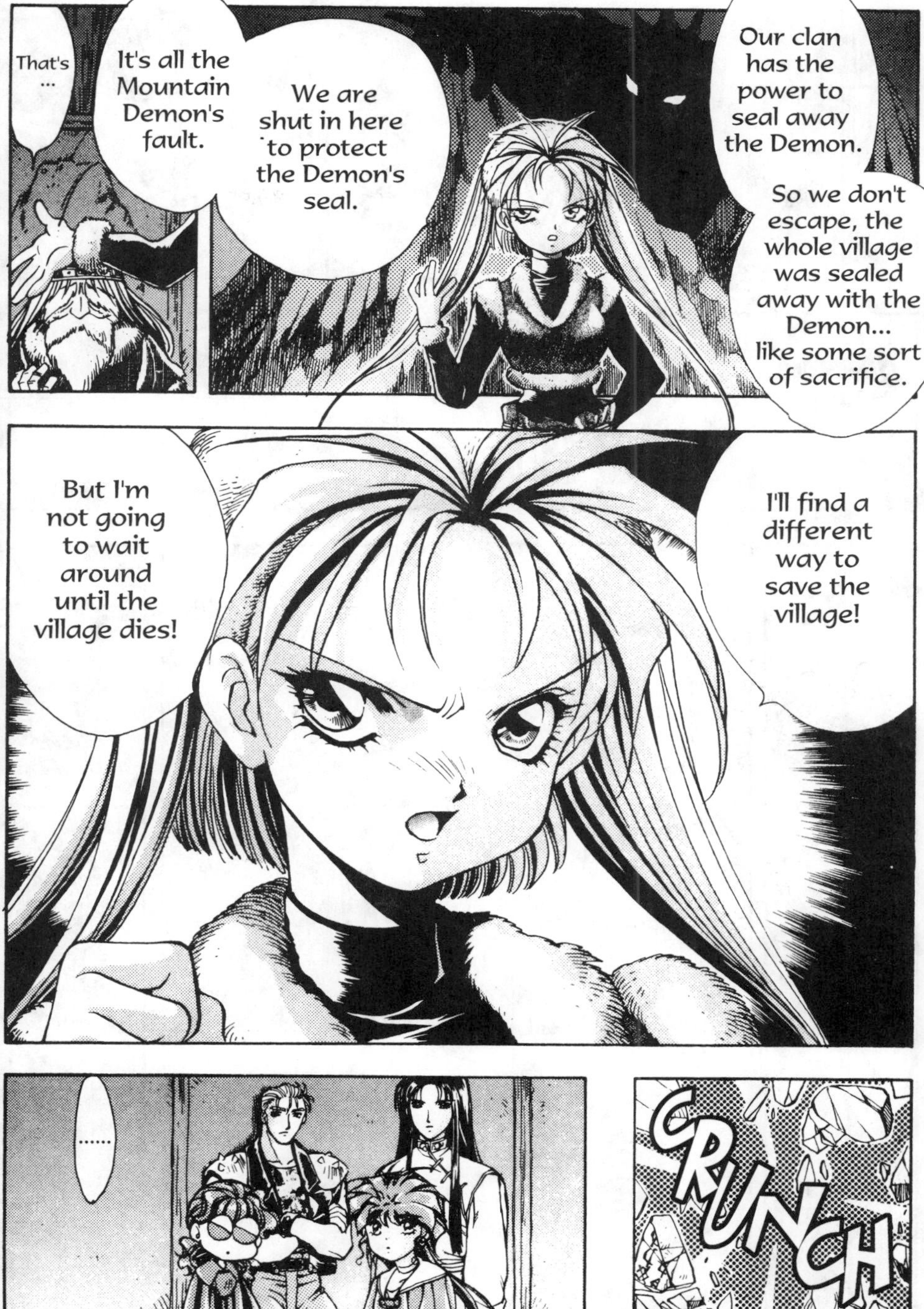

That's ...
It's all the Mountain Demon's fault.
We are shut in here to protect the Demon's seal.
Our clan has the power to seal away the Demon.
So we don't escape, the whole village was sealed away with the Demon... like some sort of sacrifice.
But I'm not going to wait around until the village dies!
I'll find a different way to save the village!
......
CRUNCH

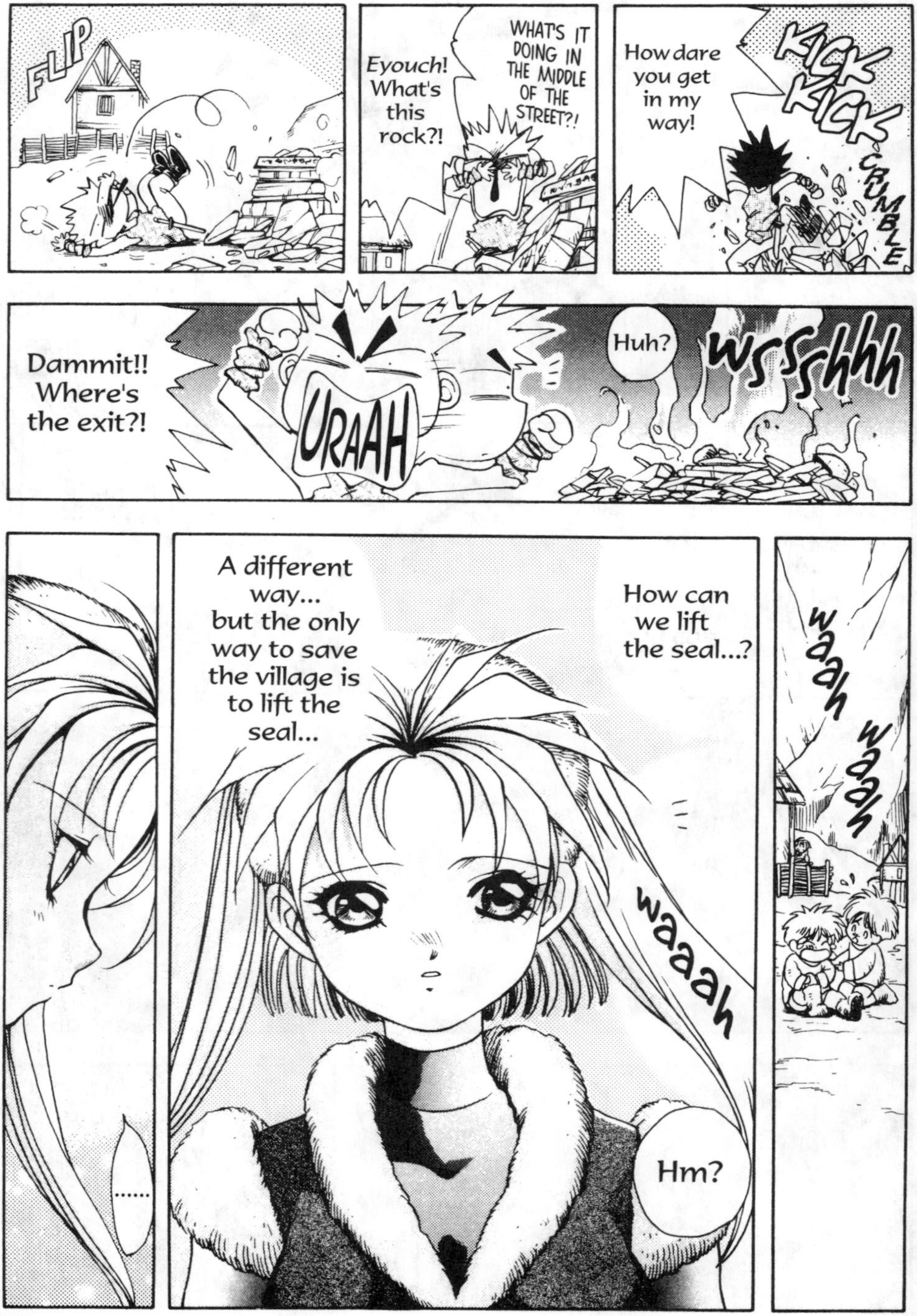

FLIP
Eyouch! What's this rock?!
WHAT'S IT DOING IN THE MIDDLE OF THE STREET?!
How dare you get in my way!
KICK KICK
CRUMBLE
Dammit!! Where's the exit?!
URAAH
Huh?
WSSShhh
......
A different way... but the only way to save the village is to lift the seal...
How can we lift the seal...?
waaaah
Hm?
waaah waaah

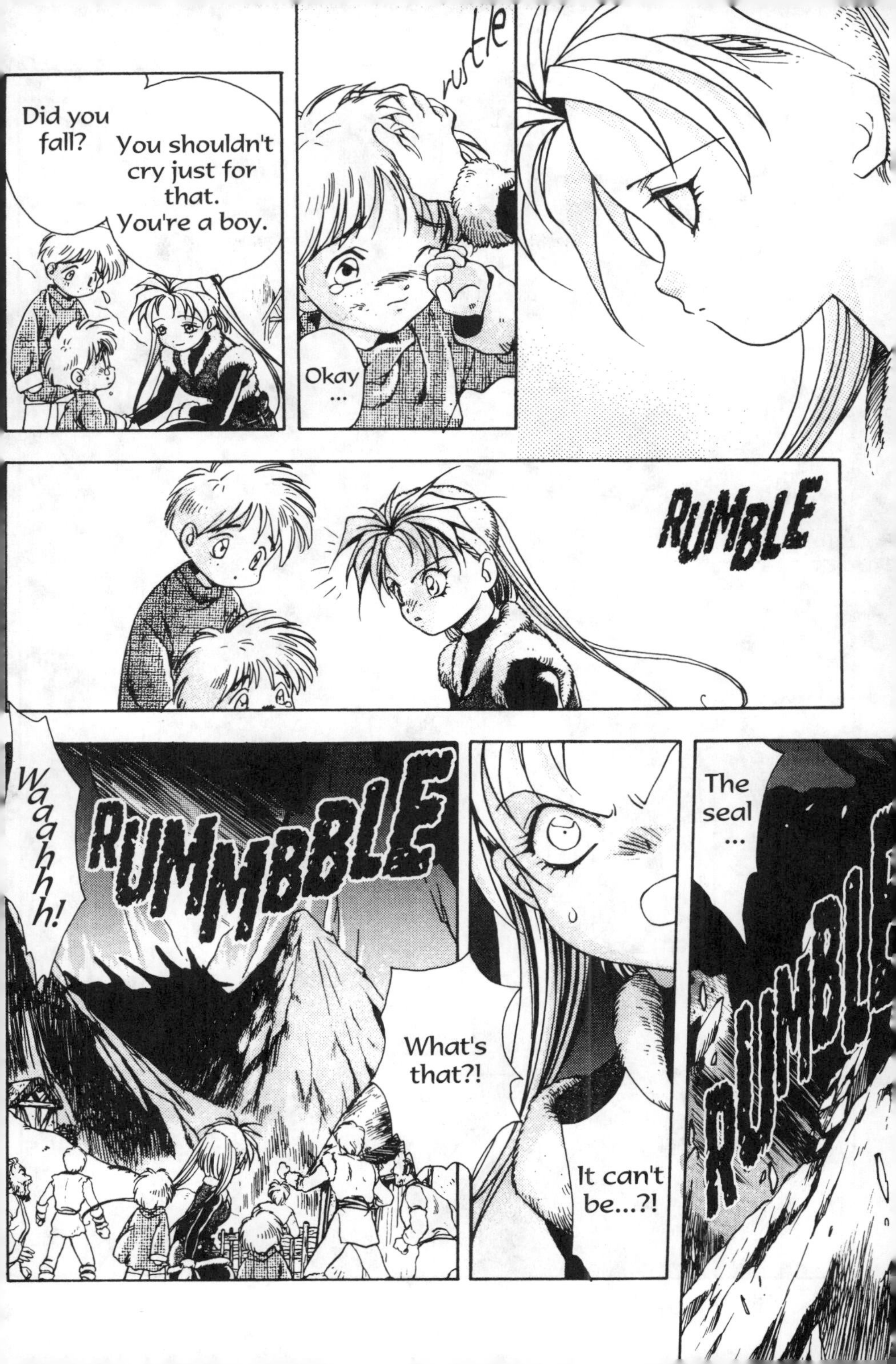
Did you fall?
You shouldn't cry just for that. You're a boy.
rustle
Okay ...
RUMBLE
Waaahhh!
RUMMBBLE
What's that?!
It can't be...?!
The seal ...
RUMBLE

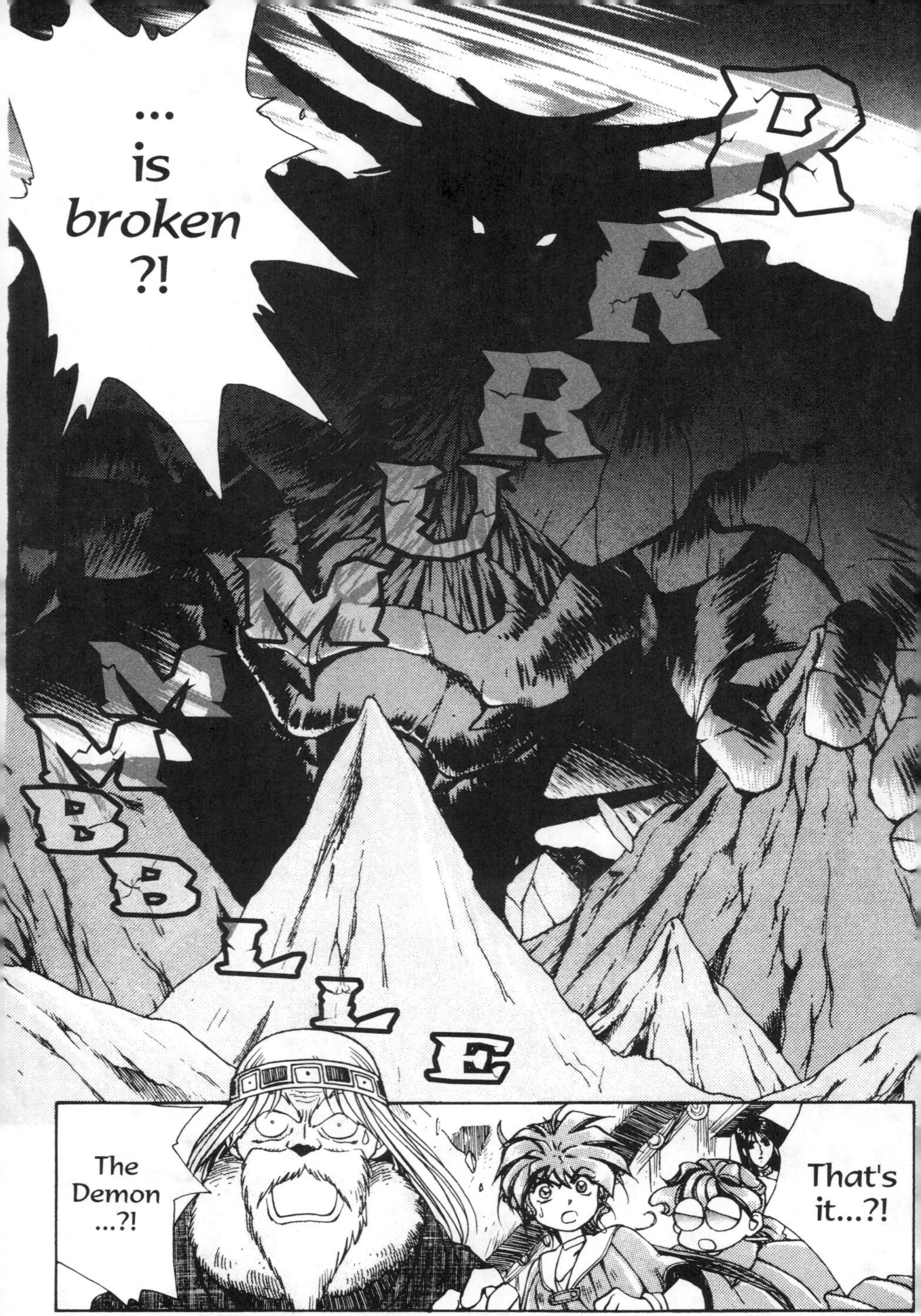
... is broken ?!
RRRUMMMBBLLE
That's it...?!
The Demon ...?!

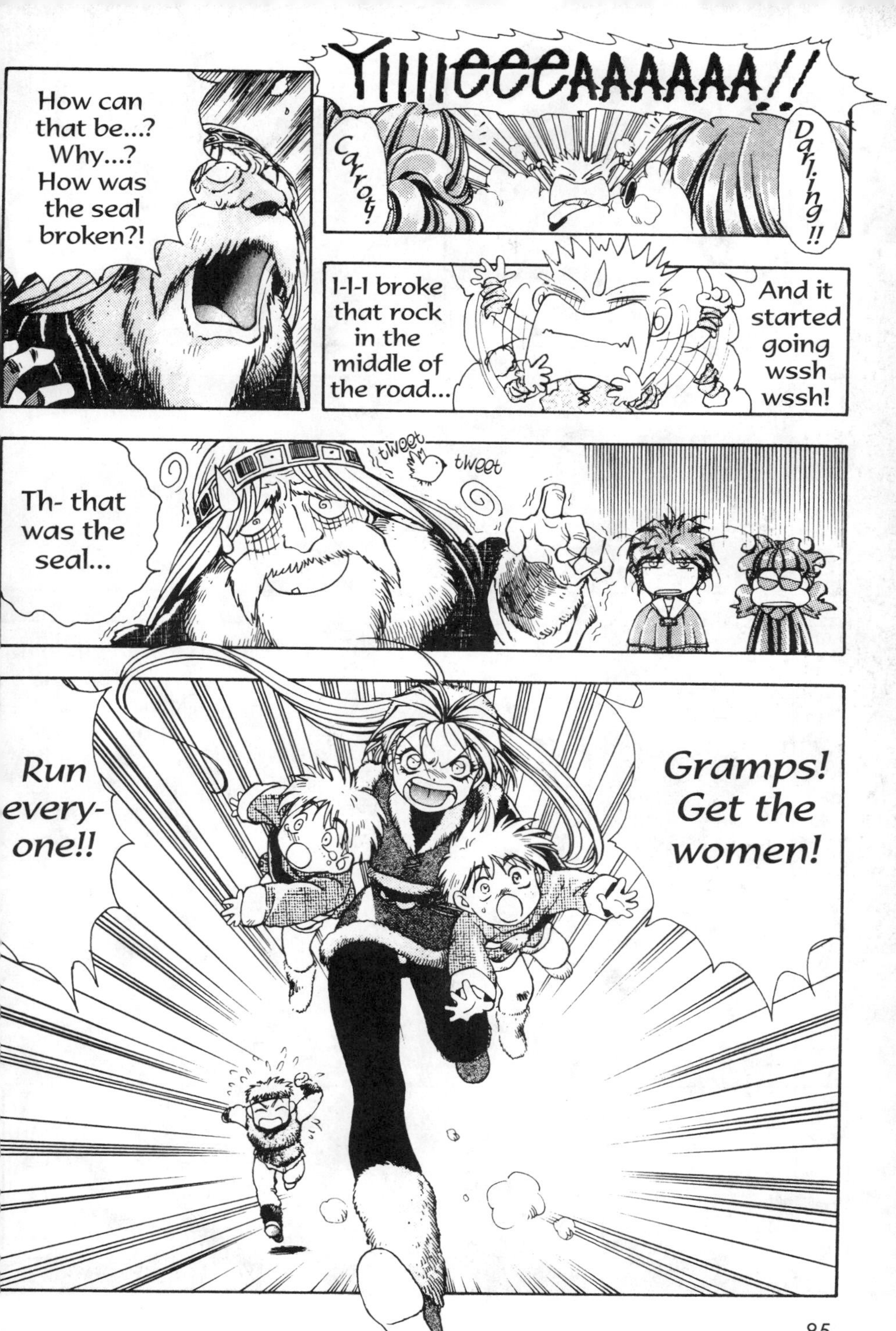
How can that be...? Why...? How was the seal broken?!
YIIIEEEAAAAAA!!
Carrot!
Darling!!
I-I-I broke that rock in the middle of the road...
And it started going wssh wssh!
Th- that was the seal...
tweet
tweet
Run every-one!!
Gramps! Get the women!

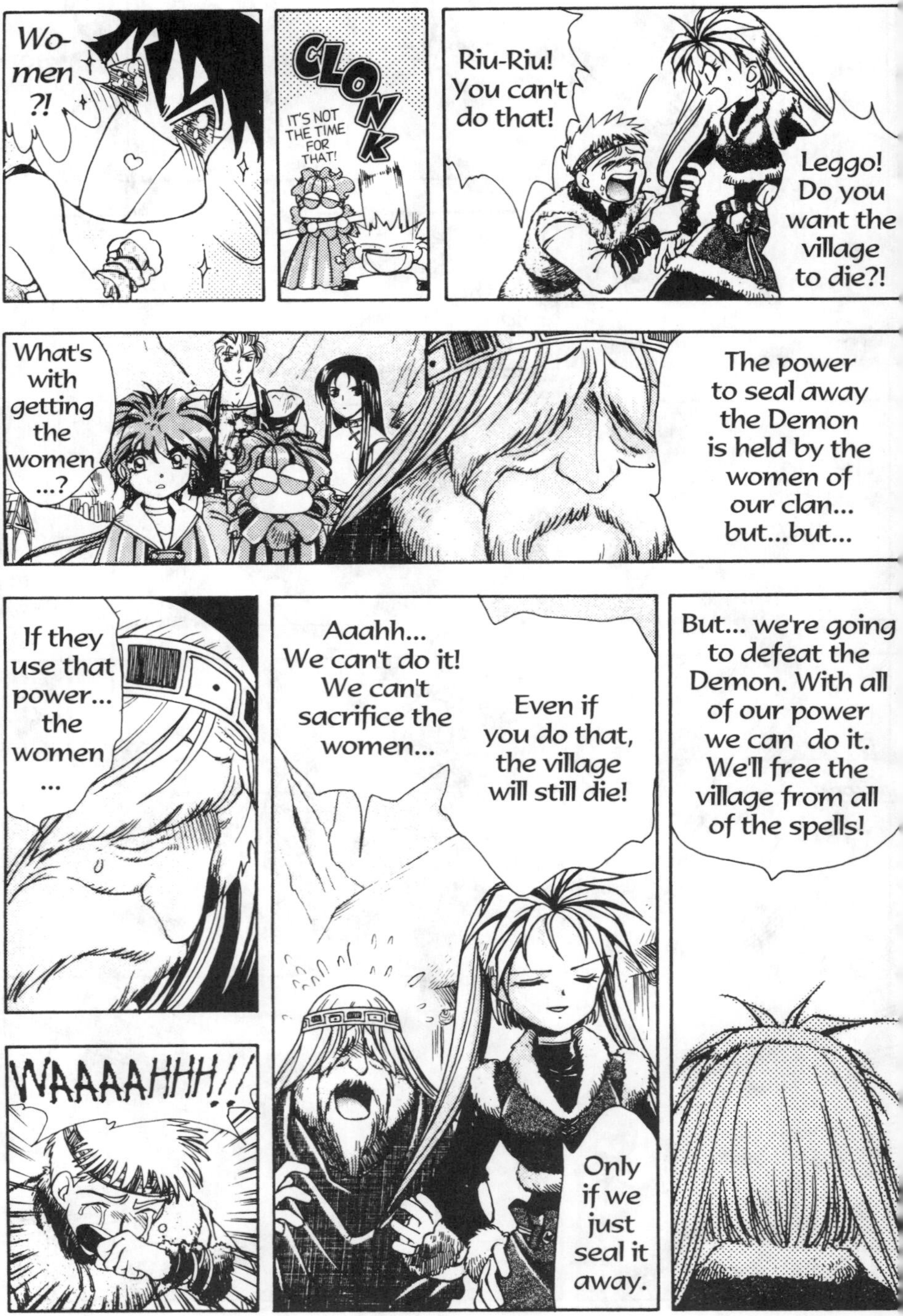
Wo-men?!
CLONK
IT'S NOT THE TIME FOR THAT!
Riu-Riu! You can't do that!
Leggo! Do you want the village to die?!
What's with getting the women...?
The power to seal away the Demon is held by the women of our clan... but...but...
If they use that power... the women...
Aaahh... We can't do it! We can't sacrifice the women...
Even if you do that, the village will still die!
Only if we just seal it away.
But... we're going to defeat the Demon. With all of our power we can do it. We'll free the village from all of the spells!
WAAAAHHH!!

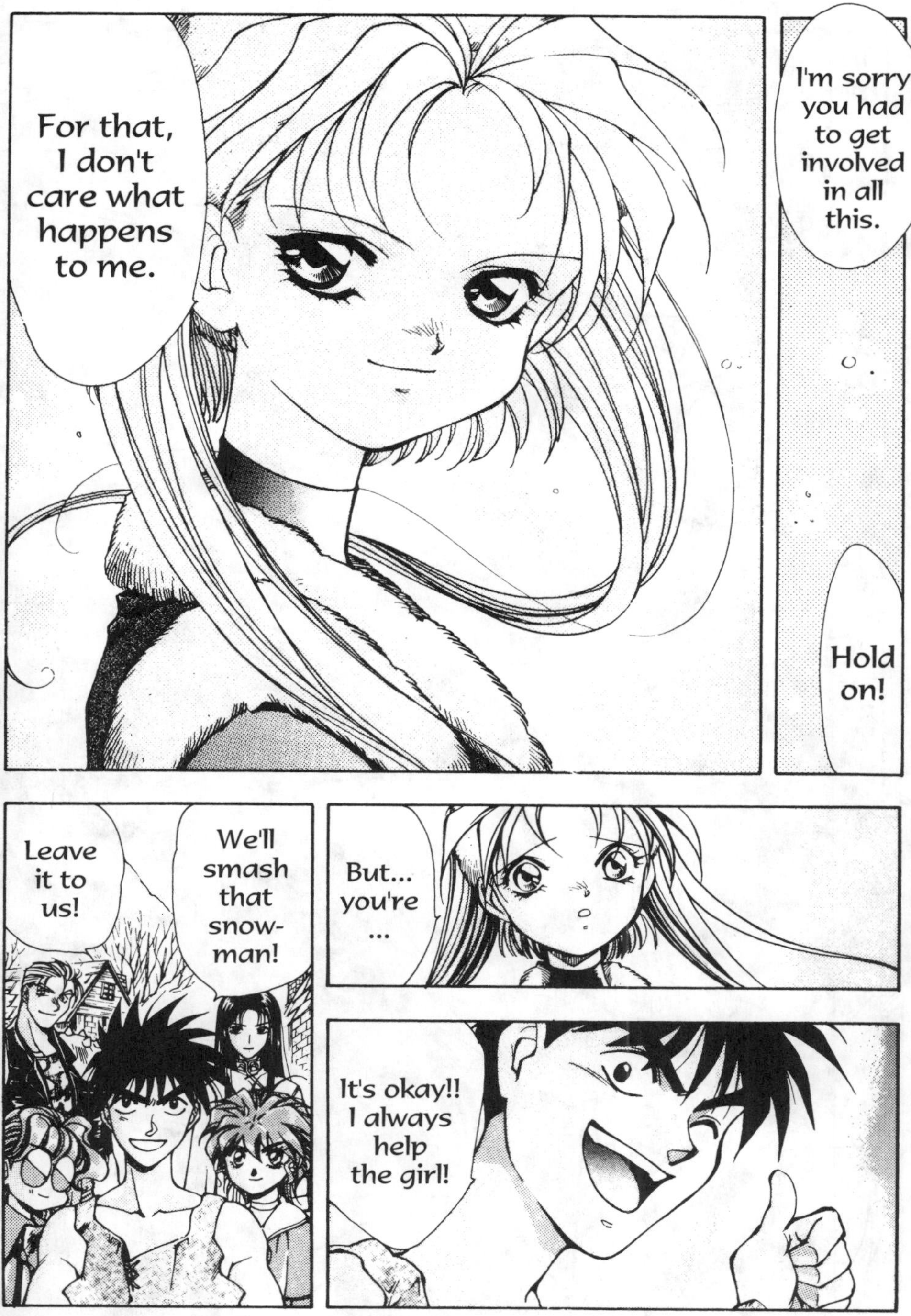
I'm sorry you had to get involved in all this.
Hold on!
For that, I don't care what happens to me.
But... you're ...
It's okay!! I always help the girl!
We'll smash that snow-man!
Leave it to us!

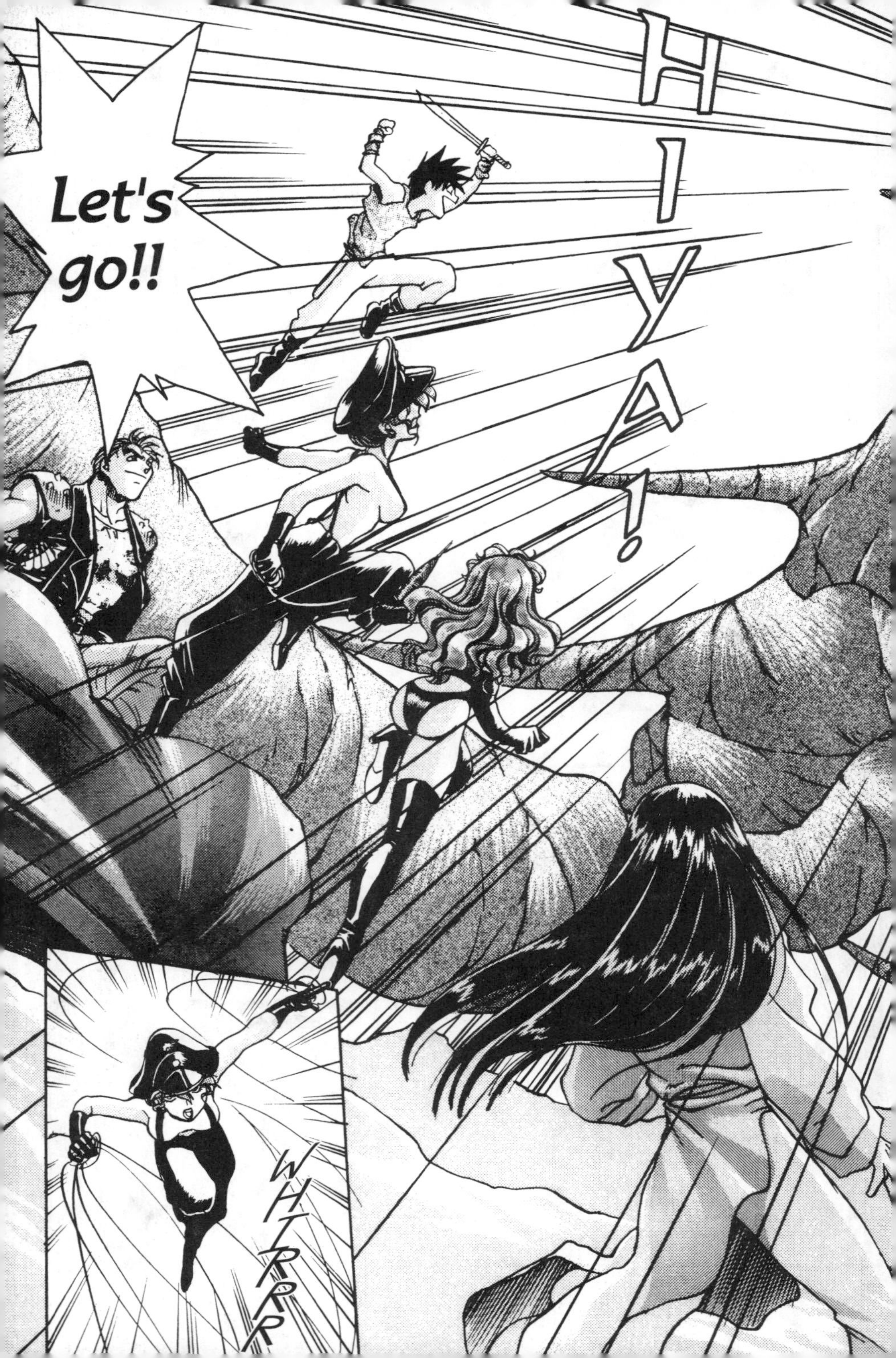
HIYAA!
Let's go!!
WHIRRR

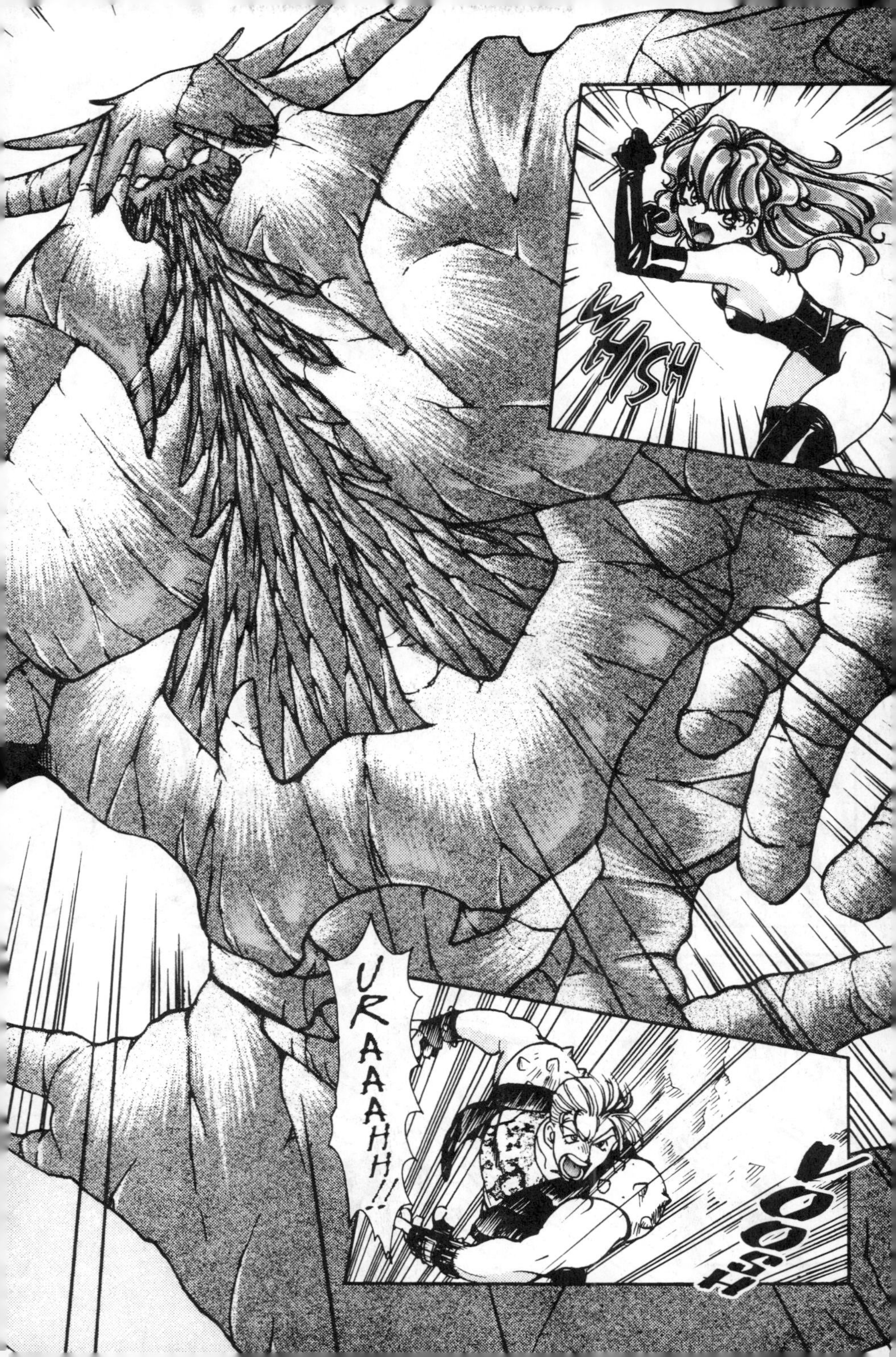
WHISH
URAAAAHH!!
VOOSH

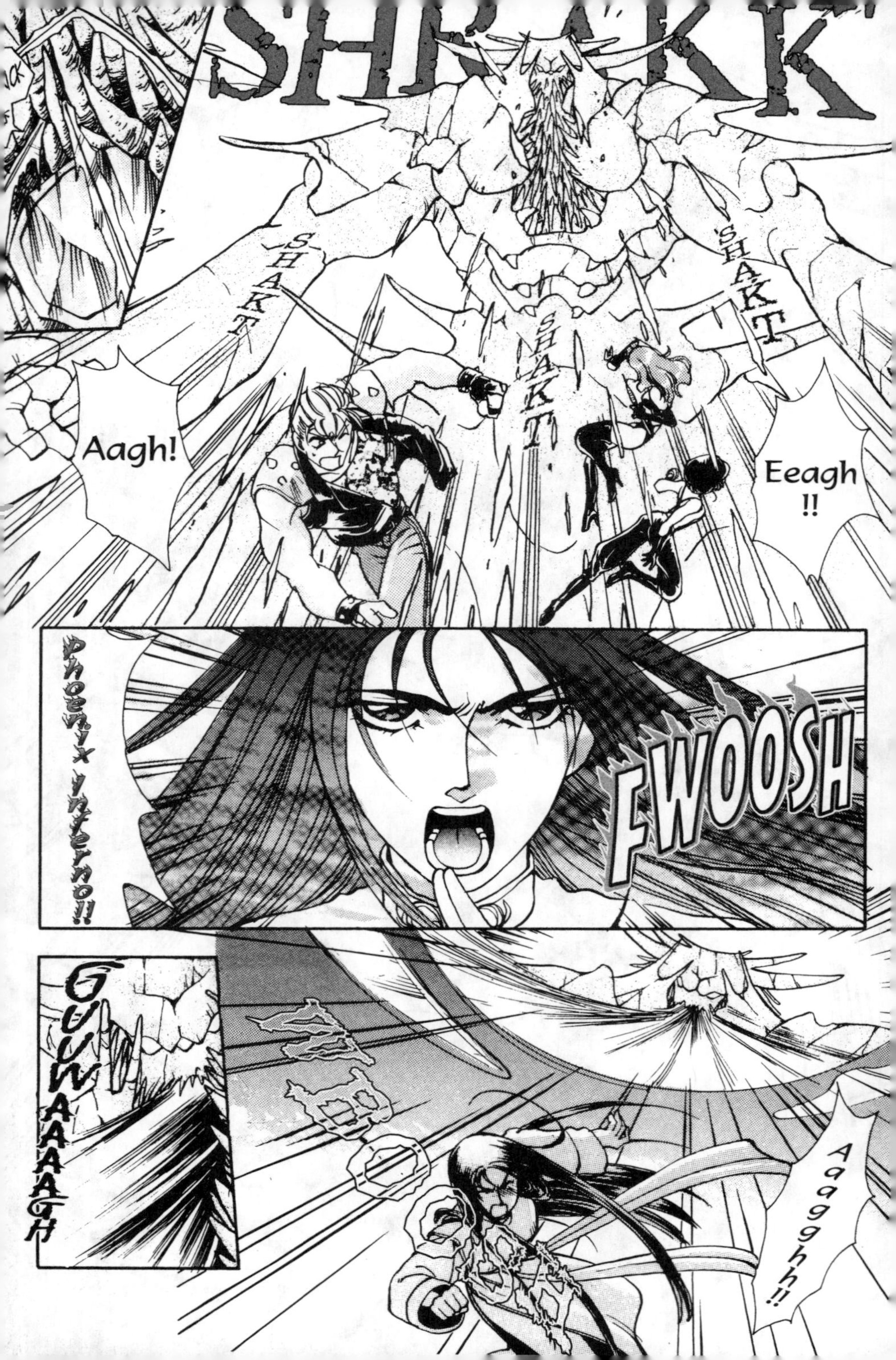
SHRAKK
SHAKT
SHAKT
SHAKT
Eeagh !!
Aagh!
FWOOSH
Phoenix Inferno!!
Aaagghh!!
GUUWAAAAAGH

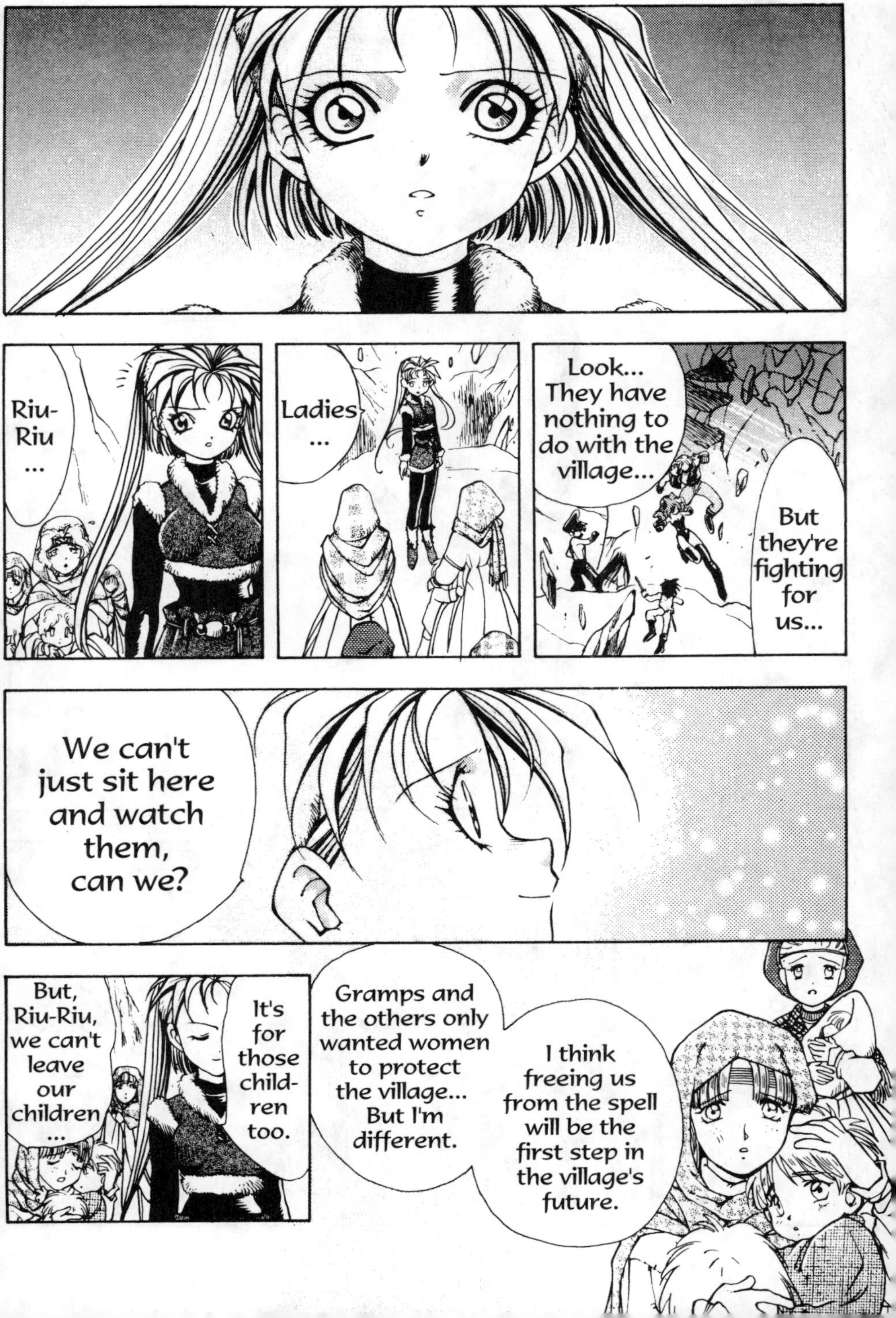
Riu-Riu ...
Ladies ...
Look... They have nothing to do with the village...
But they're fighting for us...
We can't just sit here and watch them, can we?
But, Riu-Riu, we can't leave our children ...
It's for those child-ren too.
Gramps and the others only wanted women to protect the village... But I'm different.
I think freeing us from the spell will be the first step in the village's future.

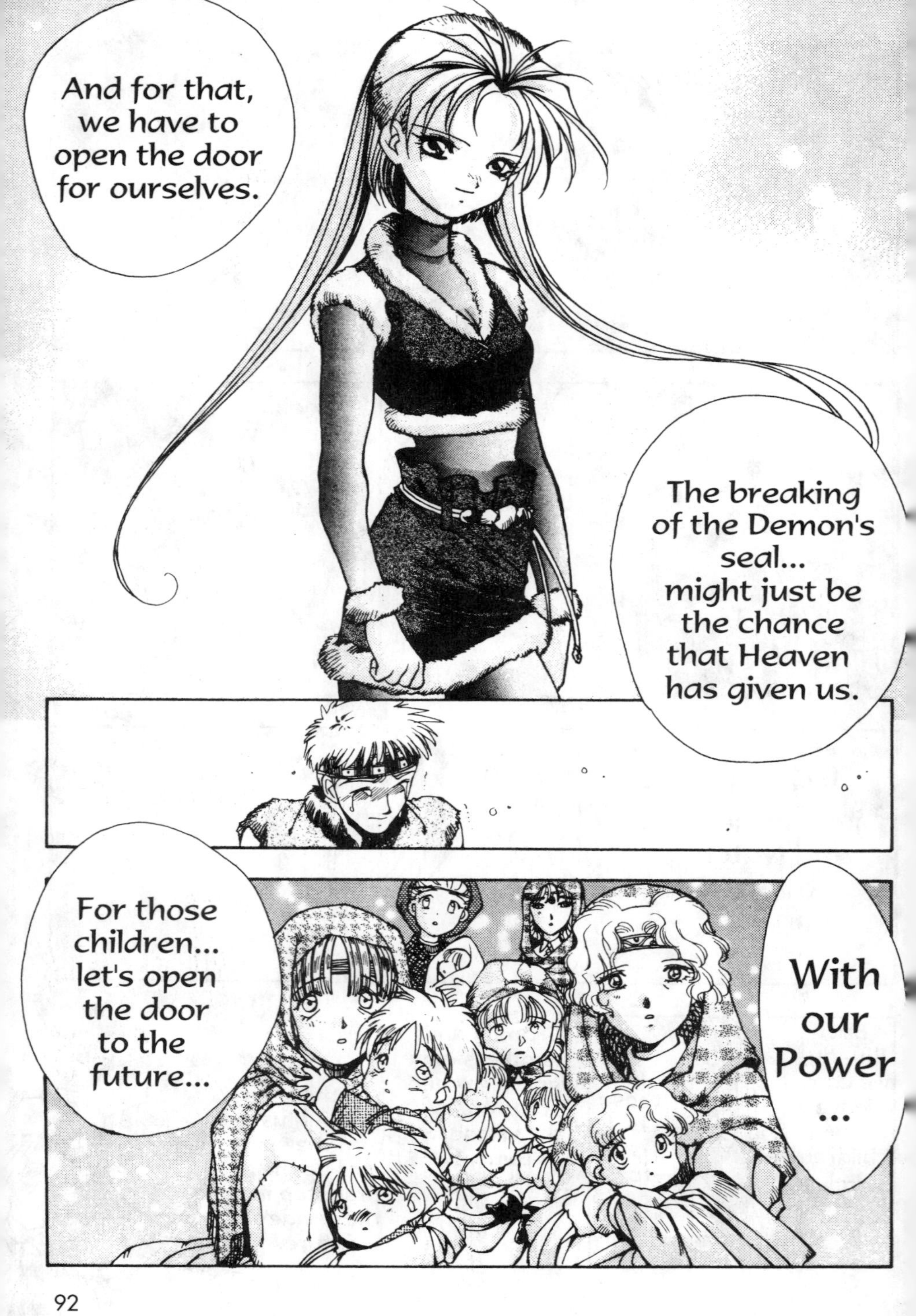
And for that, we have to open the door for ourselves.
The breaking of the Demon's seal... might just be the chance that Heaven has given us.
With our Power...
For those children... let's open the door to the future...

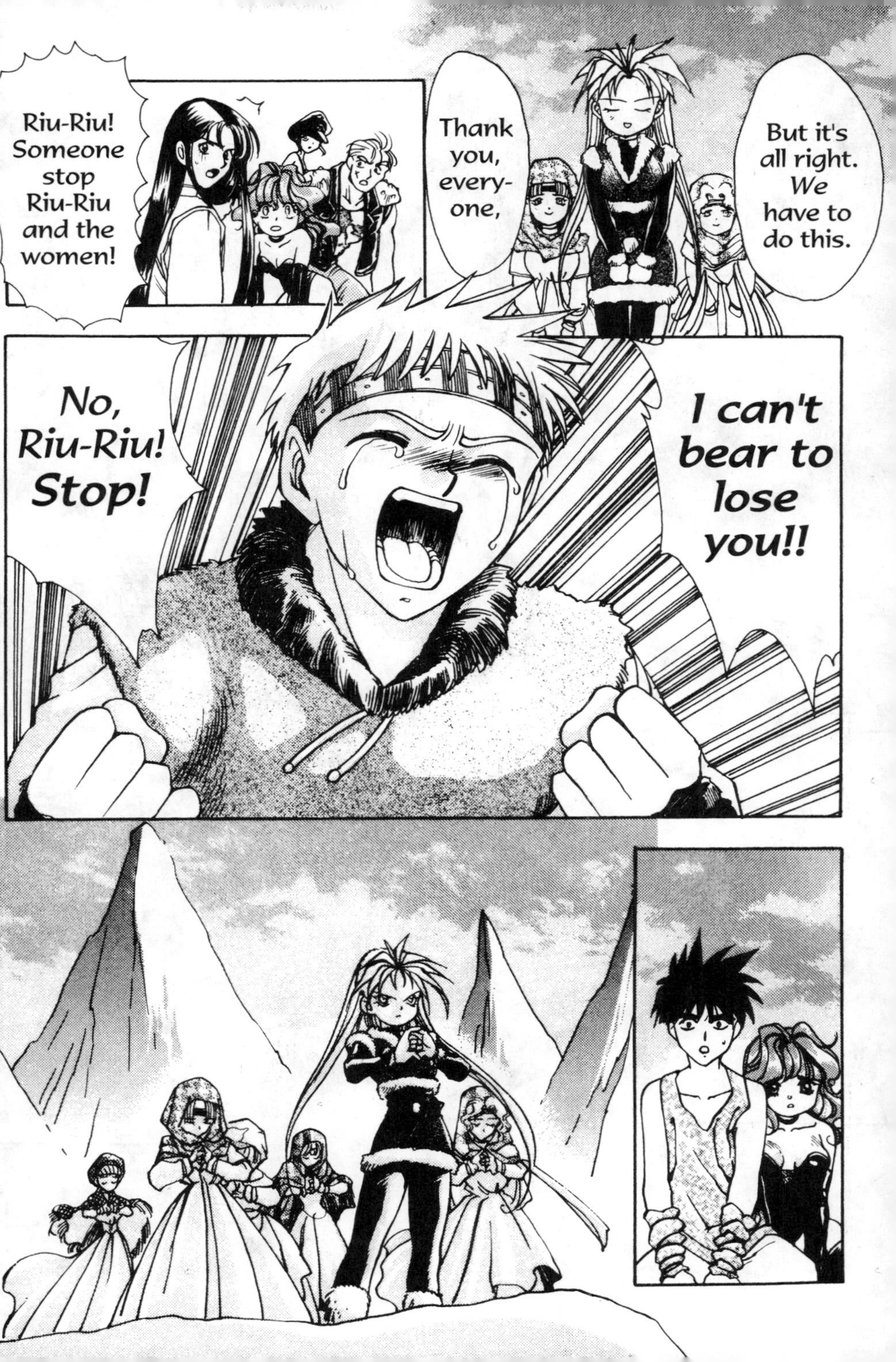
Riu-Riu! Someone stop Riu-Riu and the women!
Thank you, every-one,
But it's all right. We have to do this.
No, Riu-Riu! Stop!
I can't bear to lose you!!

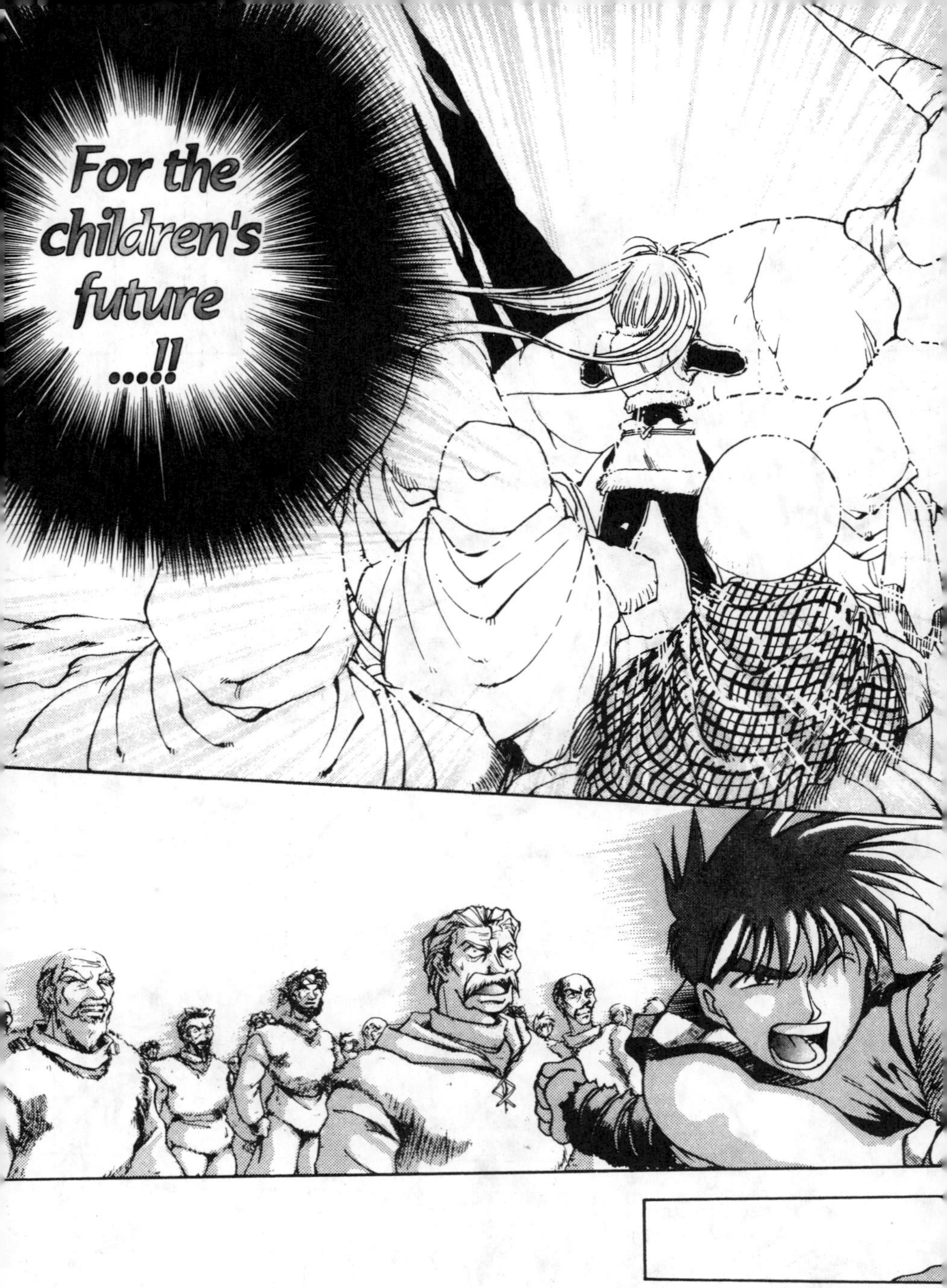
For the children's future ...!!

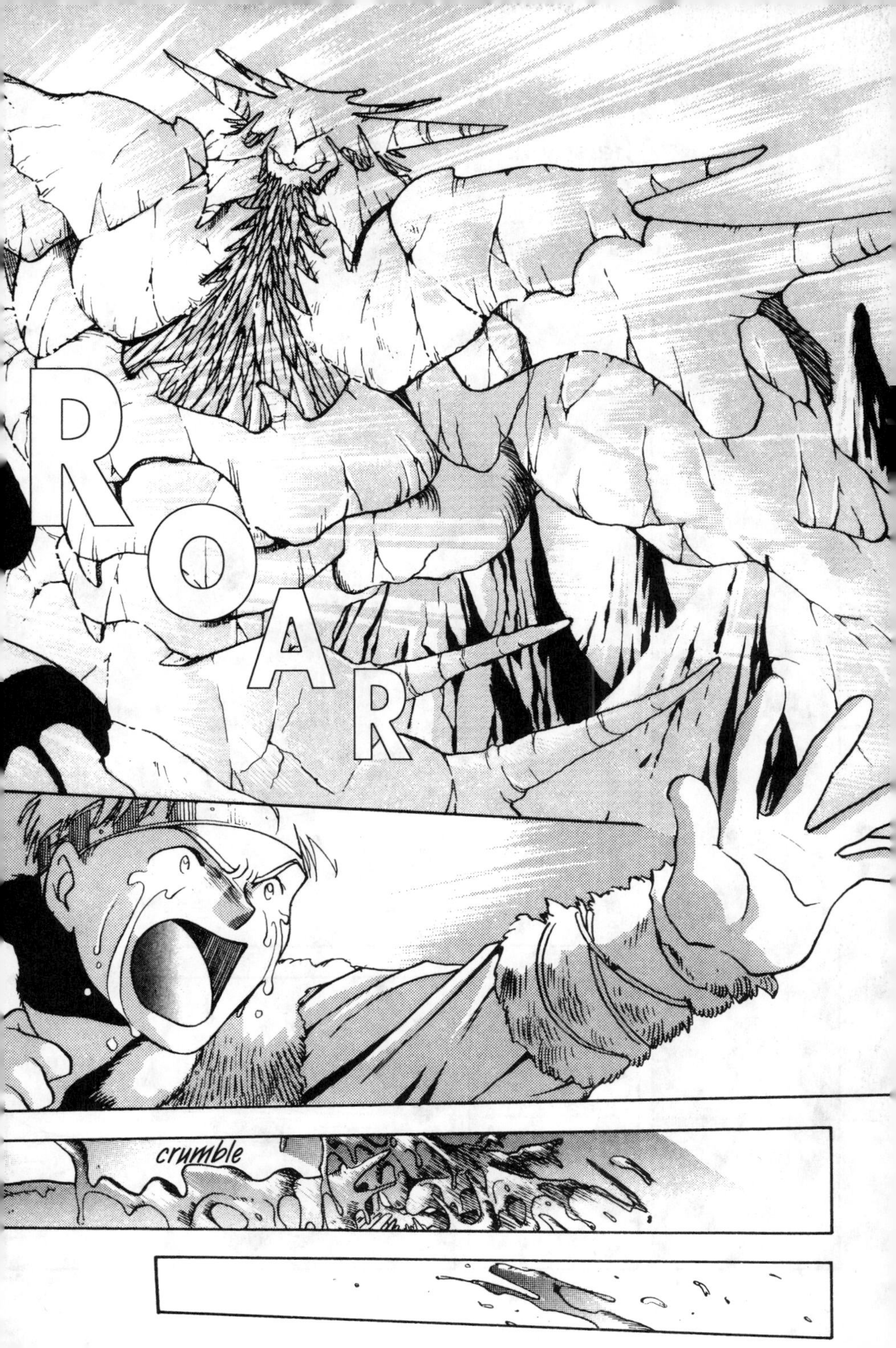
ROAR
crumble

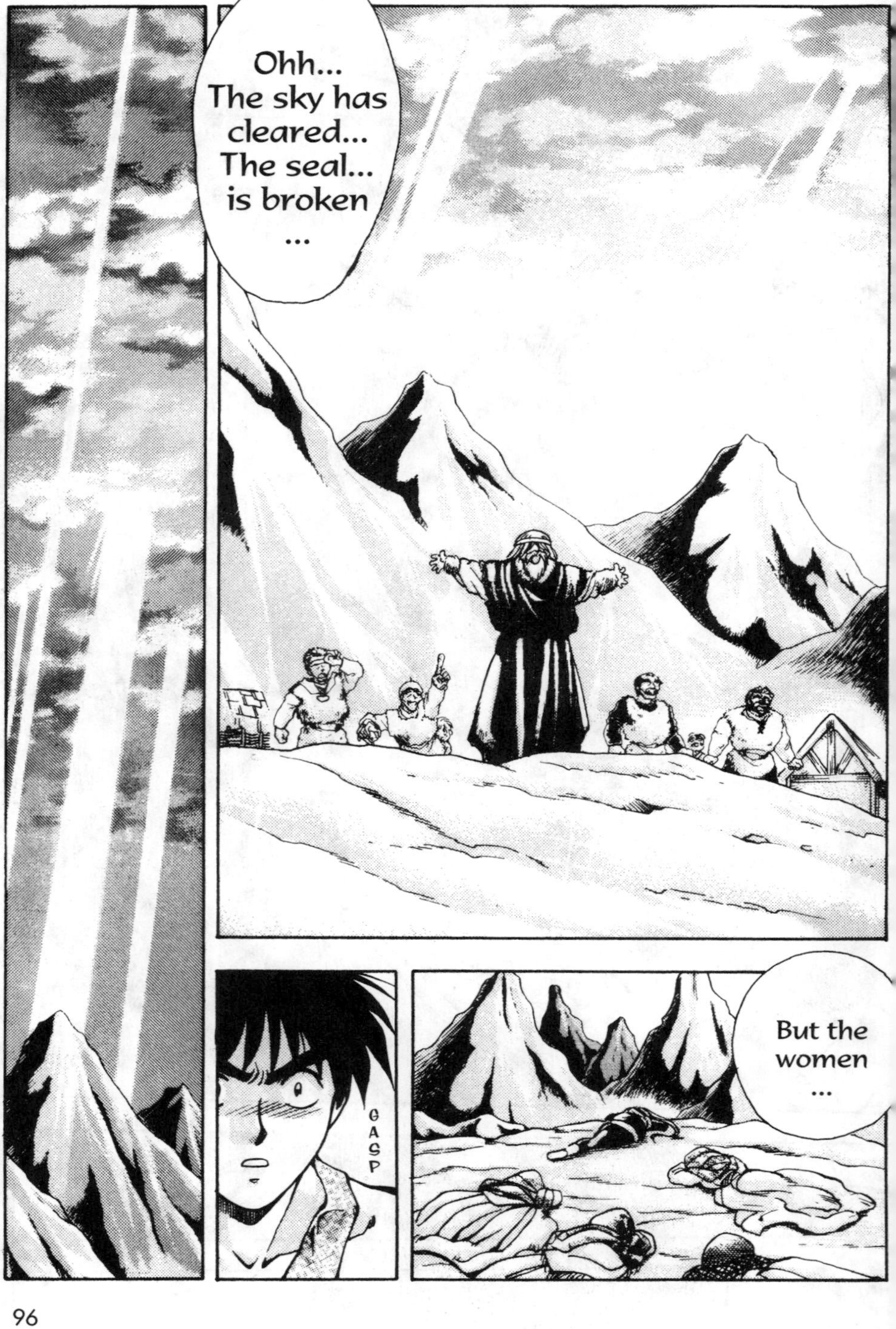
Ohh... The sky has cleared... The seal... is broken ...
But the women ...
GASP

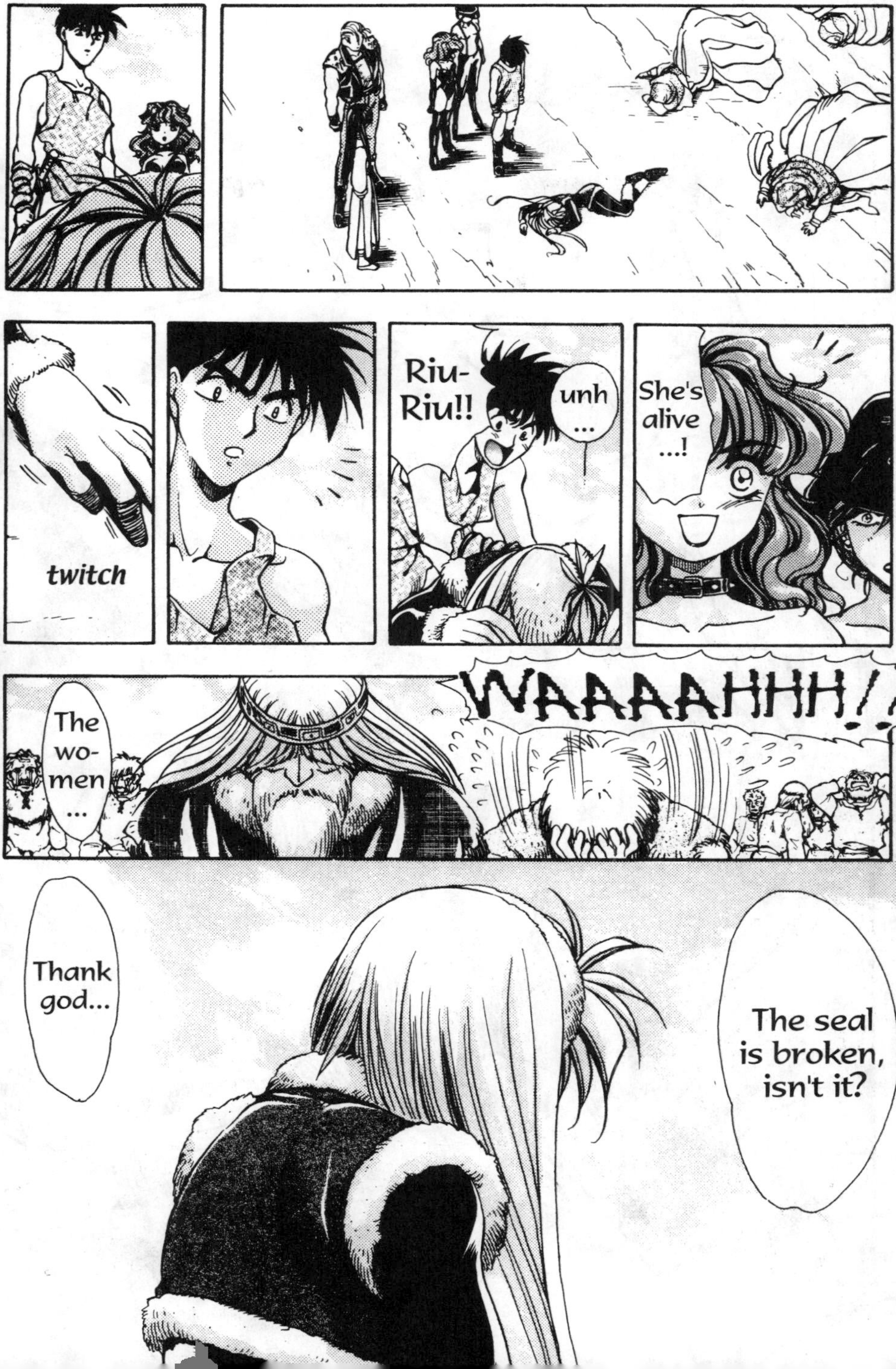
twitch
Riu-Riu!!
unh ...
She's alive ...!
The wo-men ...
WAAAAHH!!
Thank god...
The seal is broken, isn't it?

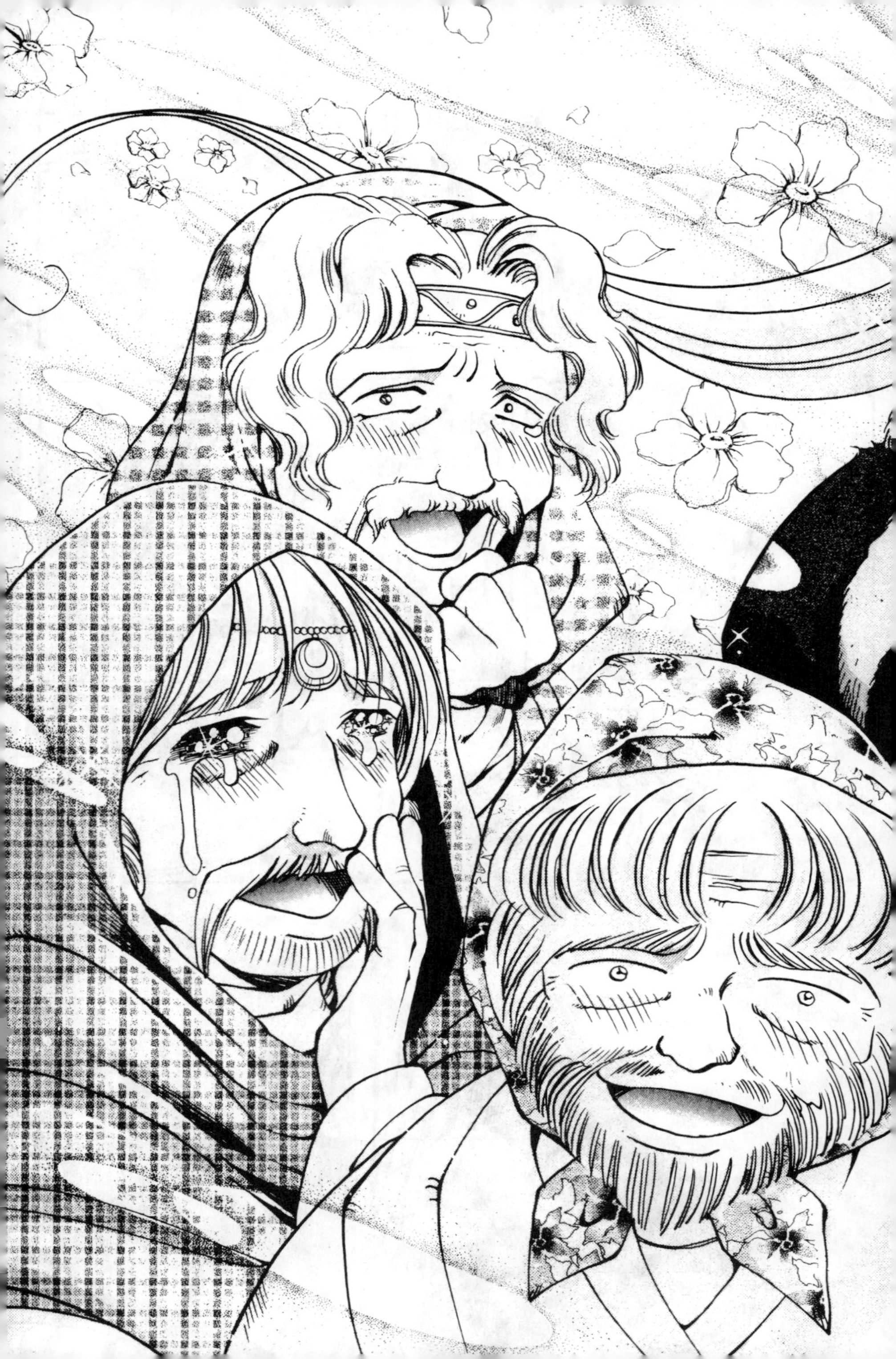

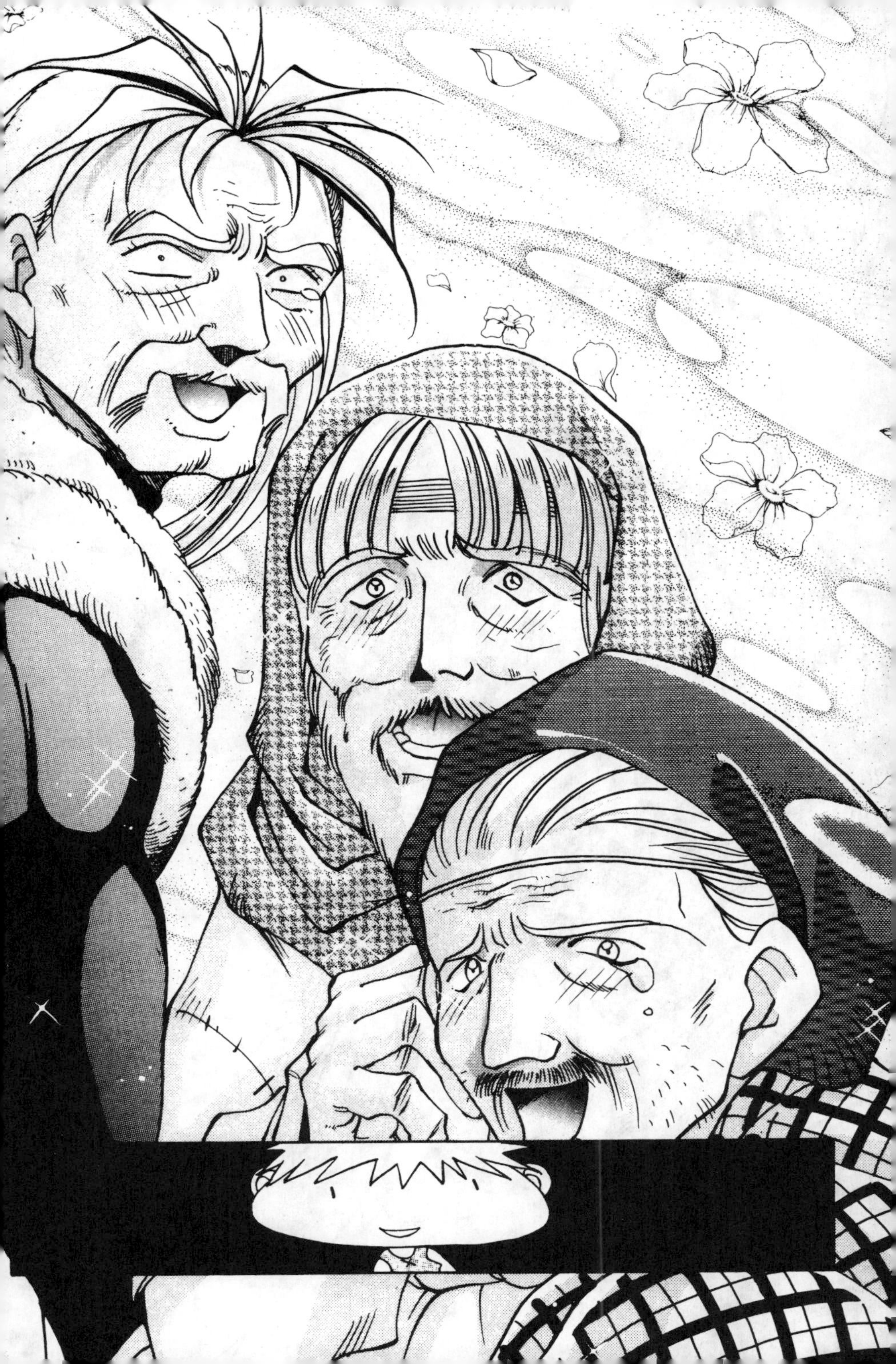

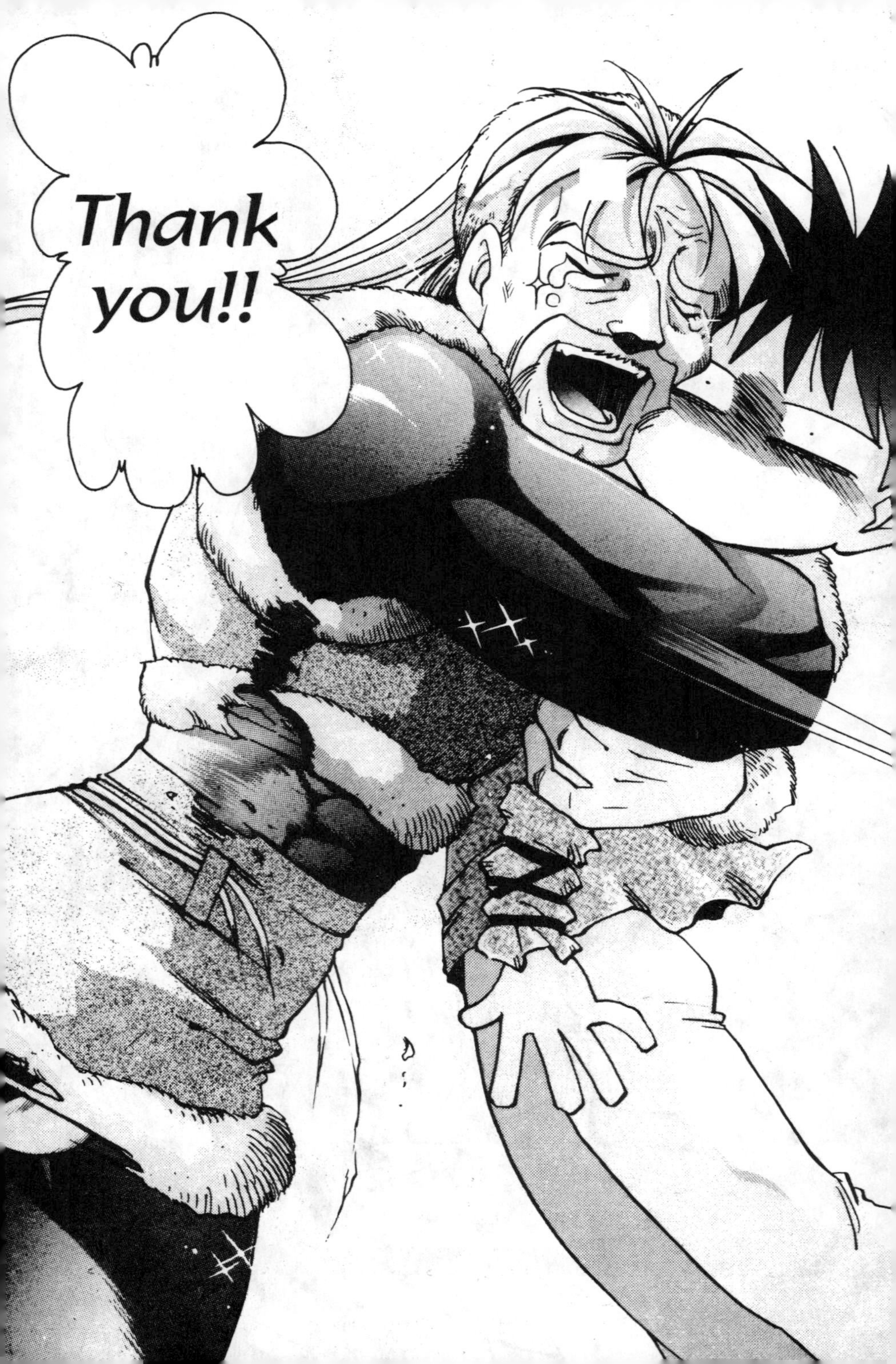
Thank you!!

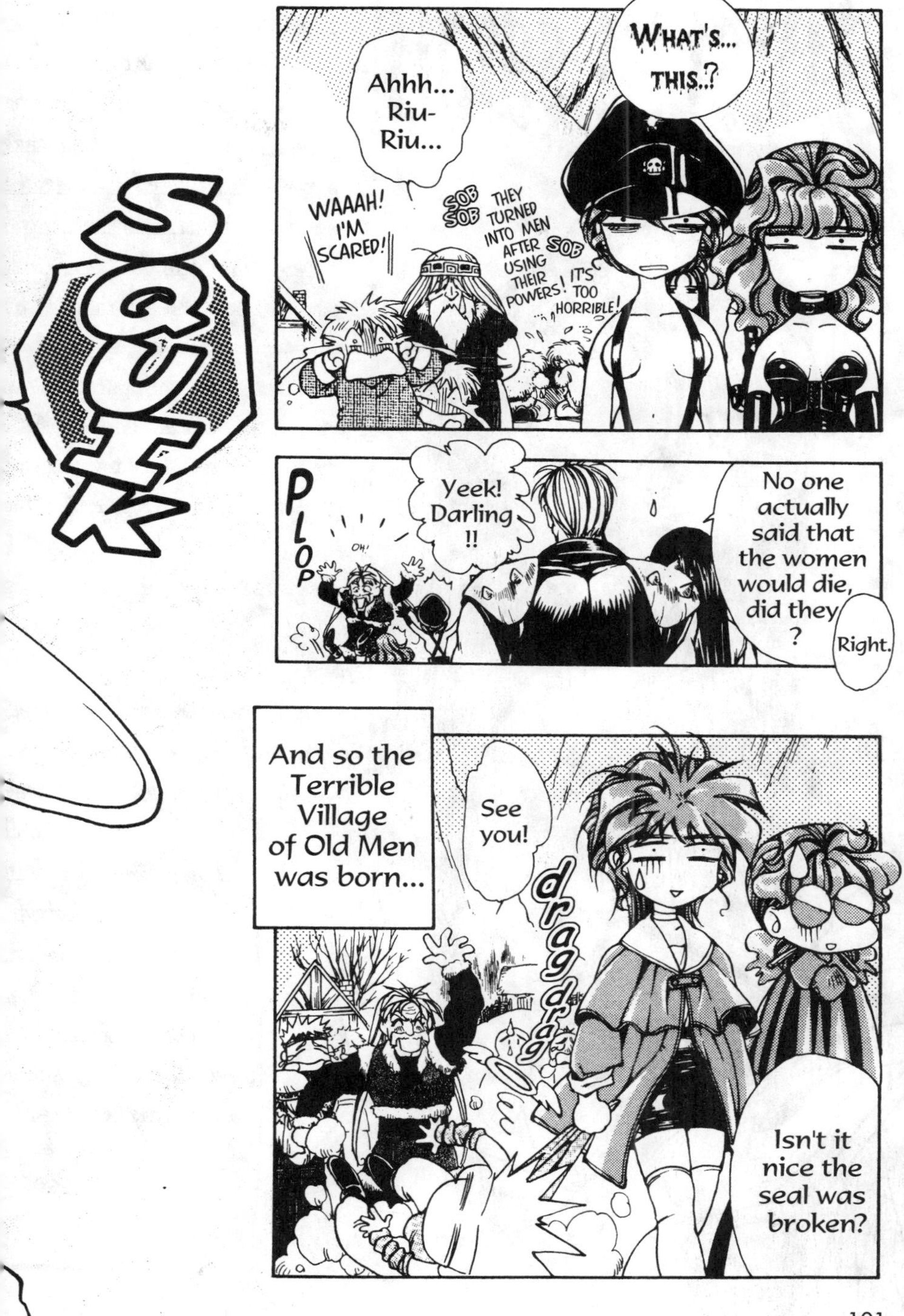
WHAT'S... THIS..?
Ahhh... Riu-Riu...
SOB SOB THEY TURNED INTO MEN AFTER SOB USING THEIR POWERS! IT'S TOO HORRIBLE!
WAAAH! I'M SCARED!
SQUIK
No one actually said that the women would die, did they?
Right.
Yeek! Darling!!
OH!
PLOP
And so the Terrible Village of Old Men was born...
Isn't it nice the seal was broken?
drag drag
See you!

Intermission

1995. 7

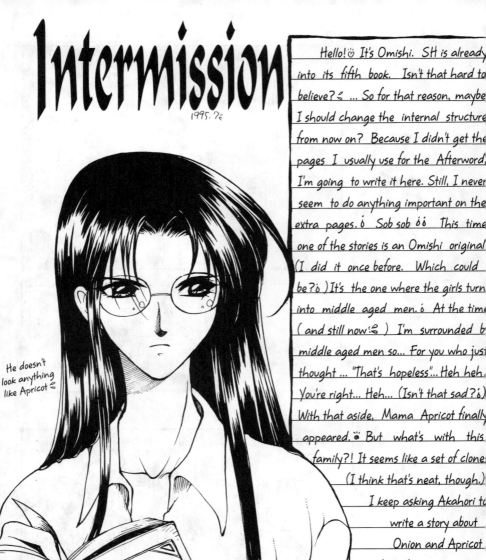

He doesn't look anything like Apricot

Hello! ♡ It's Omishi. SH is already into its fifth book. Isn't that hard to believe? ... So for that reason, maybe I should change the internal structure from now on? Because I didn't get the pages I usually use for the Afterword, I'm going to write it here. Still, I never seem to do anything important on the extra pages. Sob sob This time one of the stories is an Omishi original (I did it once before. Which could be?) It's the one where the girls turn into middle aged men. At the time (and still now:) I'm surrounded by middle aged men so... For you who just thought ... "That's hopeless"... Heh heh. You're right... Heh... (Isn't that sad?) With that aside, Mama Apricot finally appeared. But what's with this family?! It seems like a set of clones (I think that's neat, though.)

I keep asking Akahori to write a story about Onion and Apricot when they were young. This is all for now.
....What should I do with the extra pages next time...?

7-1995 Rei Omishi

We had decided that Marron uses glasses when he reads... but it never appears in the story so I'm drawing it here ...

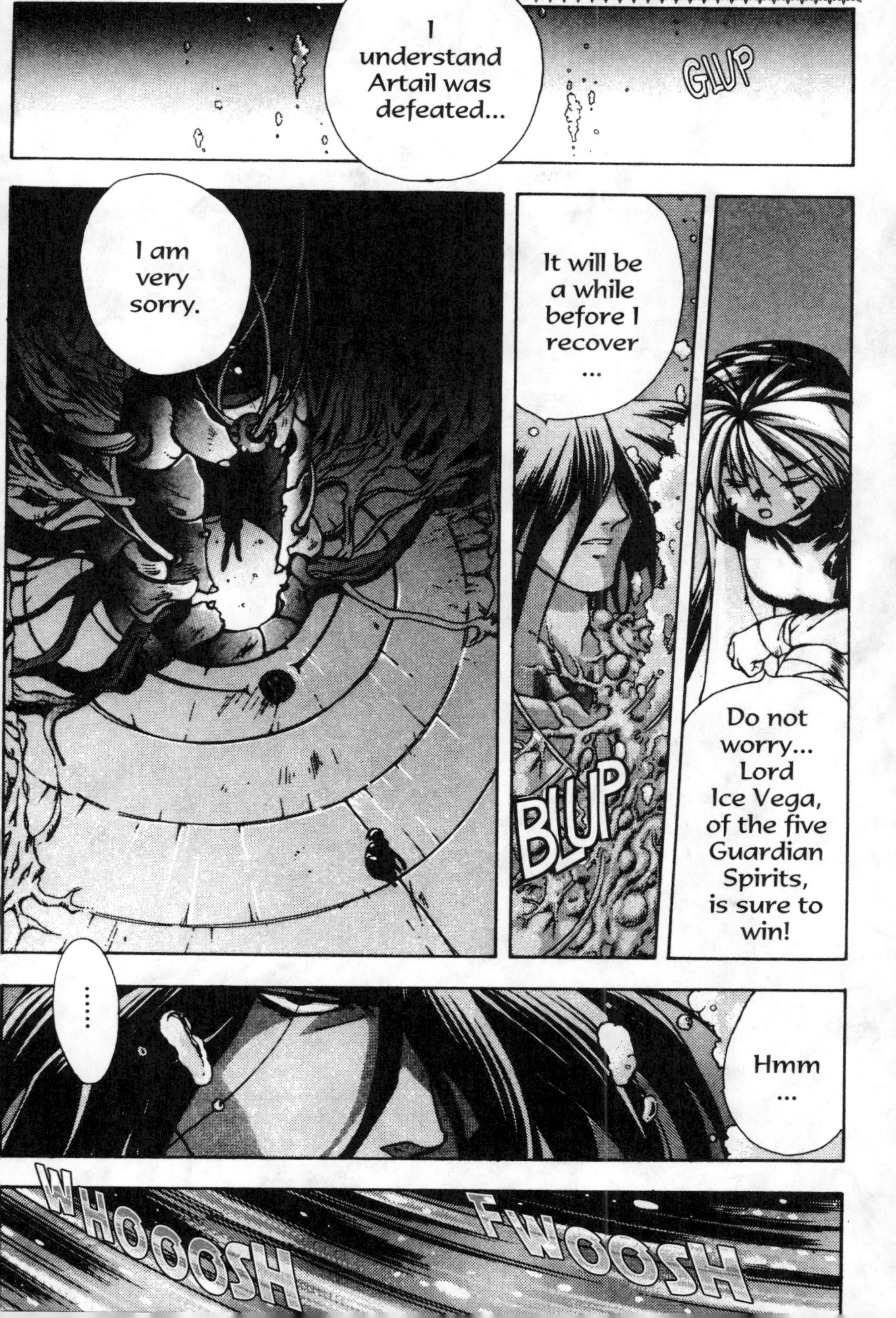
I understand Artail was defeated...
GLUP
I am very sorry.
It will be a while before I recover ...
BLUP
Do not worry... Lord Ice Vega, of the five Guardian Spirits, is sure to win!
......
Hmm ...
WHOOOSH
FWOOSH

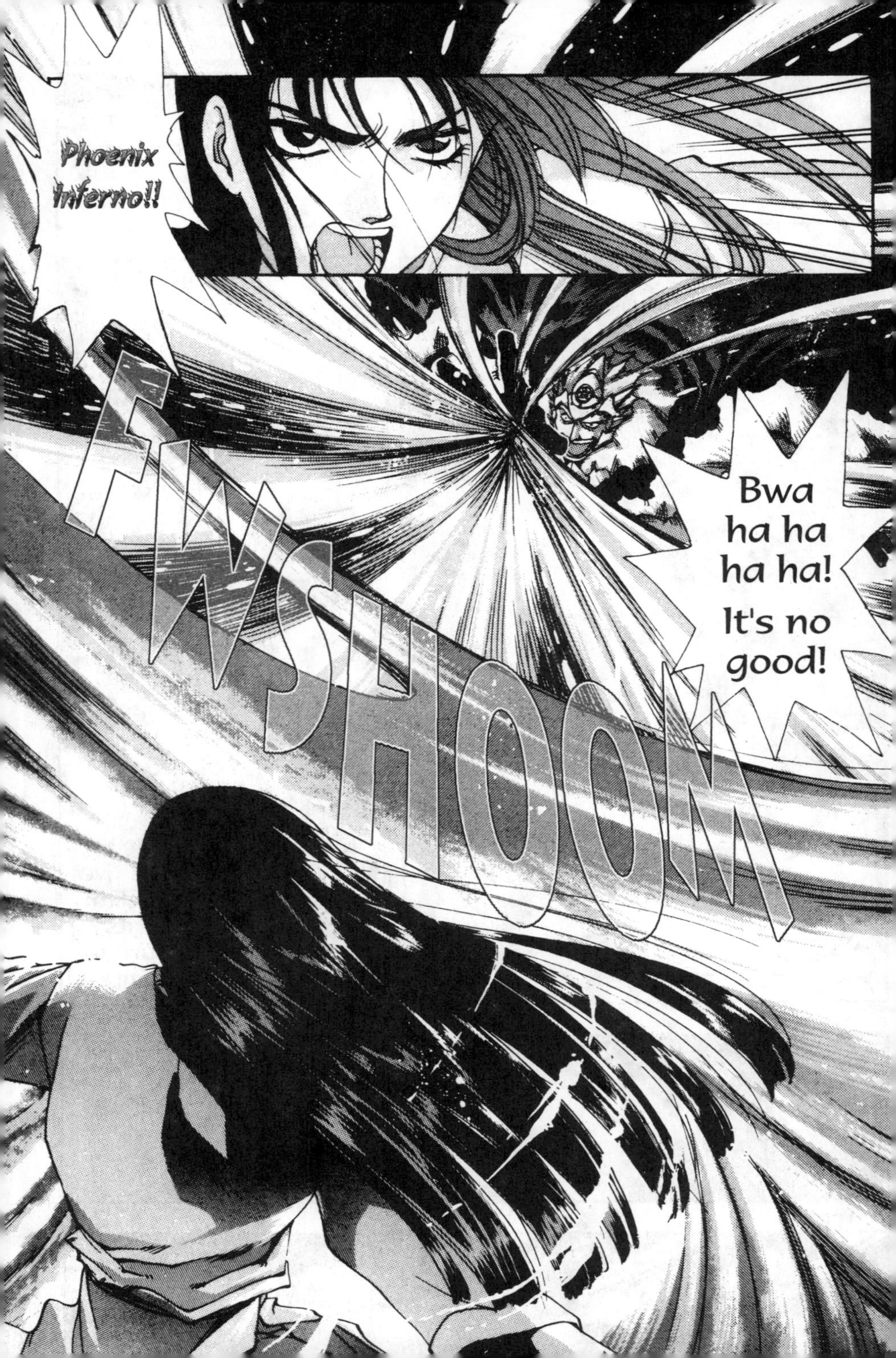
Phoenix Inferno!!
Bwa ha ha ha ha! It's no good!
FWSHOOM

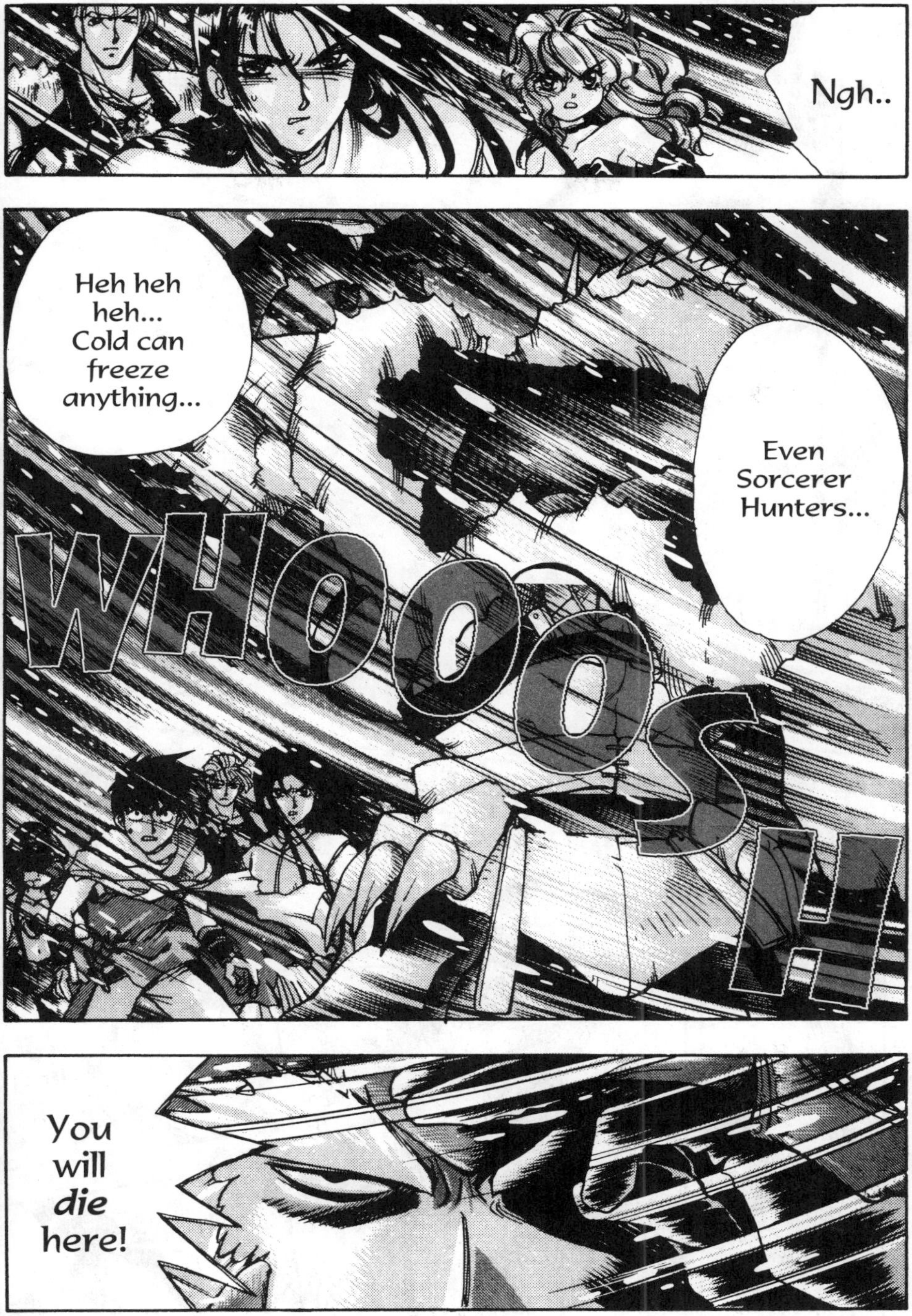

Ngh..
Even Sorcerer Hunters...
Heh heh heh... Cold can freeze anything...
WHOOOOSH!!
You will *die* here!

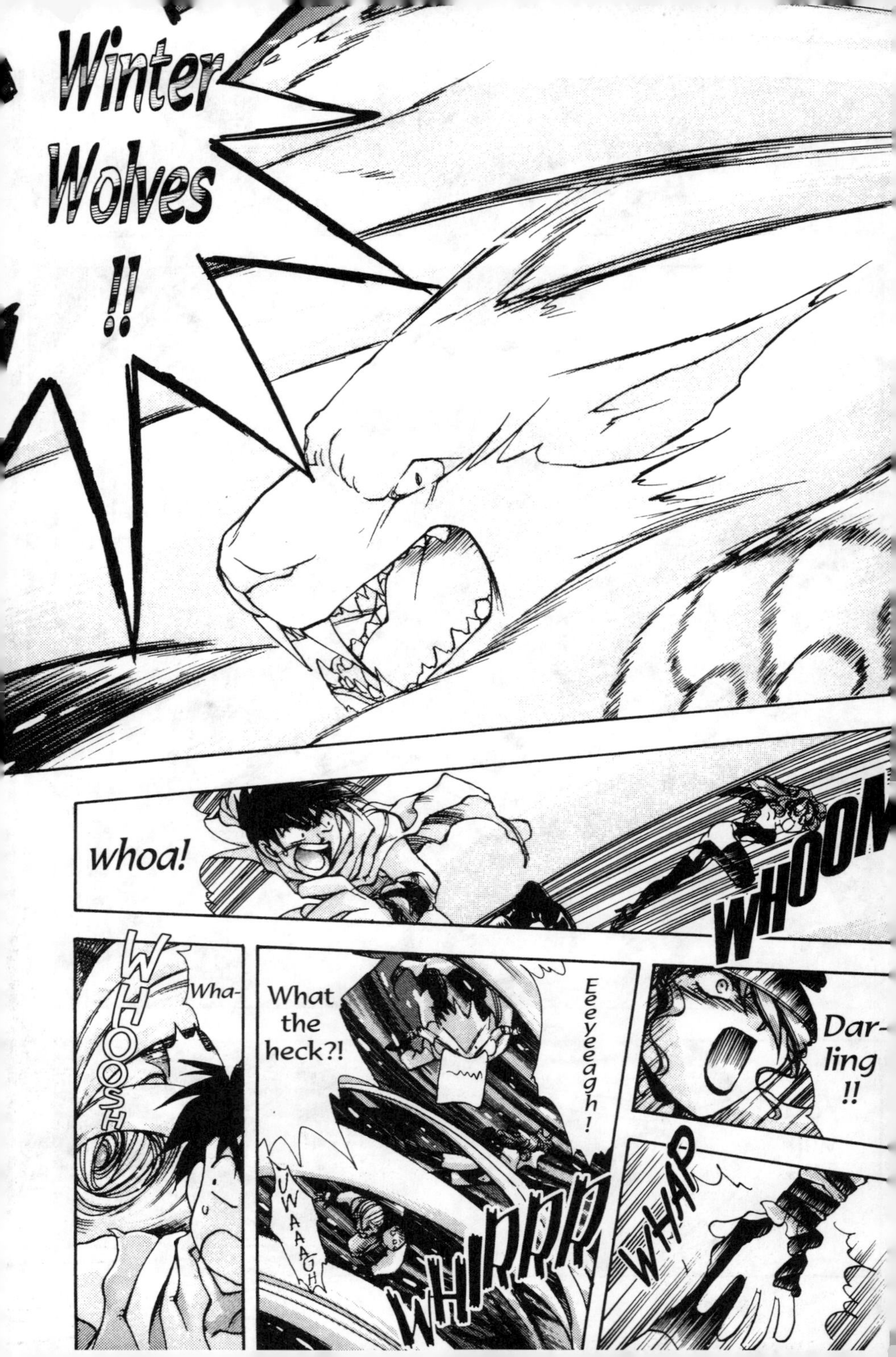
Winter Wolves !!
WHOOOM
whoa!
Darling !!
WHAP
Eeeyeeagh!
What the heck?!
UWAAAAGH!
WHIRRRR
Wha-
WHOOOSH

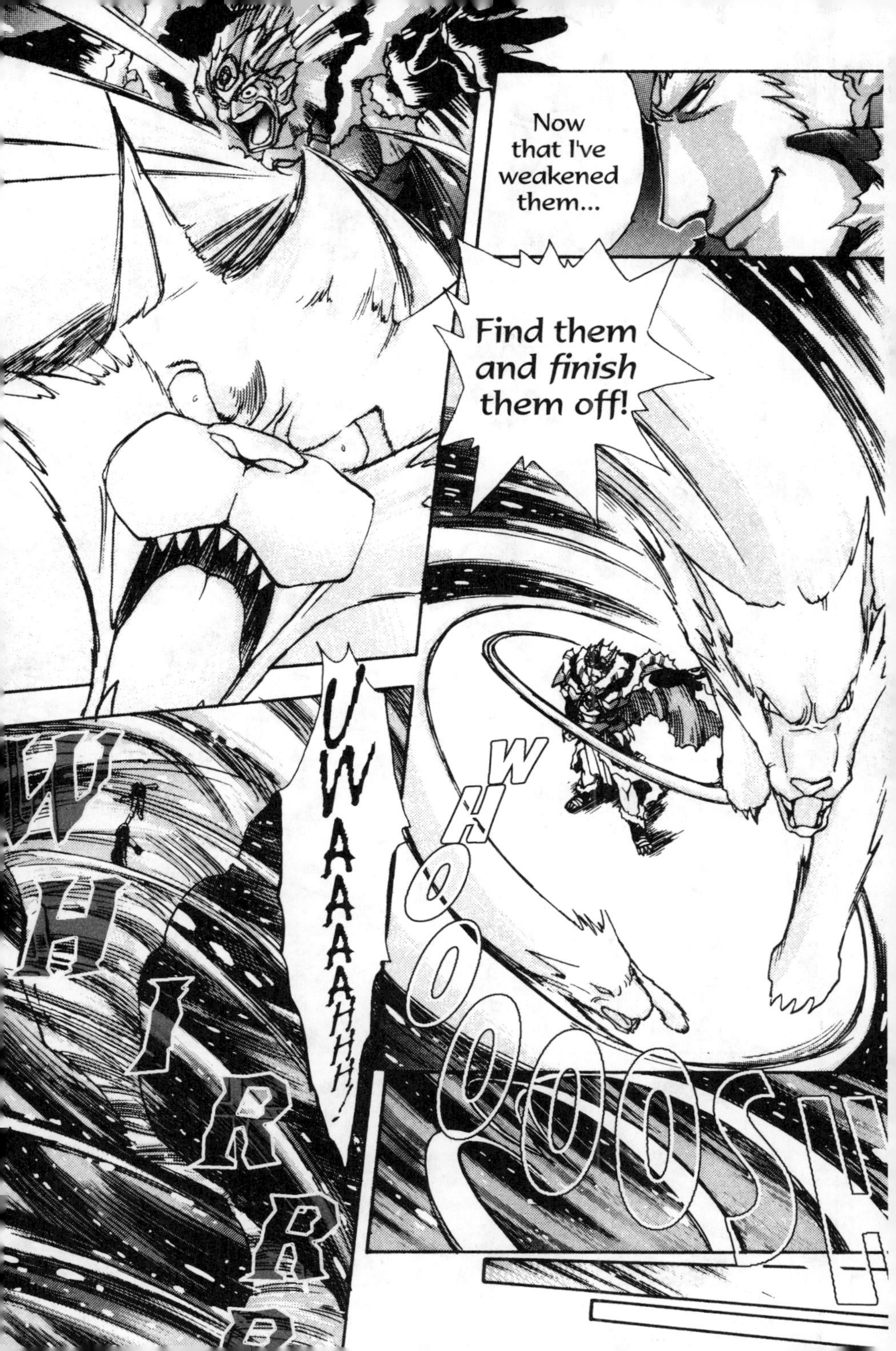
Now that I've weakened them...
Find them and *finish* them off!
WHOOOOOOSH
UWAAAAAAHHHH!

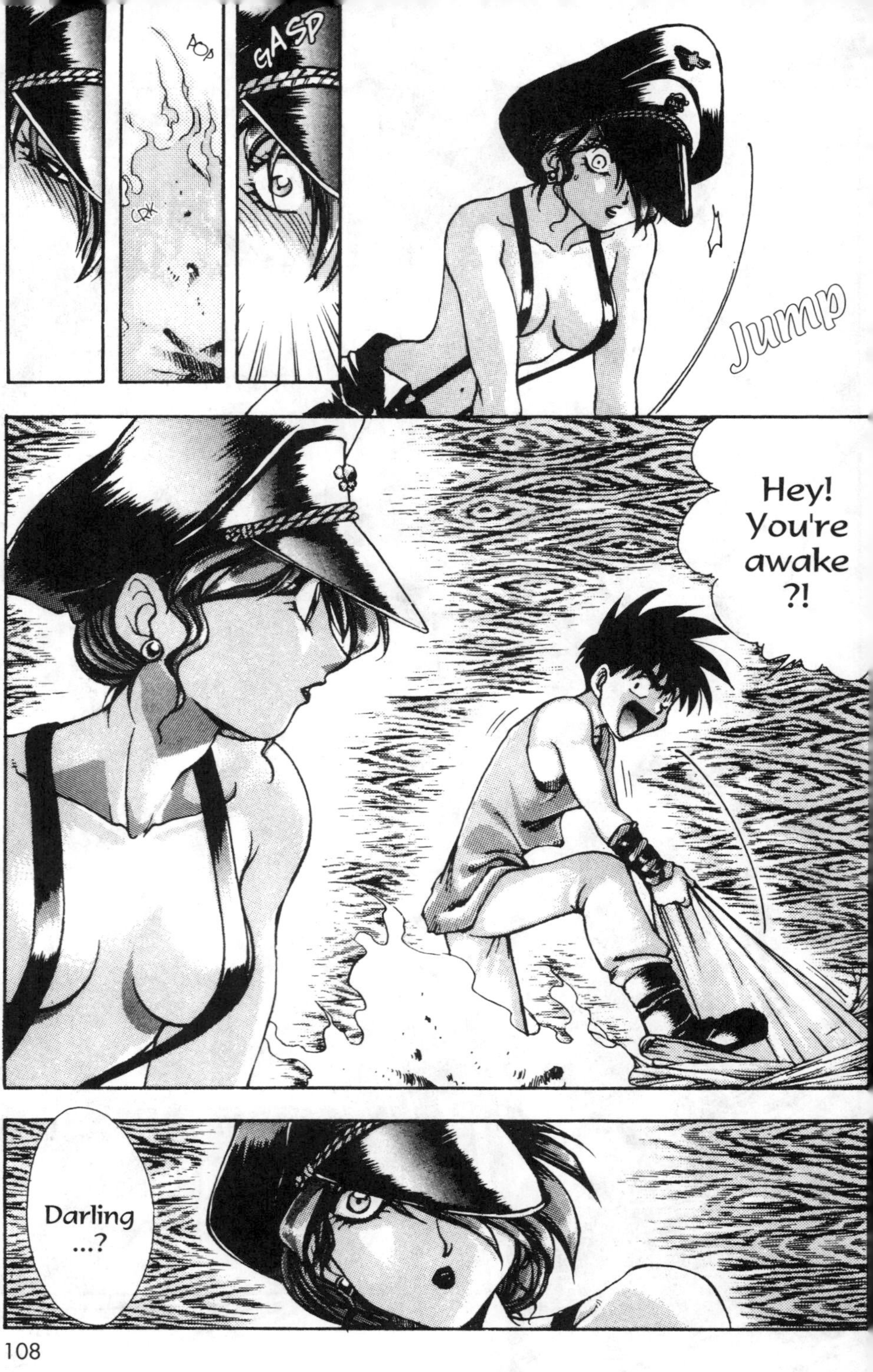
Jump
GASP
POP
CRK
Hey! You're awake ?!
Darling ...?

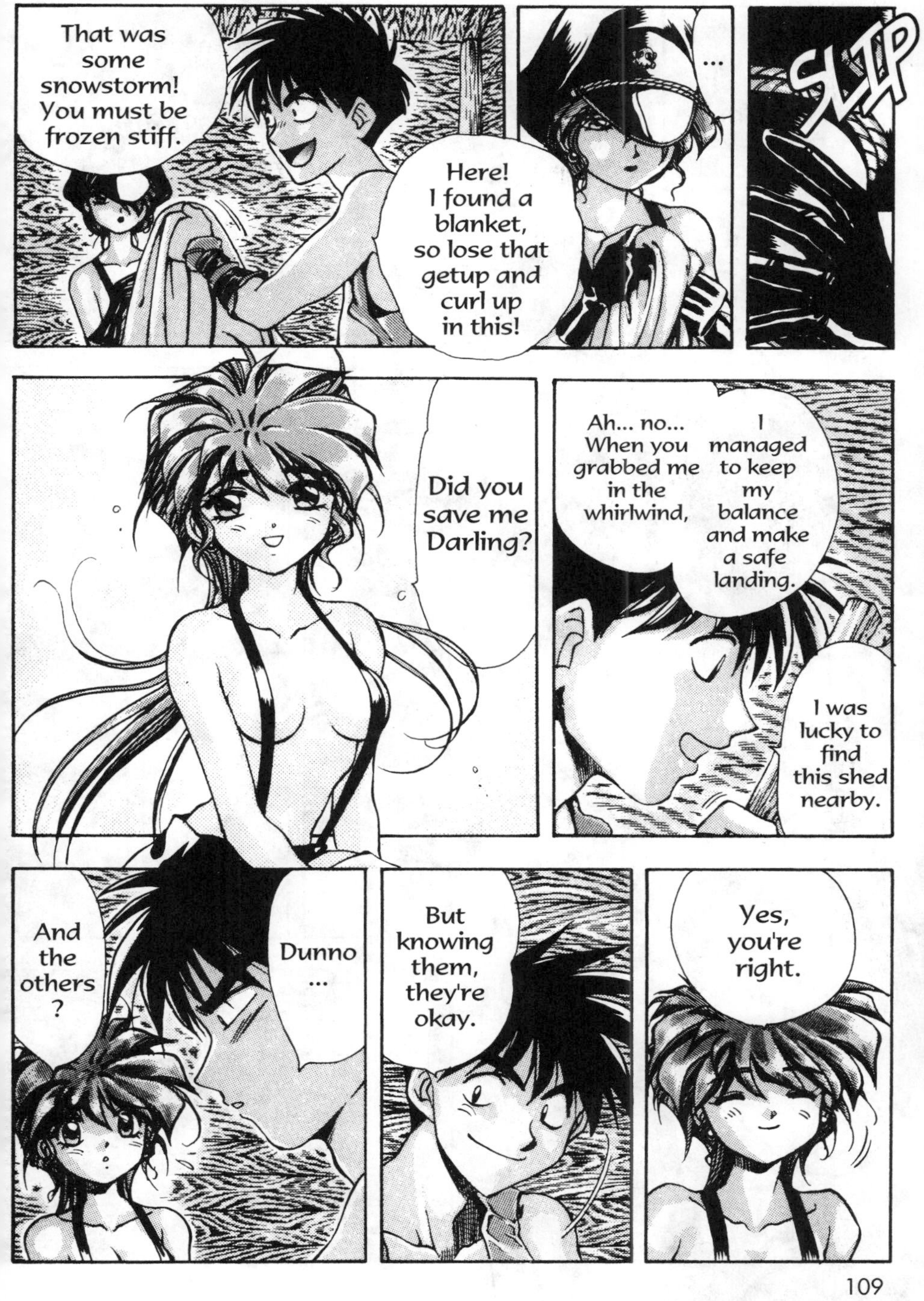
That was some snowstorm! You must be frozen stiff.
Here! I found a blanket, so lose that getup and curl up in this!
...
SLIP
Did you save me Darling?
Ah... no... When you grabbed me in the whirlwind,
I managed to keep my balance and make a safe landing.
I was lucky to find this shed nearby.
And the others?
Dunno...
But knowing them, they're okay.
Yes, you're right.

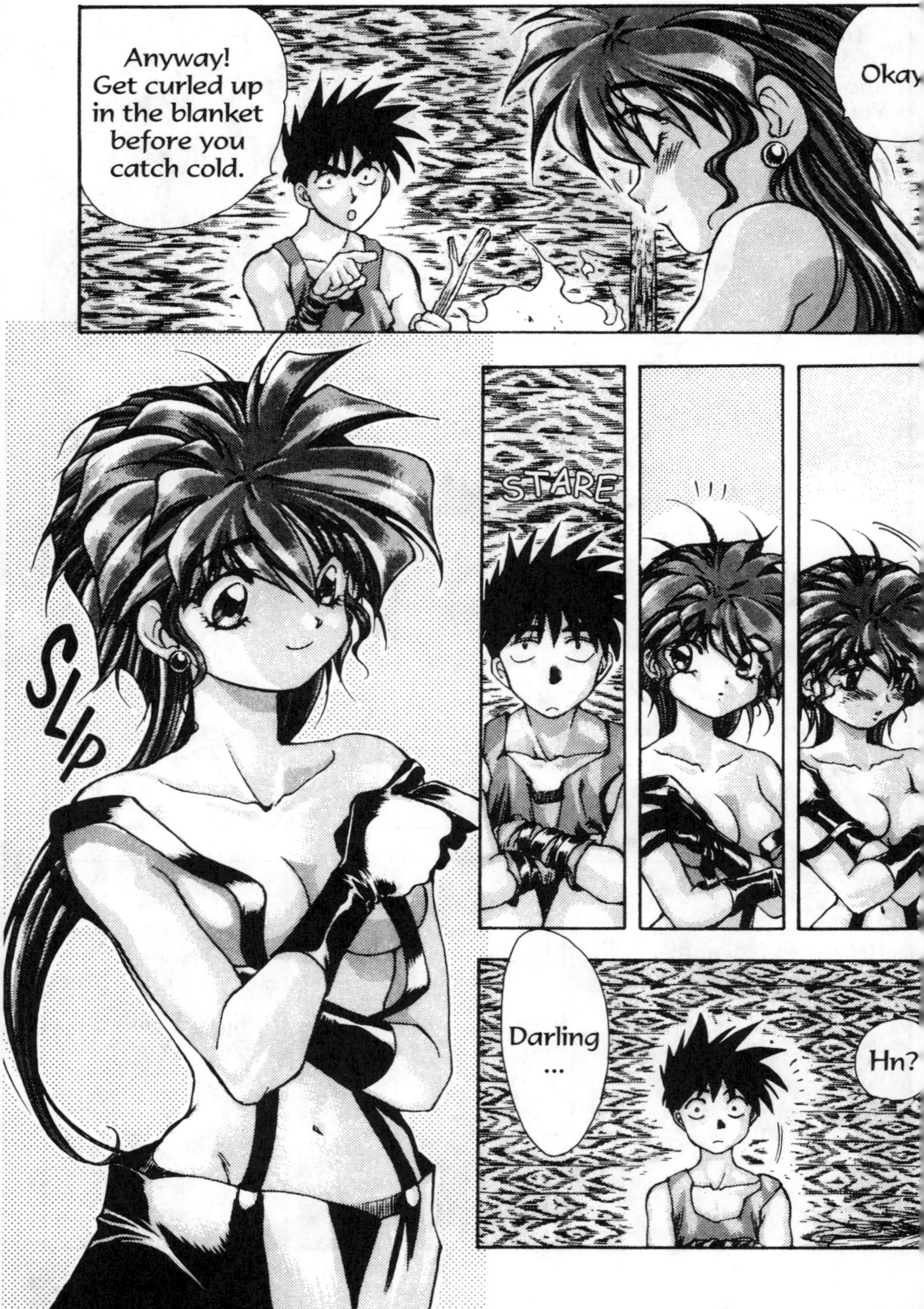
Anyway! Get curled up in the blanket before you catch cold.
Okay
SLIP
STARE
Darling ...
Hn?

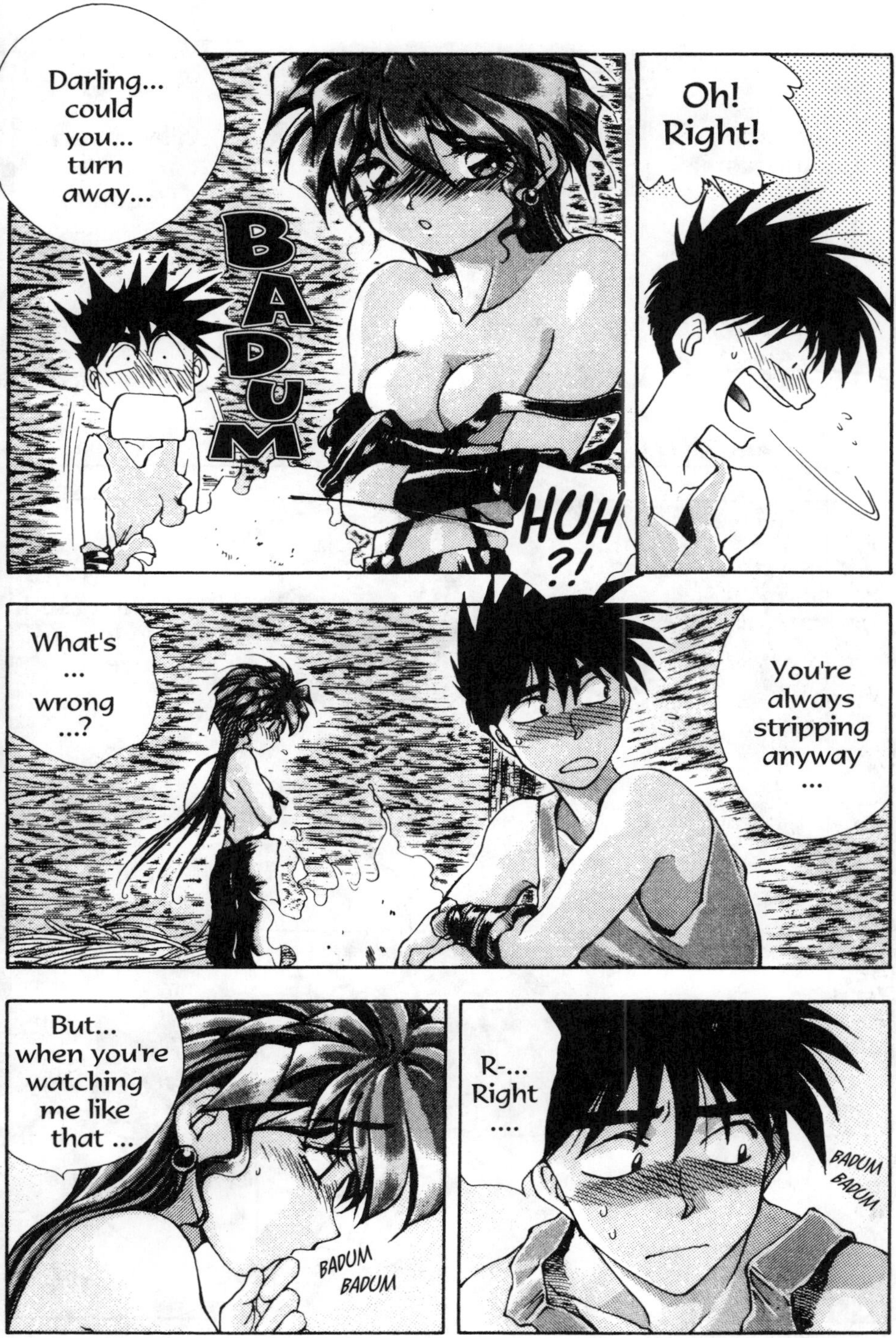
Darling... could you... turn away...
BADUM
HUH ?!
Oh! Right!
What's ... wrong ...?
You're always stripping anyway ...
But... when you're watching me like that ...
BADUM BADUM
R-... Right ....
BADUM BADUM

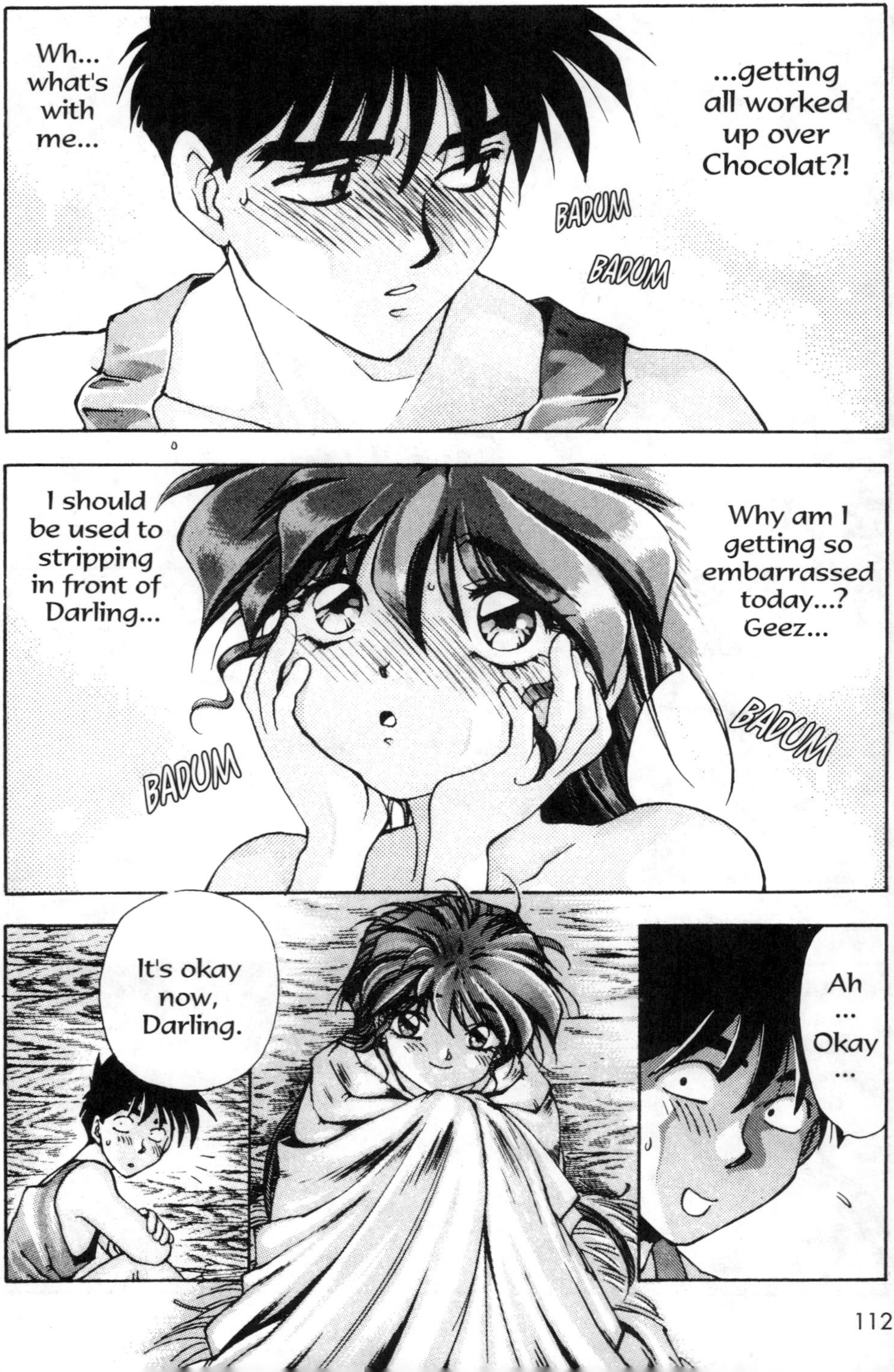
Wh... what's with me...
...getting all worked up over Chocolat?!
BADUM
BADUM
I should be used to stripping in front of Darling...
Why am I getting so embarrassed today...? Geez...
BADUM
BADUM
It's okay now, Darling.
Ah ... Okay ...

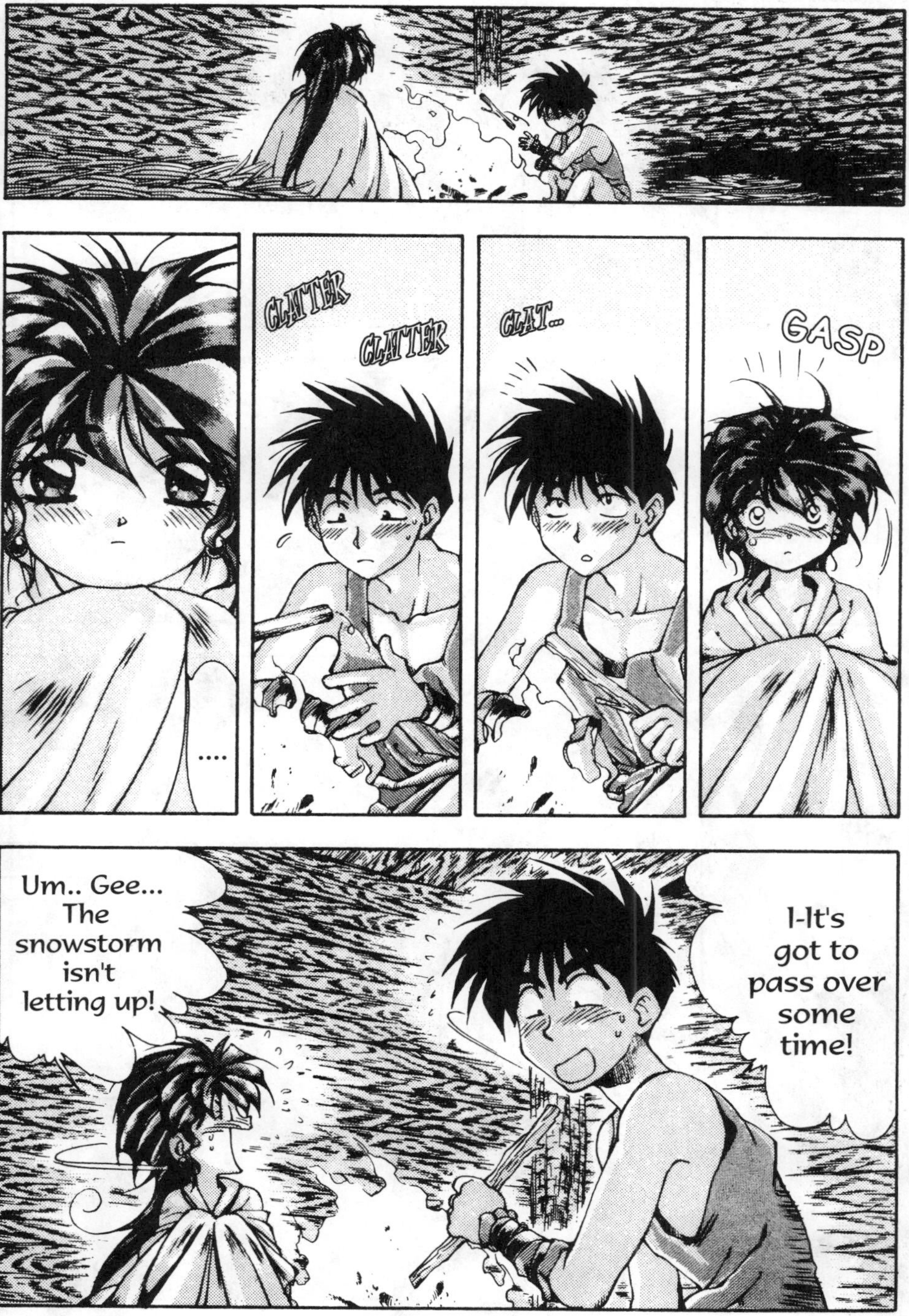
....
CLATTER
CLATTER
CLAT...
GASP
Um.. Gee... The snowstorm isn't letting up!
I-It's got to pass over some time!

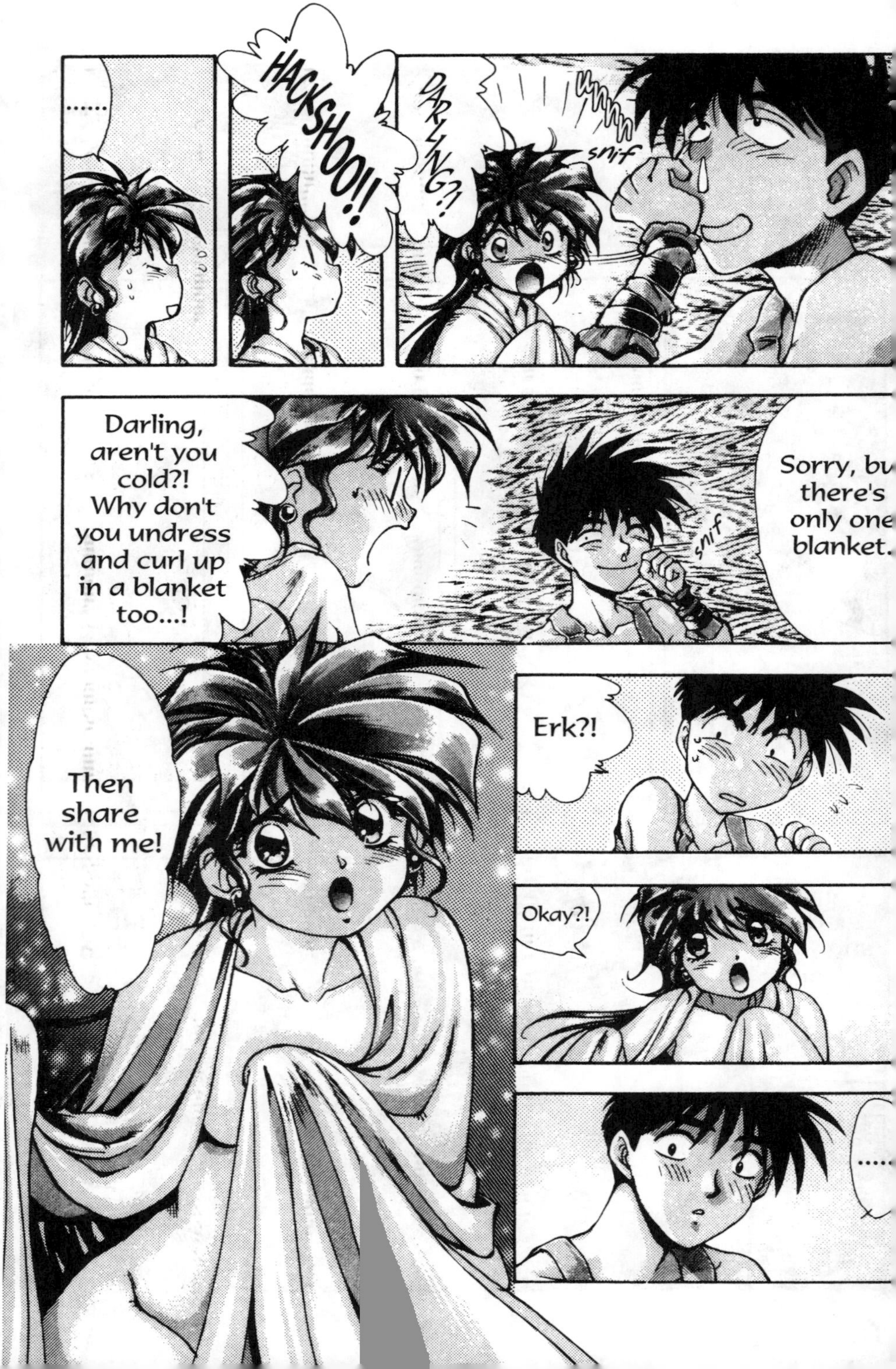
......
HACKSHOO!!
DARLING?!
unnnn
snif
Darling, aren't you cold?! Why don't you undress and curl up in a blanket too...!
snif
Sorry, bu there's only one blanket.
Then share with me!
Erk?!
Okay?!
.....

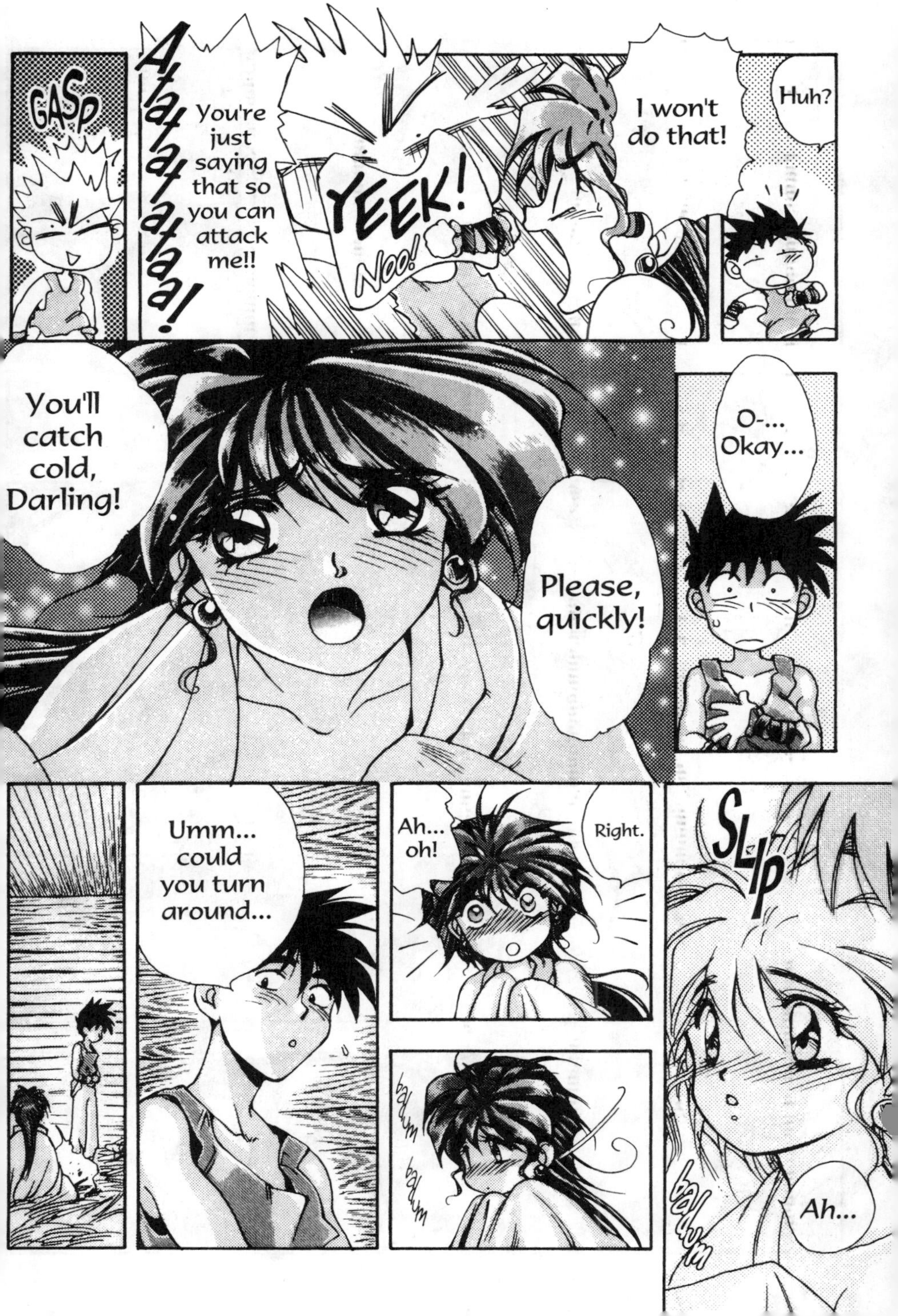
GASP
Atatatataa!
You're just saying that so you can attack me!!
YEEK!
Noo!
I won't do that!
Huh?
You'll catch cold, Darling!
Please, quickly!
O-... Okay...
Umm... could you turn around...
Ah... oh!
Right.
badum
badum
SLIP
badum
Ah...

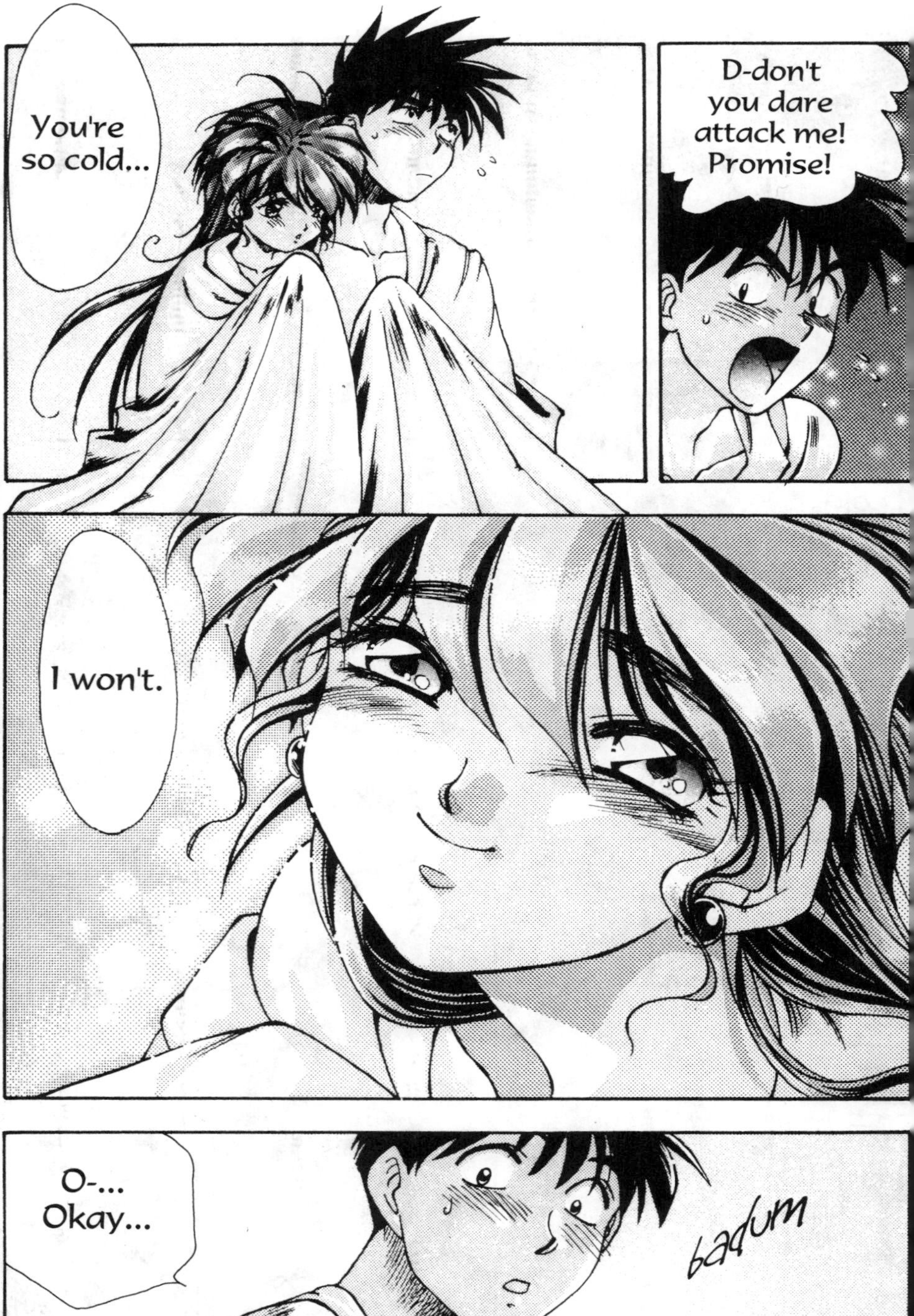
You're so cold...
D-don't you dare attack me! Promise!
I won't.
O-... Okay...
badum

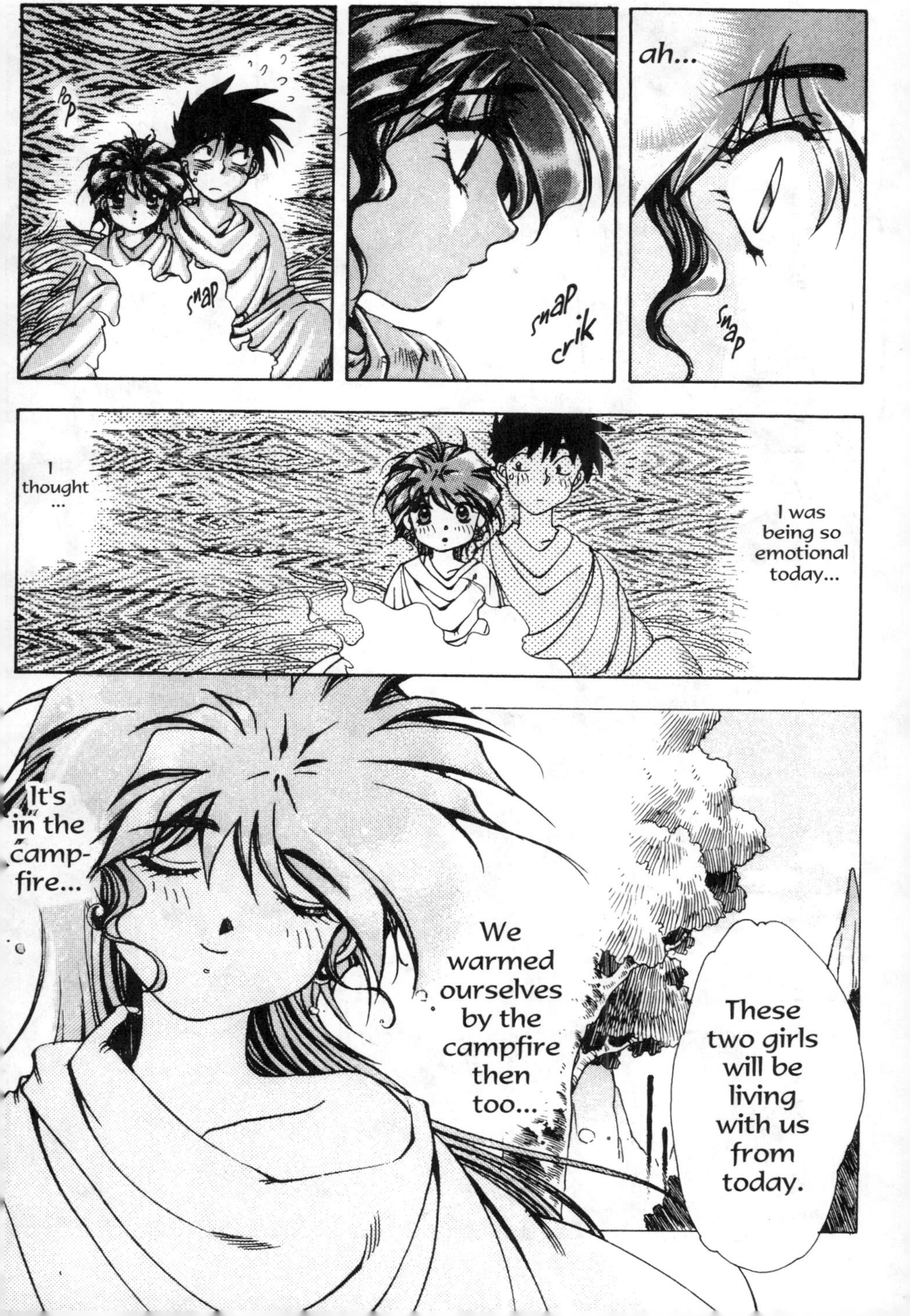
pop
snap
snap
crik
ah...
snap
I thought...
I was being so emotional today...
It's in the campfire...
We warmed ourselves by the campfire then too...
These two girls will be living with us from today.

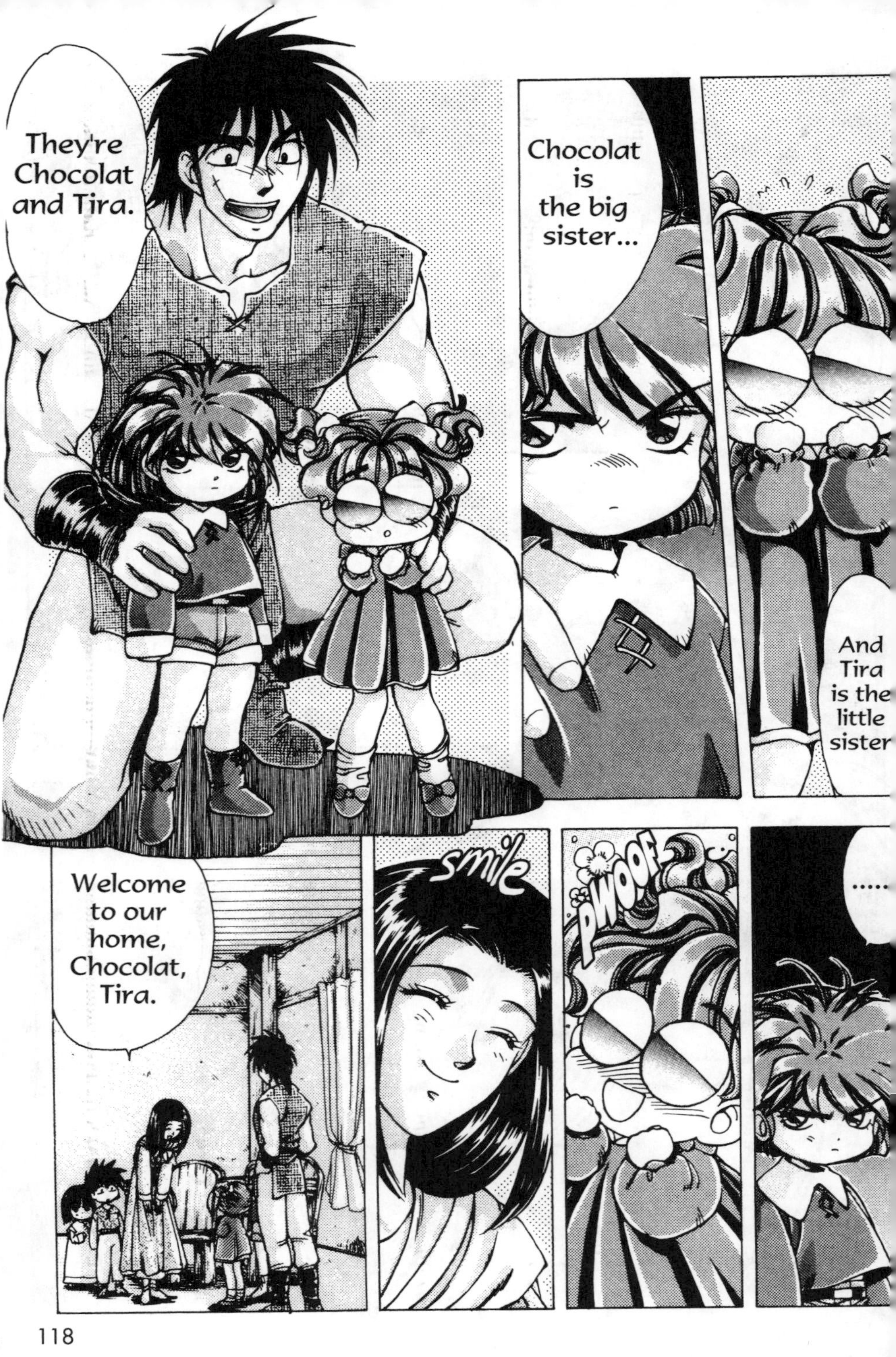
They're Chocolat and Tira.
Chocolat is the big sister...
And Tira is the little sister
Welcome to our home, Chocolat, Tira.
smile
pwoof
.....

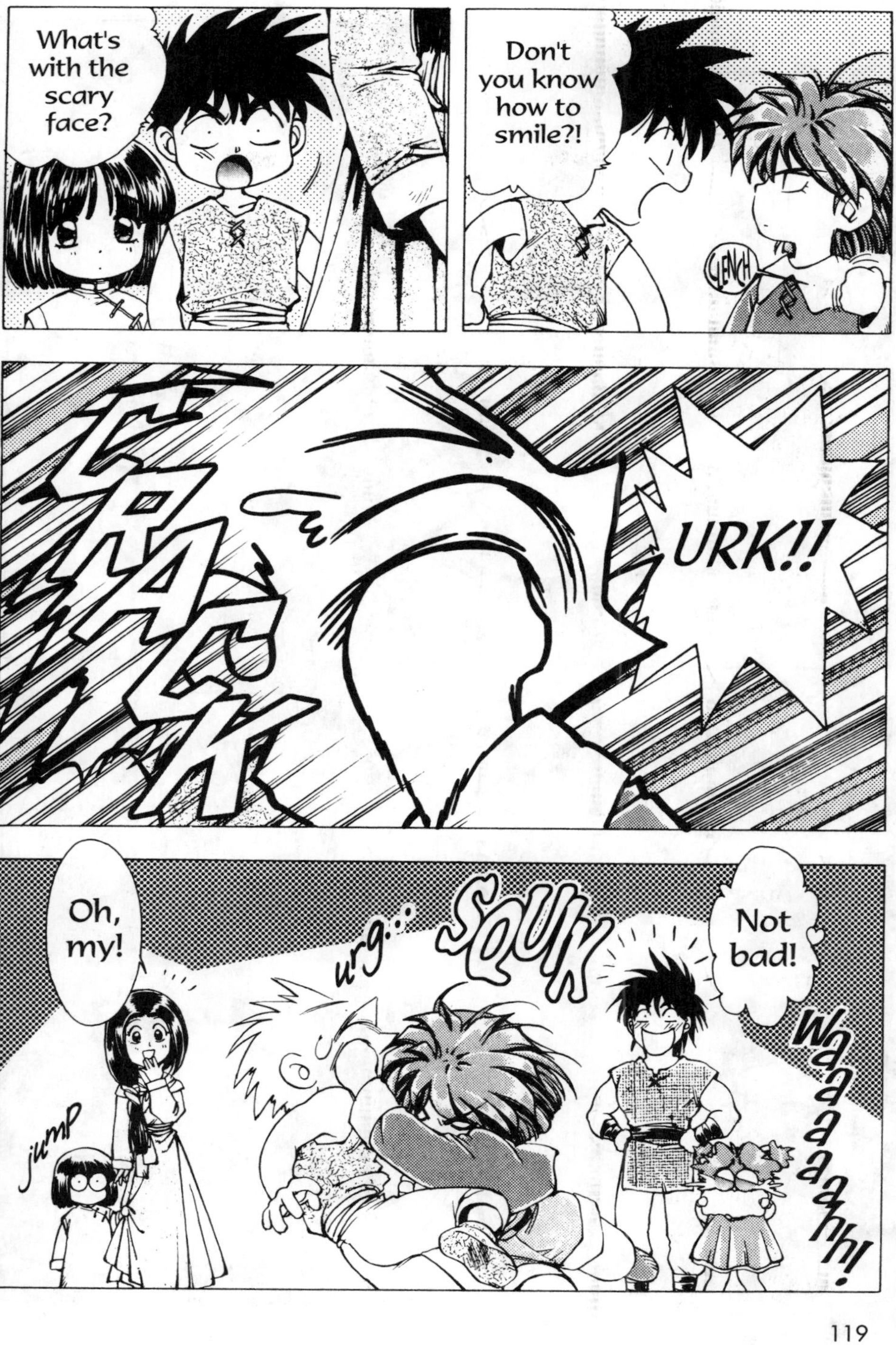
What's with the scary face?
Don't you know how to smile?!
CLENCH
CRACK
URK!!
Oh, my!
jump
urg...
SQUIK
Not bad!
Waaaaaahh!

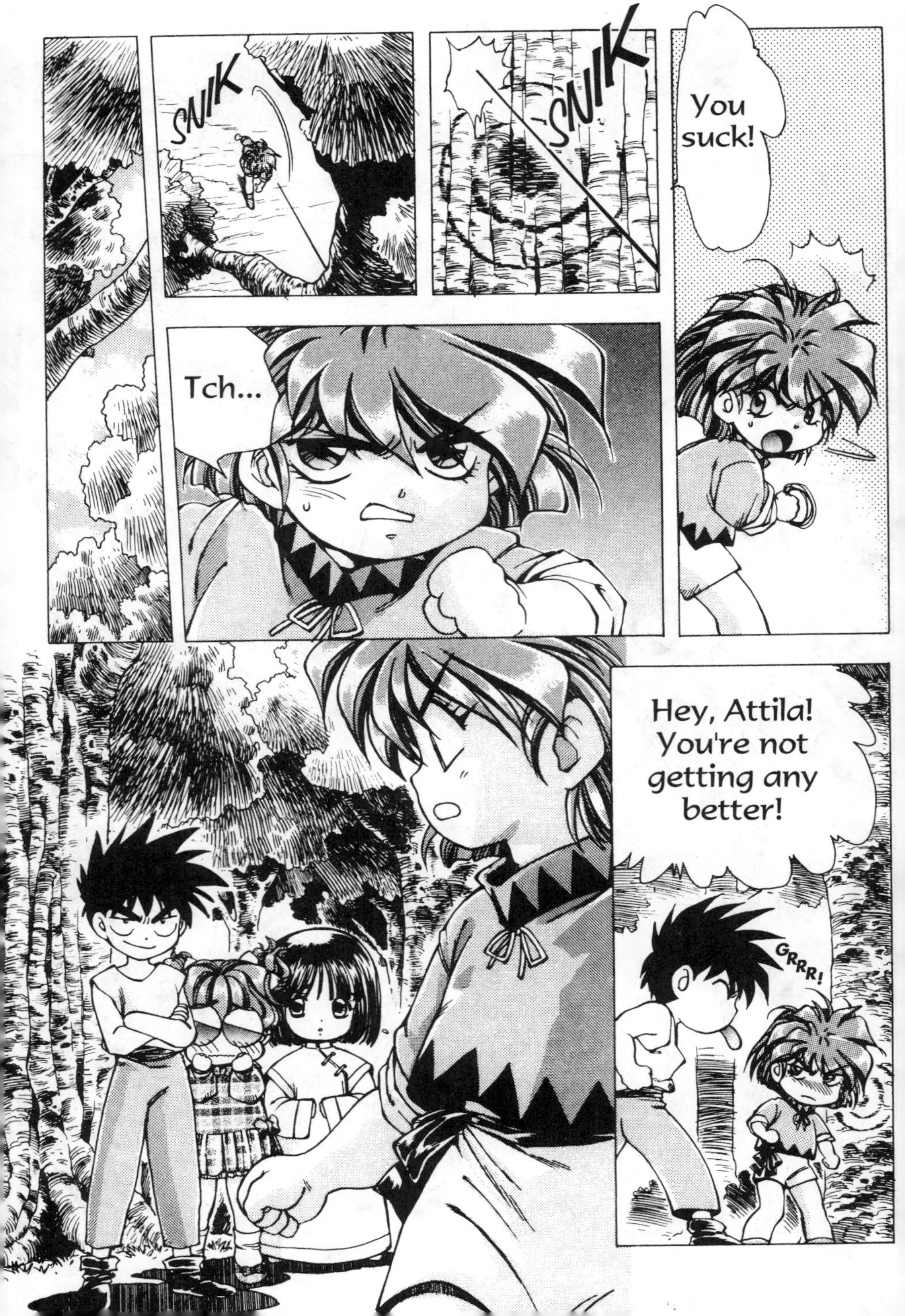
You suck!
SNIK
SNIK
Tch...
Hey, Attila! You're not getting any better!
GRRR!

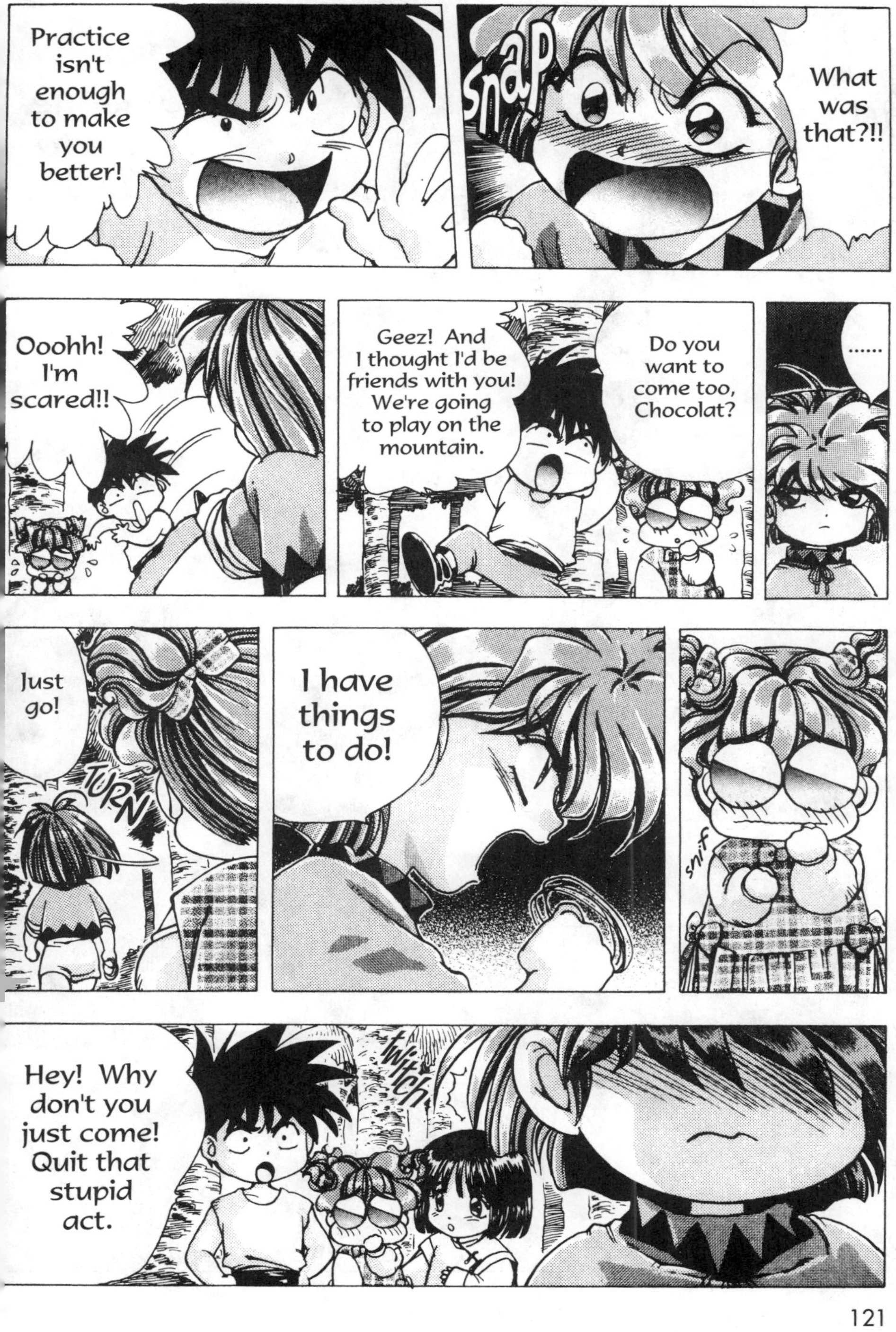
Practice isn't enough to make you better!
SNAP
What was that?!!
Ooohh! I'm scared!!
Geez! And I thought I'd be friends with you! We're going to play on the mountain.
Do you want to come too, Chocolat?
......
Just go!
TURN
I have things to do!
snif
Hey! Why don't you just come! Quit that stupid act.
twitch

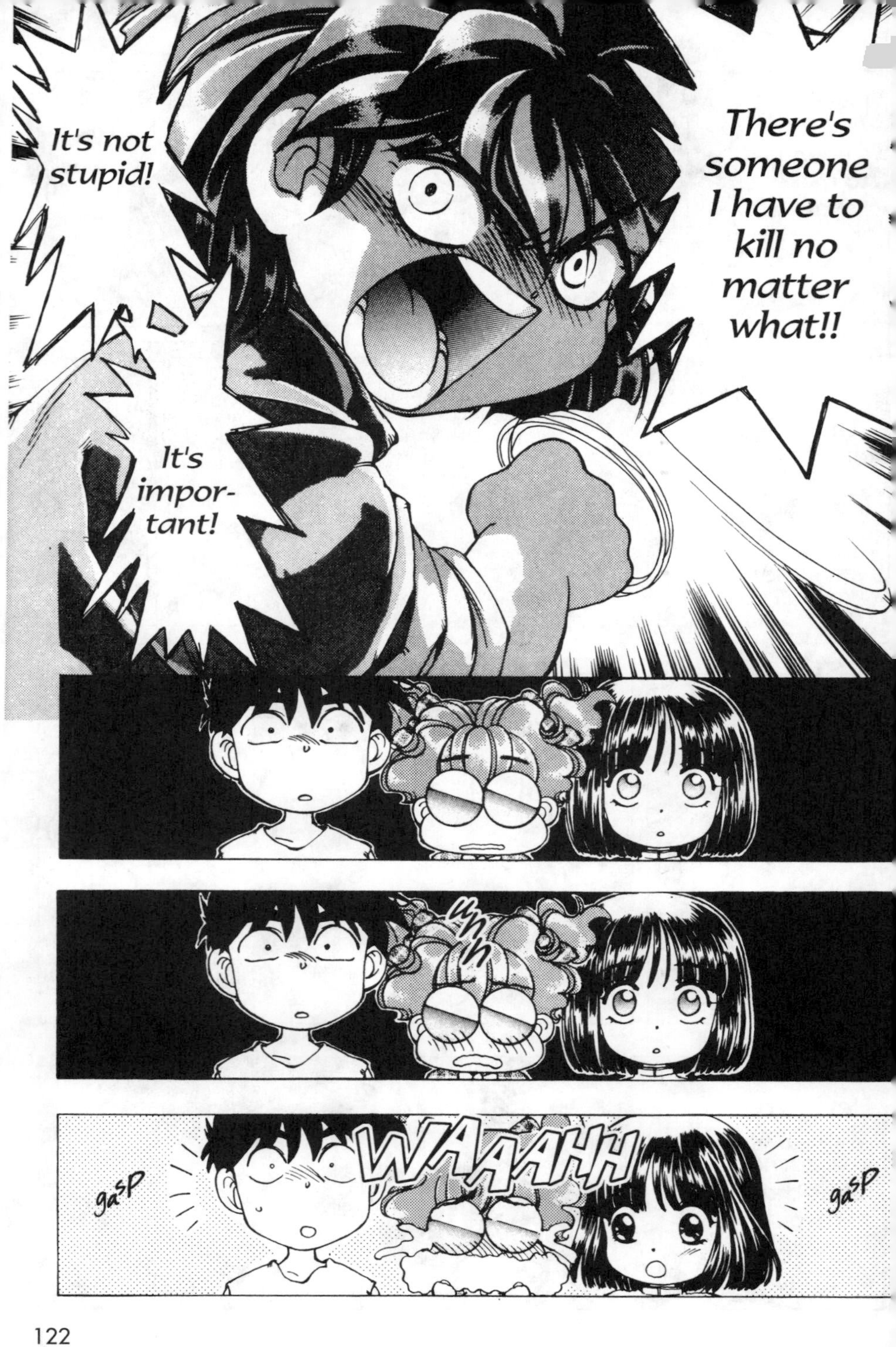
There's someone I have to kill no matter what!!
It's not stupid!
It's impor-tant!
WAAAHH
gasp
gasp

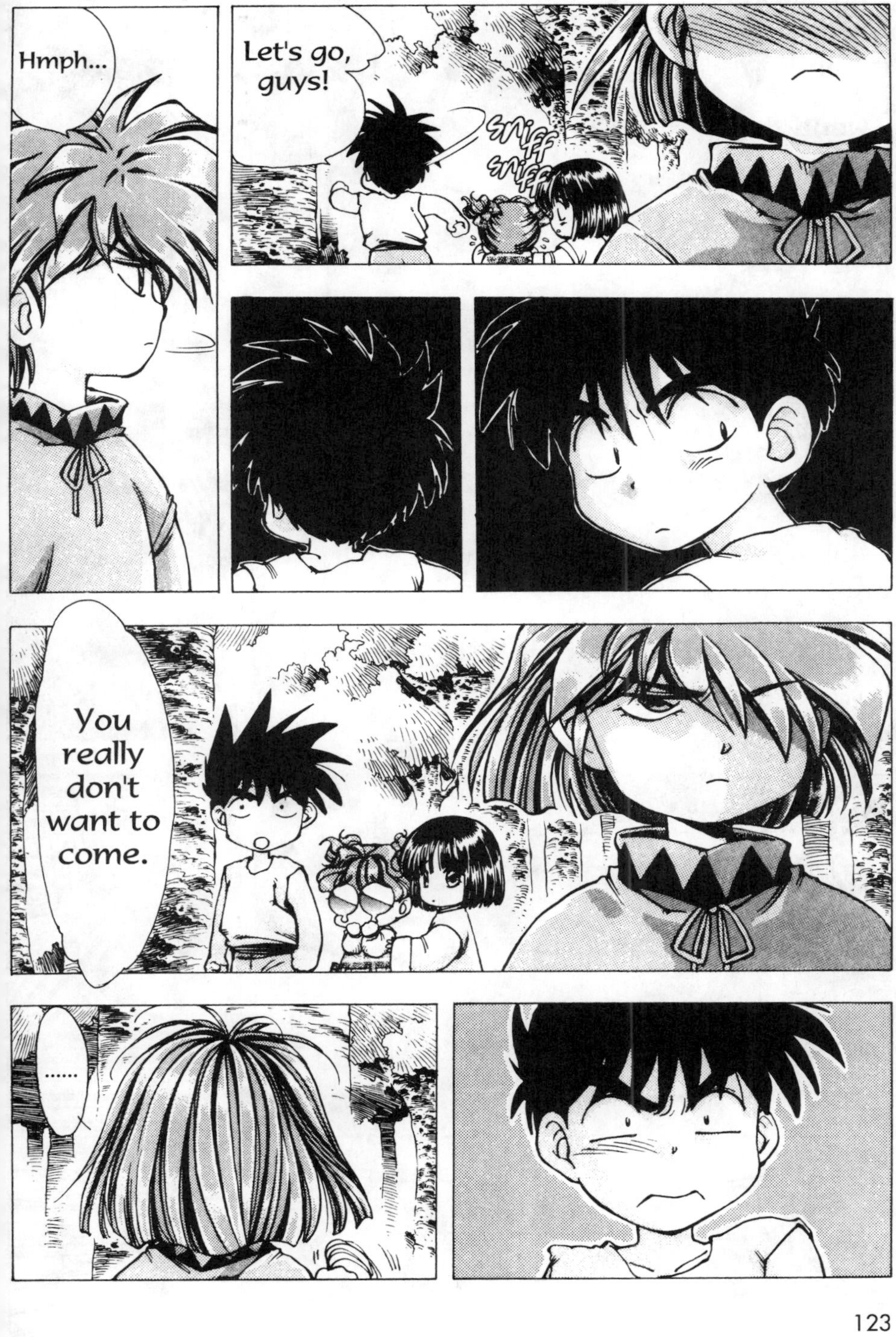
Let's go, guys!
sniff sniff
Hmph...
You really don't want to come.
......

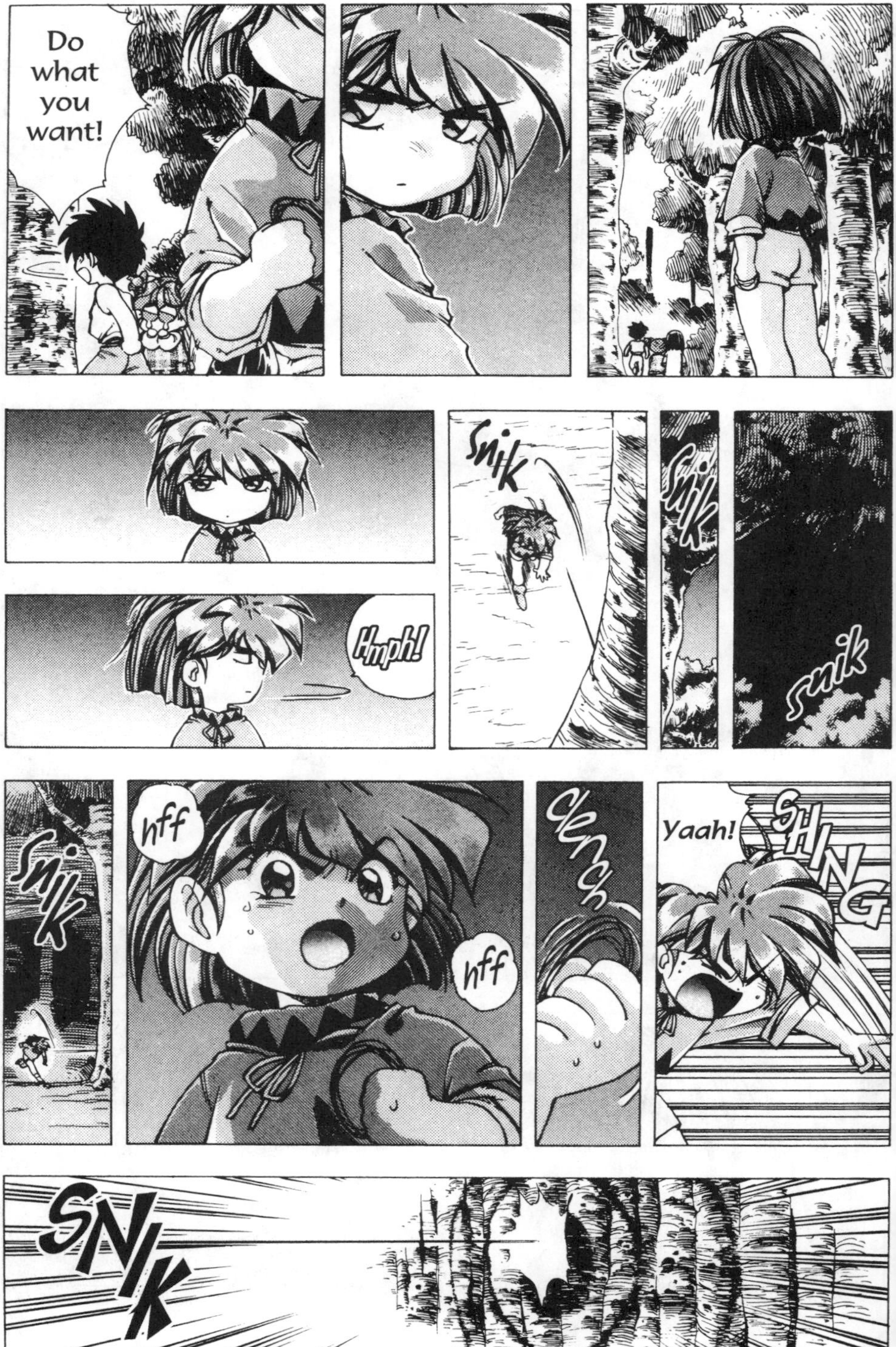
Do what you want!
Hmph!
Snik
Snik
snik
Snik
hff
hff
clench
Yaah!
SHING
SNIK

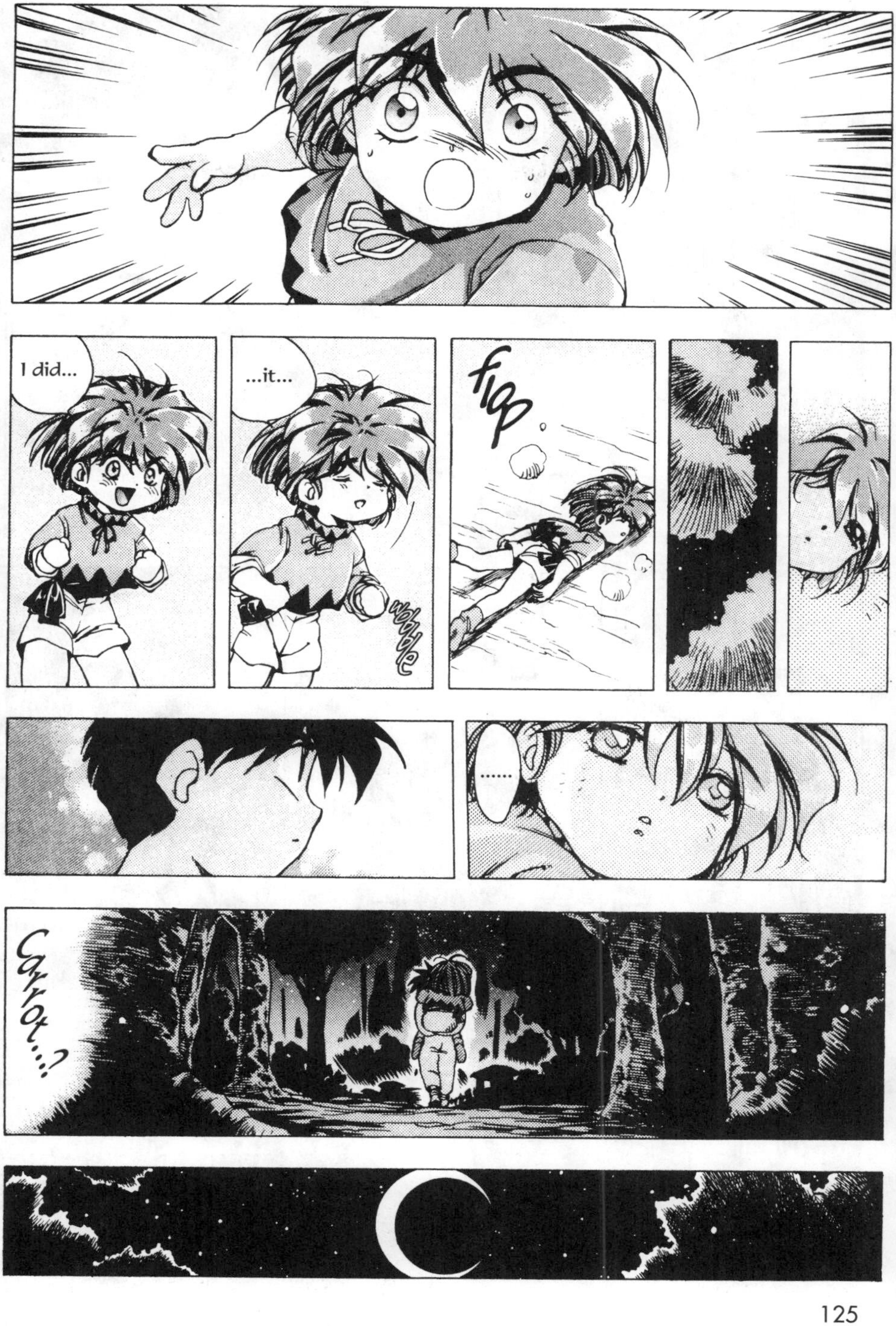

I did...
...it...
wobble
flop
......
Carrot...?

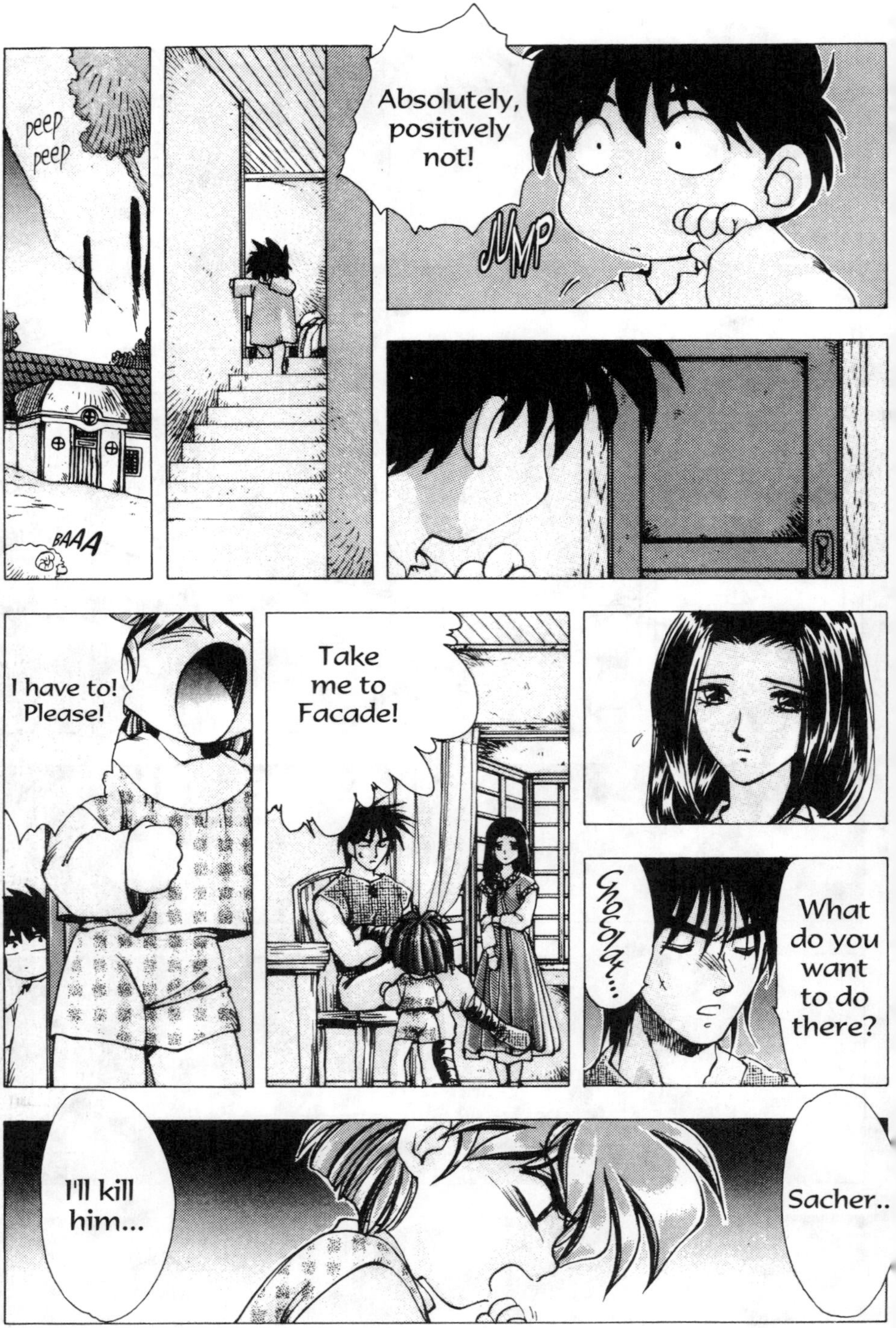
Absolutely, positively not!
JUMP
peep peep
BAAA
Chocolat...
What do you want to do there?
Take me to Facade!
I have to! Please!
Sacher..
I'll kill him...

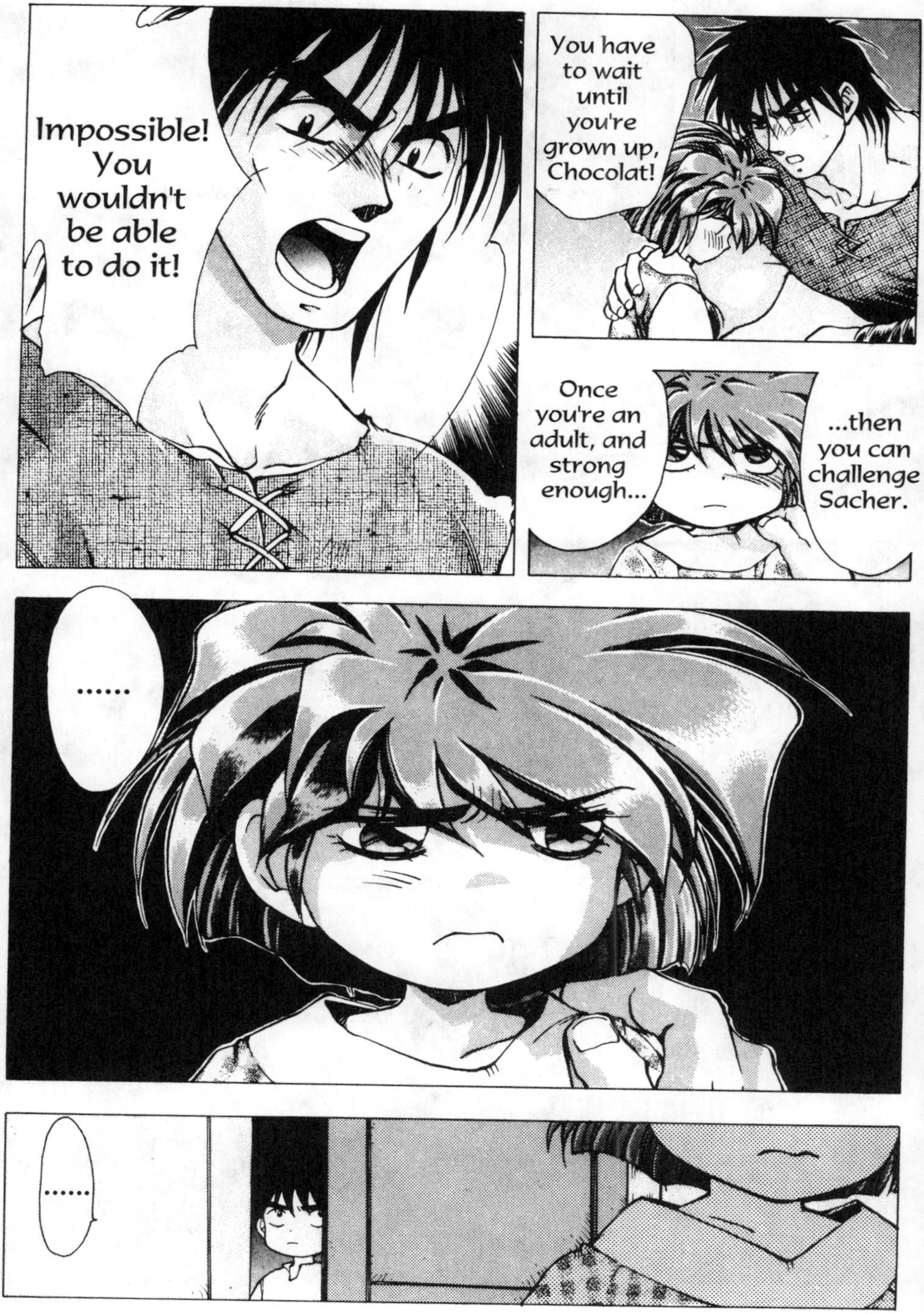
Impossible! You wouldn't be able to do it!
You have to wait until you're grown up, Chocolat!
Once you're an adult, and strong enough...
...then you can challenge Sacher.
......
......

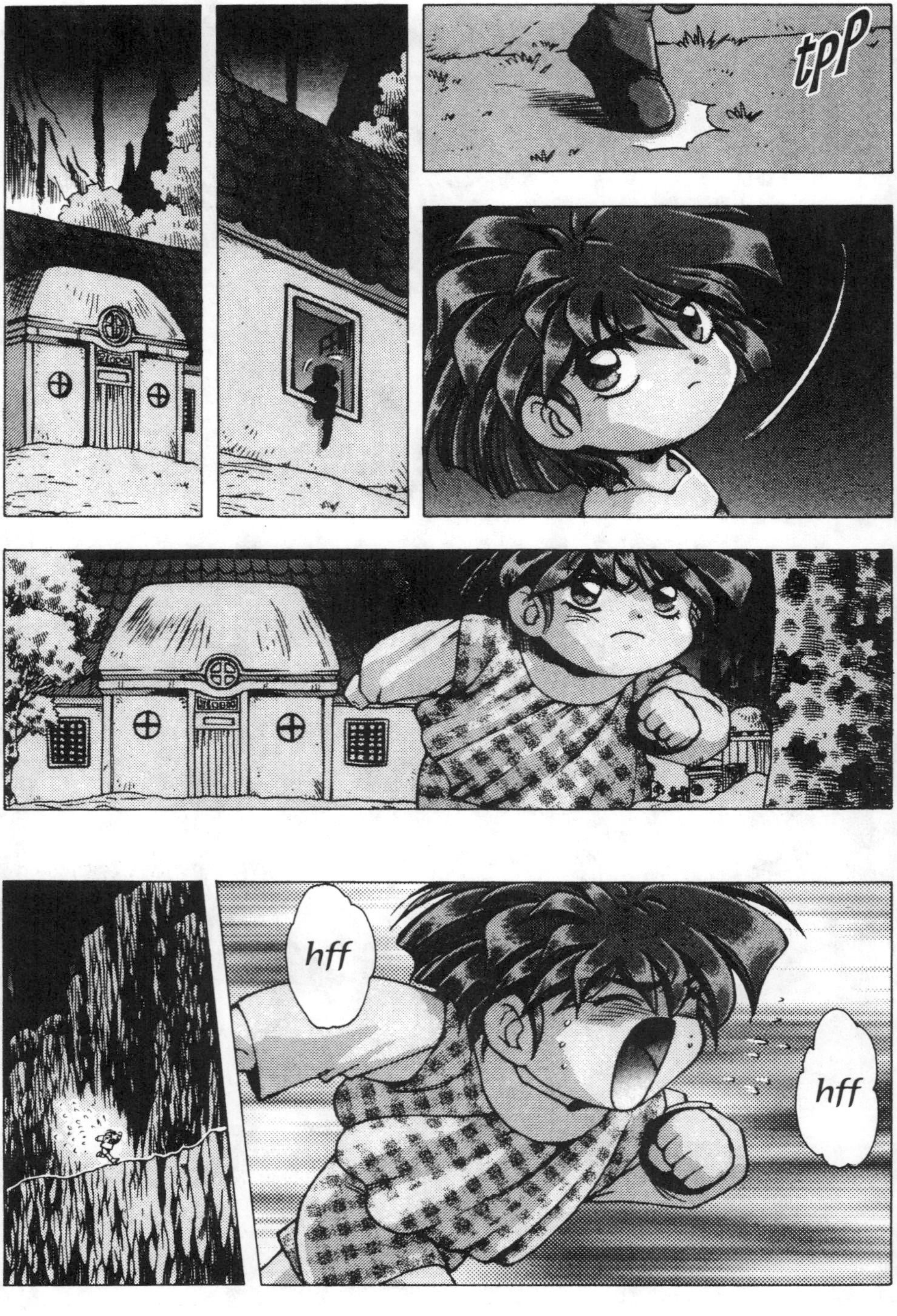
tpp
hff
hff

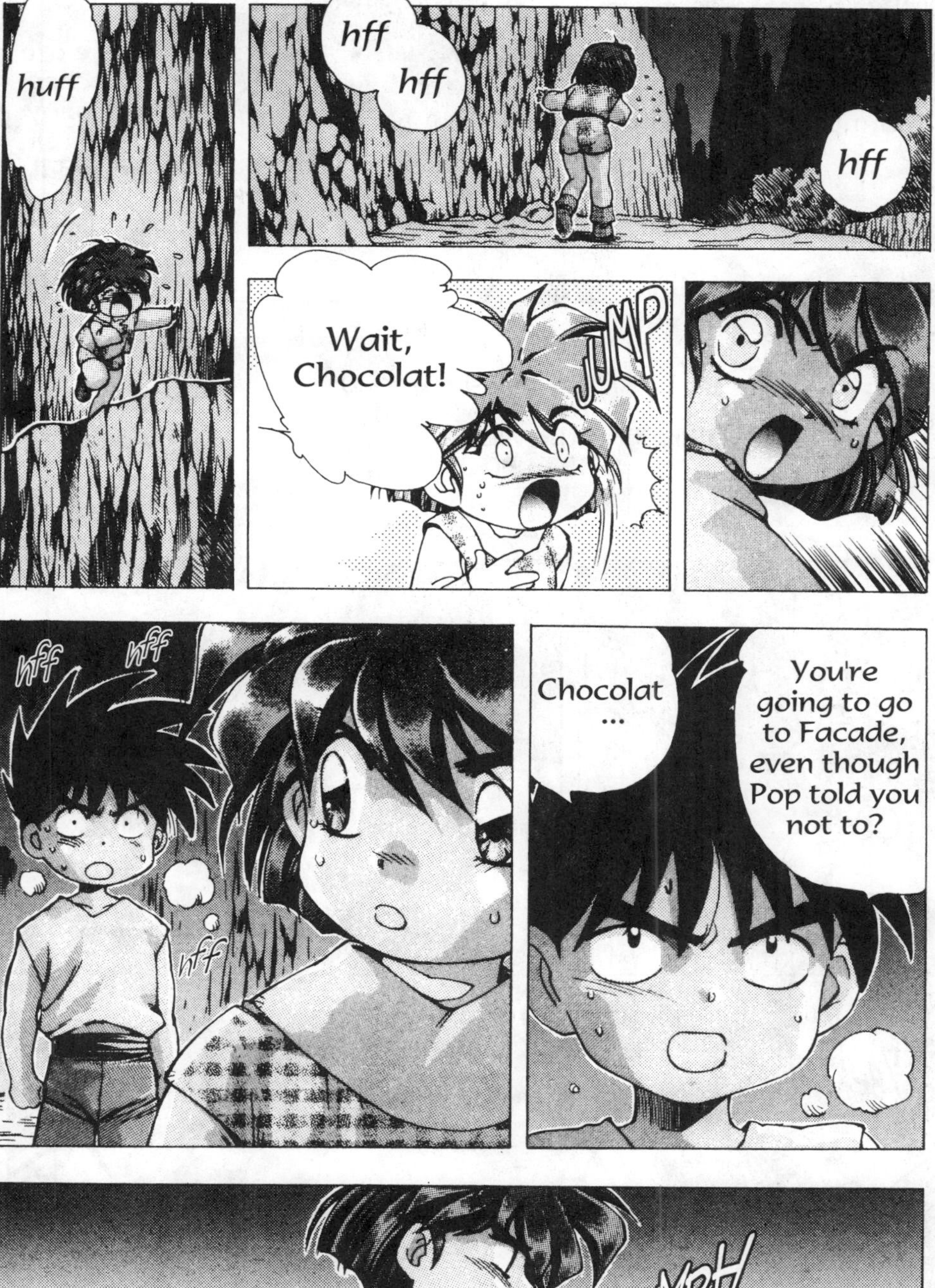
hff
hff
hff
Wait, Chocolat!
JUMP
huff
Chocolat ...
You're going to go to Facade, even though Pop told you not to?
hff
hff
hff
HMPH

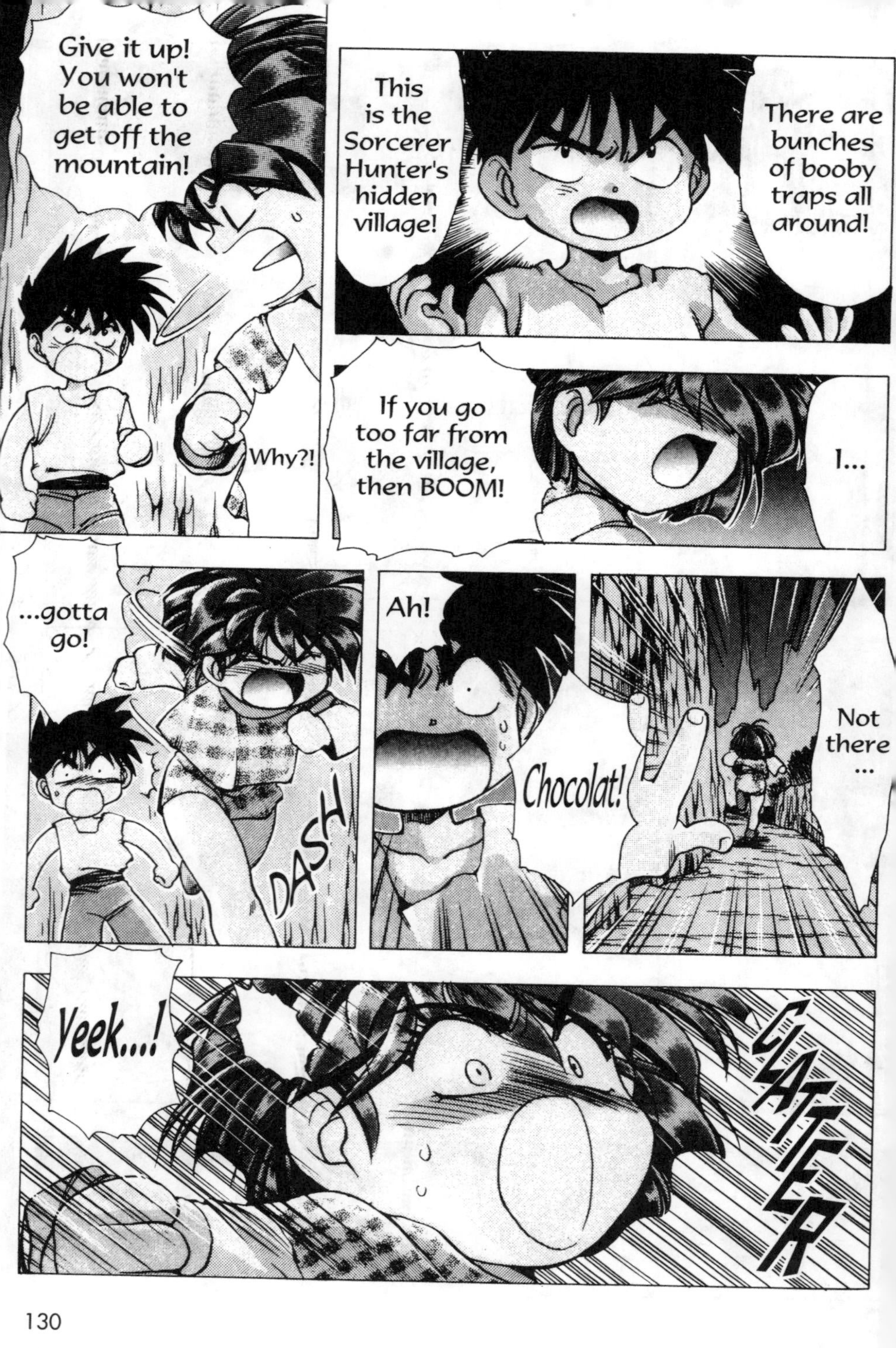
Give it up! You won't be able to get off the mountain!
Why?!
This is the Sorcerer Hunter's hidden village!
There are bunches of booby traps all around!
If you go too far from the village, then BOOM!
I...
...gotta go!
DASH
Ah!
Chocolat!
Not there ...
Yeek...!
CLATTER

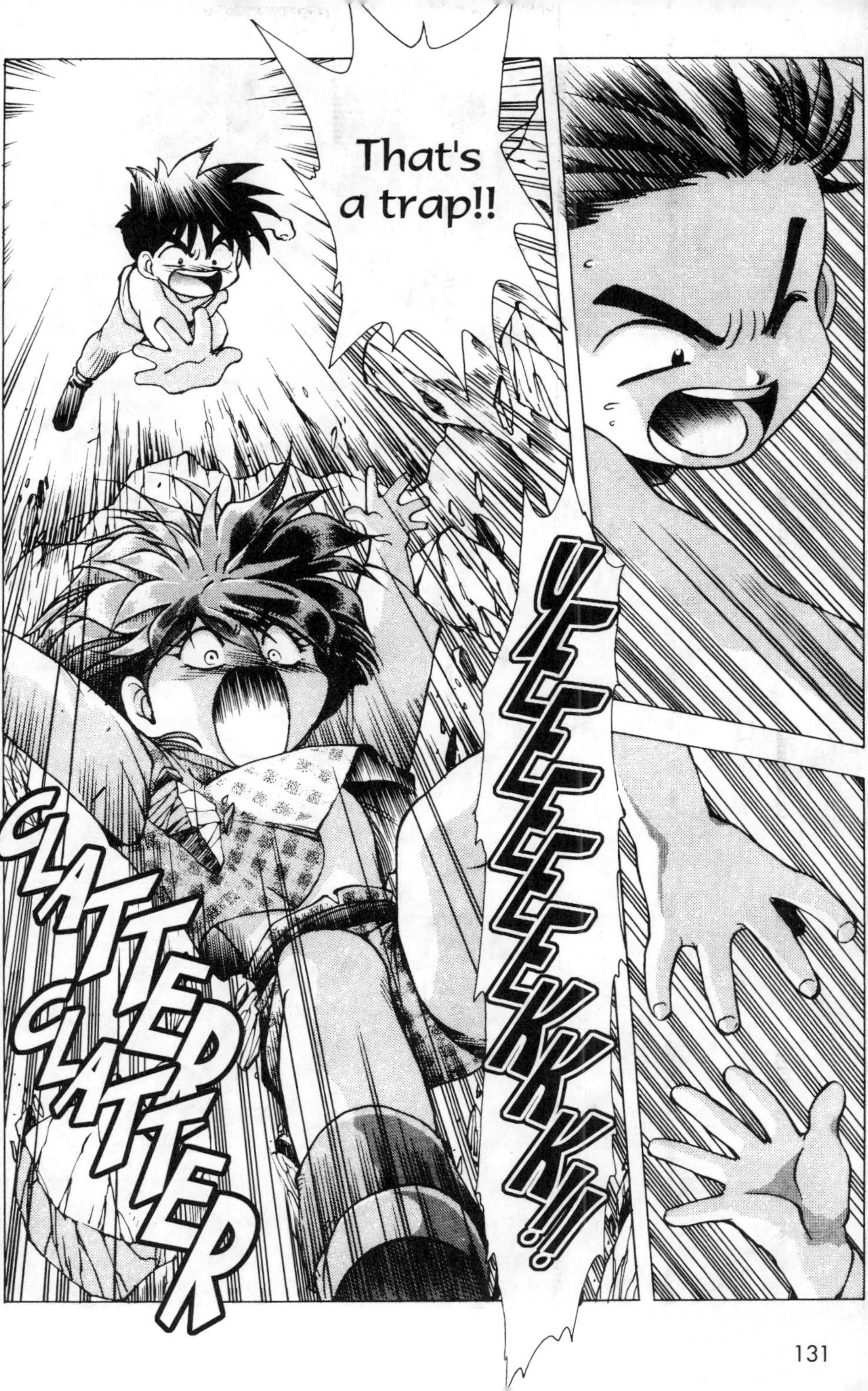
YEEEEEEEKKK!!
That's a trap!!
CLATTER CLATTER

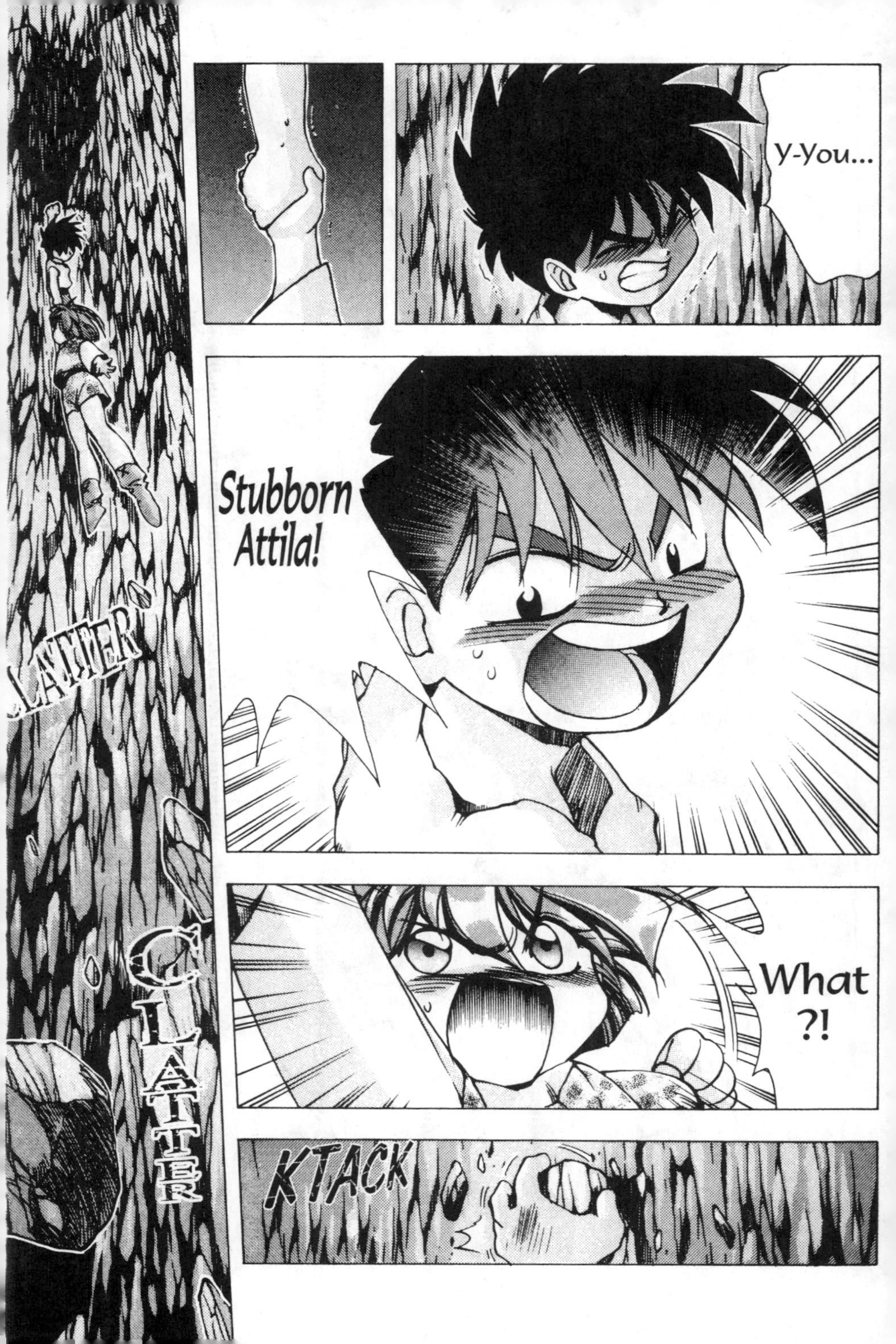
Y-You...
Stubborn Attila!
What ?!
KTACK
CLATTER

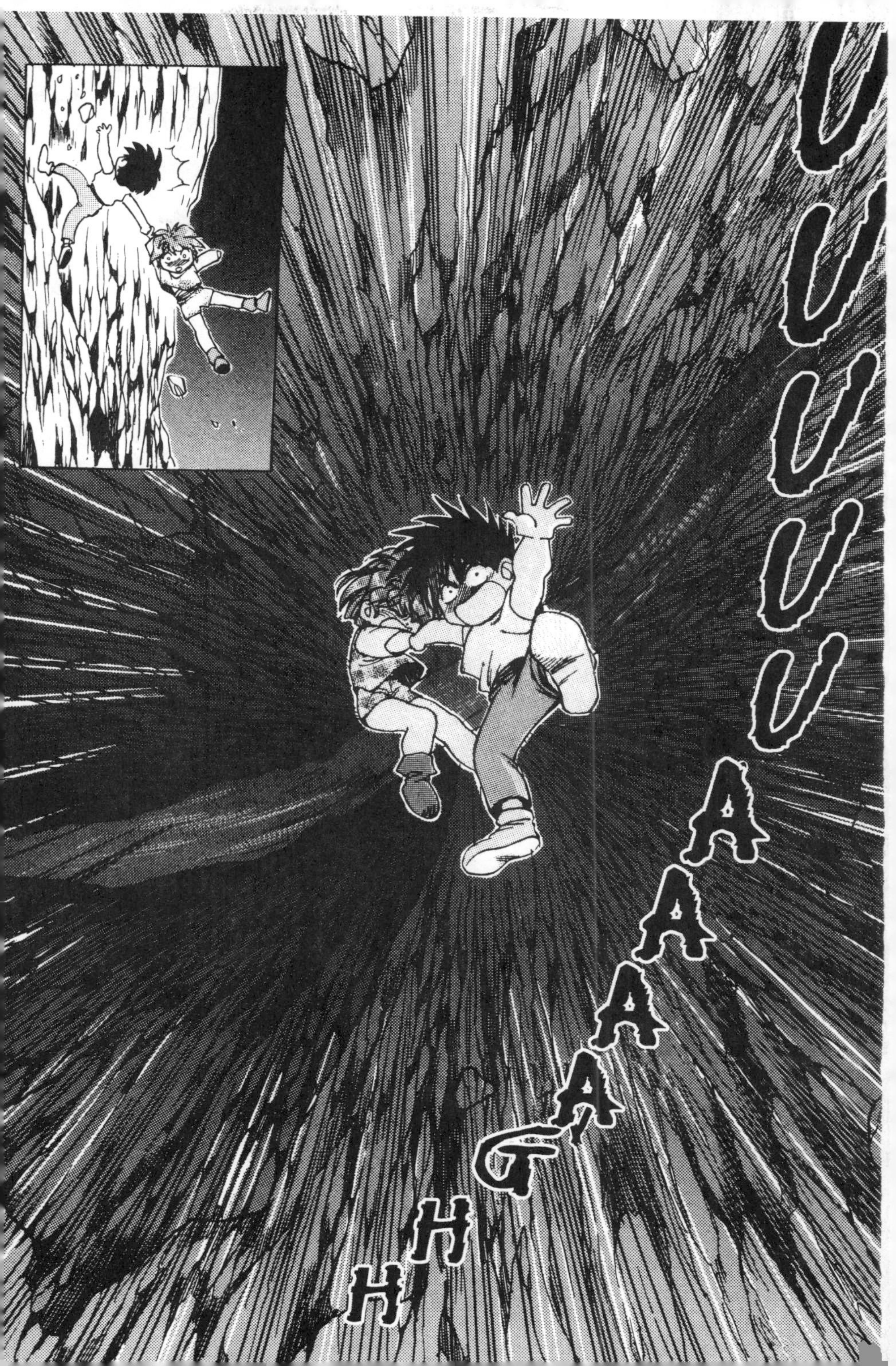
HHGAAAAUUUUUUUU

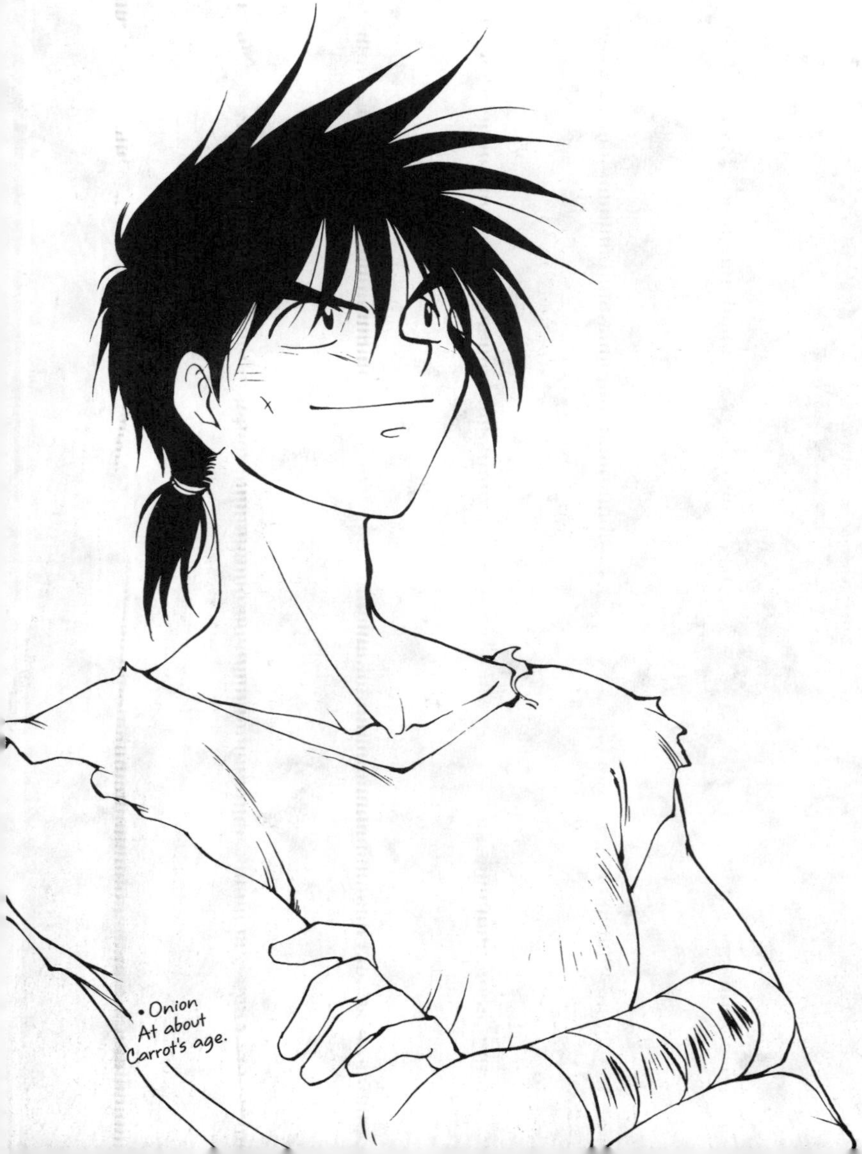
•Onion
At about
Carrot's age.

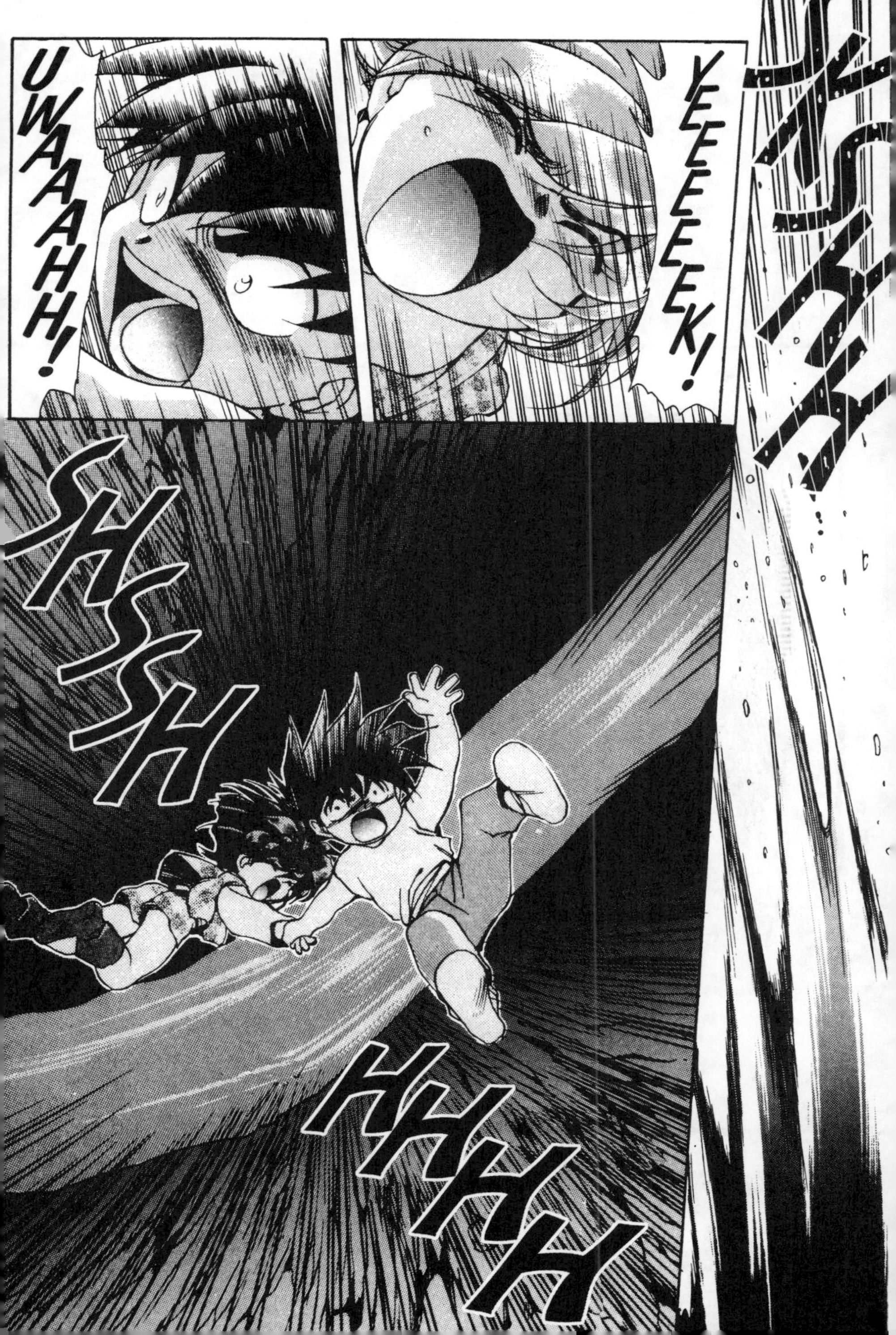
YEEEEEK!
UWAAAHH!
SHSHSH
HHHHH

Memories by the Campfire (Part 2)

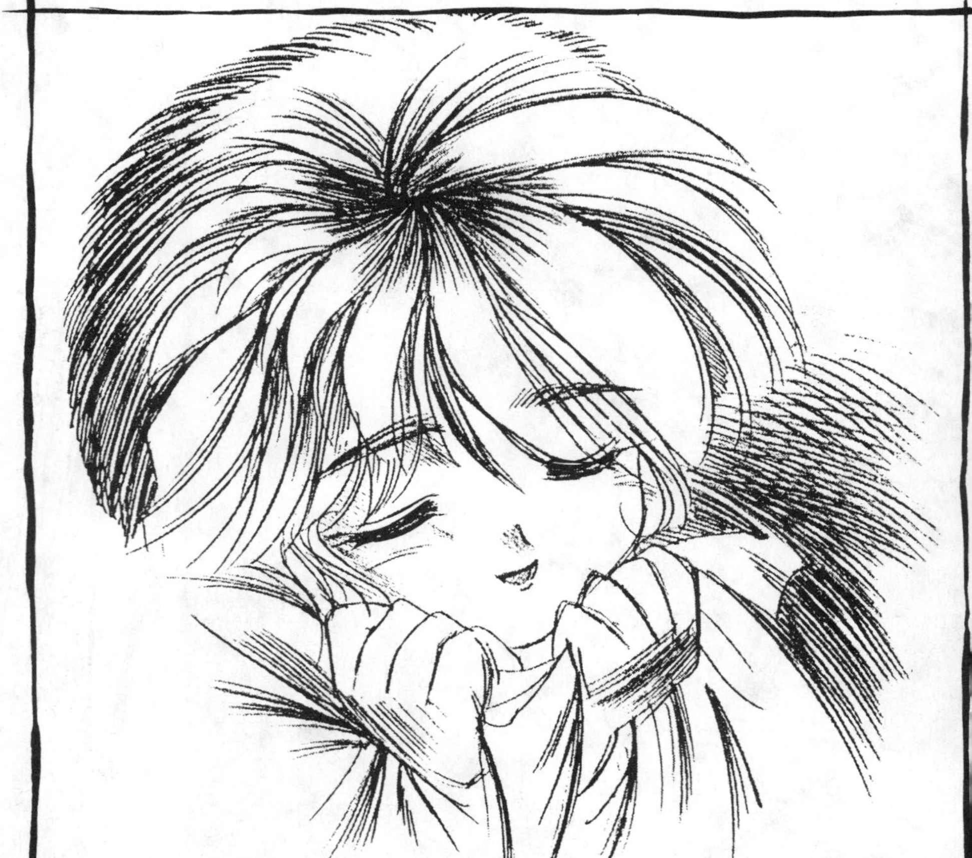

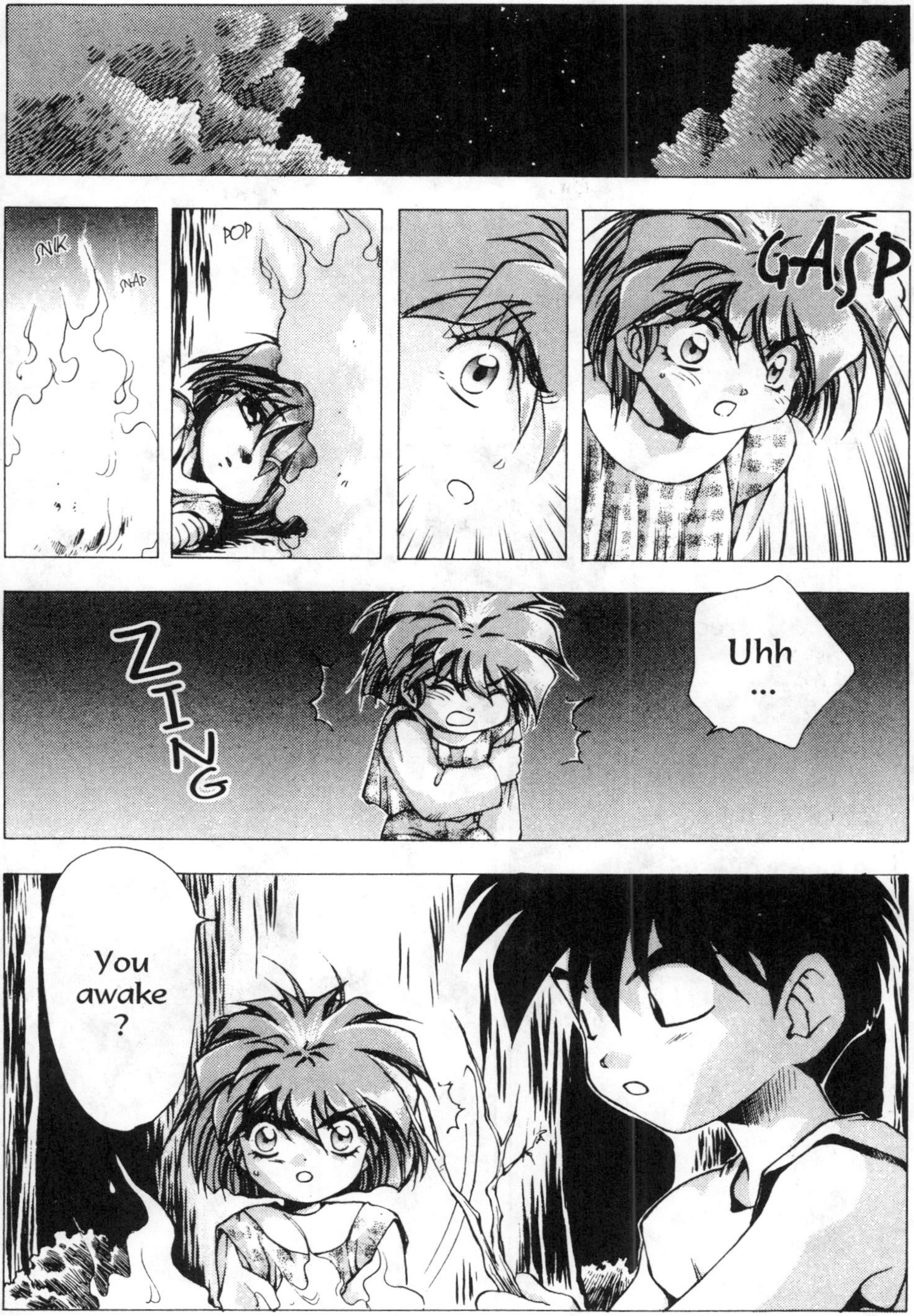
GASP
POP
SNIK
SNAP
Uhh ...
ZING
You awake?

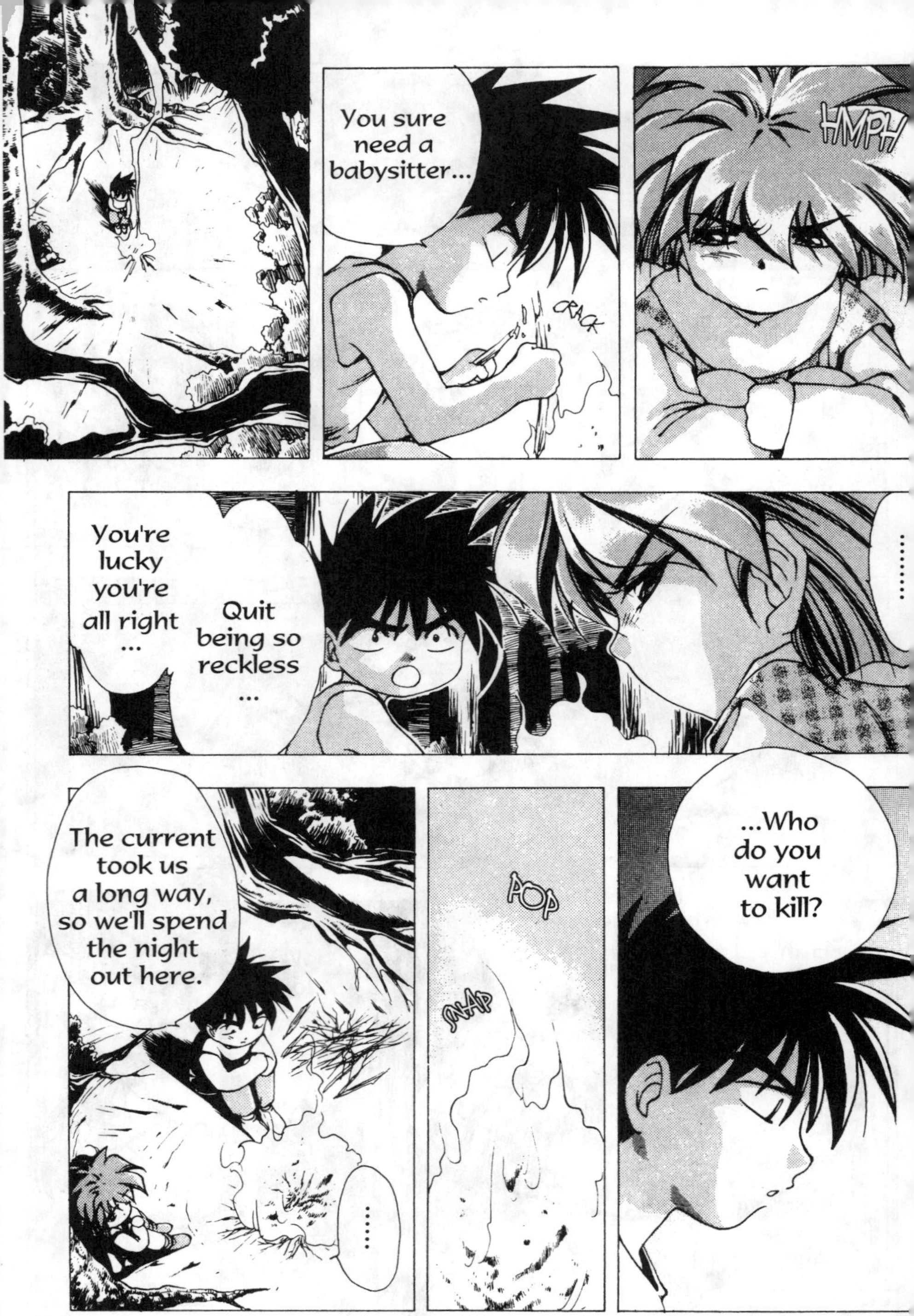
HMPH
You sure need a babysitter...
CRACK
......
Quit being so reckless ...
You're lucky you're all right ...
...Who do you want to kill?
POP
SNAP
The current took us a long way, so we'll spend the night out here.
......

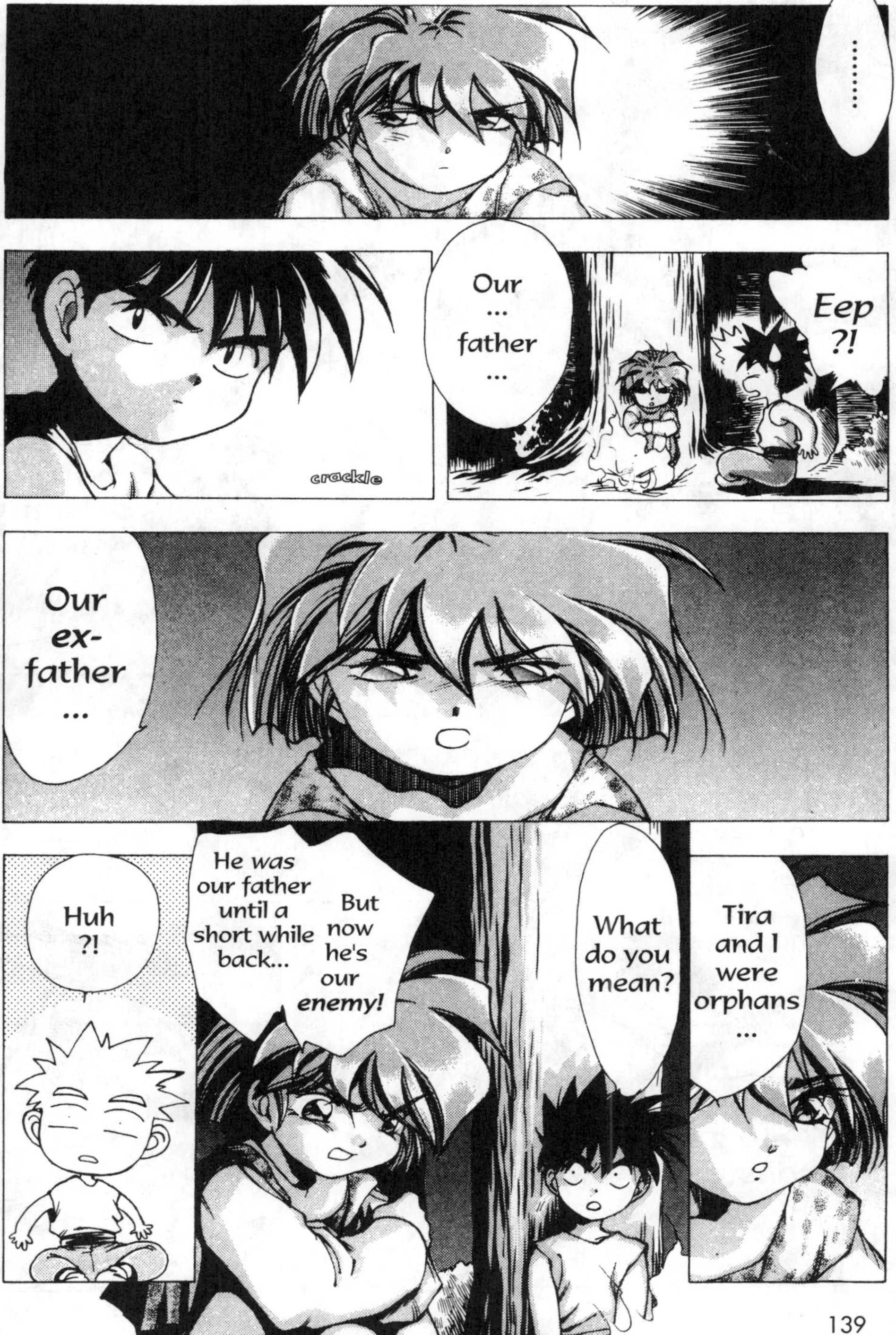
......
Eep ?!
Our ... father ...
crackle
Our ex-father ...
Tira and I were orphans ...
What do you mean?
He was our father until a short while back...
But now he's our enemy!
Huh ?!

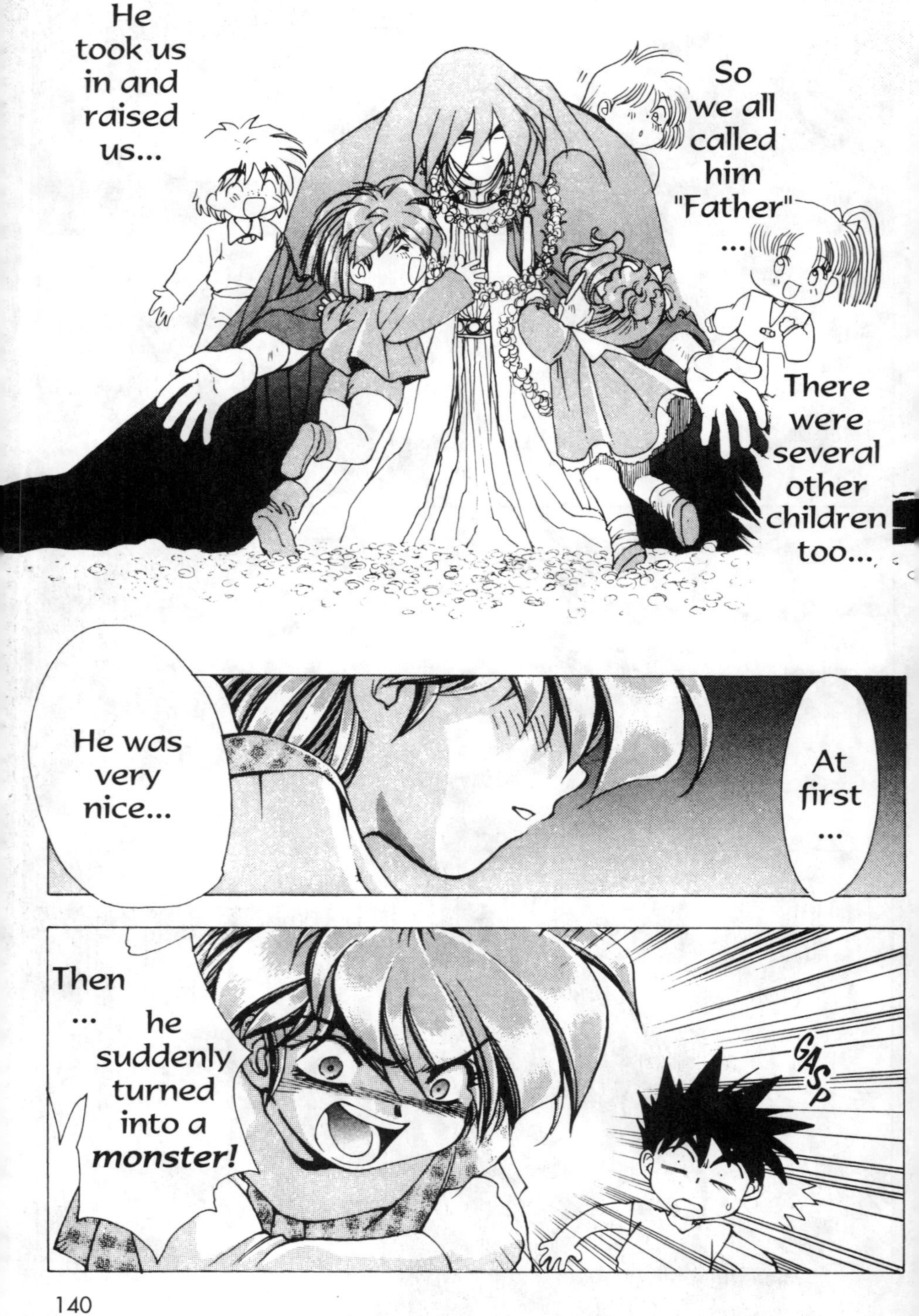
So we all called him "Father" ...
He took us in and raised us...
There were several other children too...
At first ...
He was very nice...
Then ... he suddenly turned into a monster!
GASP

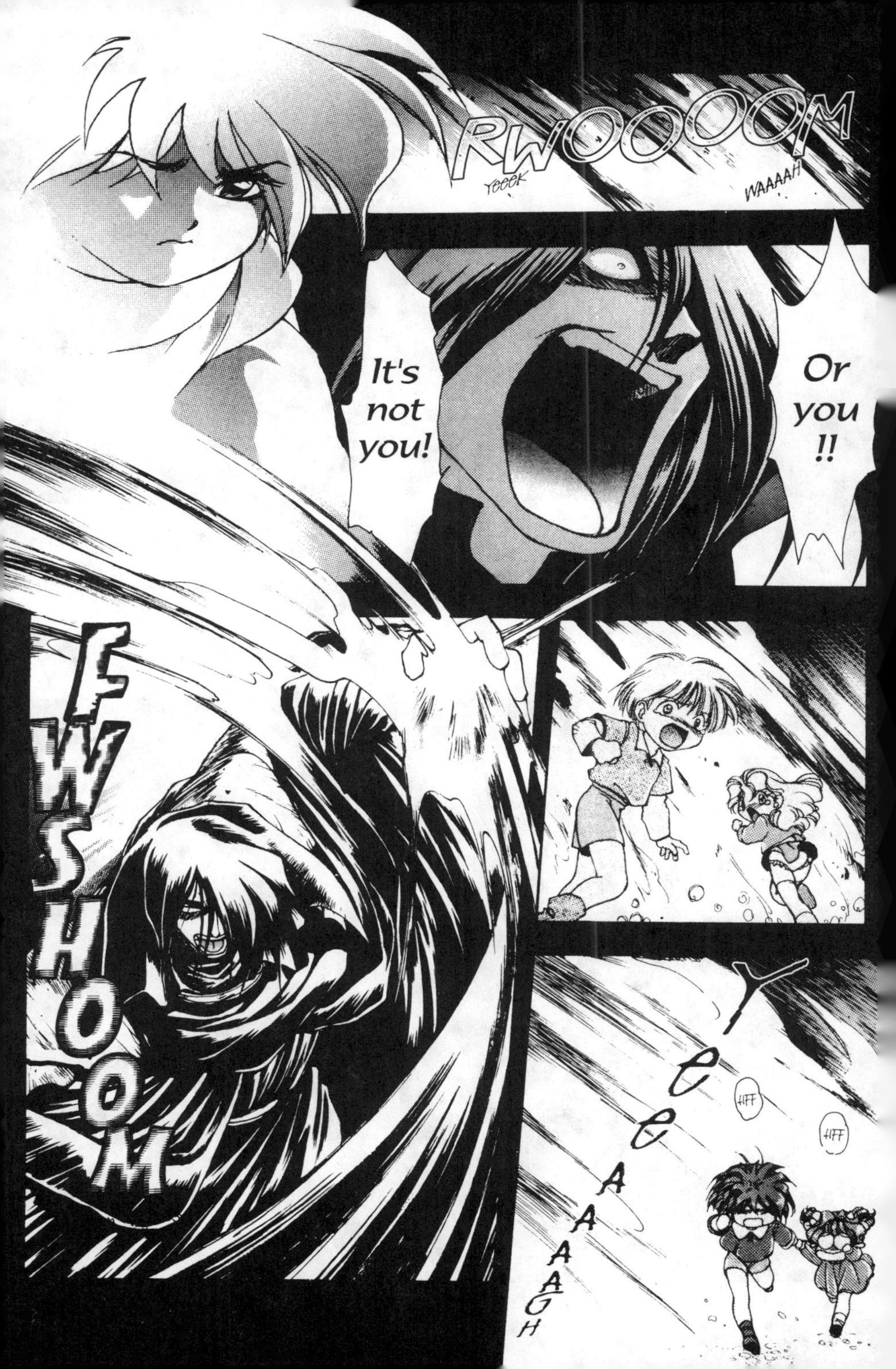
RWOOOOOM
YEEEK
WAAAAH
It's not you!
Or you !!
FWSHOOOM
YEEEAAAAAAGH
HFF
HFF

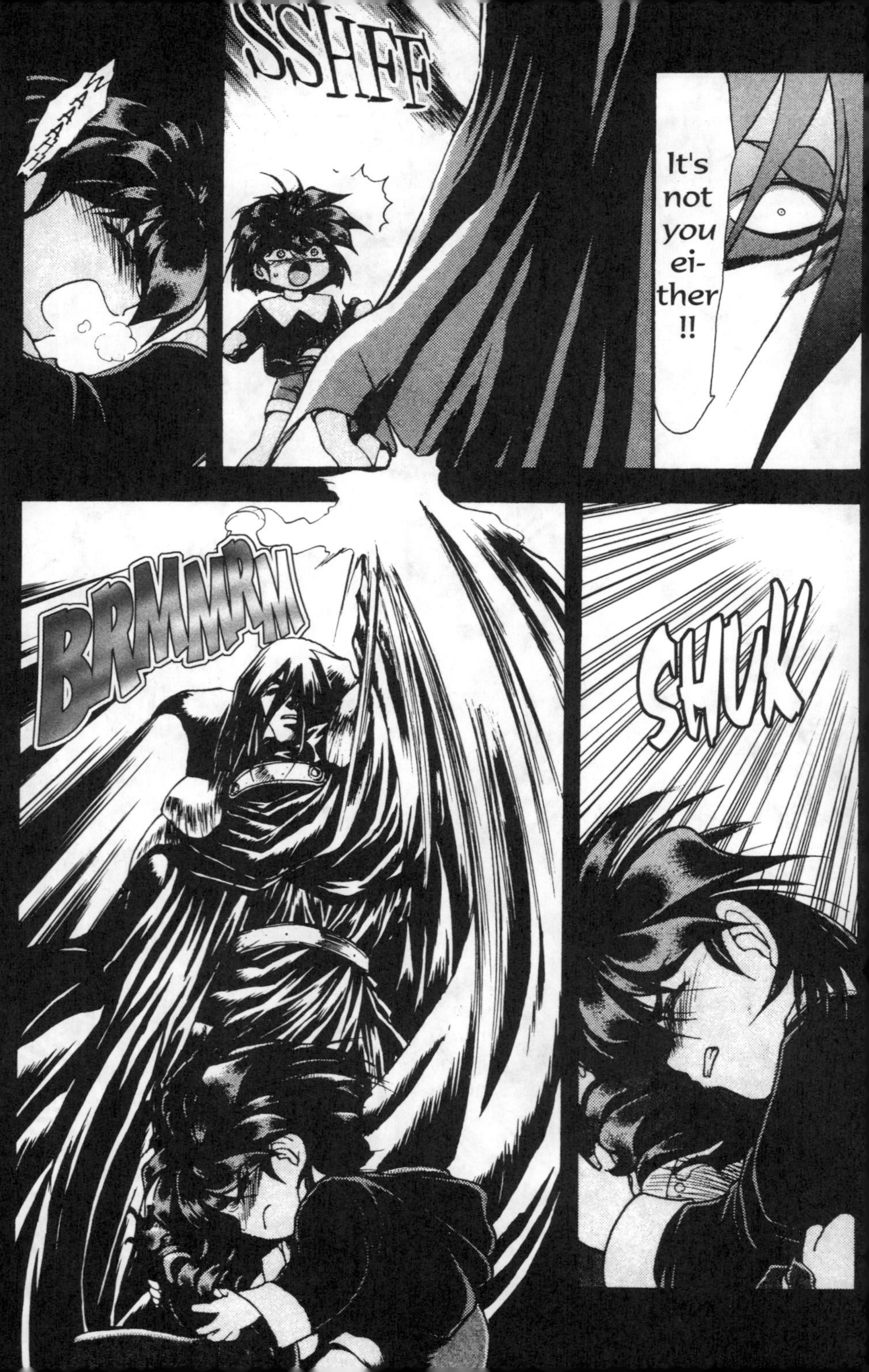
It's not you ei-ther !!
SSHFF
NAAAHH
SHUK
BRMMRM

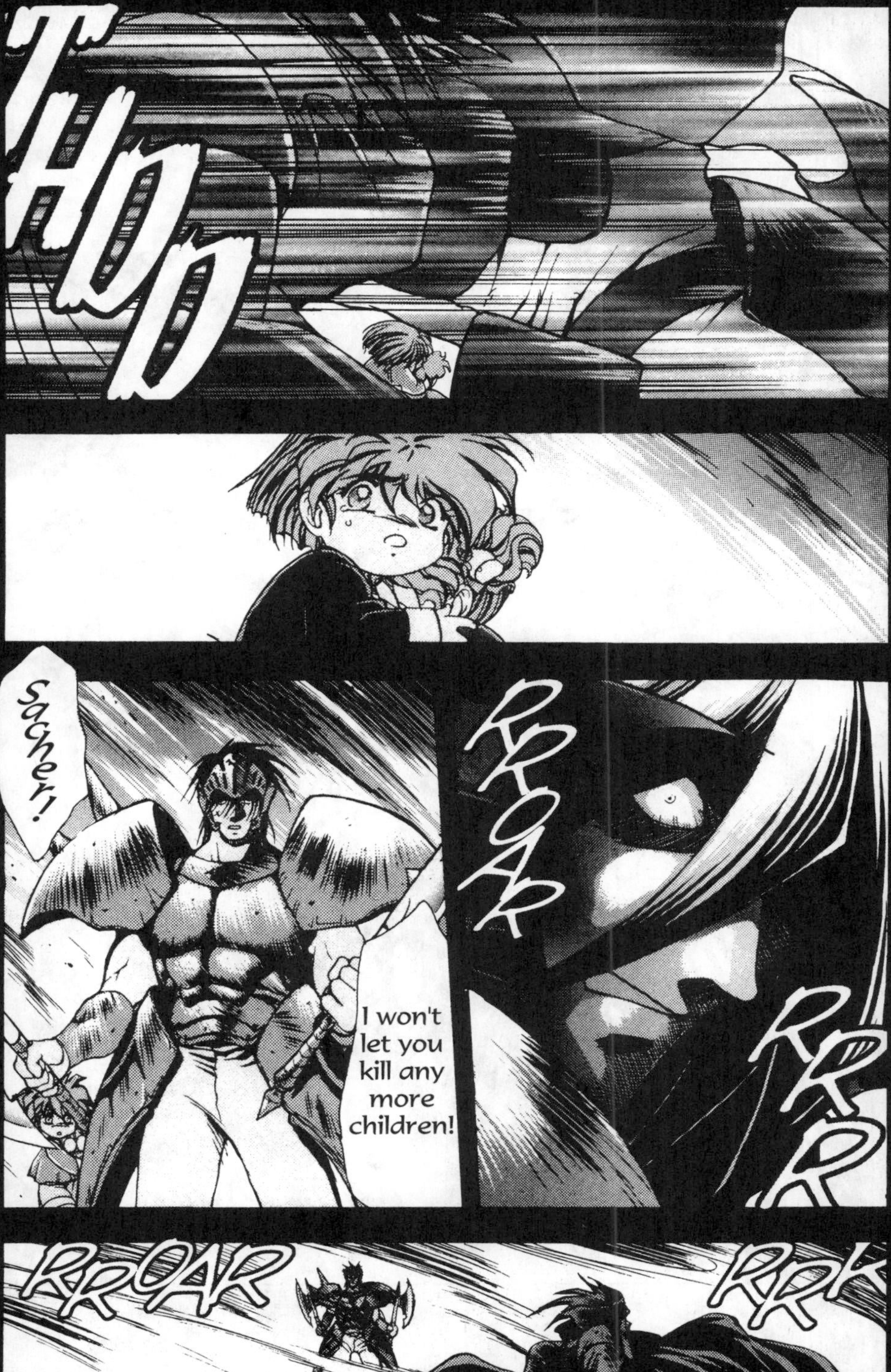
THUD
RROAR
RRR
Sacher!
I won't let you kill any more children!
RRK
RROAR

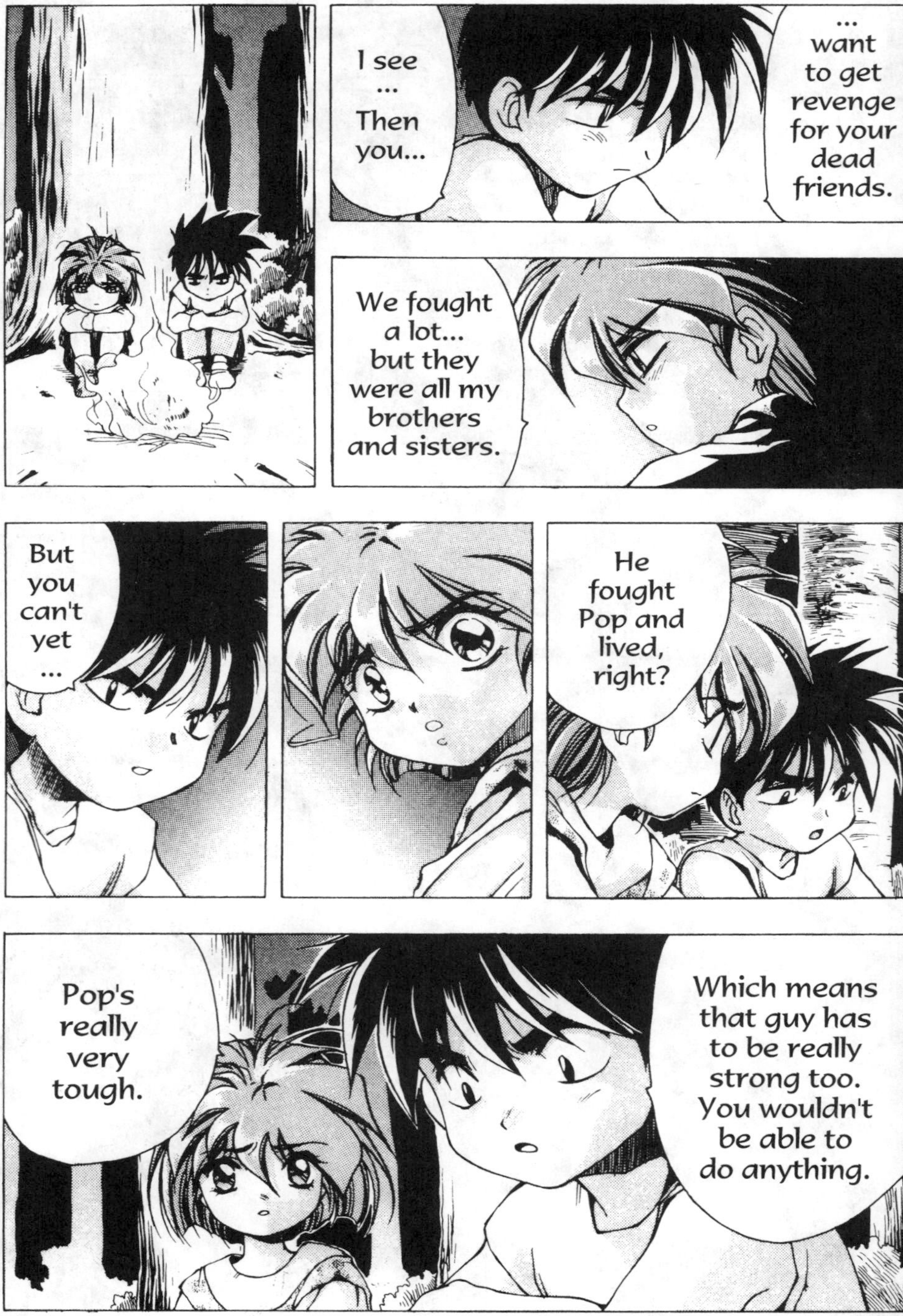
I see ... Then you...
... want to get revenge for your dead friends.
We fought a lot... but they were all my brothers and sisters.
But you can't yet ...
He fought Pop and lived, right?
Pop's really very tough.
Which means that guy has to be really strong too. You wouldn't be able to do anything.

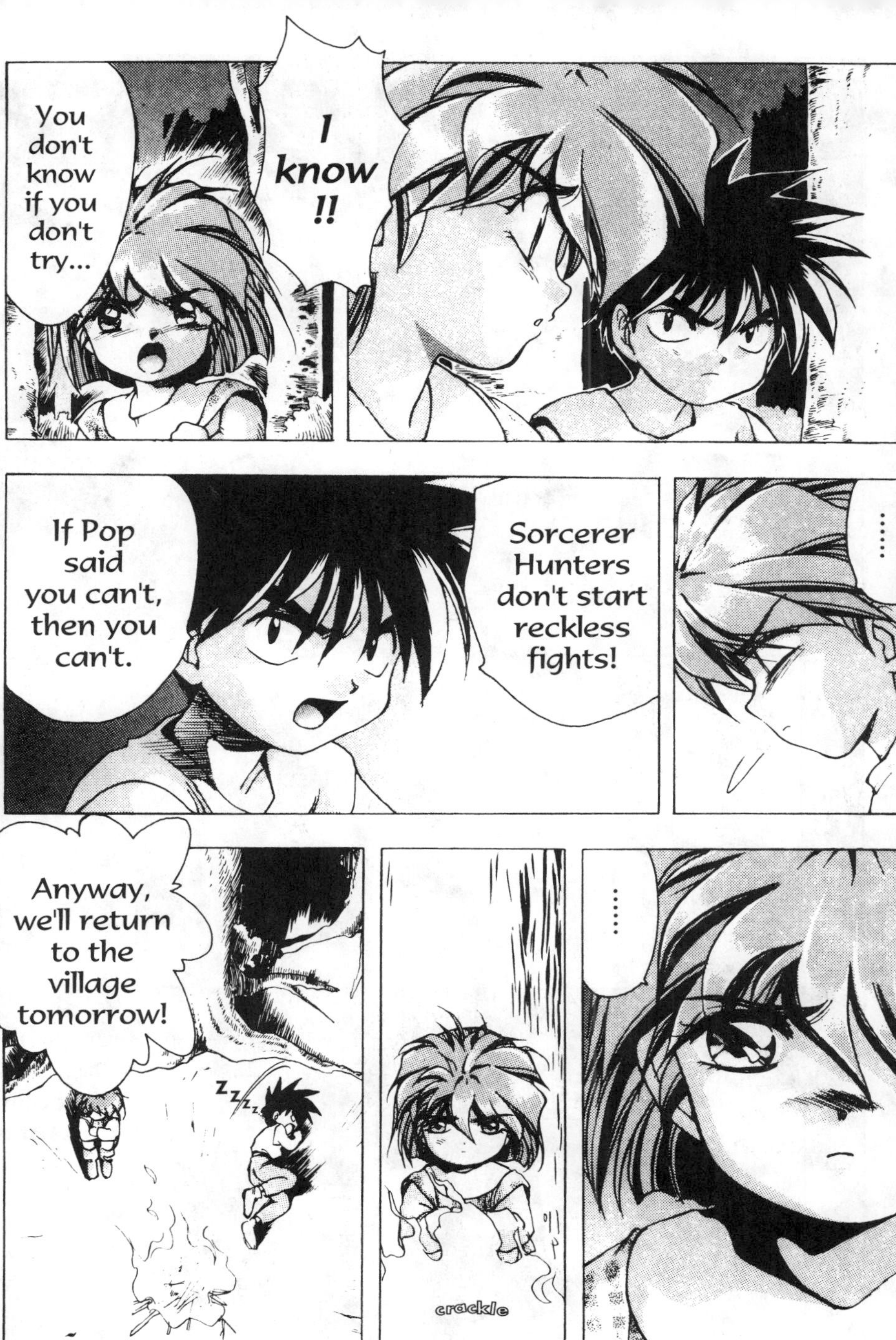
You don't know if you don't try...
I know !!
If Pop said you can't, then you can't.
Sorcerer Hunters don't start reckless fights!
......
Anyway, we'll return to the village tomorrow!
zzz
crackle
......

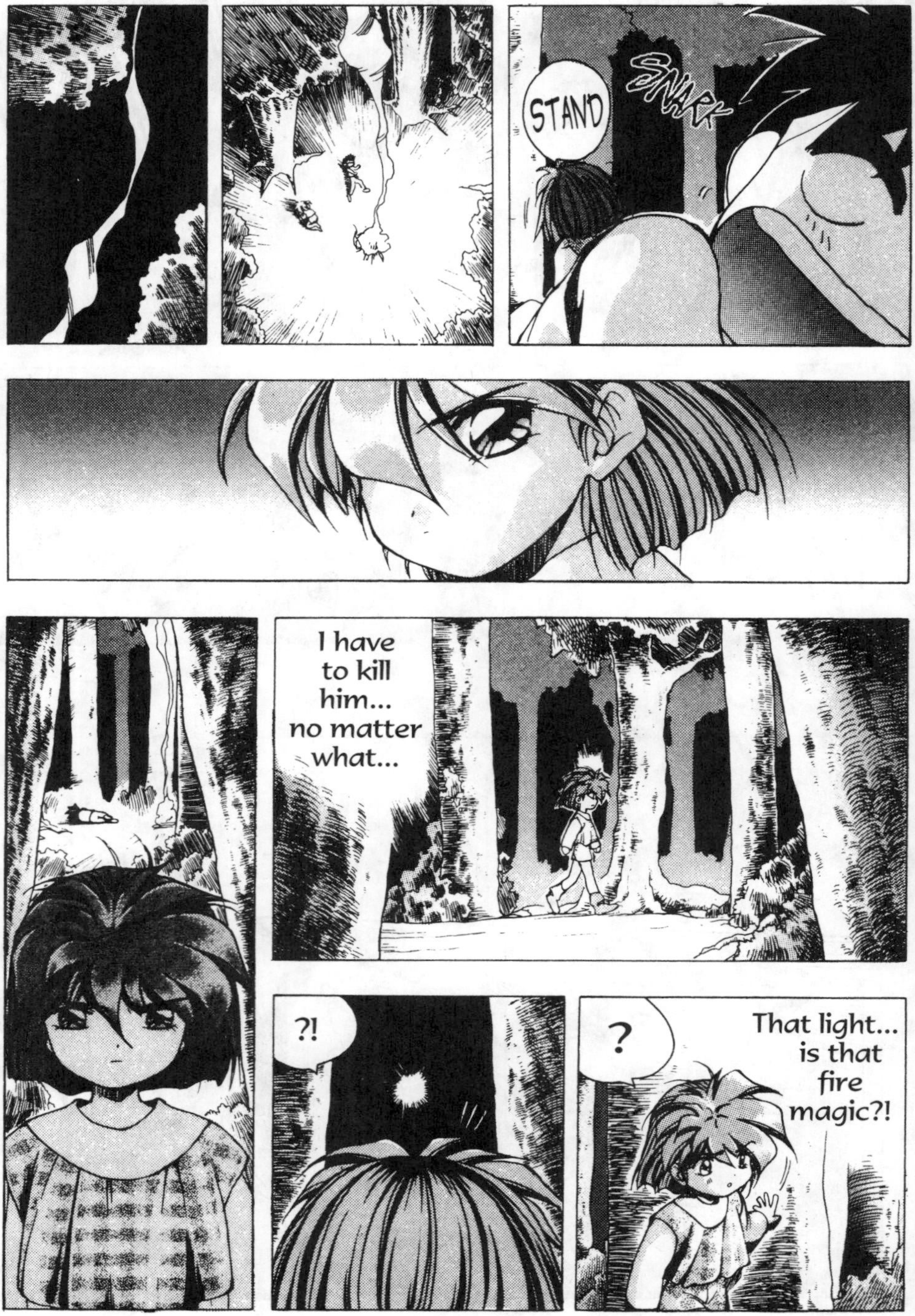
STAND'
SNARK
I have to kill him... no matter what...
?
That light... is that fire magic?!
?!

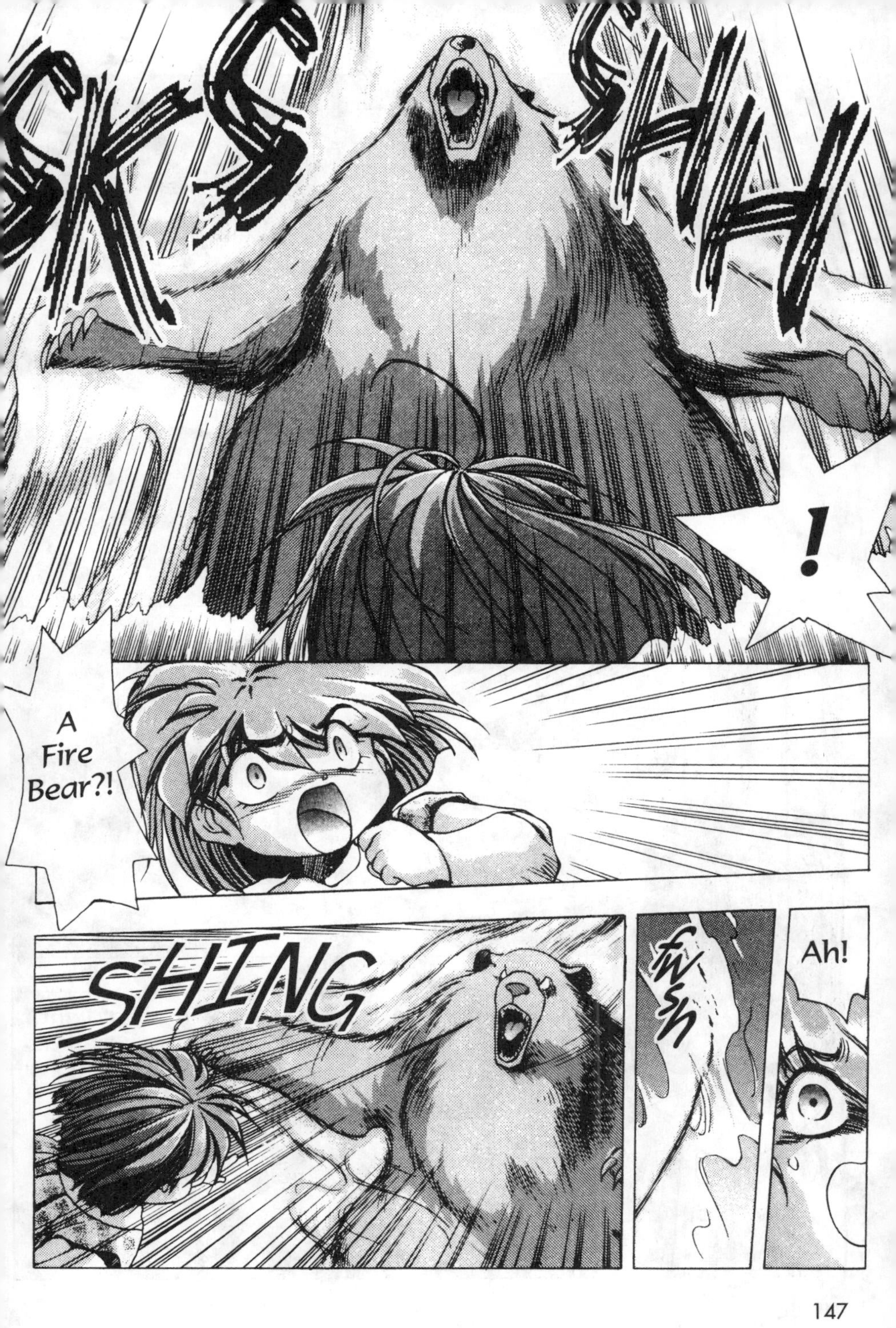
SKSSHHH
!
A Fire Bear?!
Ah!
fwsh
SHING

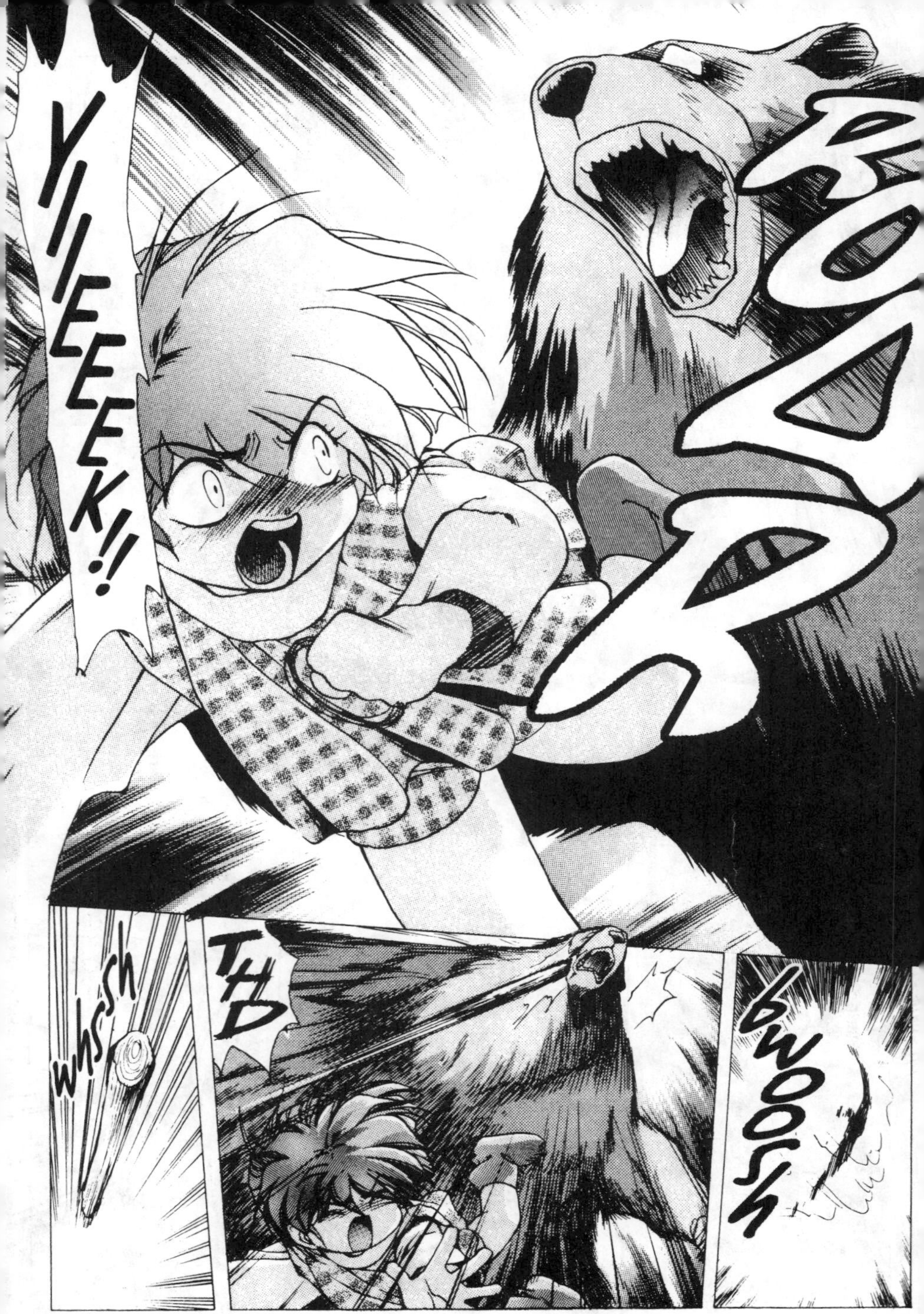
ROAR
YIIIEEEEK!!!
bwoosh
THD
whssh

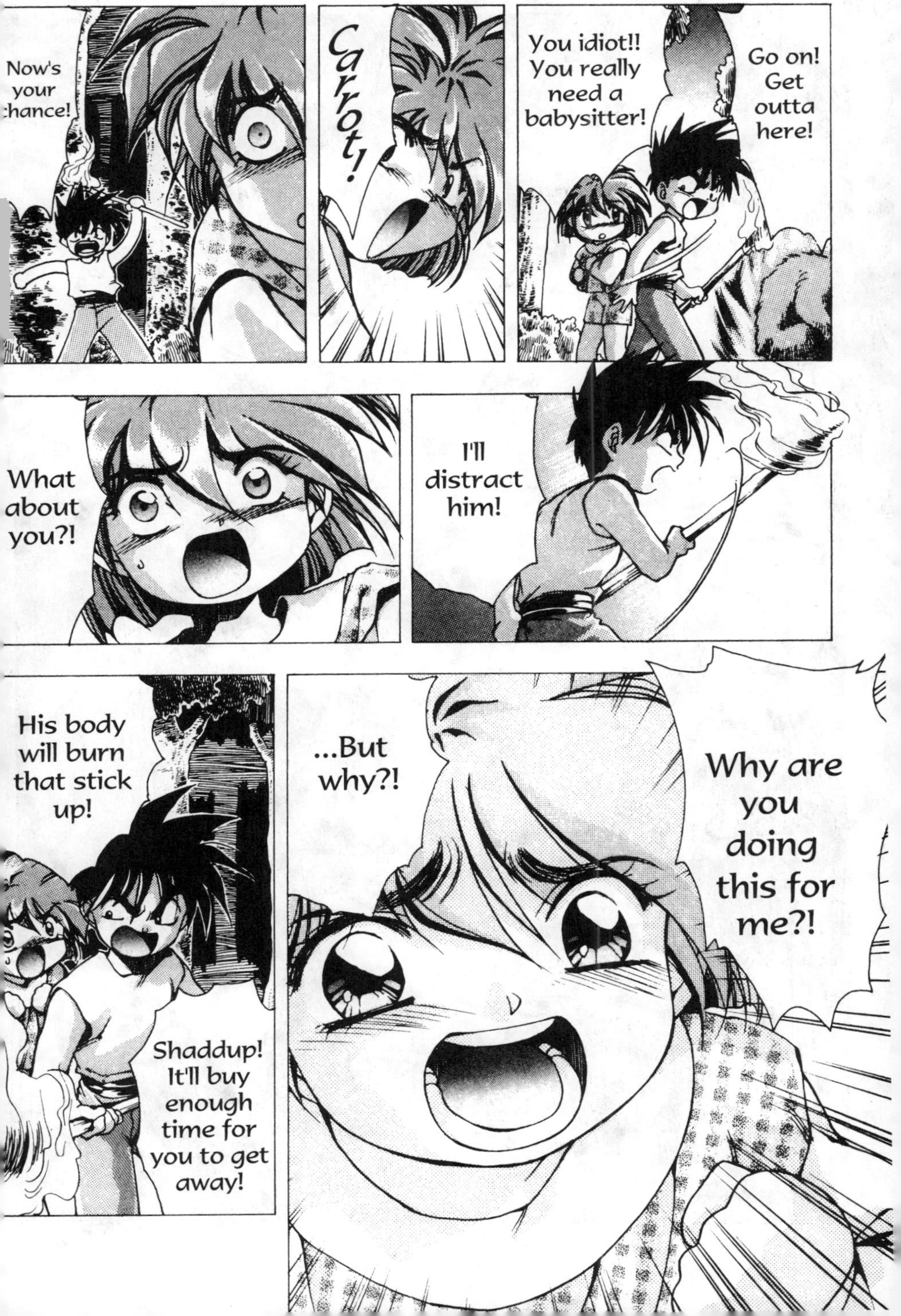

Now's your chance!
Carrot!
You idiot!! You really need a babysitter!
Go on! Get outta here!
What about you?!
I'll distract him!
His body will burn that stick up!
Shaddup! It'll buy enough time for you to get away!
...But why?!
Why are you doing this for me?!

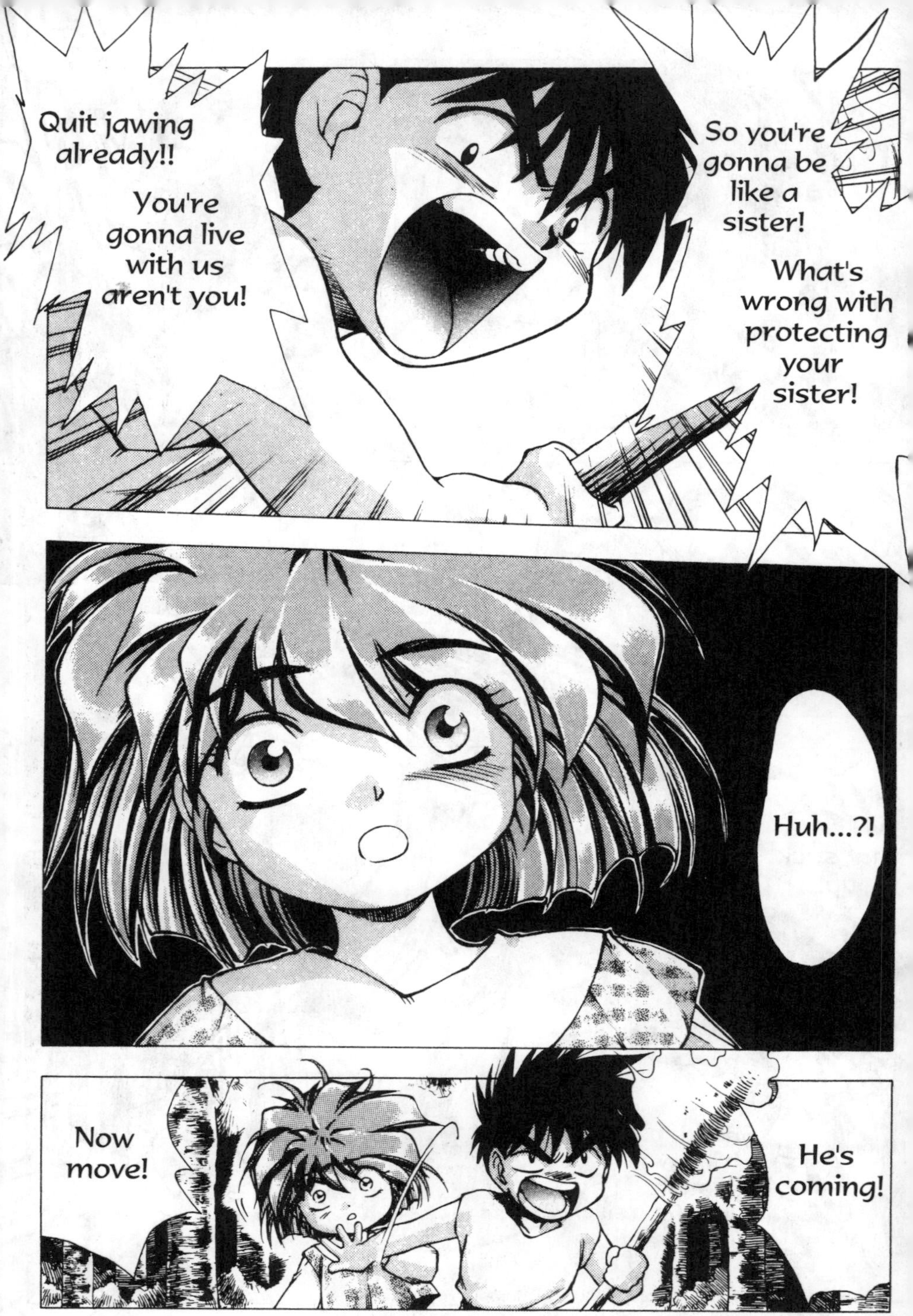
So you're gonna be like a sister!
What's wrong with protecting your sister!
Quit jawing already!!
You're gonna live with us aren't you!
Huh...?!
He's coming!
Now move!

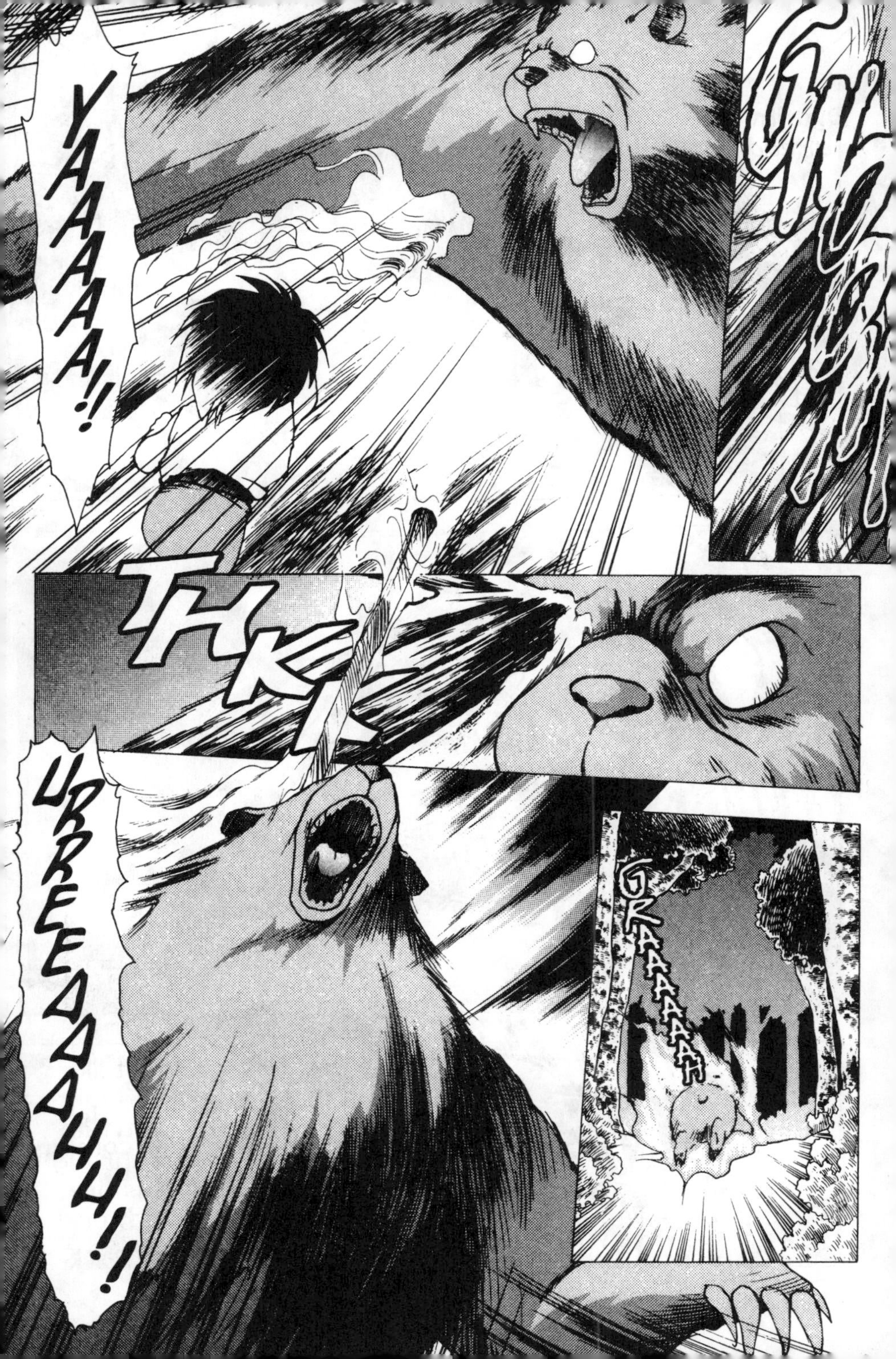
YAAAAAA!!
THK!
GRAAAAAAH
URREEAAAHH!!

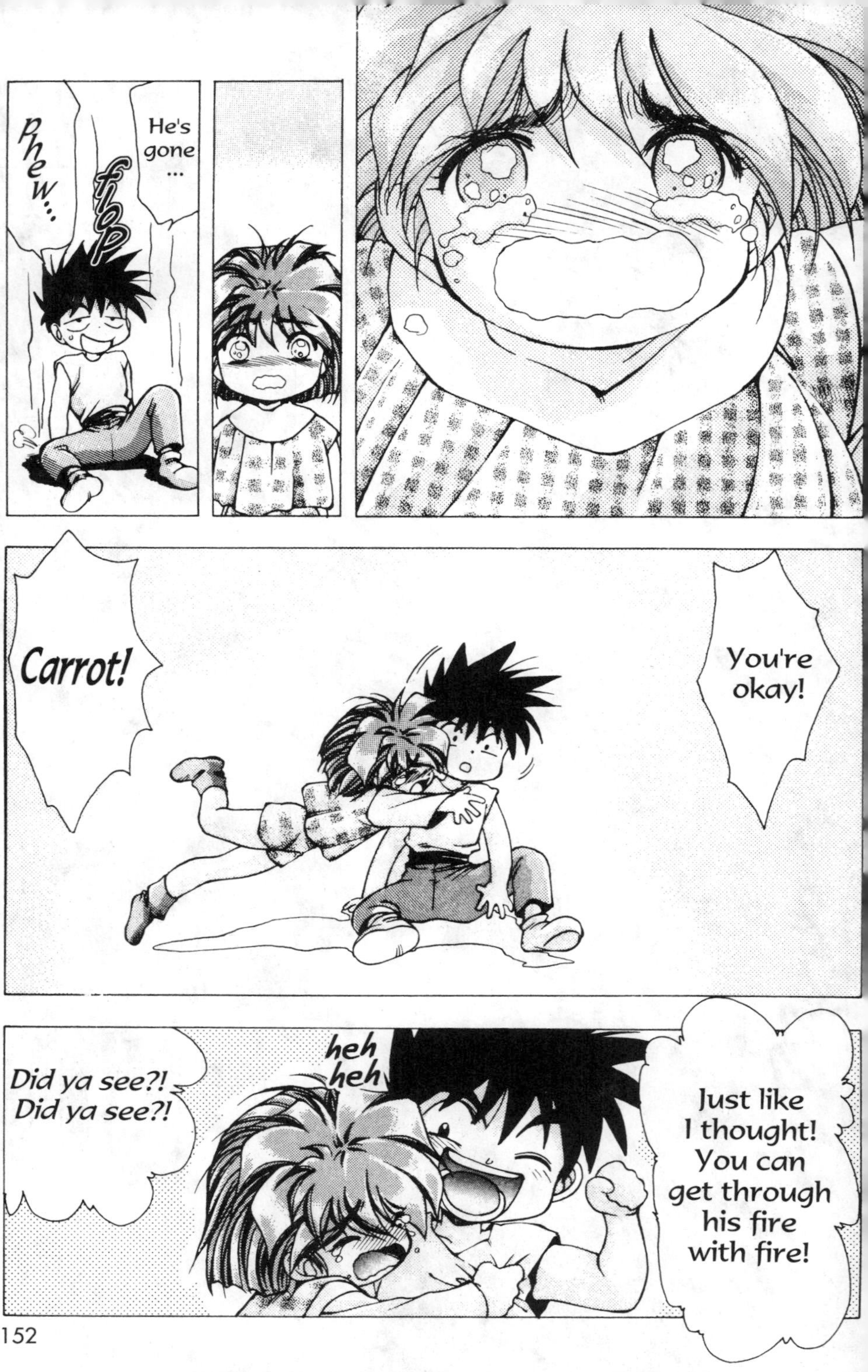
phew...
flop
He's gone ...
Carrot!
You're okay!
Did ya see?! Did ya see?!
heh heh
Just like I thought! You can get through his fire with fire!

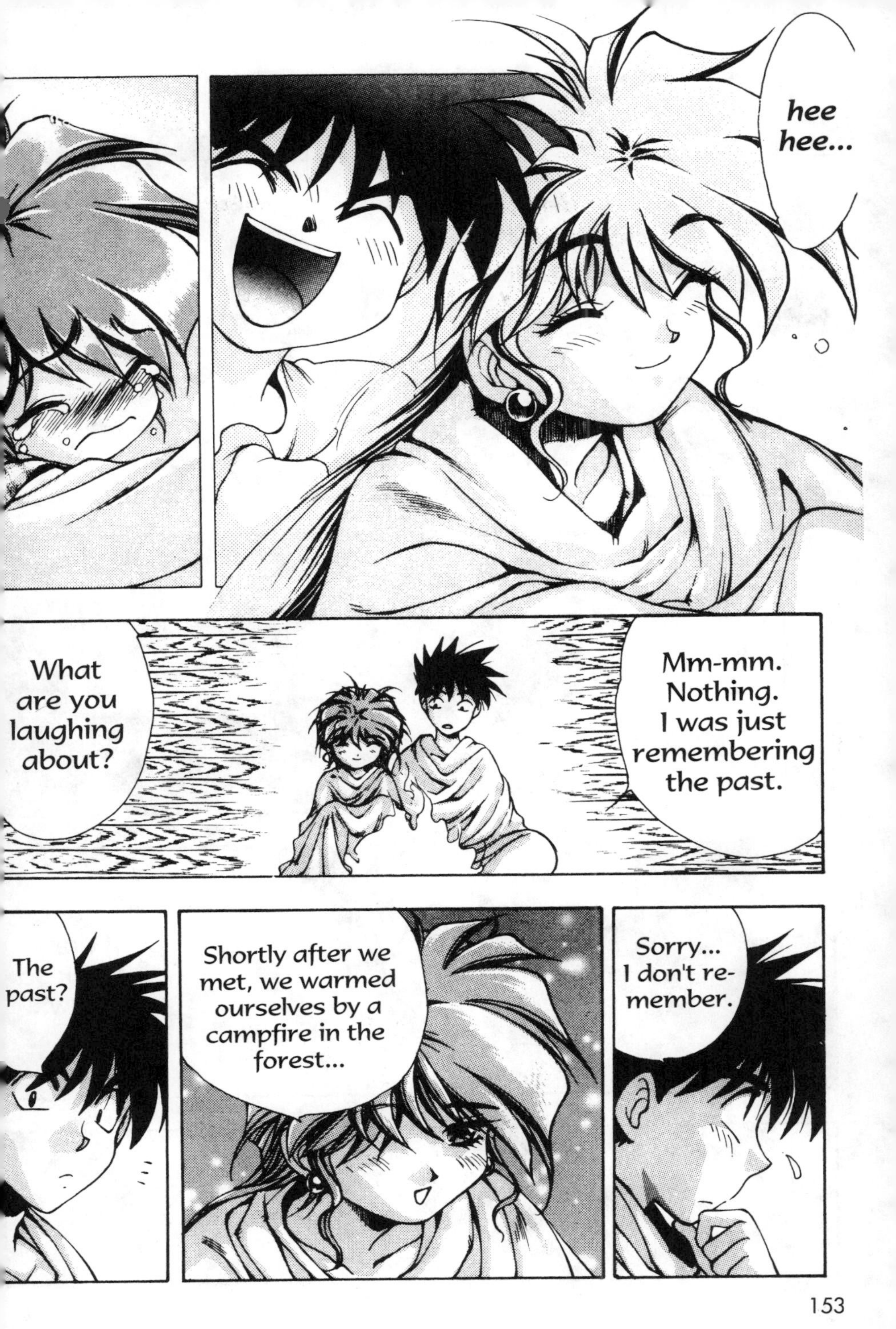
hee hee...
Mm-mm. Nothing. I was just remembering the past.
What are you laughing about?
Sorry... I don't re-member.
Shortly after we met, we warmed ourselves by a campfire in the forest...
The past?

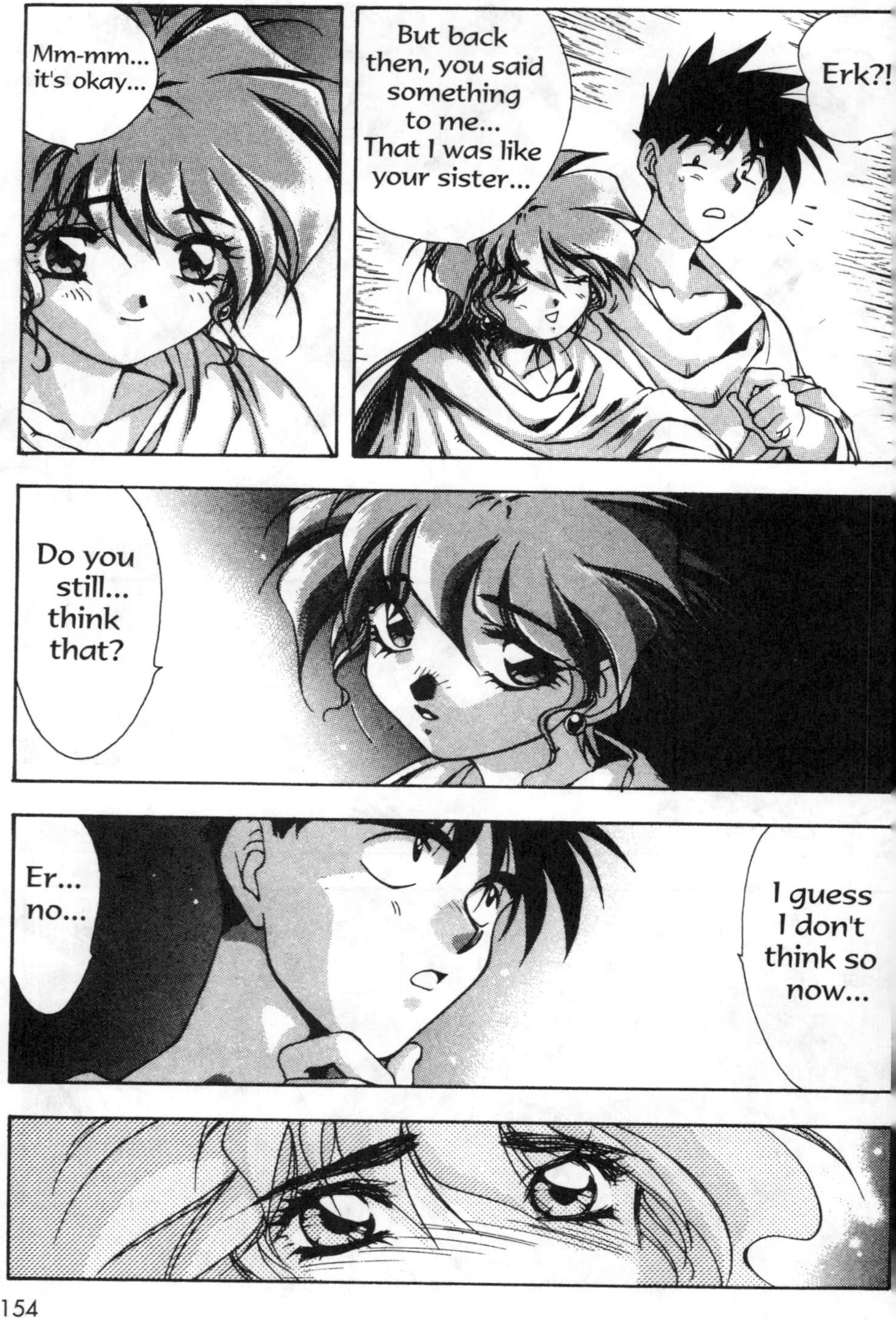
Mm-mm... it's okay...
But back then, you said something to me... That I was like your sister...
Erk?!
Do you still... think that?
Er... no...
I guess I don't think so now...

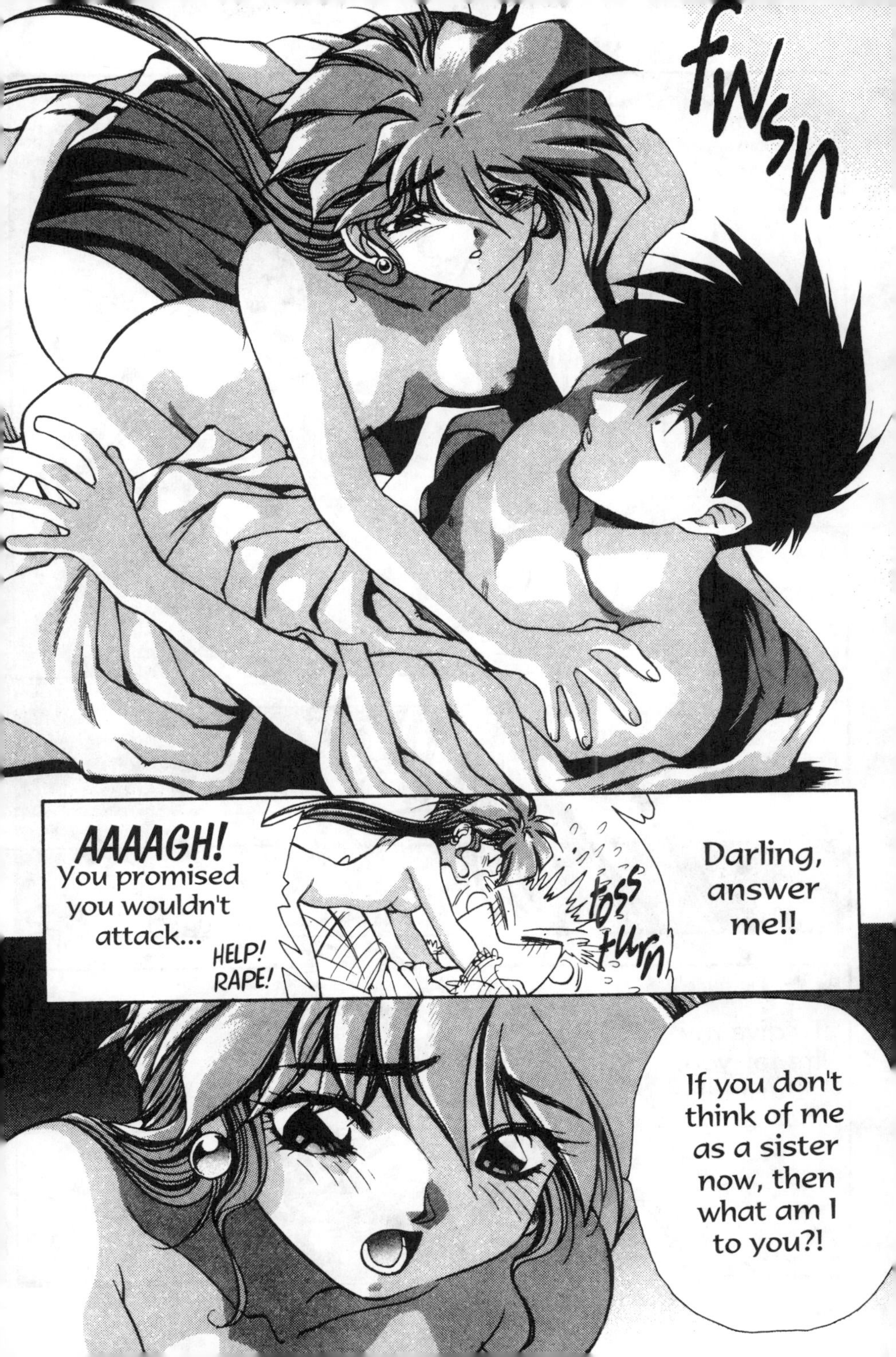
fwsh
Darling, answer me!!
toss turn
AAAAGH! You promised you wouldn't attack...
HELP! RAPE!
If you don't think of me as a sister now, then what am I to you?!

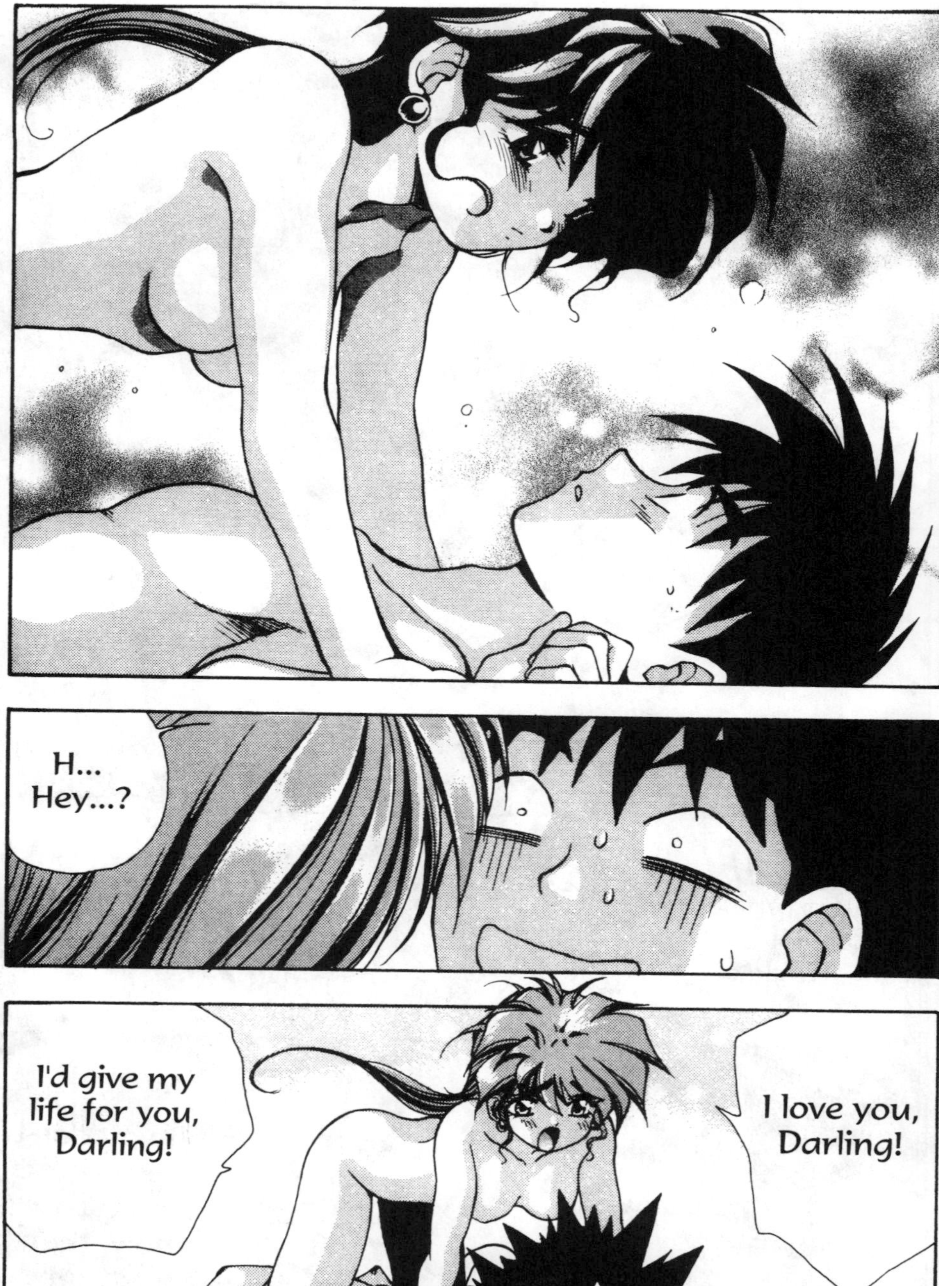
H... Hey...?
I love you, Darling!
I'd give my life for you, Darling!

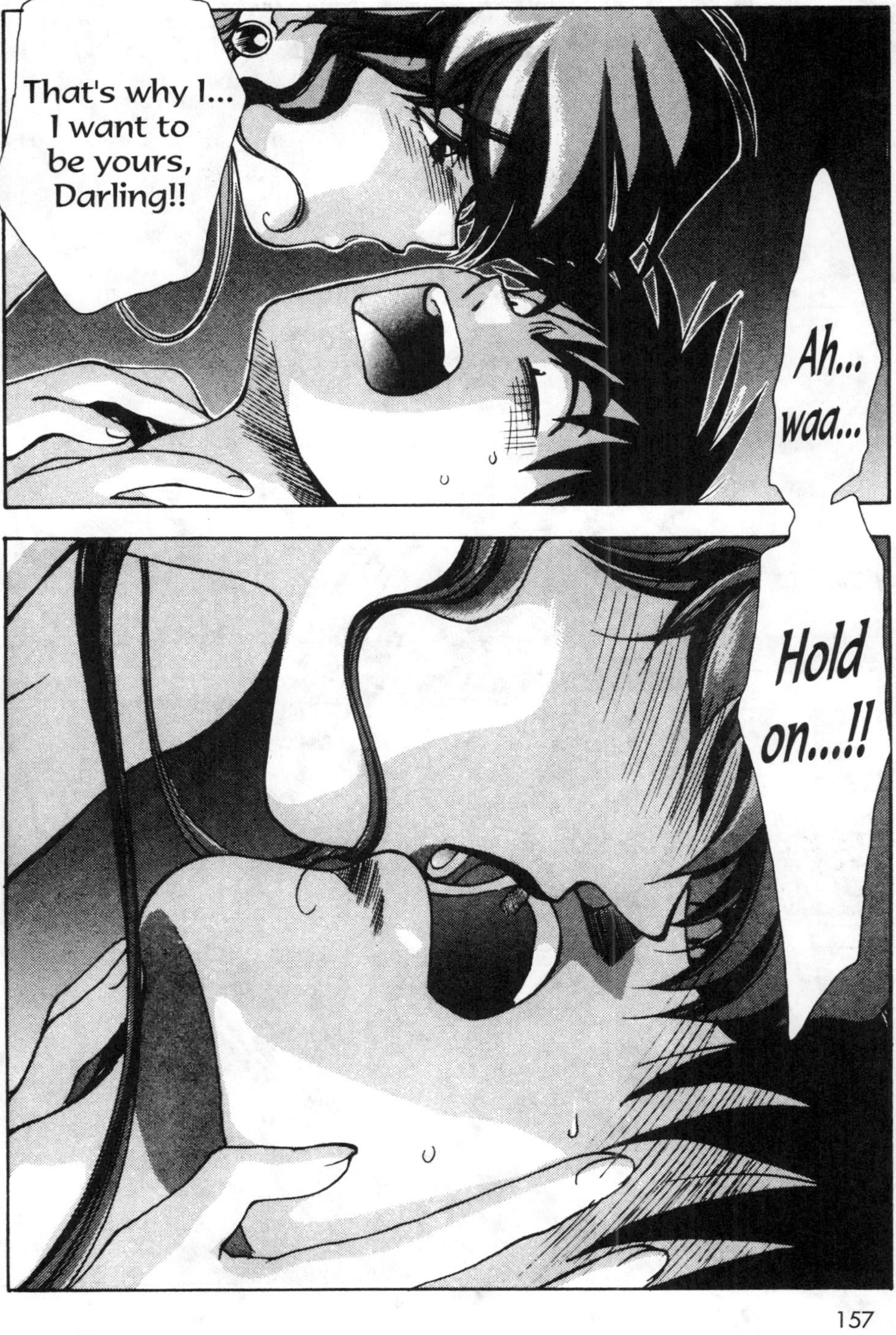
That's why I... I want to be yours, Darling!!
Ah... waa...
Hold on...!!

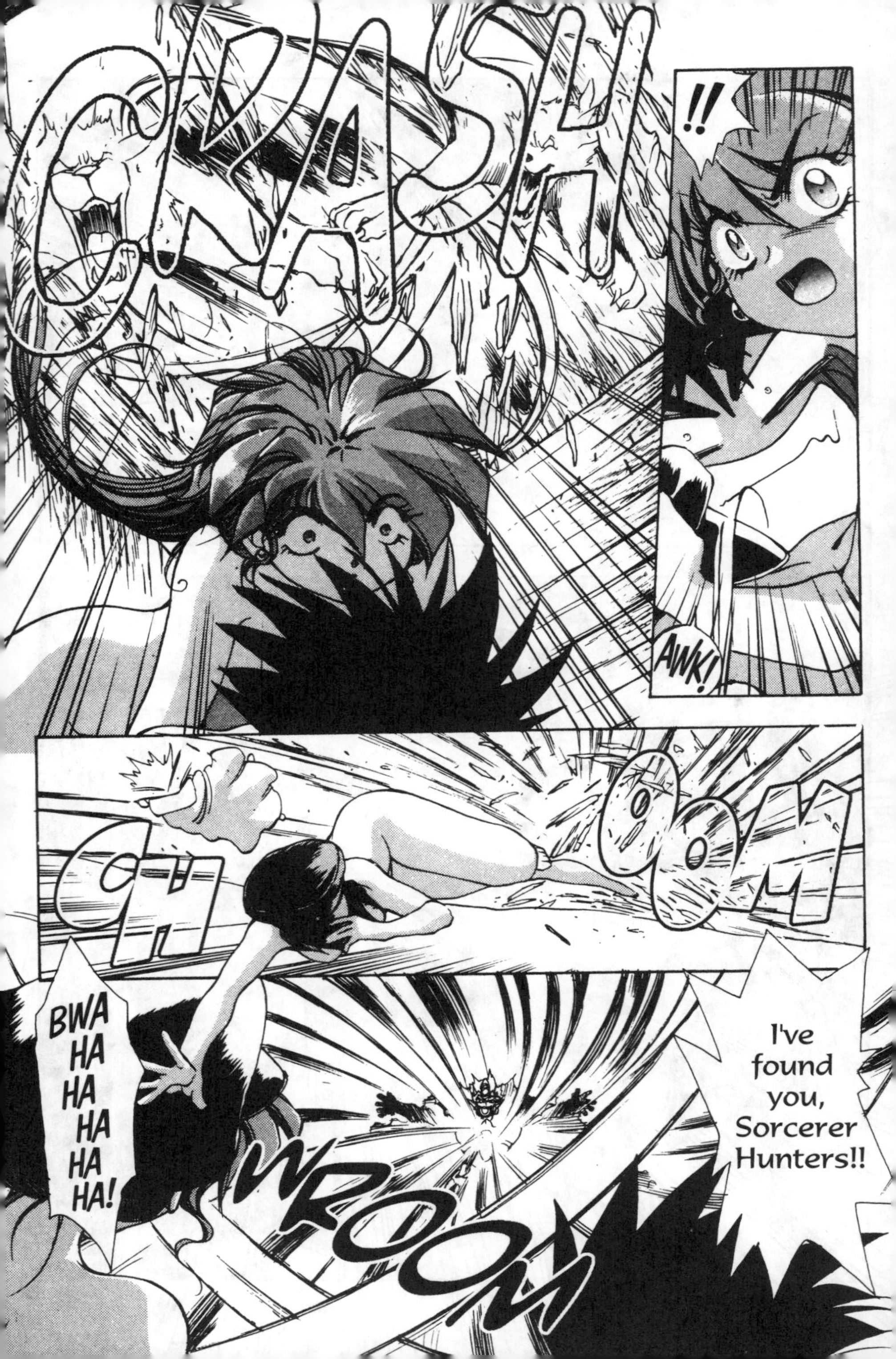
!!
CRASH
AWK!
OOOM
CH
I've found you, Sorcerer Hunters!!
WROOM
BWA HA HA HA HA HA!

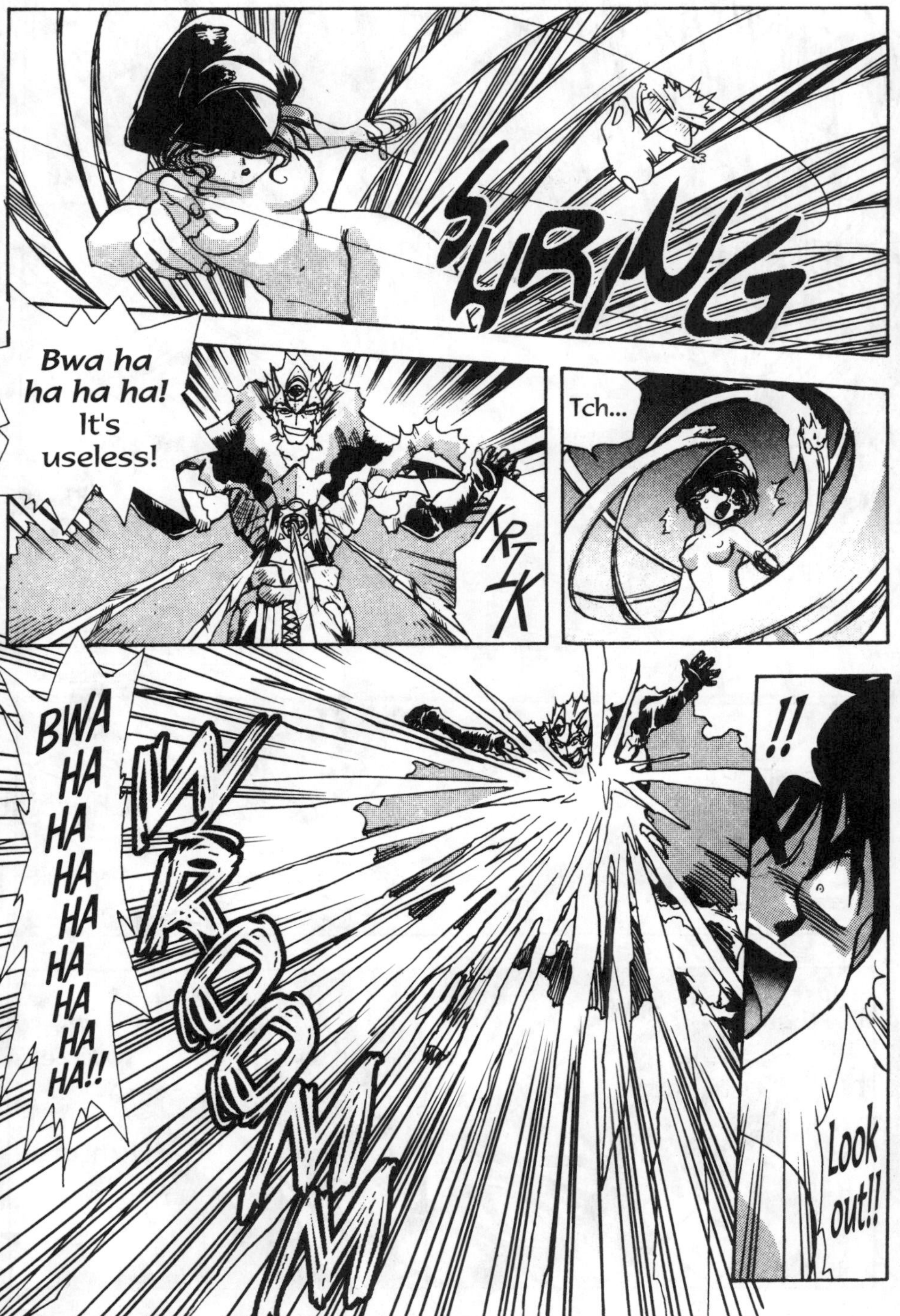
SHRING
Tch...
Bwa ha ha ha ha! It's useless!
KRIK
!!
Look out!!
BWA HA HA HA HA HA HA HA HA!!

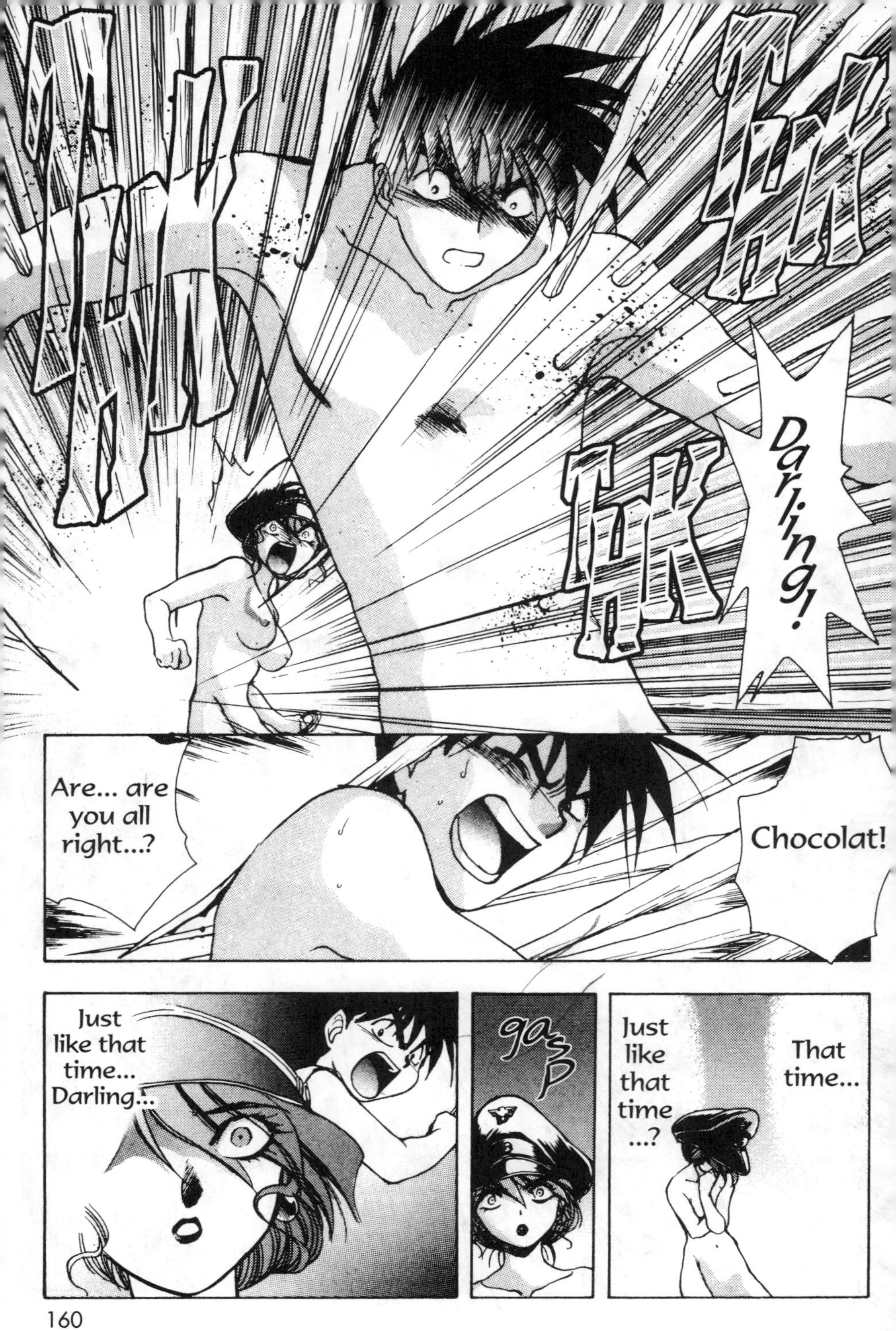
THK
Darling!
THK
THK
Chocolat!
Are... are you all right...?
That time...
Just like that time ...?
gasp
Just like that time... Darling...

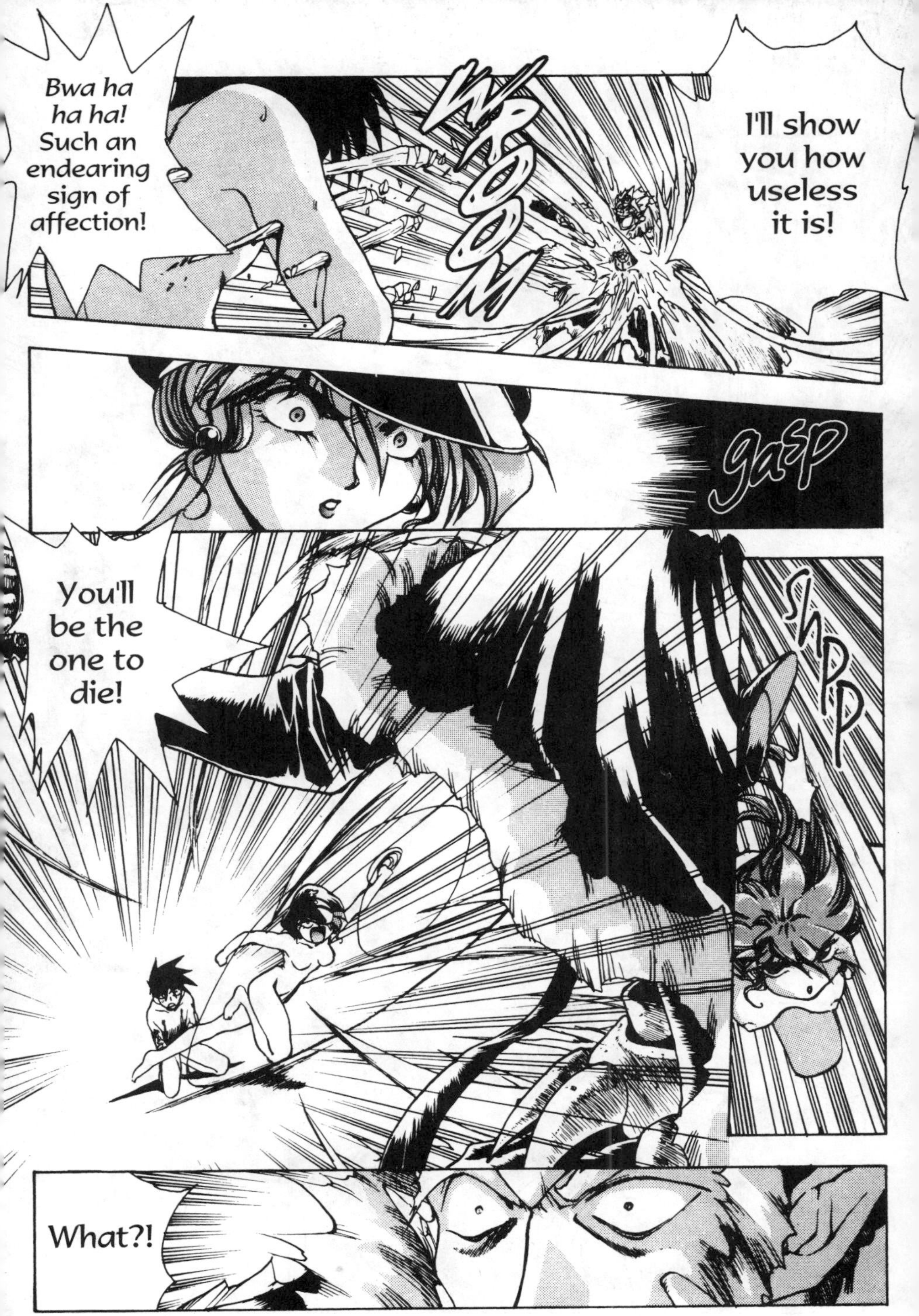
I'll show you how useless it is!
WHOOOM
Bwa ha ha ha! Such an endearing sign of affection!
gasp
SHPP
You'll be the one to die!
What?!

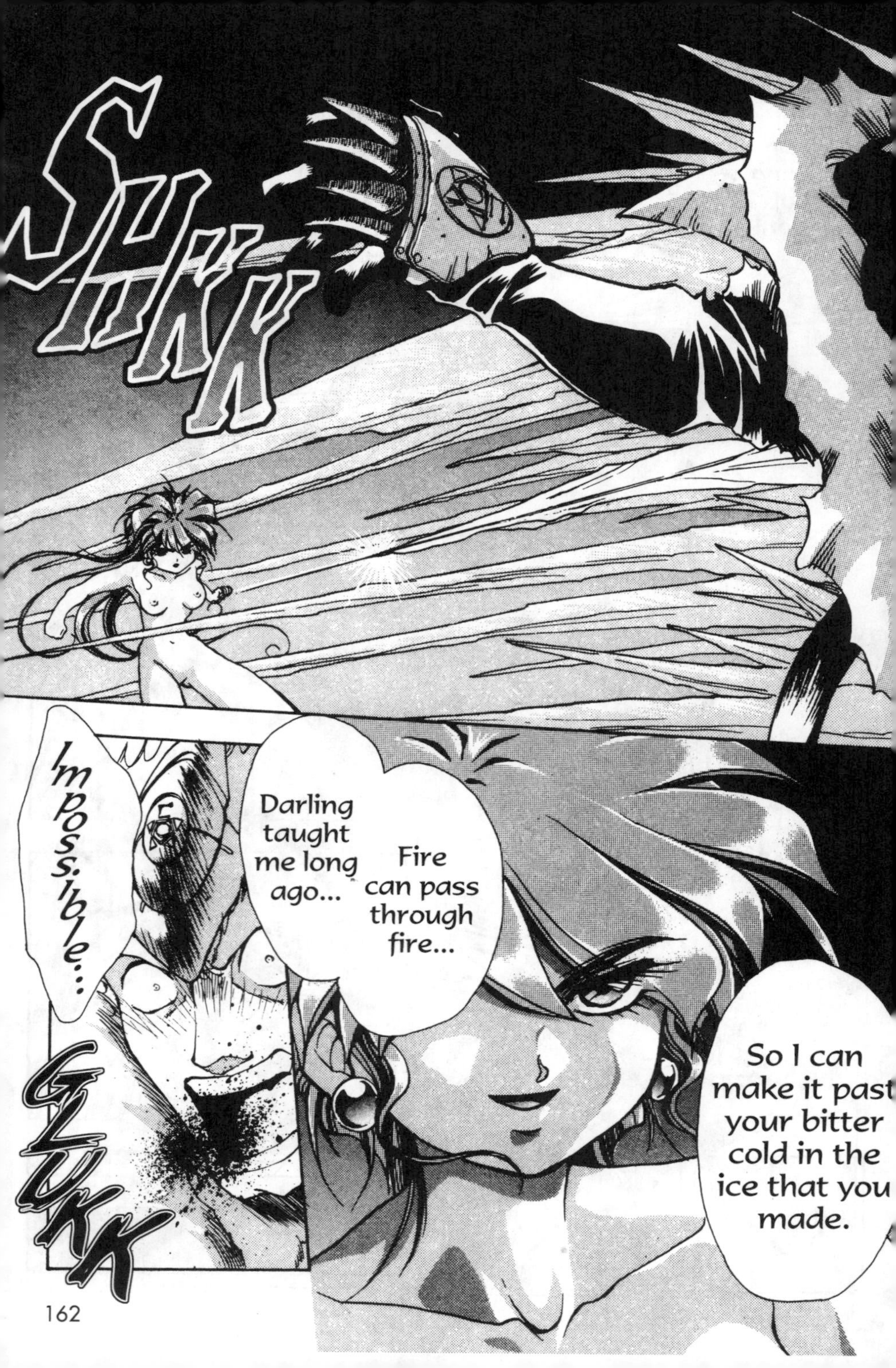
SHUKK
Darling taught me long ago...
Fire can pass through fire...
So I can make it past your bitter cold in the ice that you made.
Impossible...
GLUKK

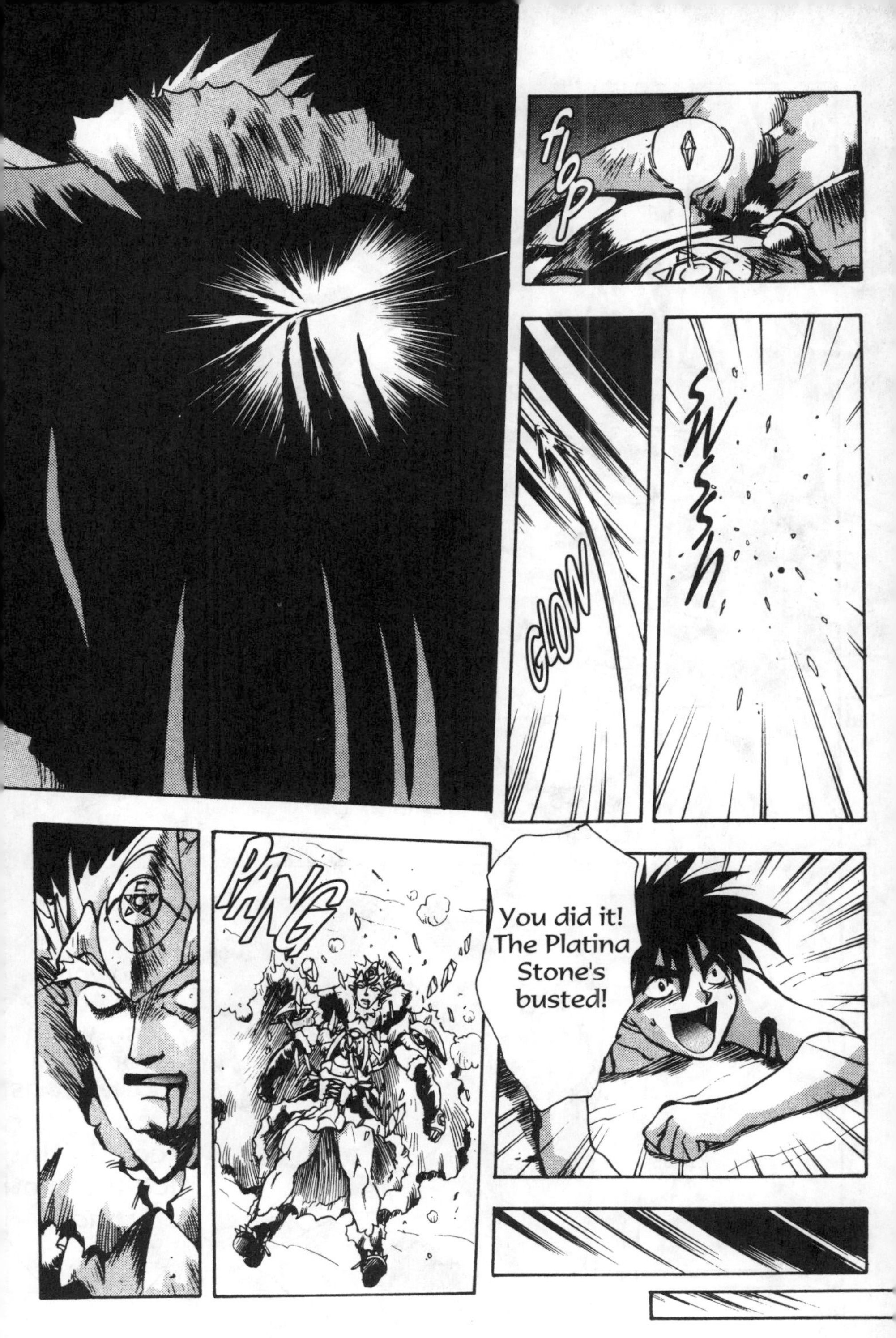
flop
GLOW
You did it! The Platina Stone's busted!
PANG

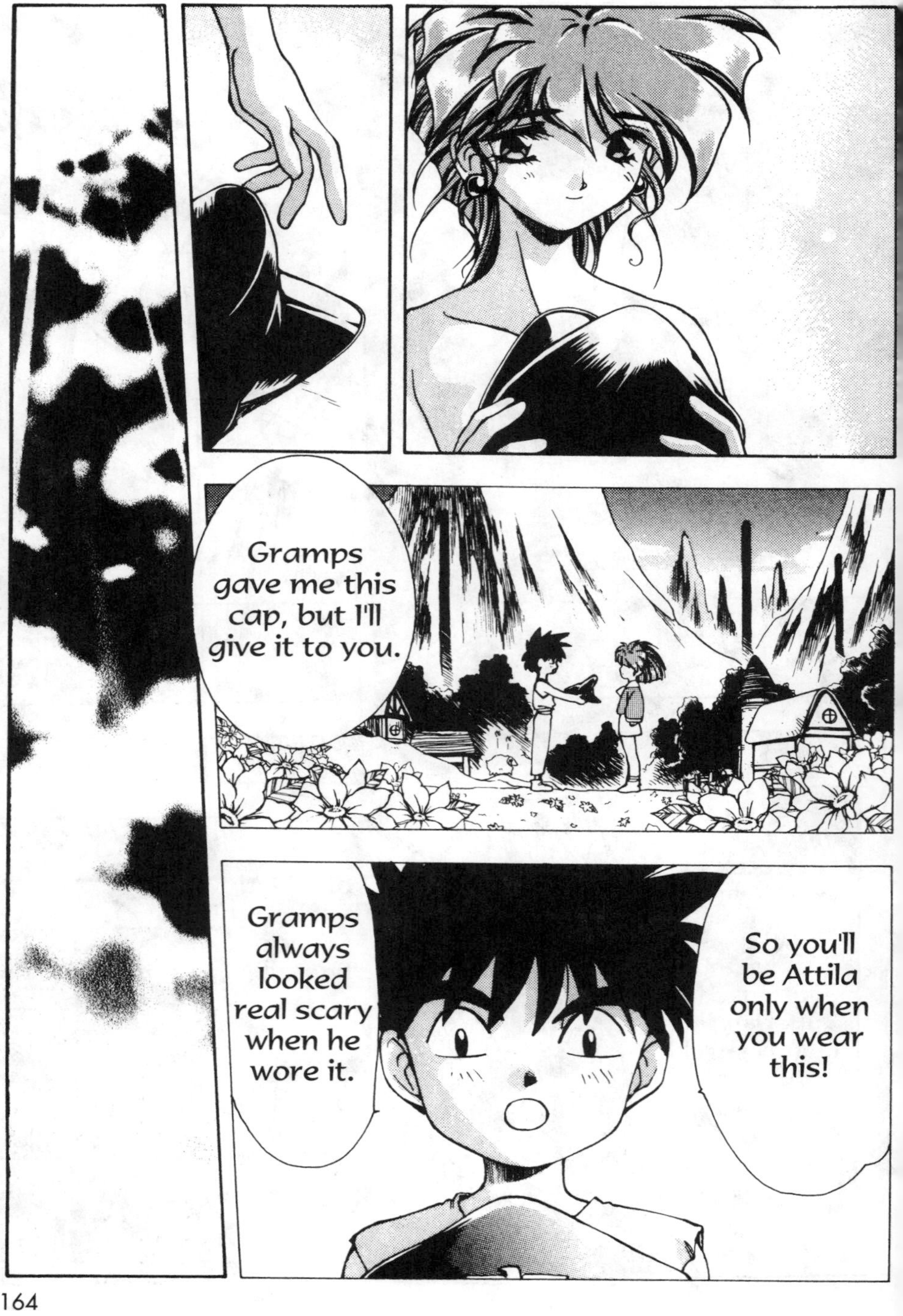
Gramps gave me this cap, but I'll give it to you.
Gramps always looked real scary when he wore it.
So you'll be Attila only when you wear this!

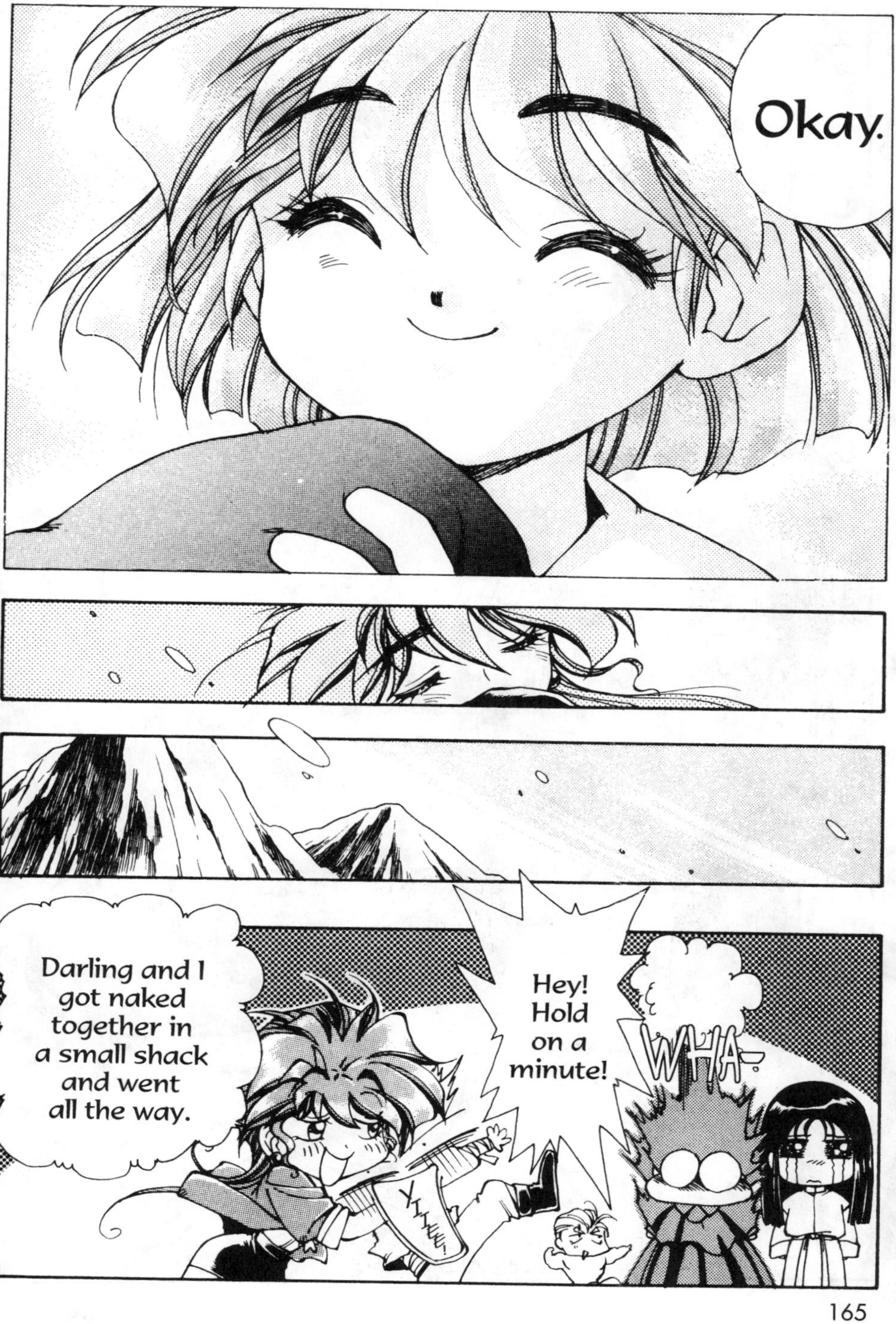
Okay.
Darling and I got naked together in a small shack and went all the way.
YIIIEEE!
Hey! Hold on a minute!
WHA

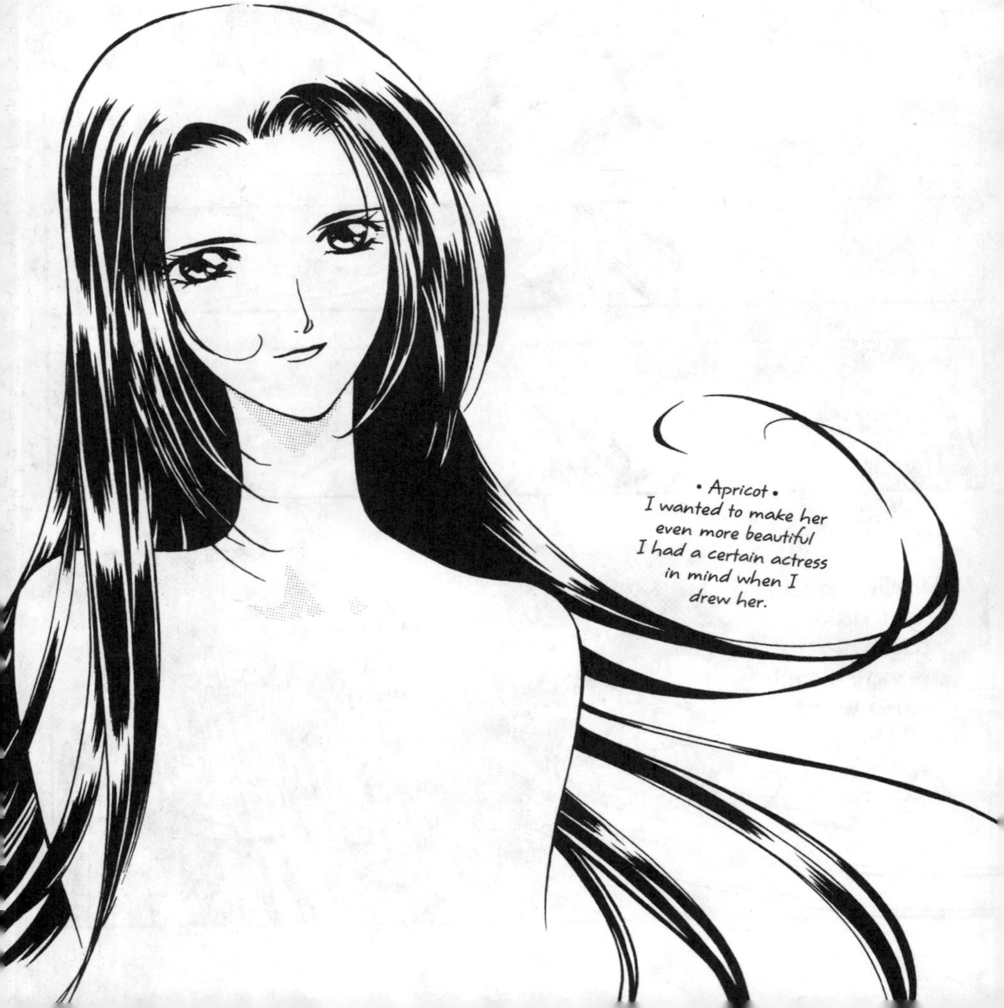
• Apricot •
I wanted to make her
even more beautiful
I had a certain actress
in mind when I
drew her.

Under the Cherry Blossoms ...?!

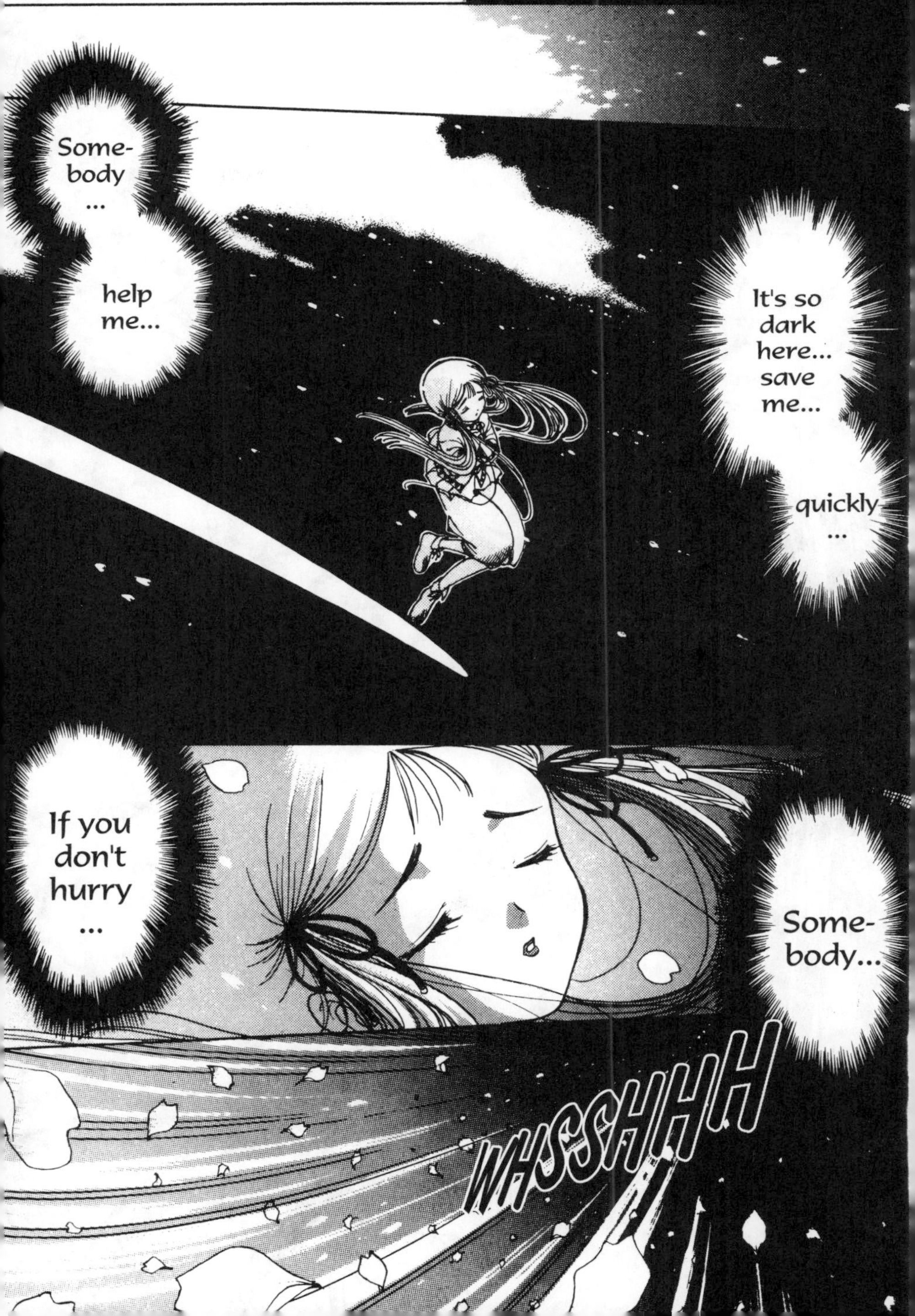
It's so dark here... save me...
quickly ...
Some-body ...
help me...
Some-body...
If you don't hurry ...
WHSSHHH

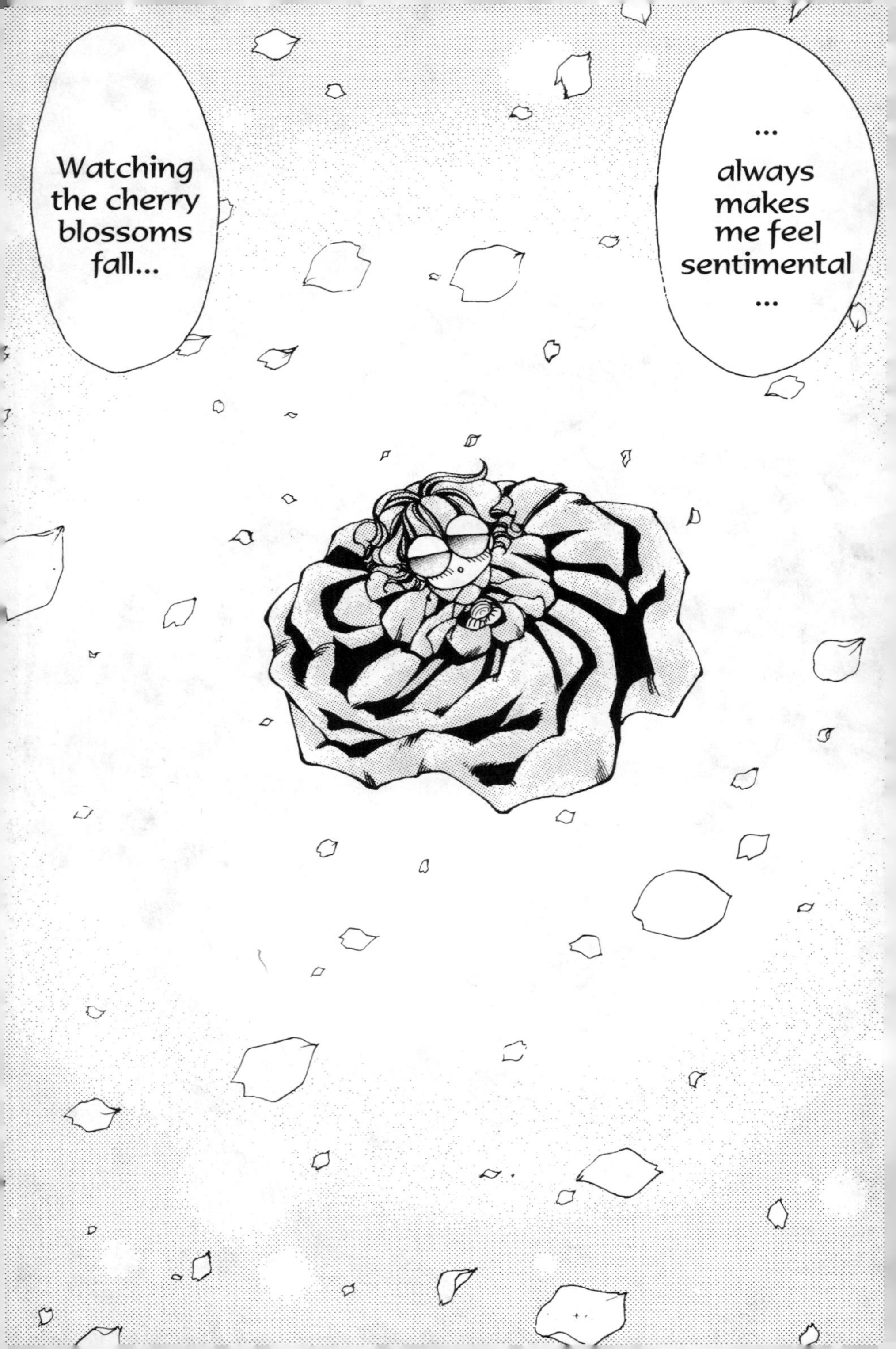
... always makes me feel sentimental ...
Watching the cherry blossoms fall...

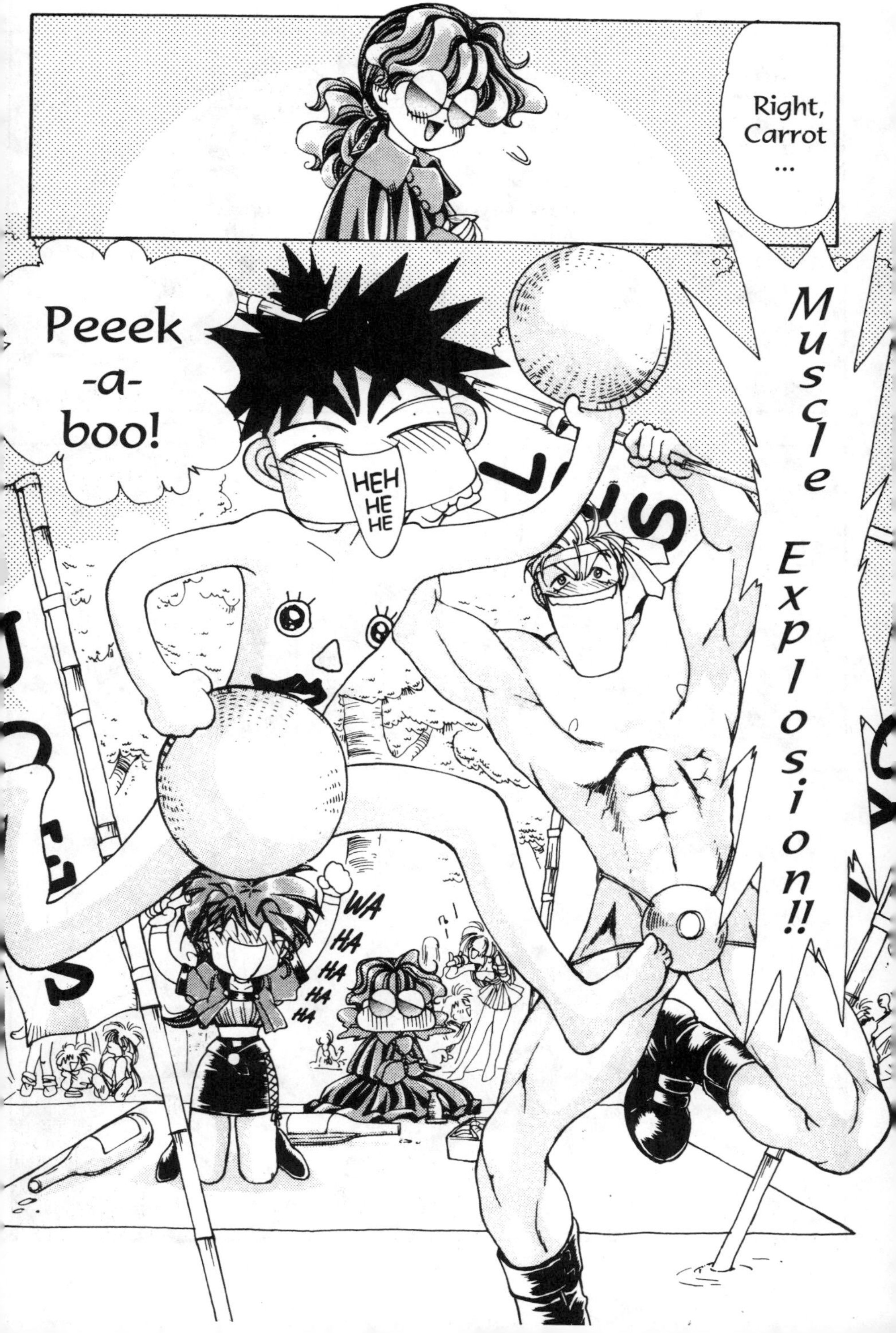
Right, Carrot ...
Muscle Explosion!!
Peeek -a- boo!
HEH HE HE
WA HA HA HA HA HA

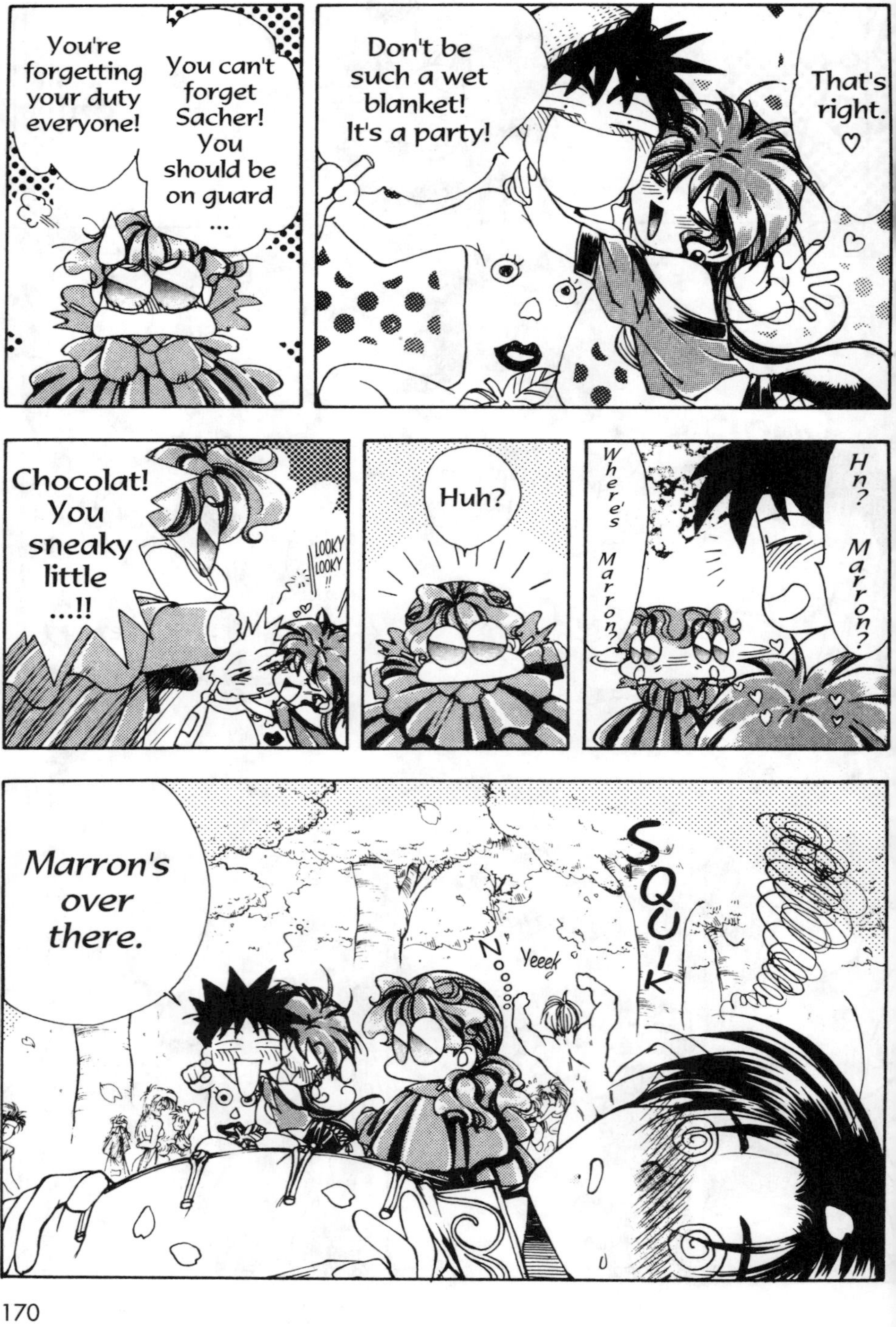
You're forgetting your duty everyone!
You can't forget Sacher! You should be on guard ...
Don't be such a wet blanket! It's a party!
That's right. ♡
Chocolat! You sneaky little ...!!
LOOKY LOOKY !!
Huh?
Where's Marron?
Hn? Marron?
Marron's over there.
Noooooo
Yeeek
SQUIK

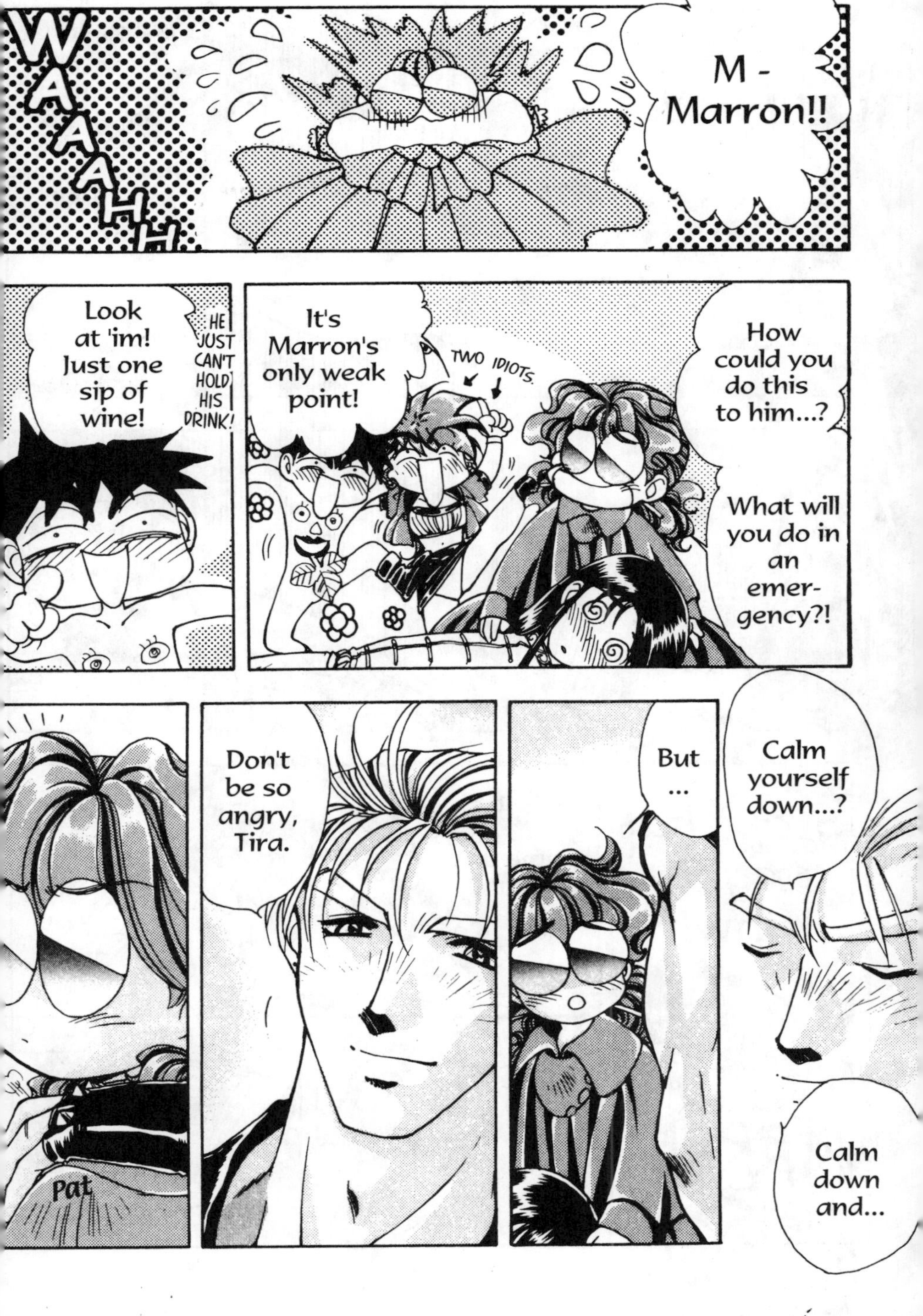
M - Marron!!
WAAAAHH
How could you do this to him...?
What will you do in an emergency?!
It's Marron's only weak point!
TWO IDIOTS.
Look at 'im! Just one sip of wine!
HE JUST CAN'T HOLD HIS DRINK!
Calm yourself down...?
Calm down and...
But ...
Don't be so angry, Tira.
Pat

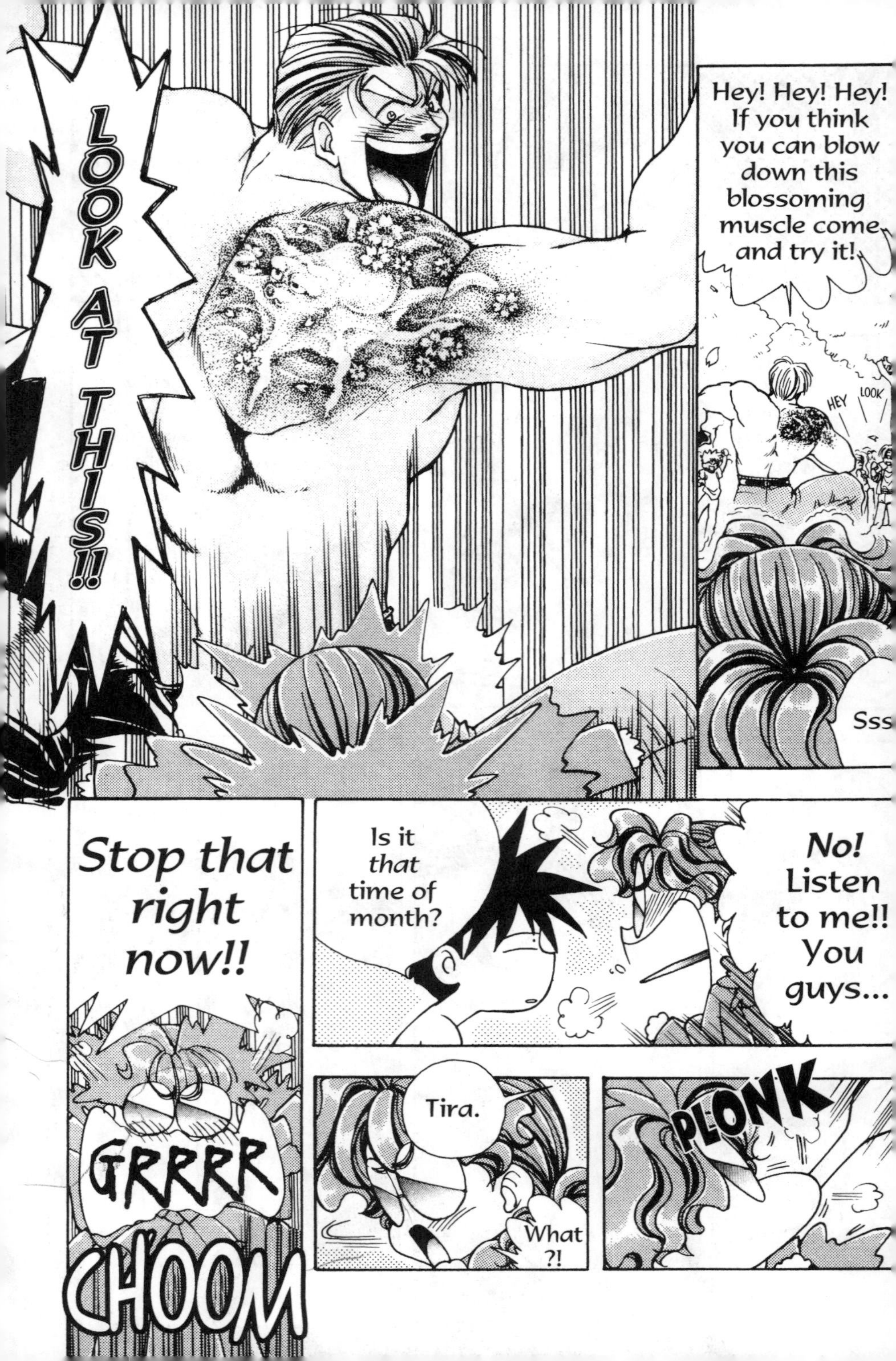
Hey! Hey! Hey! If you think you can blow down this blossoming muscle come and try it!
HEY
LOOK
Sss
LOOK AT THIS!!
No! Listen to me!! You guys...
Is it that time of month?
PLONK
Tira.
What ?!
Stop that right now!!
GRRRR
CHOOM

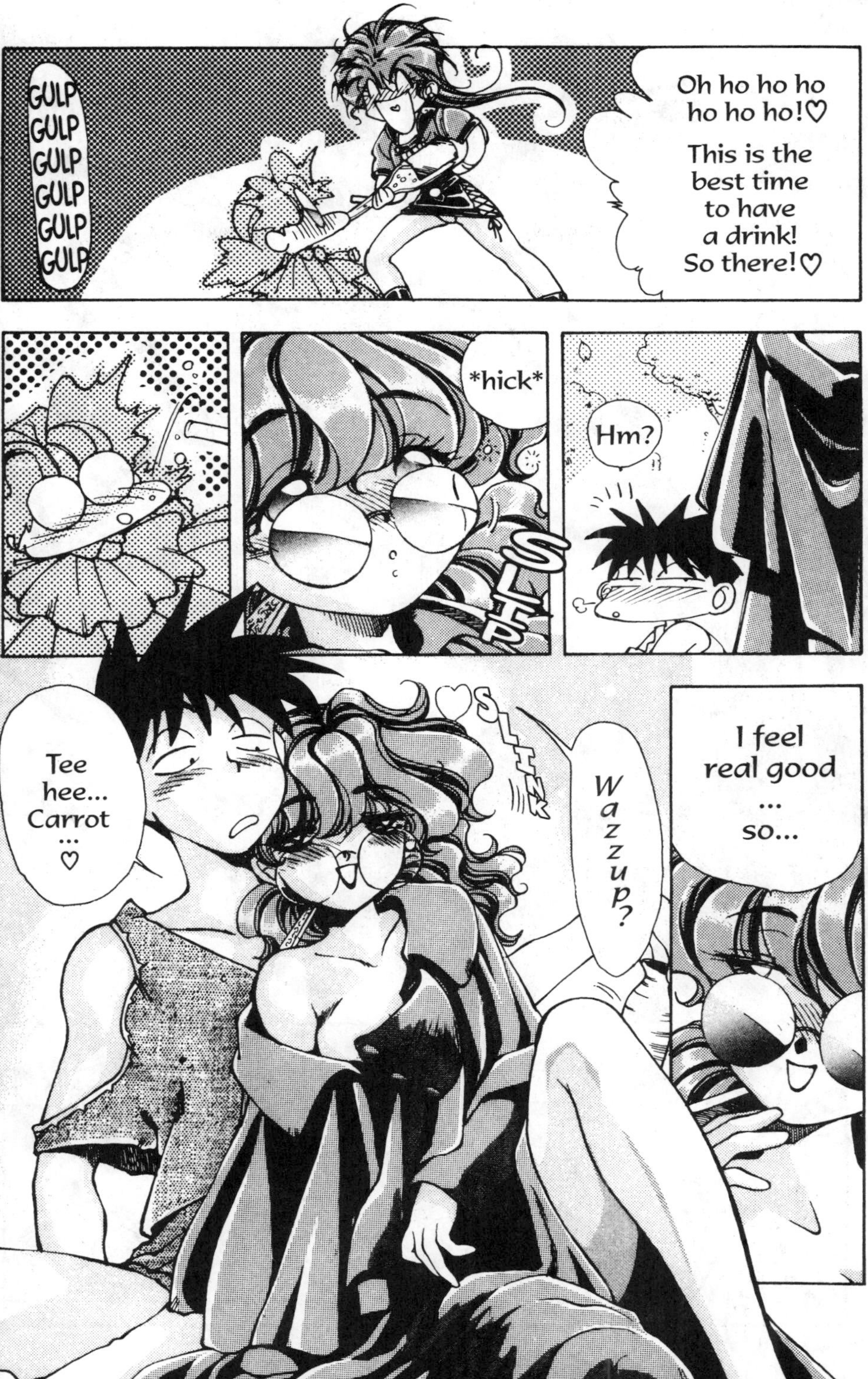
GULP GULP GULP GULP GULP GULP
Oh ho ho ho ho ho ho!♡ This is the best time to have a drink! So there!♡
hick
SLIP
Hm?
Tee hee... Carrot ...♡
SLINK
Wazzup?
I feel real good ... so...

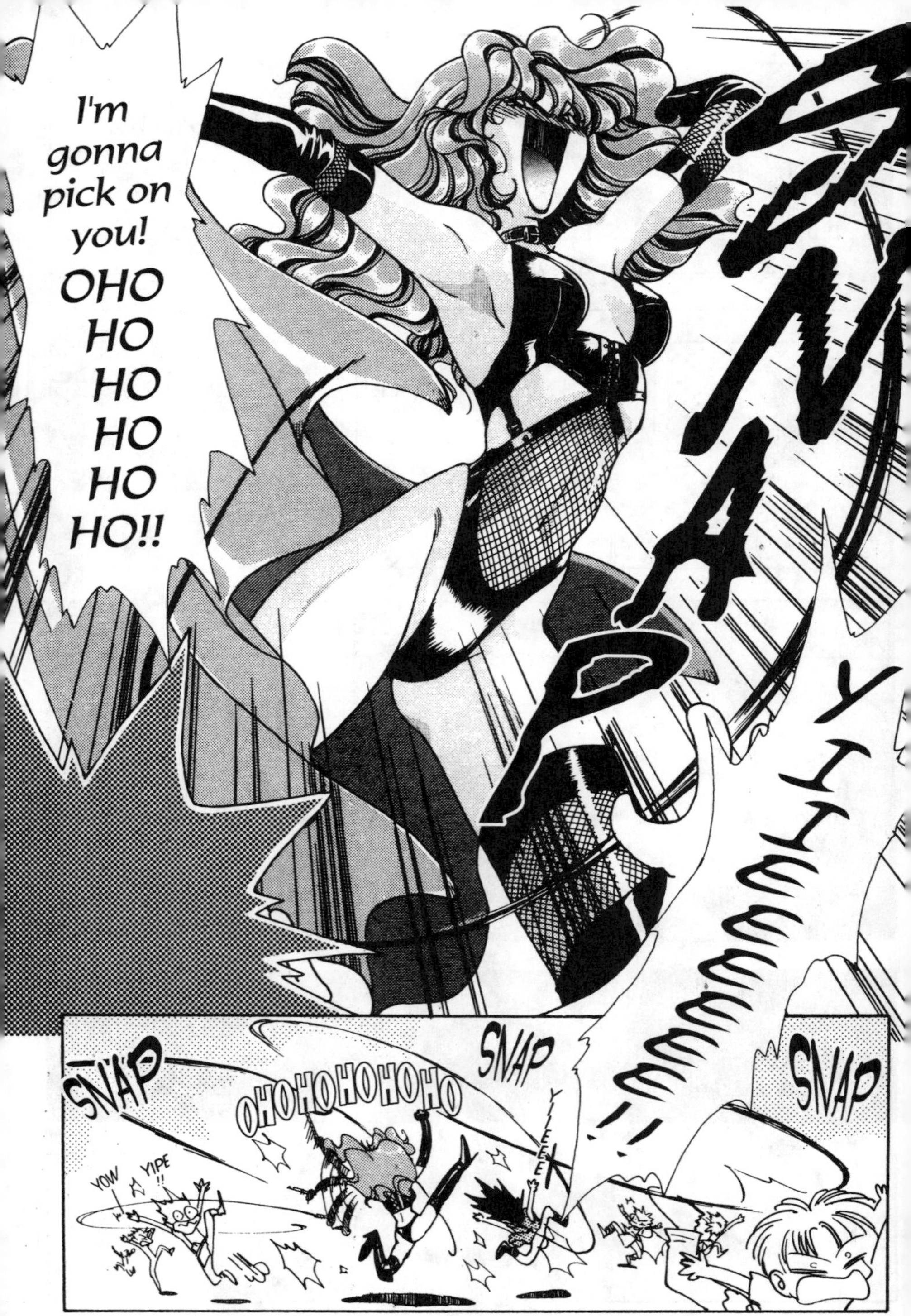
I'm gonna pick on you! OHO HO HO HO HO HO!!
YIIEEEEEEEEEE!!!
SNAP
SNAP
YIEEEE
OHOHOHOHOHOHO
SNAP
YIPE!!
YOW

Phew... What a mess.

PSSSSS SSSHHT

But ...

People really cut loose at parties!

Hee hee hee! Today I'll be doin' the wild thing with some babe!

PSS HHHT

Thath, wight!

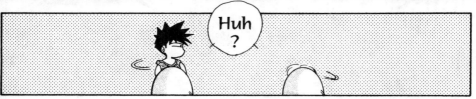

Huh ?

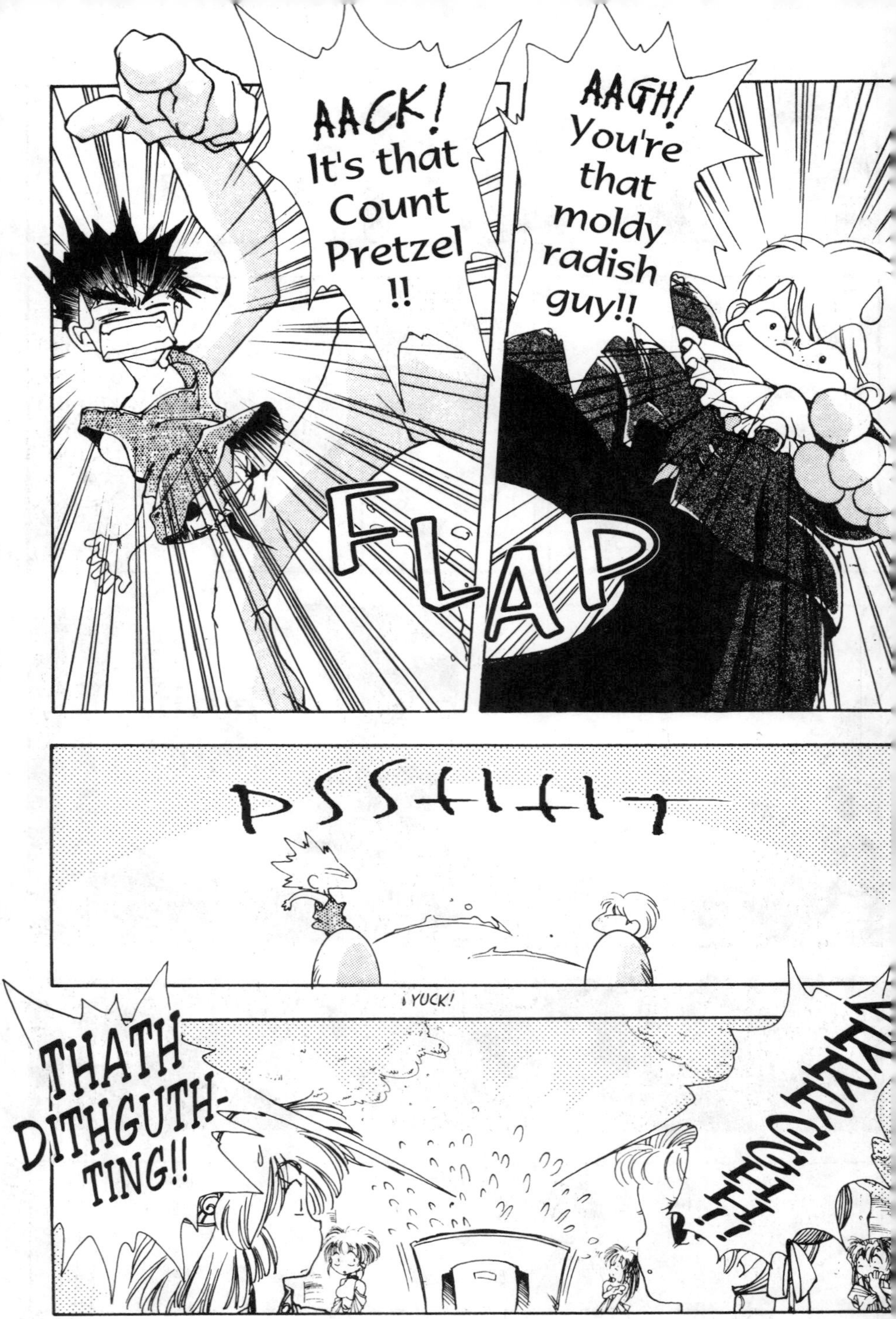
AAGH! You're that moldy radish guy!!
AACK! It's that Count Pretzel !!
FLAP
¡YUCK!
THATH DITHGUTH-TING!!

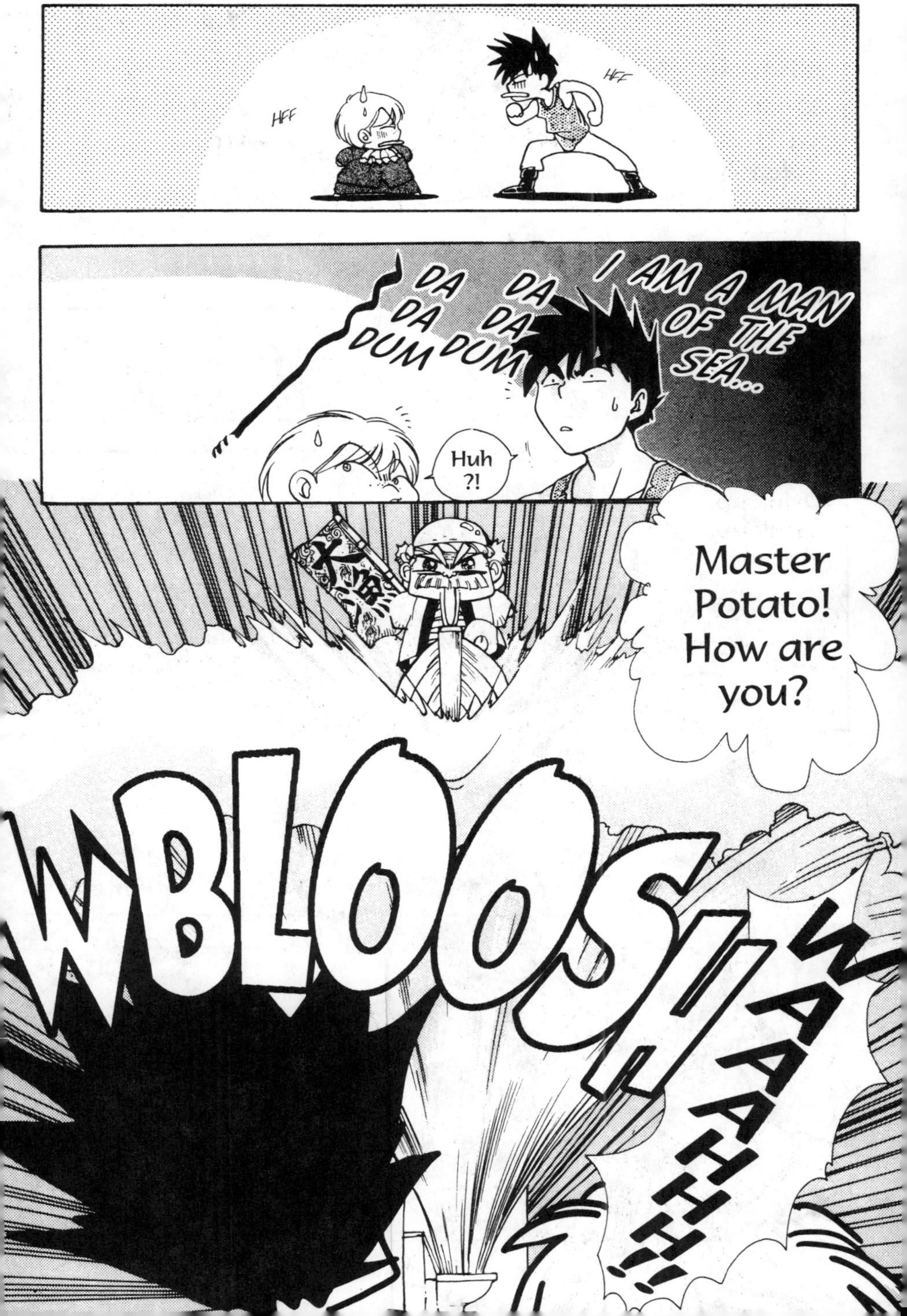
HFF
HFF
I AM A MAN OF THE SEA...
DA DA DUM
DA DA DUM
Huh ?!
Master Potato! How are you?
WBLOOSH
WAAHHH!!!

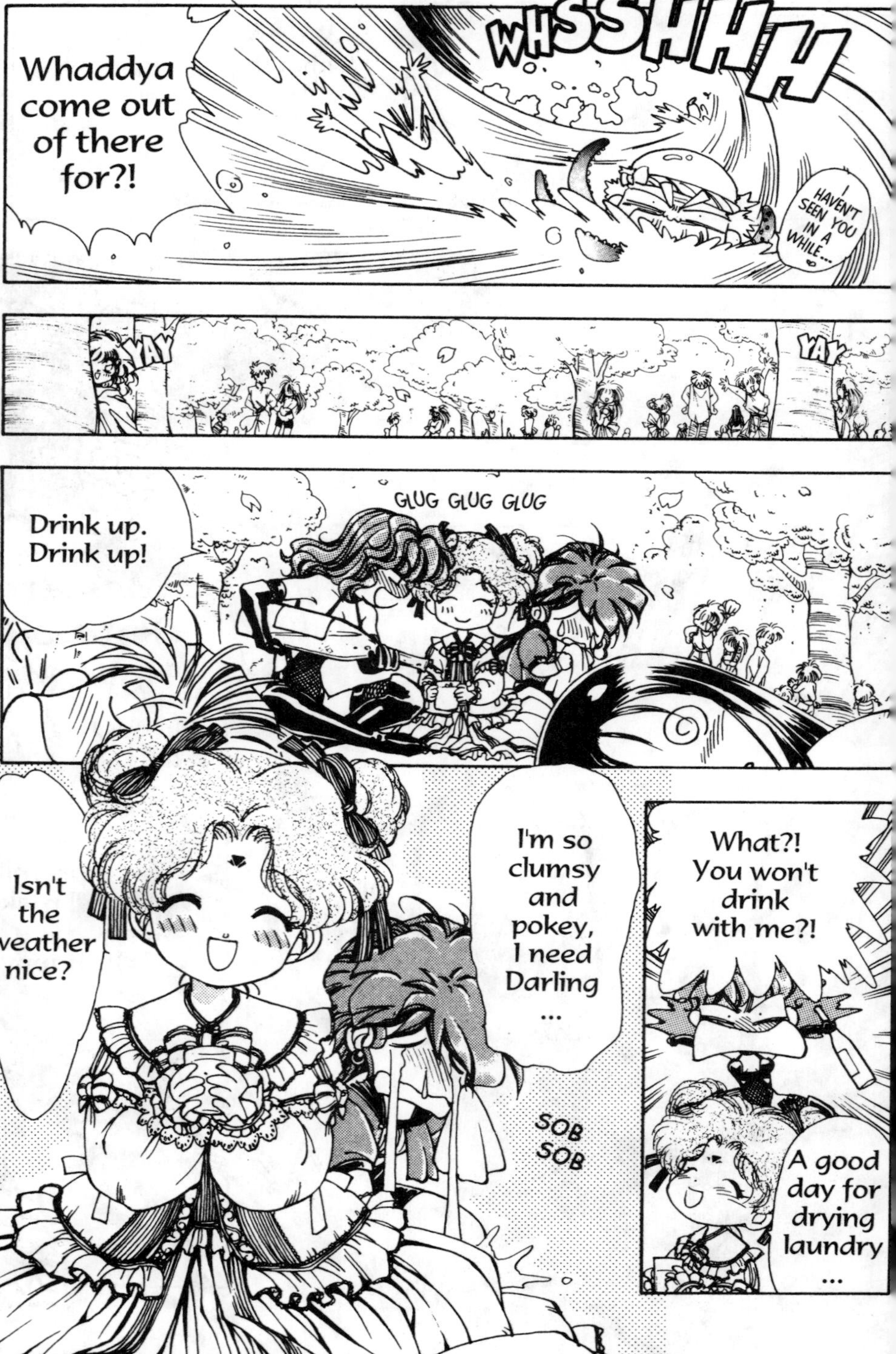
WHSSHHHH
I HAVEN'T SEEN YOU IN A WHILE...
Whaddya come out of there for?!
YAY
YAY
GLUG GLUG GLUG
Drink up. Drink up!
What?! You won't drink with me?!
A good day for drying laundry ...
I'm so clumsy and pokey, I need Darling ...
SOB SOB
Isn't the weather nice?

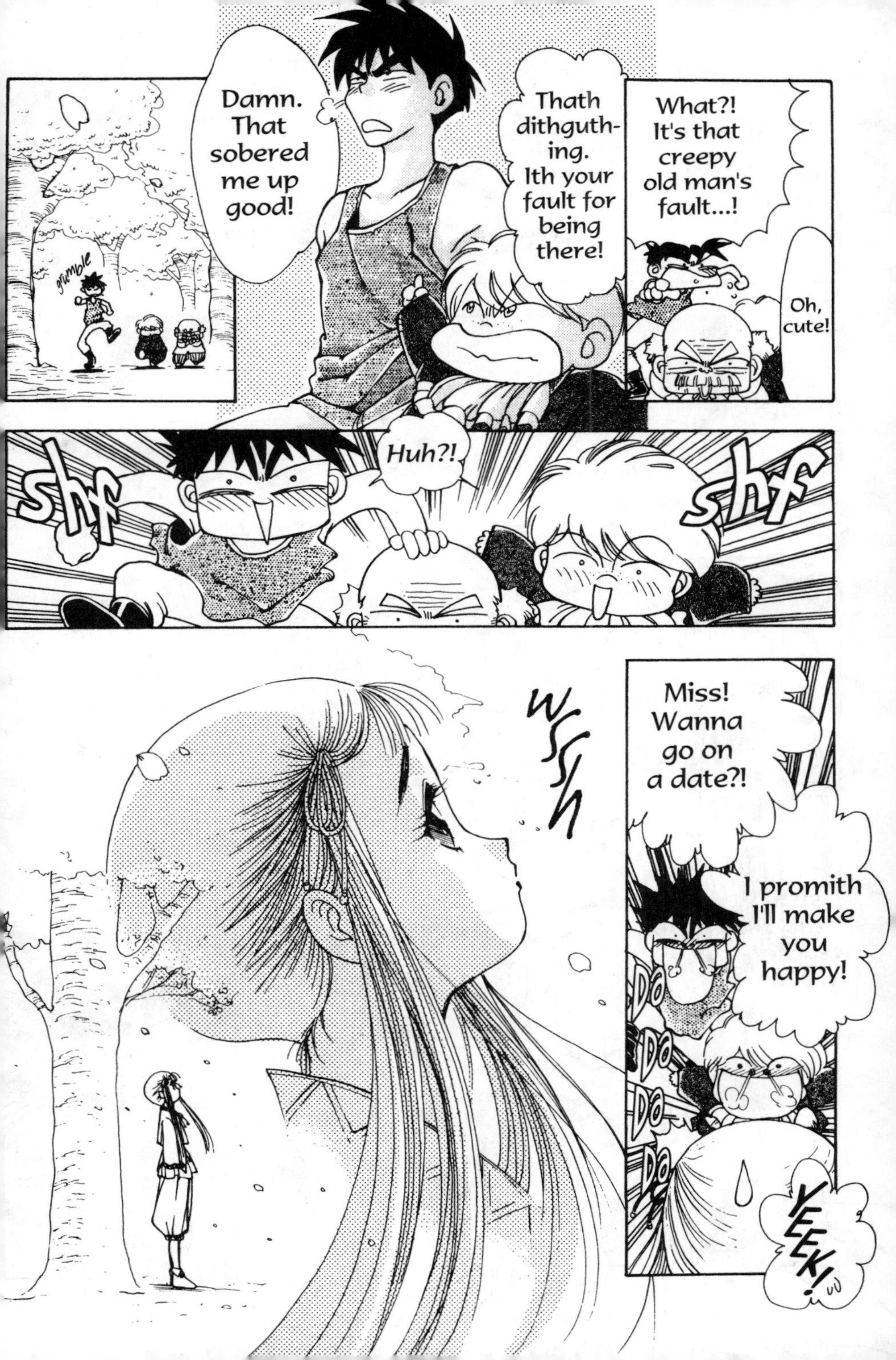
grumble
Damn. That sobered me up good!
Thath dithguthing. Ith your fault for being there!
What?! It's that creepy old man's fault...!
Oh, cute!
shf
Huh?!
shf
WSSH
Miss! Wanna go on a date?!
I promith I'll make you happy!
DO DO DO DO DO
YEEK!

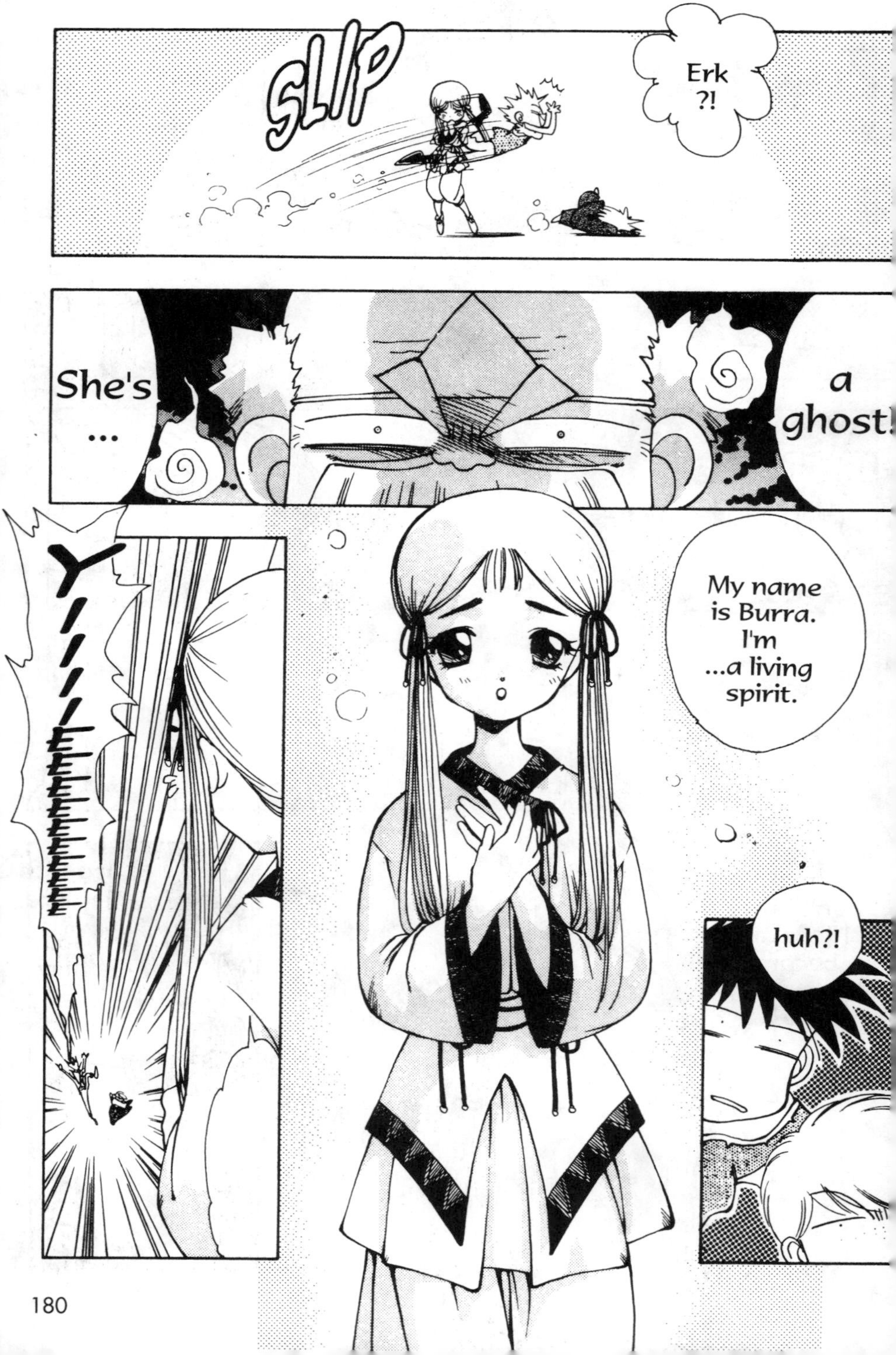
SLIP
Erk ?!
She's ...
a ghost!
YIIIIIEEEEEEEEEEEEE
My name is Burra. I'm ...a living spirit.
huh?!

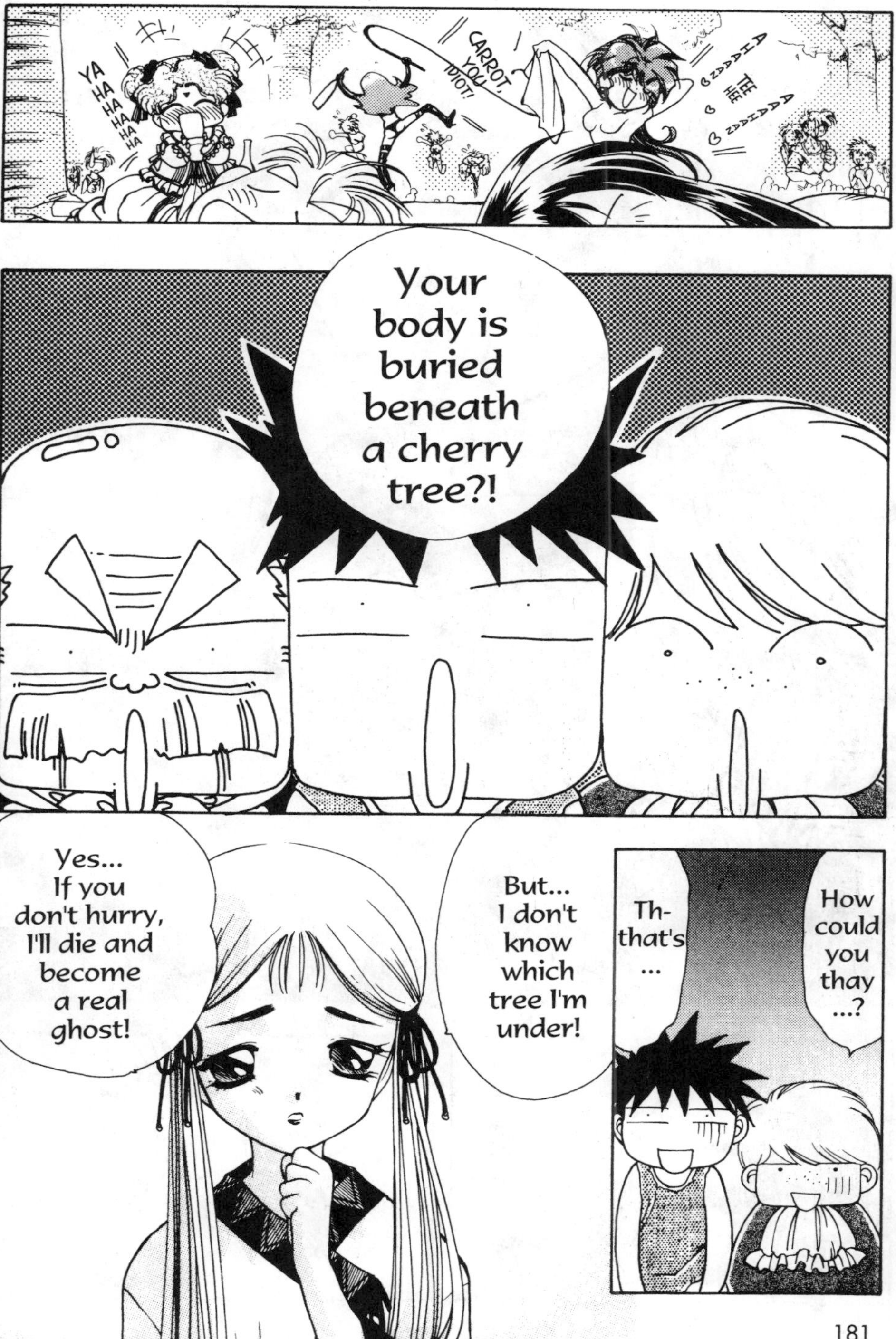
YA HA HA HA HA HA HA
CARROT, YOU IDIOT!
TEE HEE
Your body is buried beneath a cherry tree?!
Yes... If you don't hurry, I'll die and become a real ghost!
But... I don't know which tree I'm under!
Th-that's...
How could you thay...?

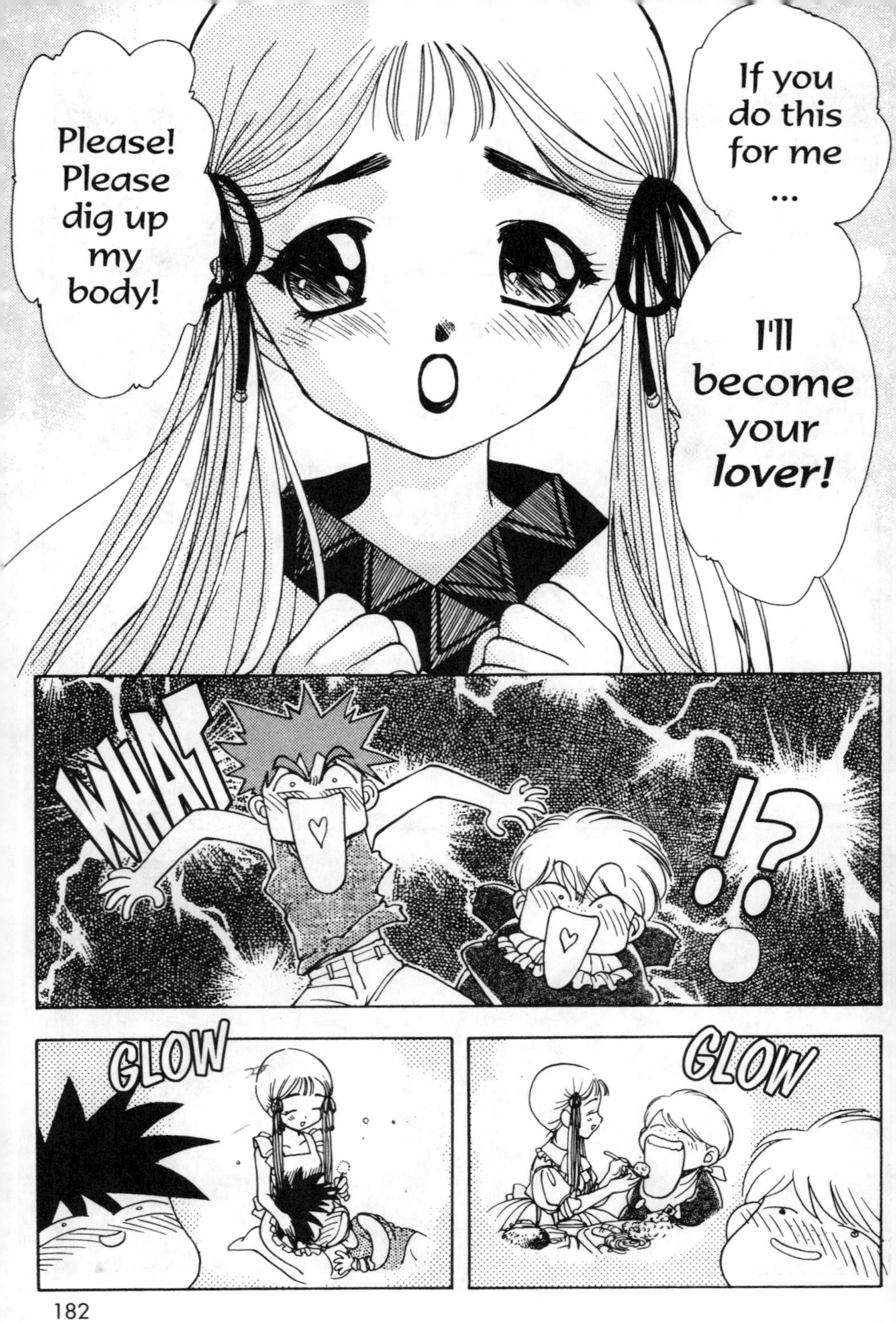
Please! Please dig up my body!
If you do this for me ...
I'll become your lover!
WHAT
!?
GLOW
GLOW

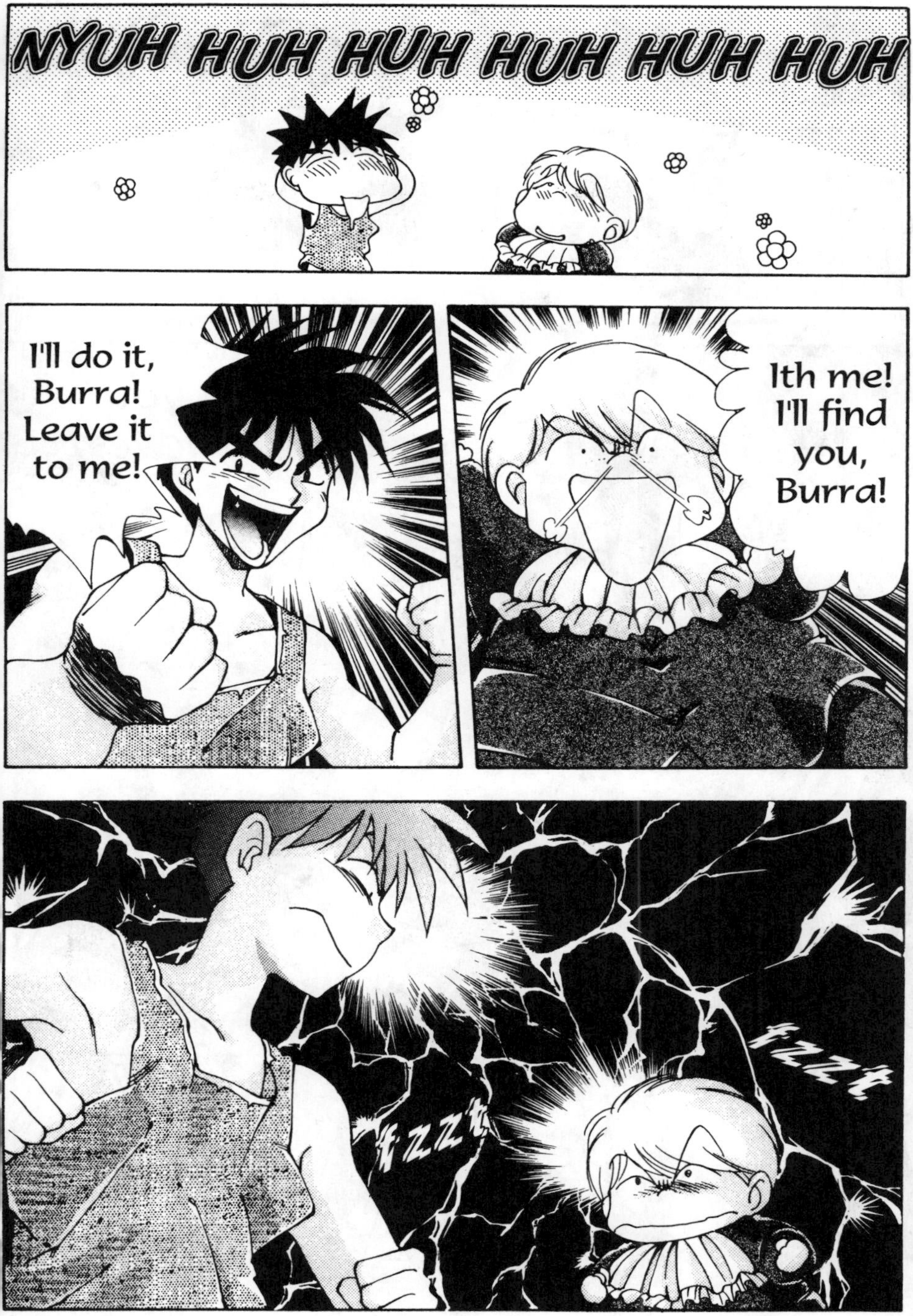
NYUH HUH HUH HUH HUH HUH
Ith me! I'll find you, Burra!
I'll do it, Burra! Leave it to me!
fzzzt
fzzzt

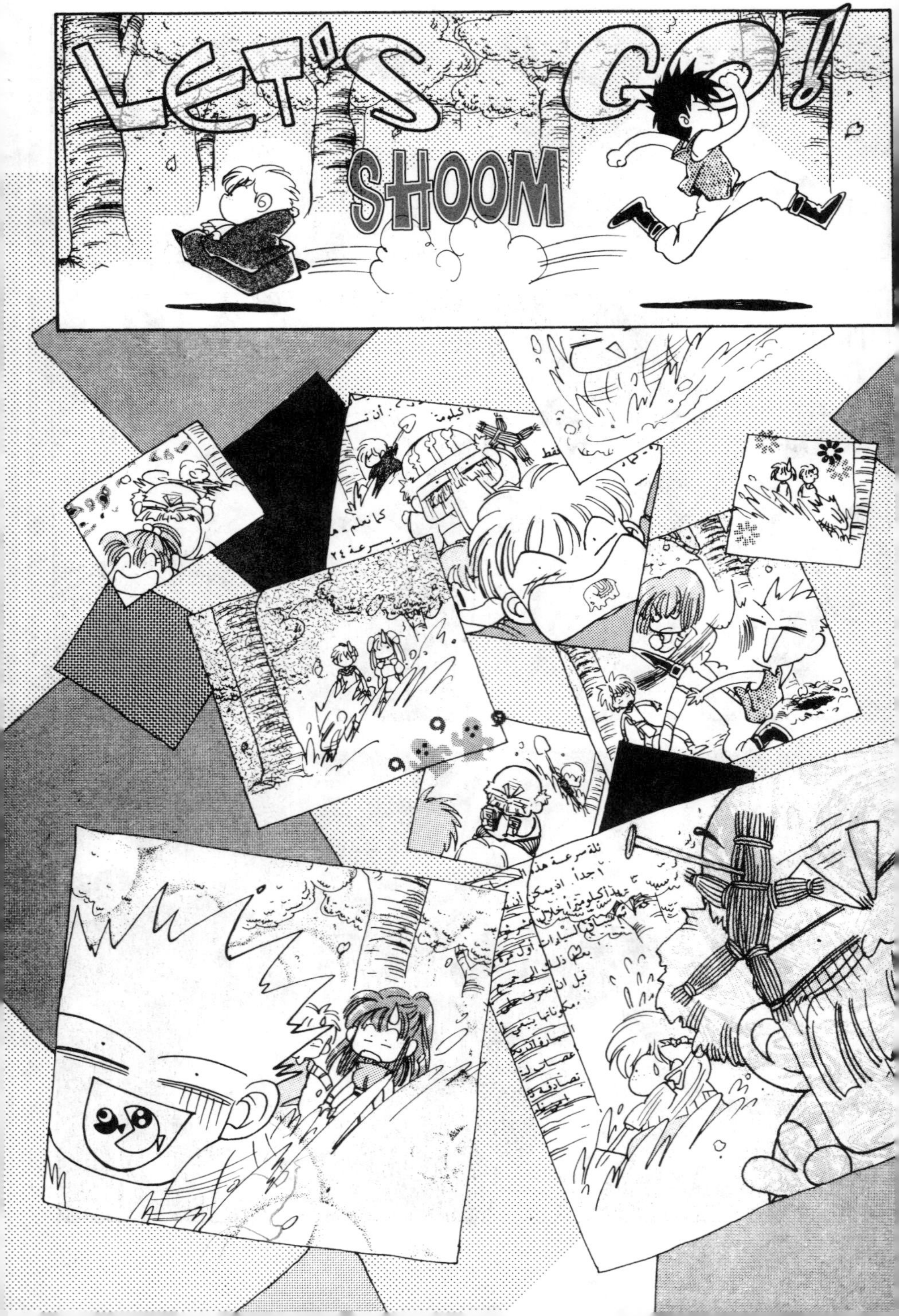
LET'S GO!
SHOOM

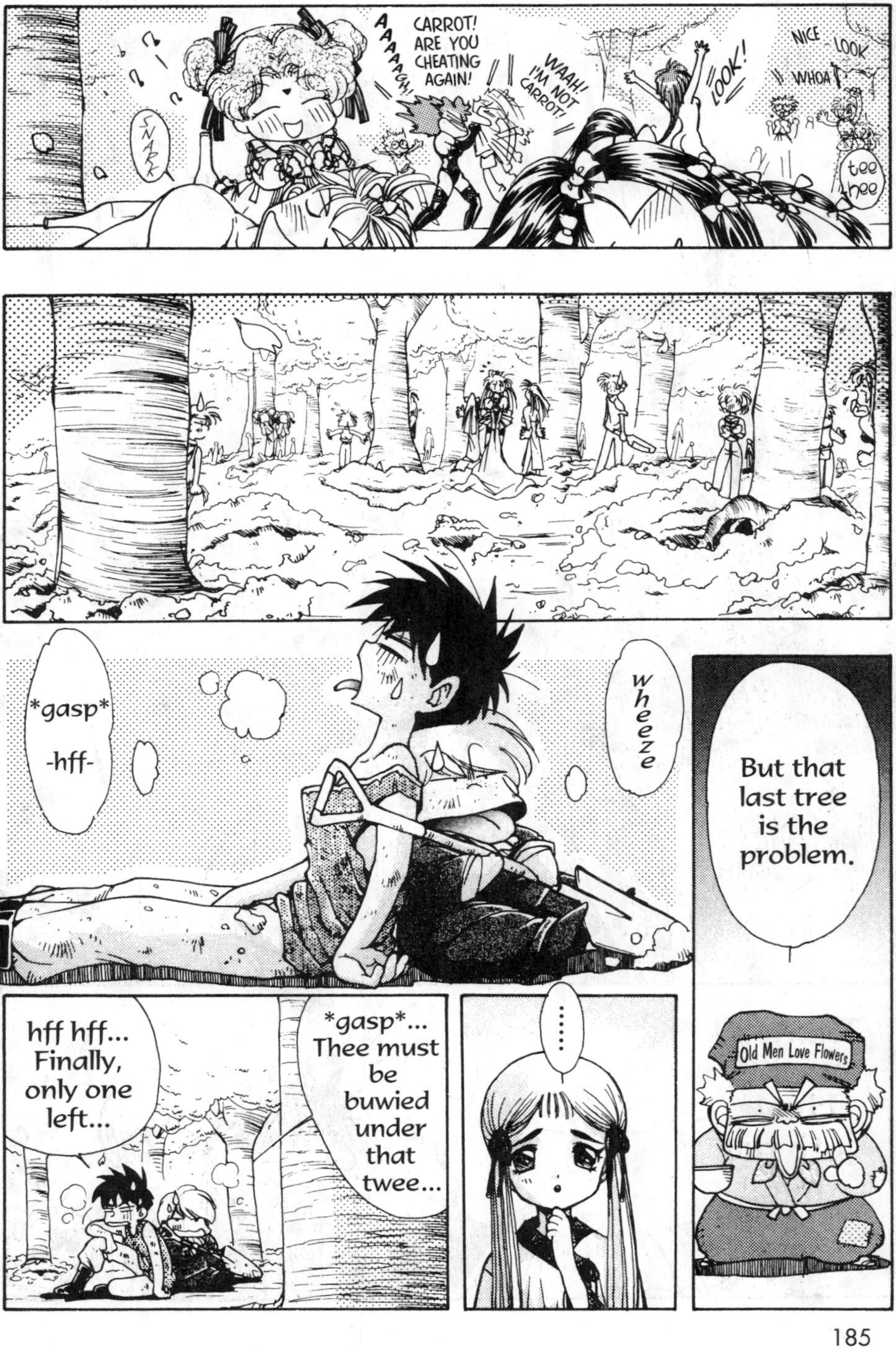
NICE
LOOK
WHOA
tee hee
LOOK!
WAAH! I'M NOT CARROT!
CARROT! ARE YOU CHEATING AGAIN!
AAAAAAGH!
SNARK
But that last tree is the problem.
wheeze
gasp
-hff-
Old Men Love Flowers
......
gasp... Thee must be buwied under that twee...
hff hff... Finally, only one left...

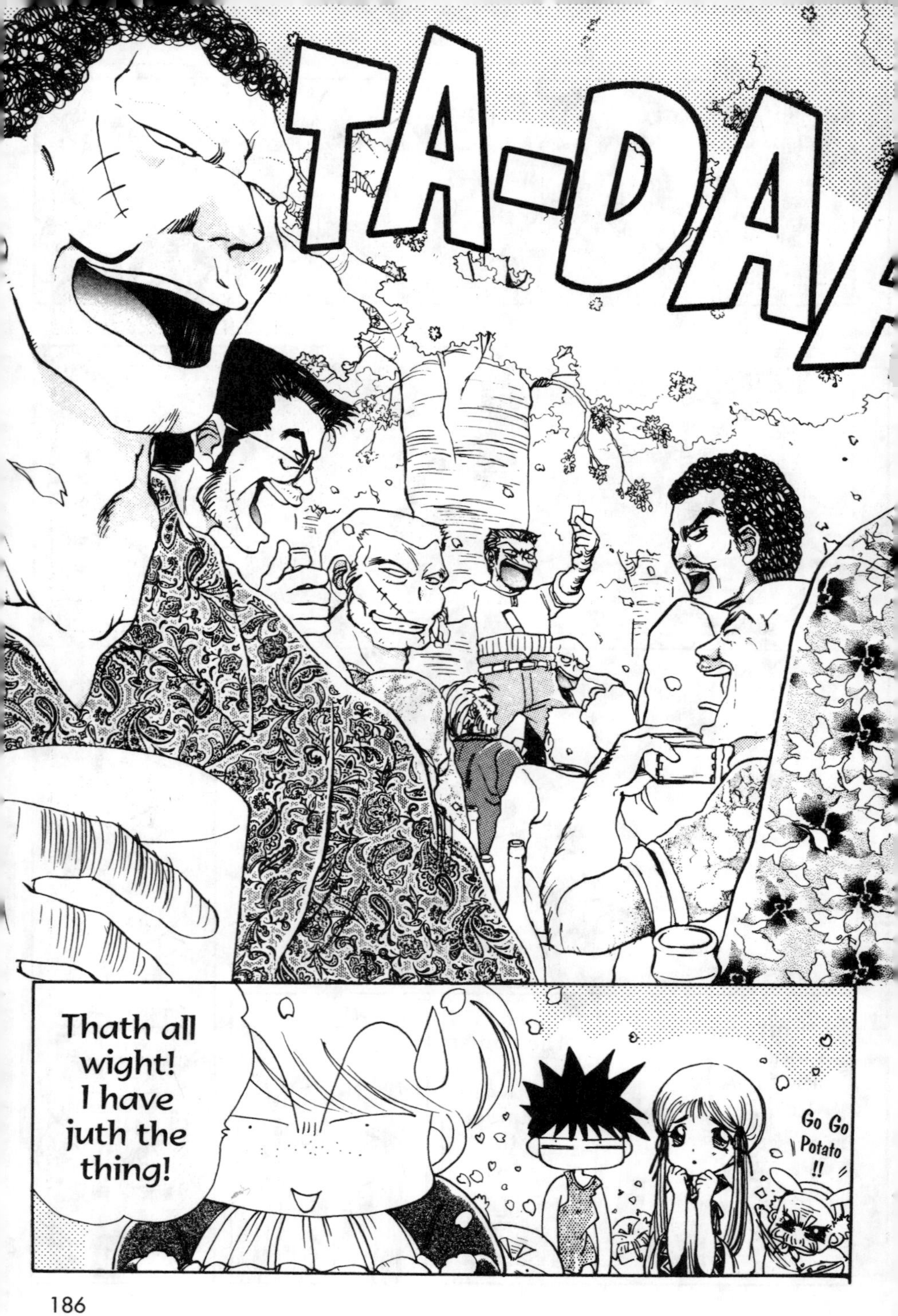
TA-DA
Go Go Potato !!
Thath all wight! I have juth the thing!

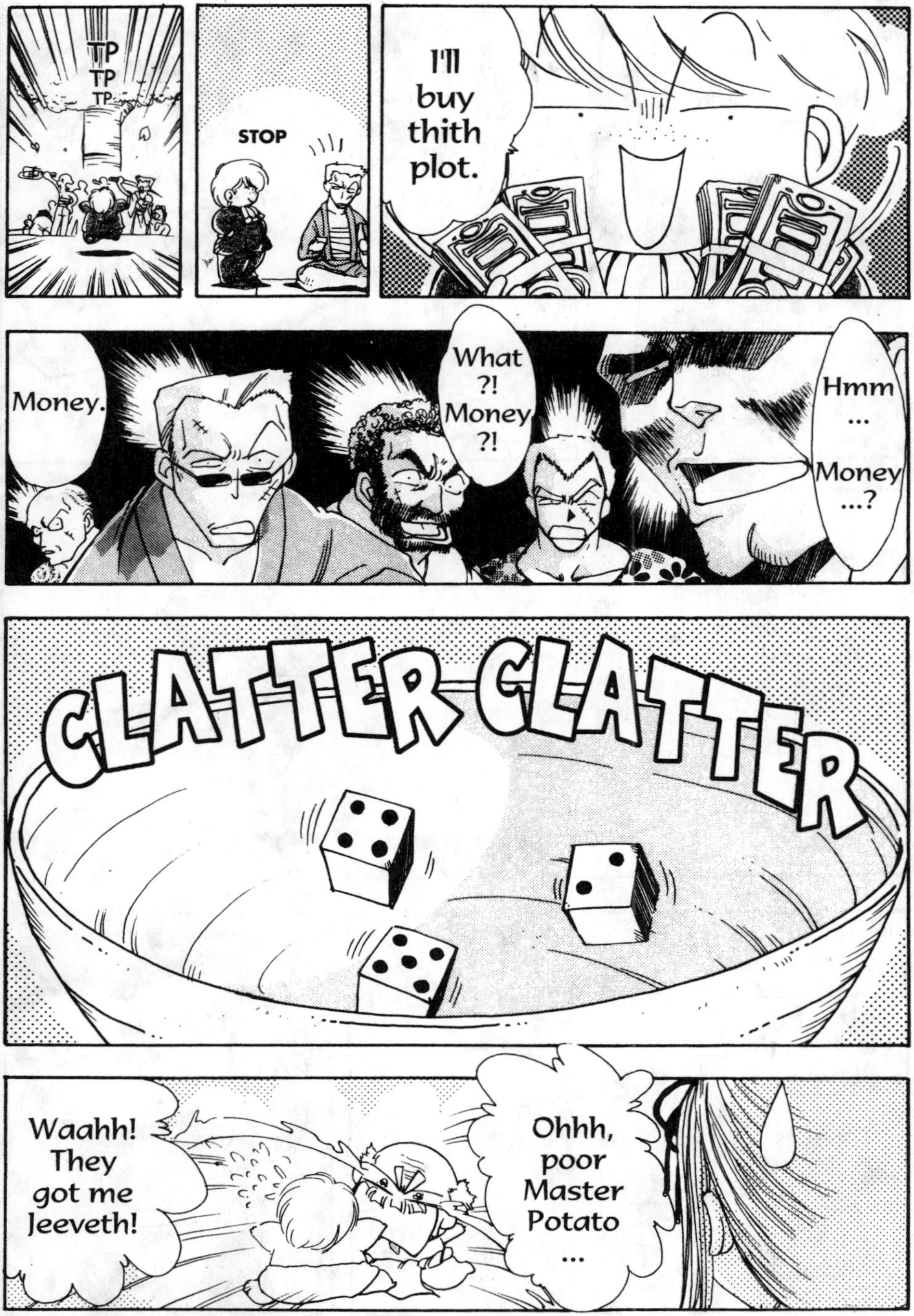
TP
TP
TP
STOP
I'll buy thith plot.
Money.
What?! Money?!
Hmm... Money...?
CLATTER CLATTER
Waahh! They got me Jeeveth!
Ohhh, poor Master Potato...

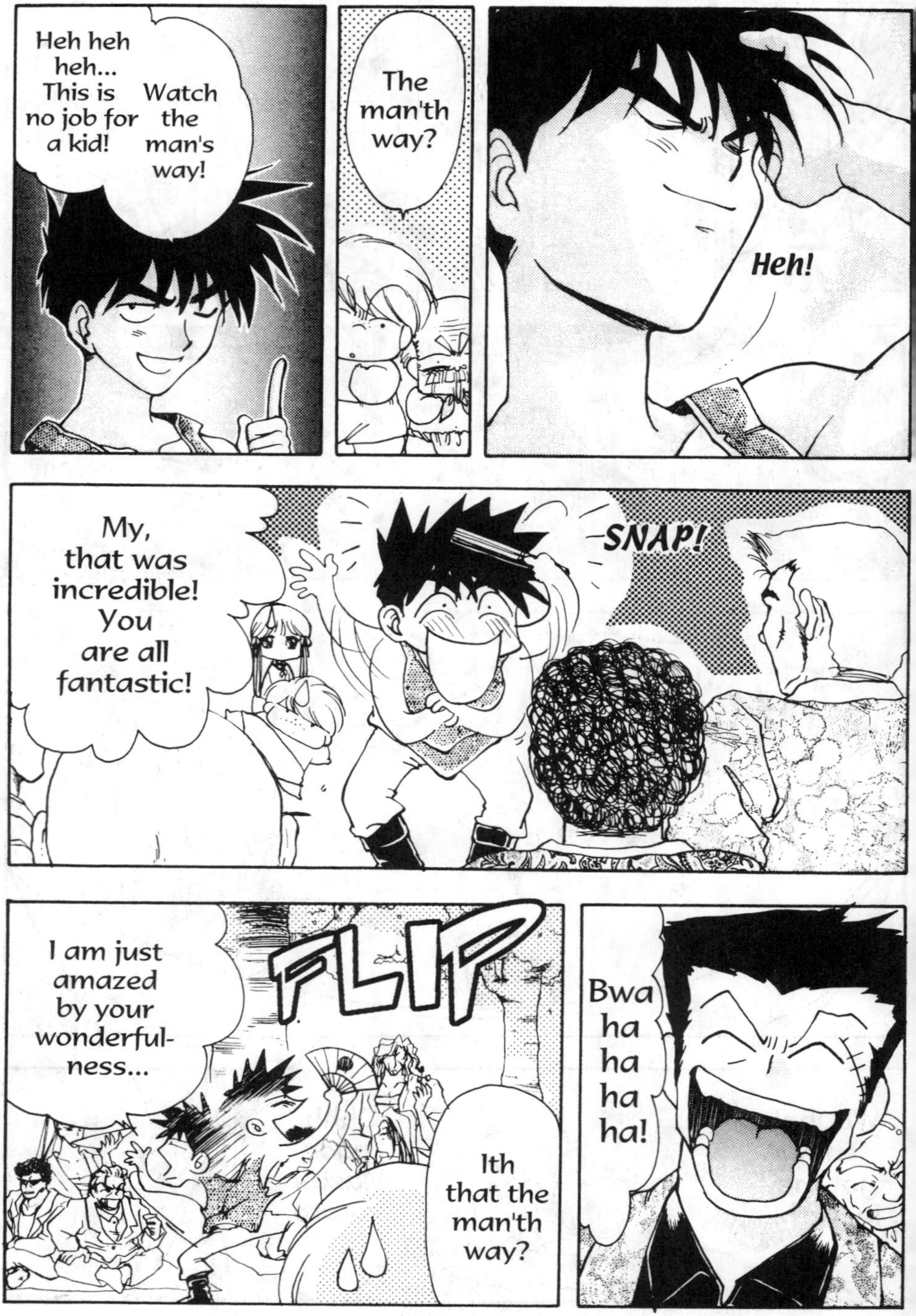

Heh heh heh... This is no job for a kid!
Watch the man's way!
The man'th way?
Heh!
My, that was incredible! You are all fantastic!
SNAP!
I am just amazed by your wonderful-ness...
FLIP
Ith that the man'th way?
Bwa ha ha ha ha!

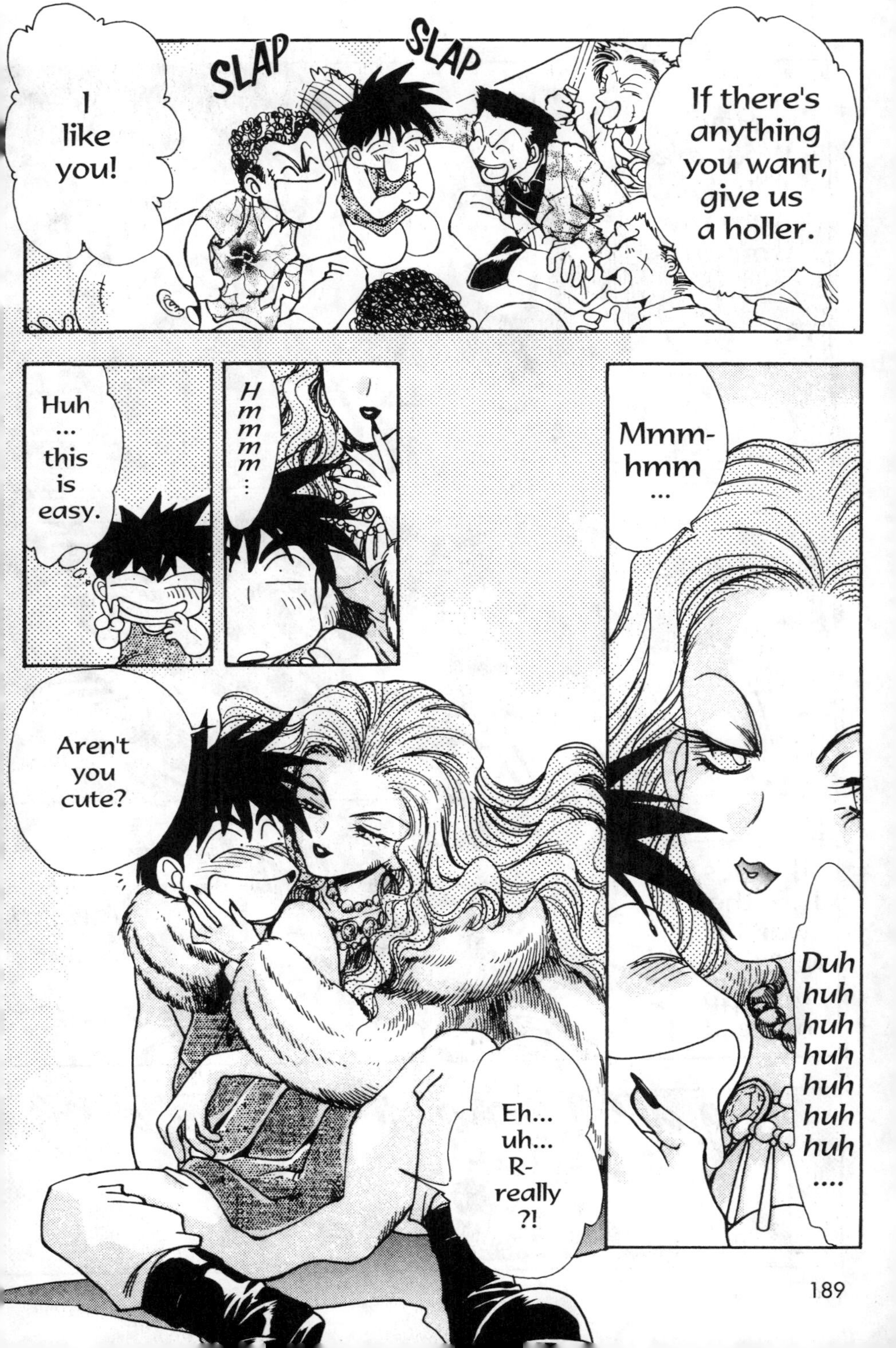
If there's anything you want, give us a holler.
SLAP
SLAP
I like you!
Mmm-hmm...
Duh huh huh huh huh huh huh....
Hmmmm...
Huh... this is easy.
Aren't you cute?
Eh... uh... R-really?!

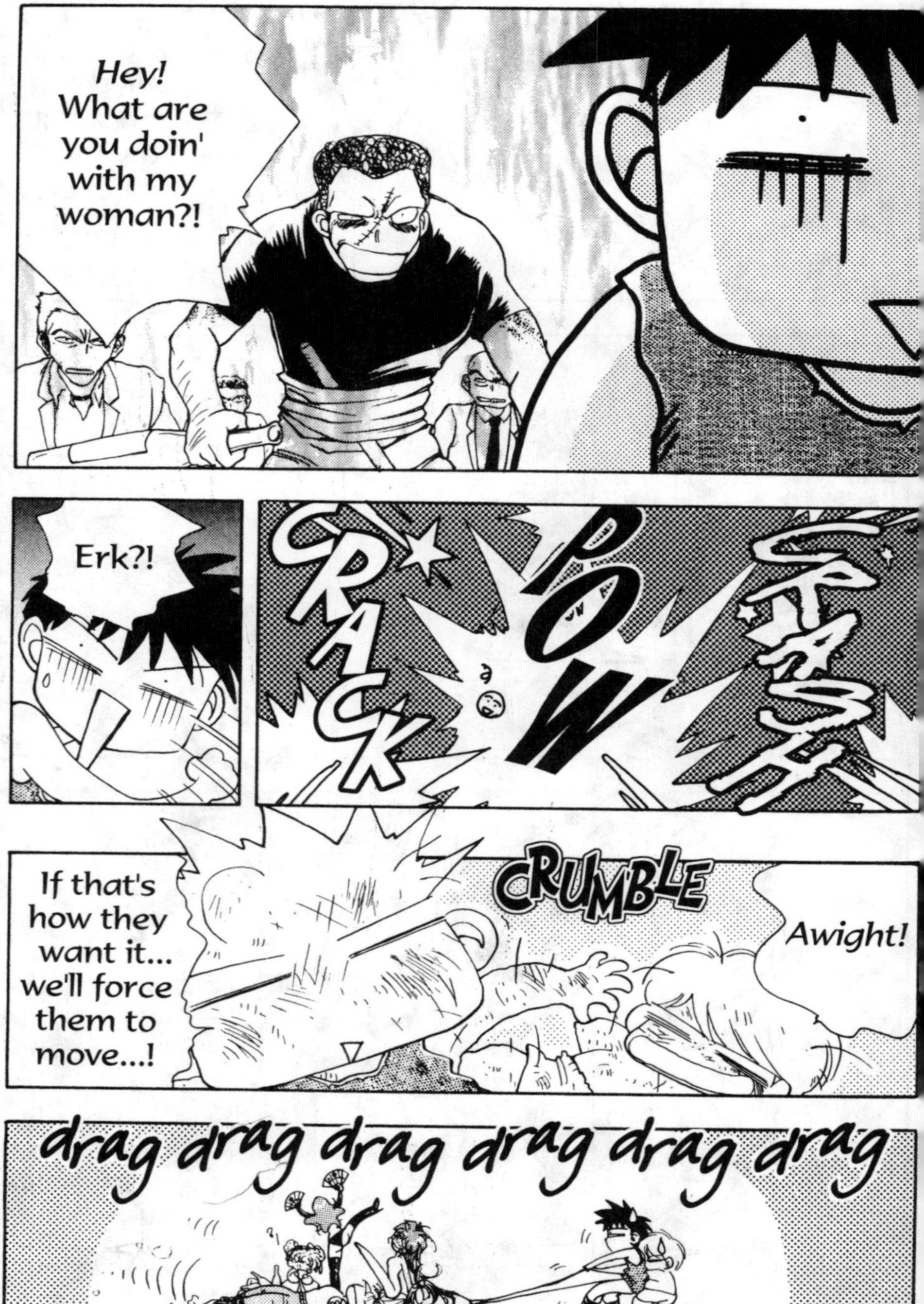
Hey! What are you doin' with my woman?!
Erk?!
CRACK
POW
CRASH
CRUMBLE
If that's how they want it... we'll force them to move...!
Awight!
drag drag drag drag drag drag

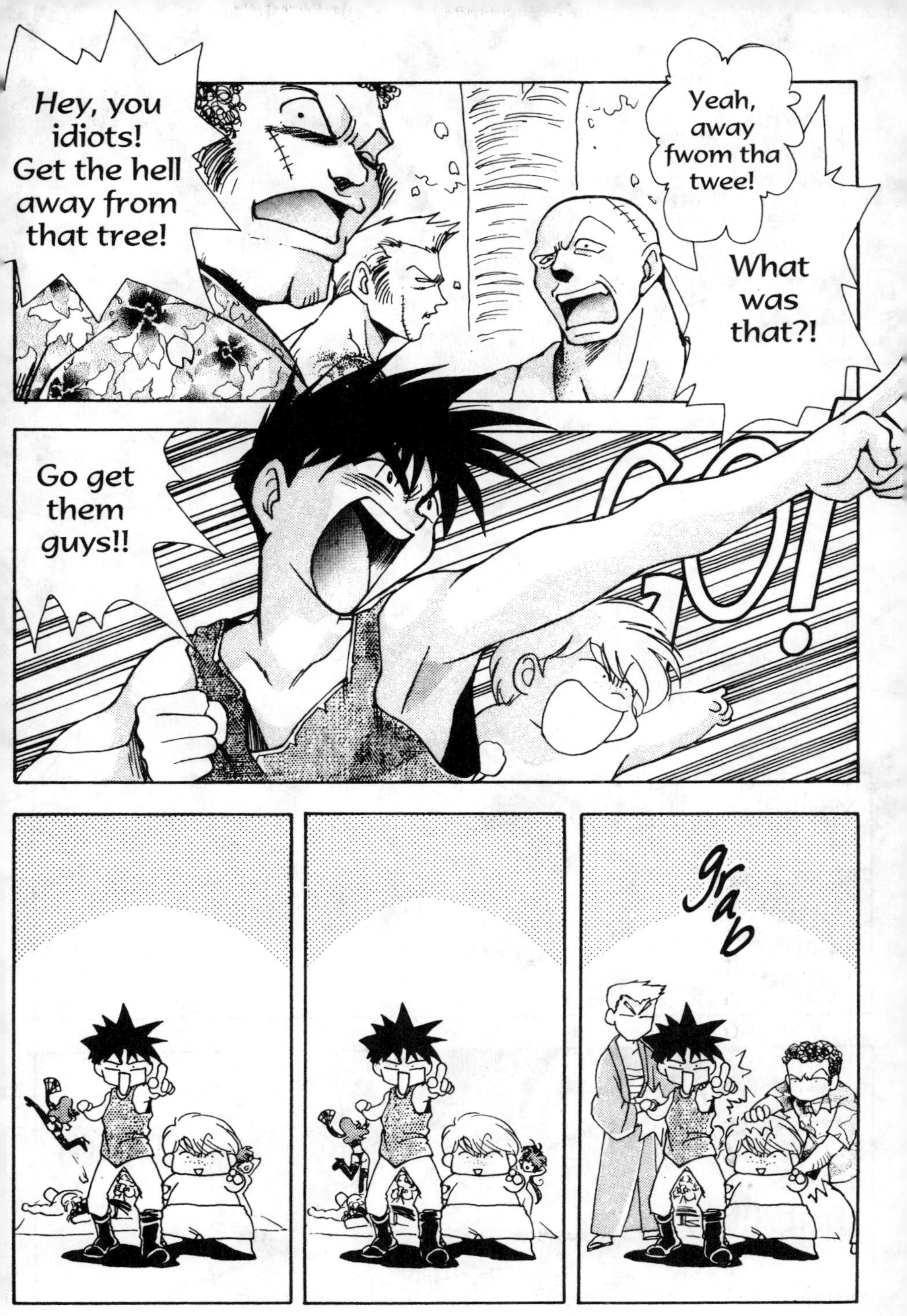
Hey, you idiots! Get the hell away from that tree!
Yeah, away fwom tha twee!
What was that?!
Go get them guys!!
GO!
grab

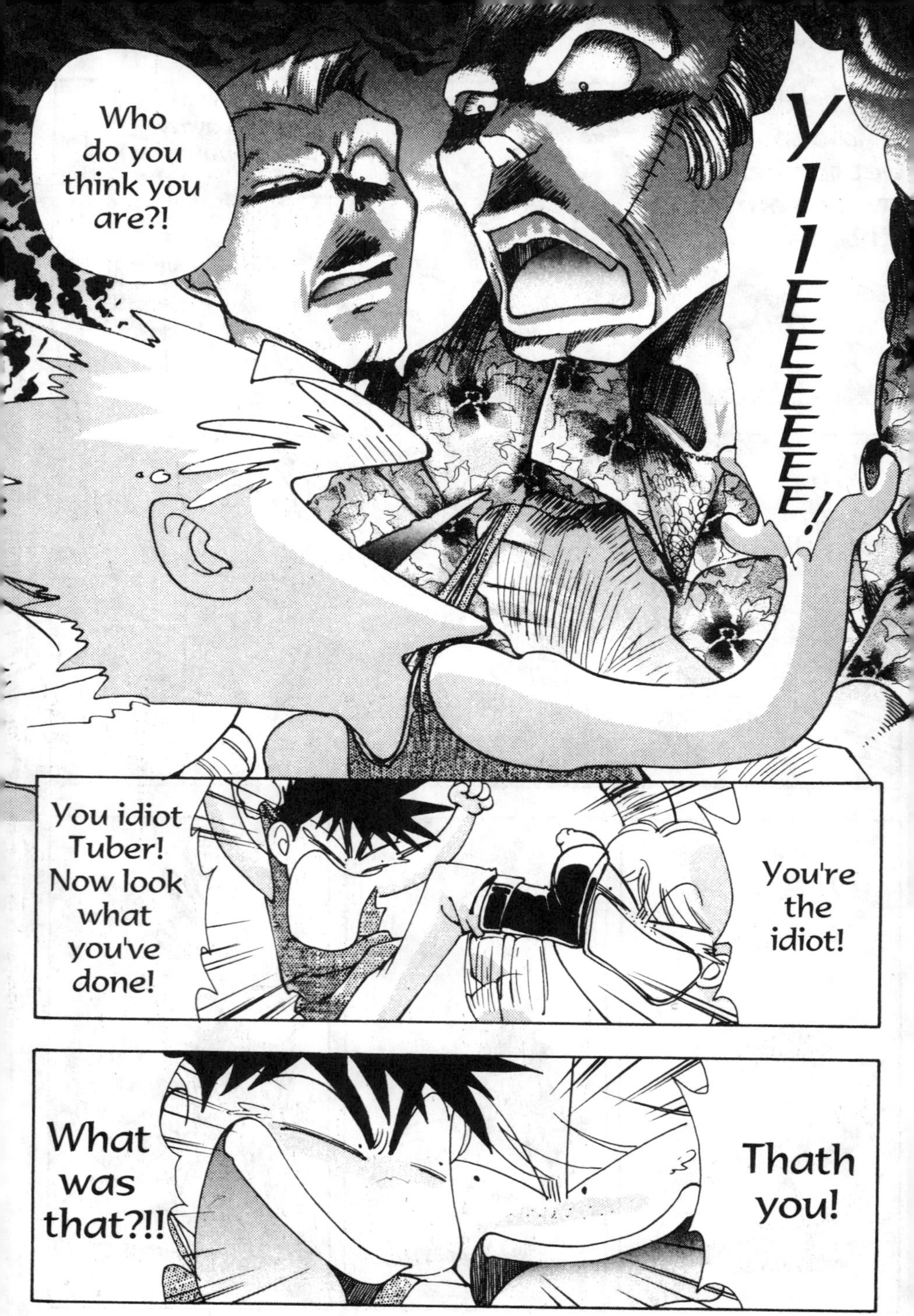

Who do you think you are?!
YIIEEEEEEE!
You idiot Tuber! Now look what you've done!
You're the idiot!
What was that?!!
Thath you!

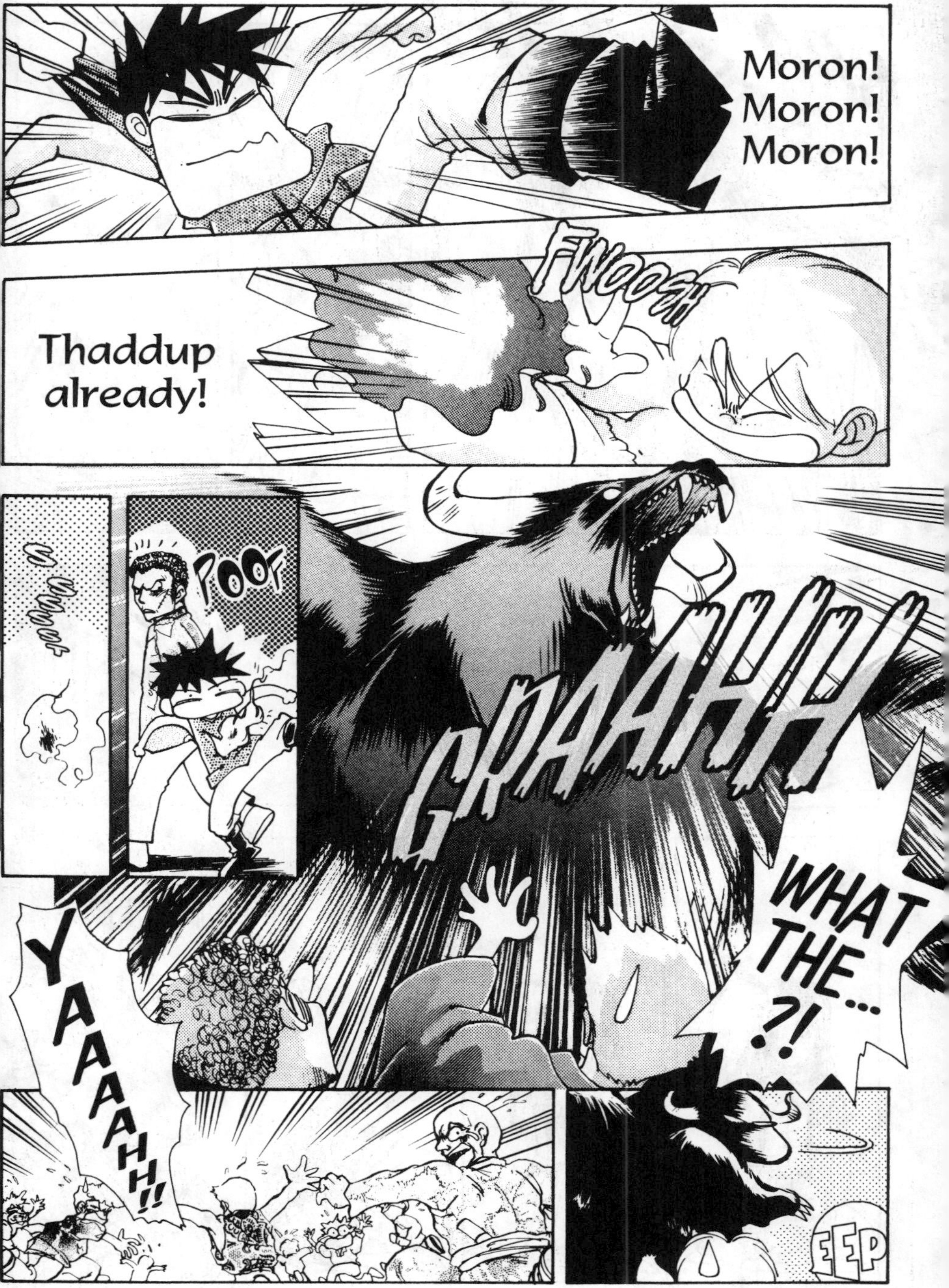
Moron! Moron! Moron!
FWOOSH
Thaddup already!
GRAAHH
POOF
WHAT THE...?!
YAAAAHH!!
EEP

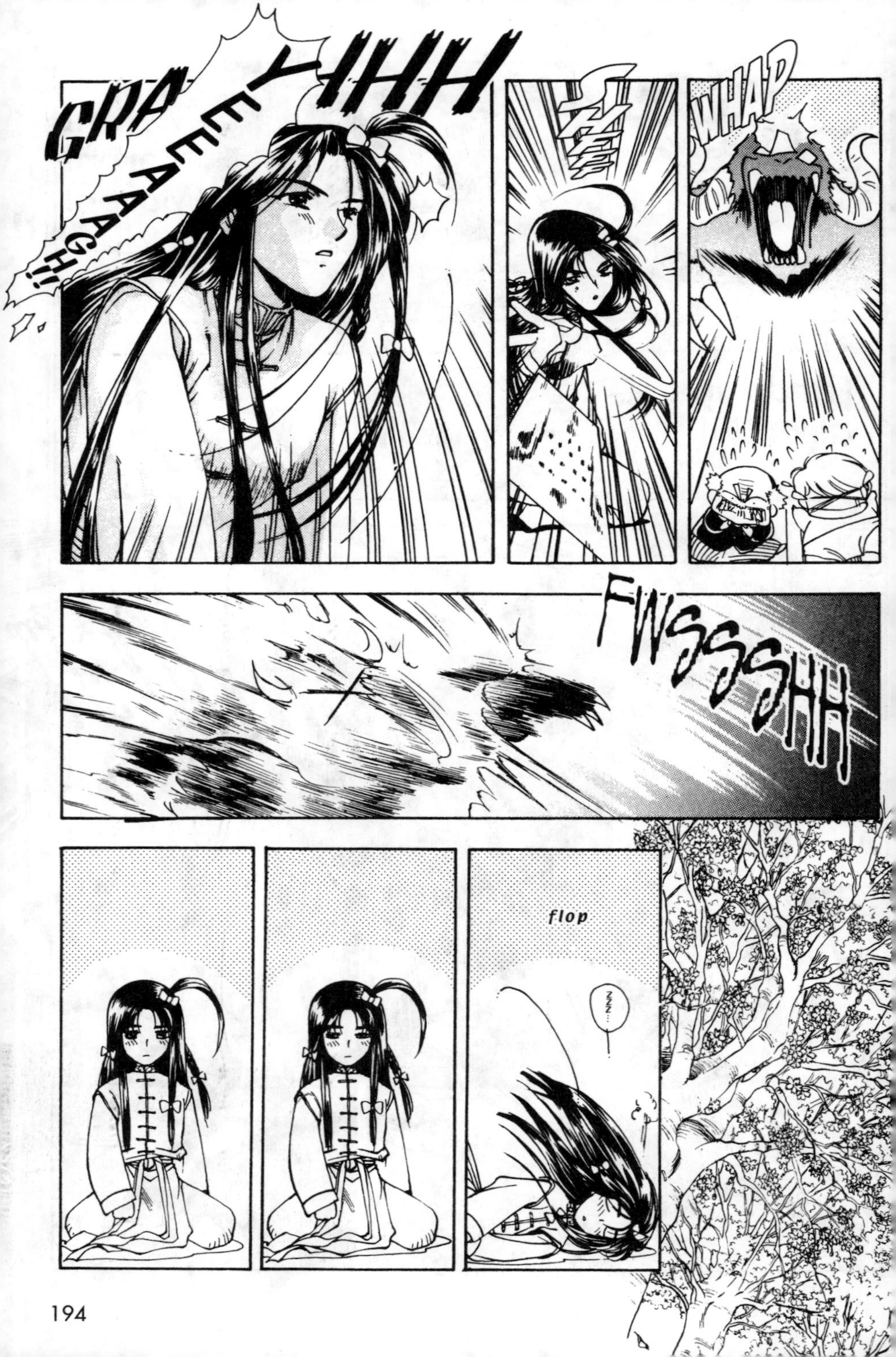
WHAP
SHEE
GRAYIHHH
EEAAAGH!!
FWSSSHH
flop
ZZZ....

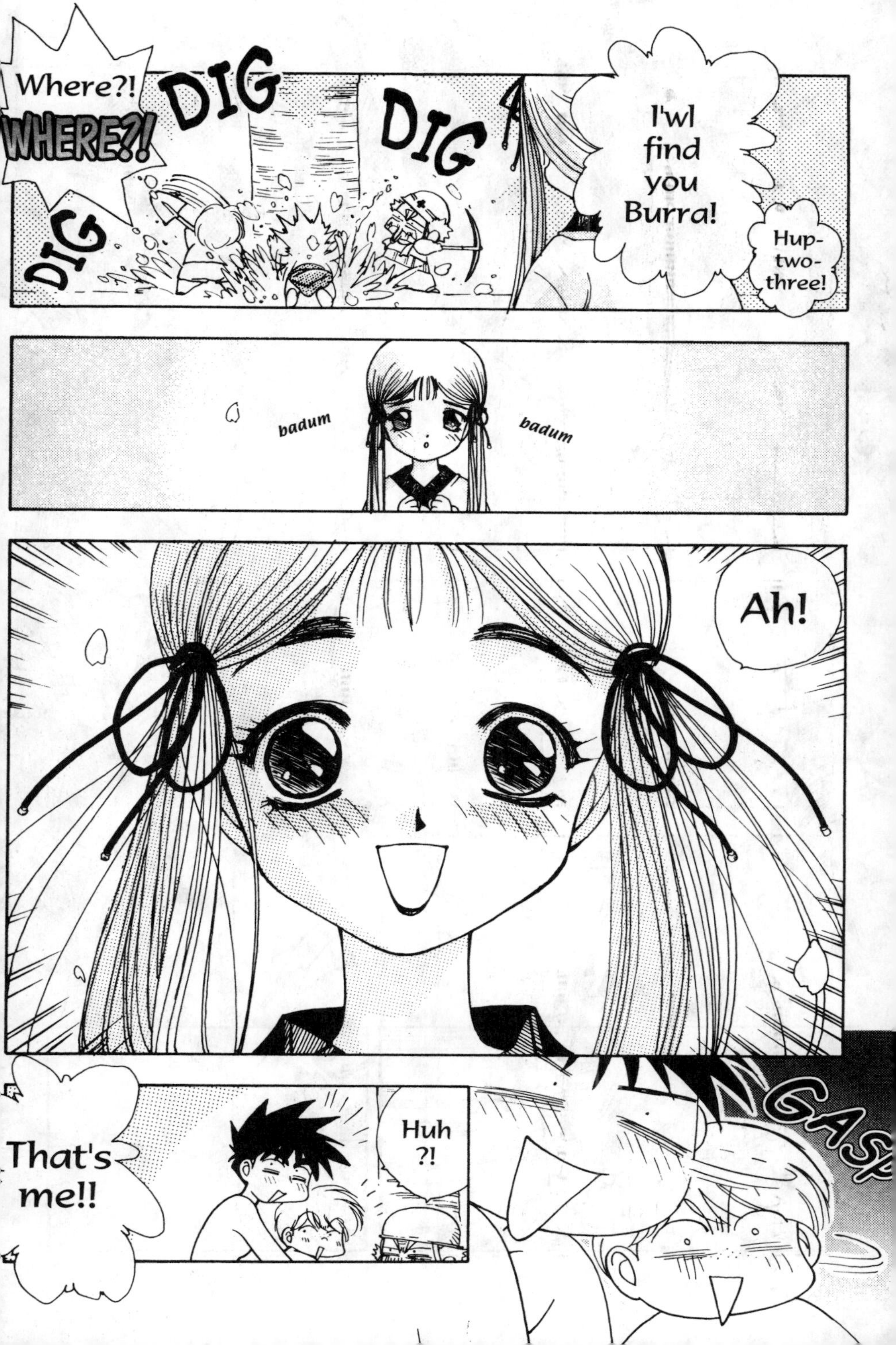
I'wl find you Burra!
Hup-two-three!
DIG
DIG
Where?! WHERE?!
DIG
badum
badum
Ah!
GASP
Huh ?!
That's me!!

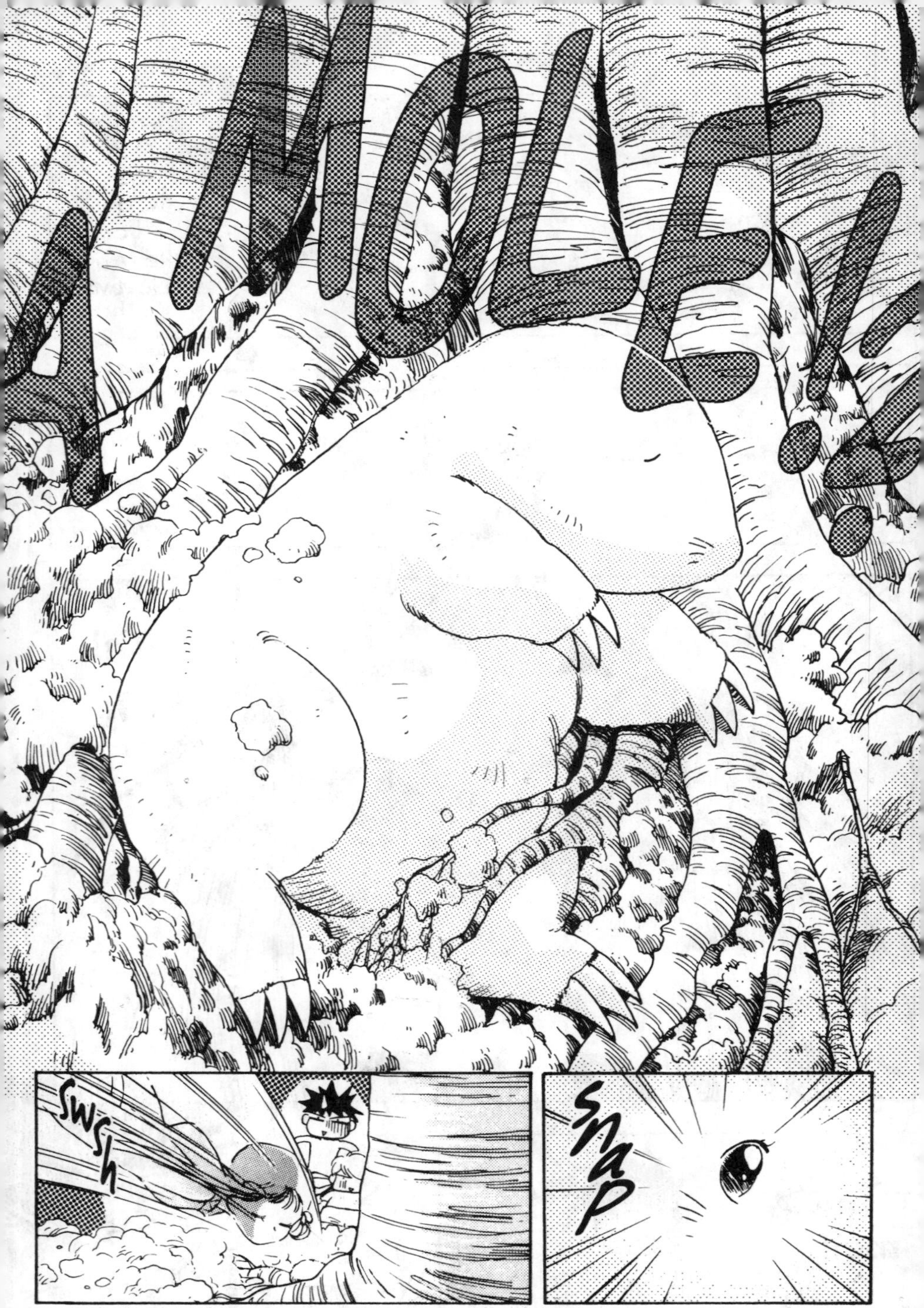
A MOLE!!?
snap
SWSH

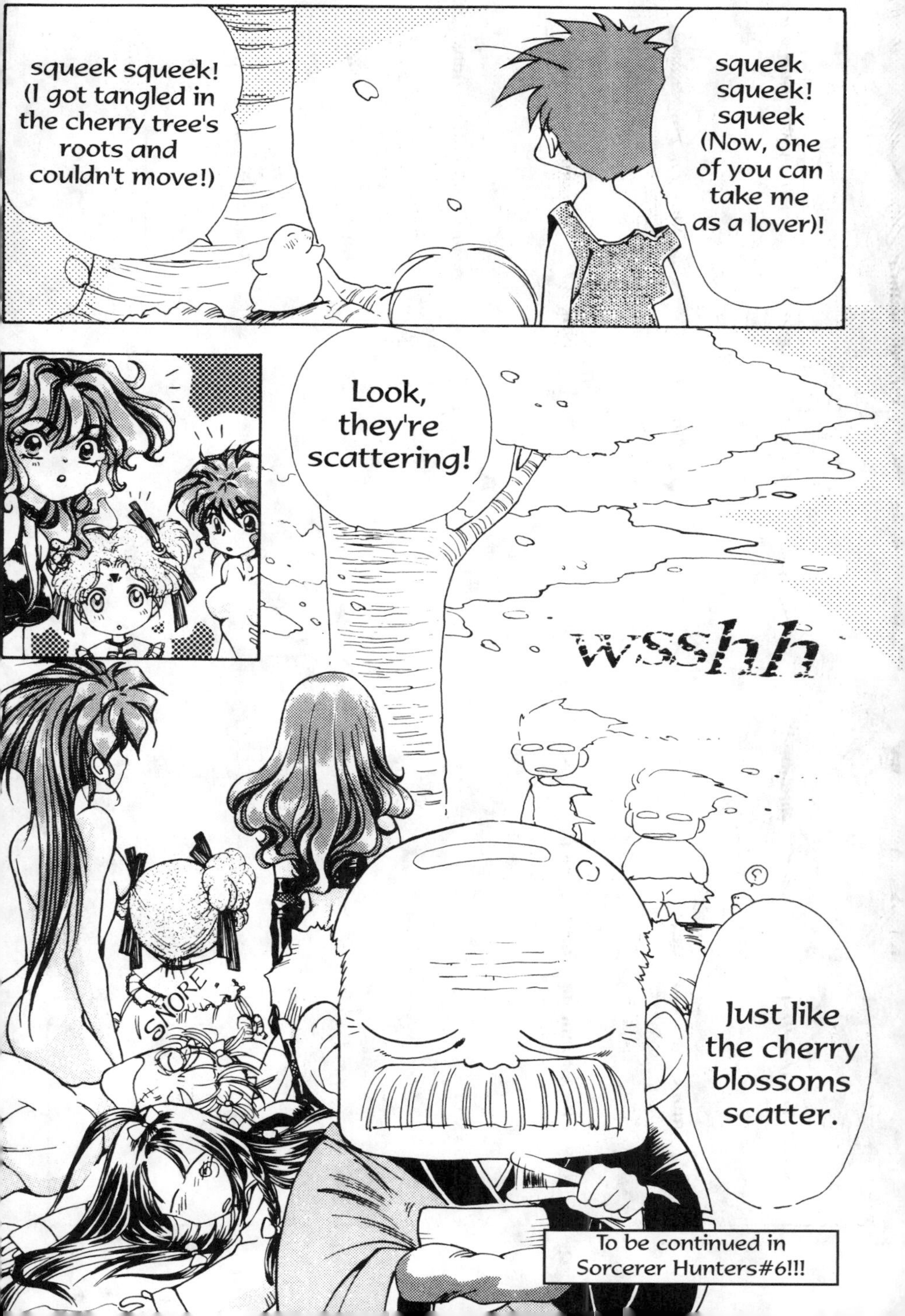
squeek squeek! squeek (Now, one of you can take me as a lover)!
squeek squeek! (I got tangled in the cherry tree's roots and couldn't move!)
Look, they're scattering!
wsshh
Just like the cherry blossoms scatter.
SNORE
To be continued in Sorcerer Hunters#6!!!

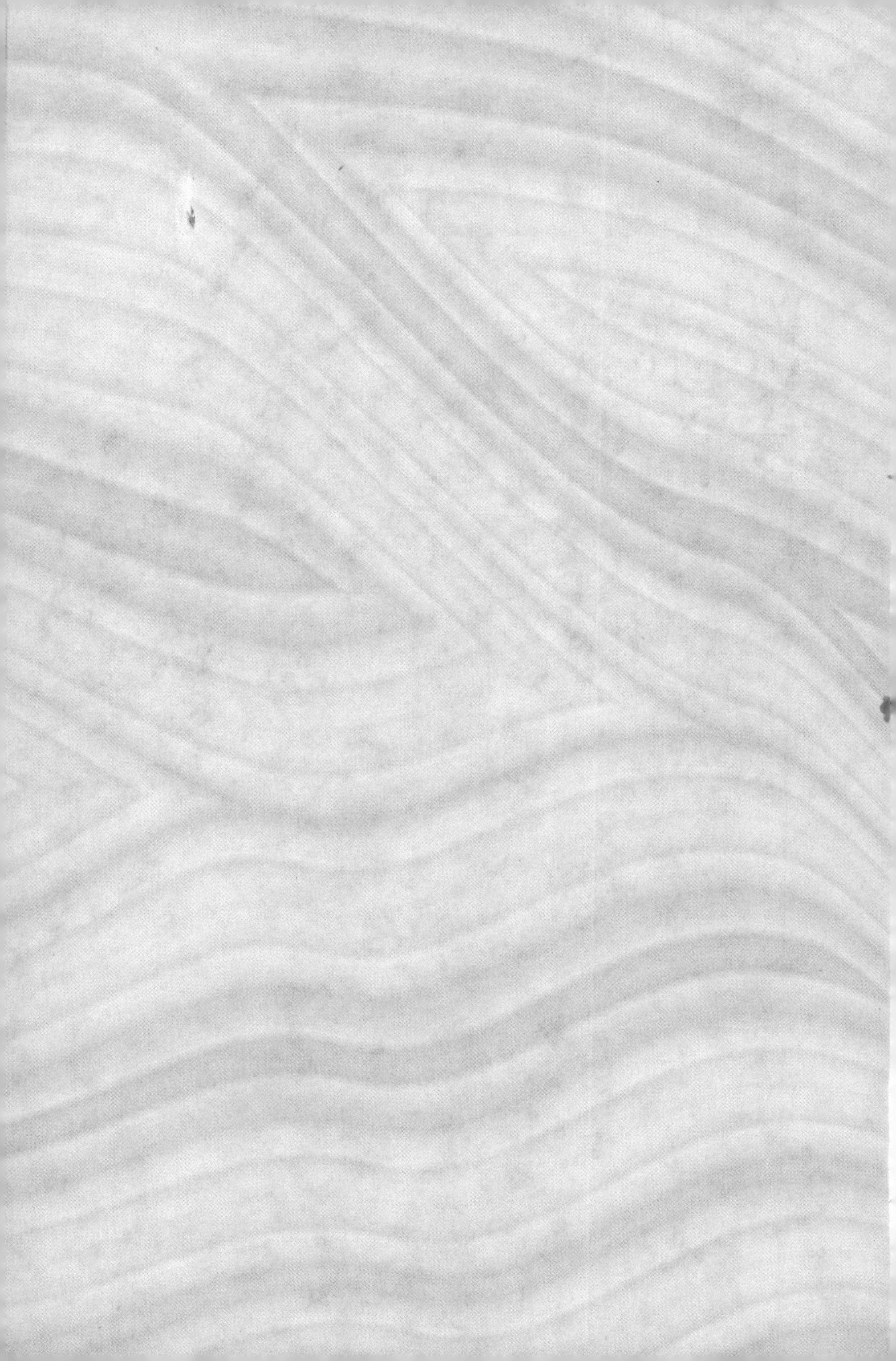

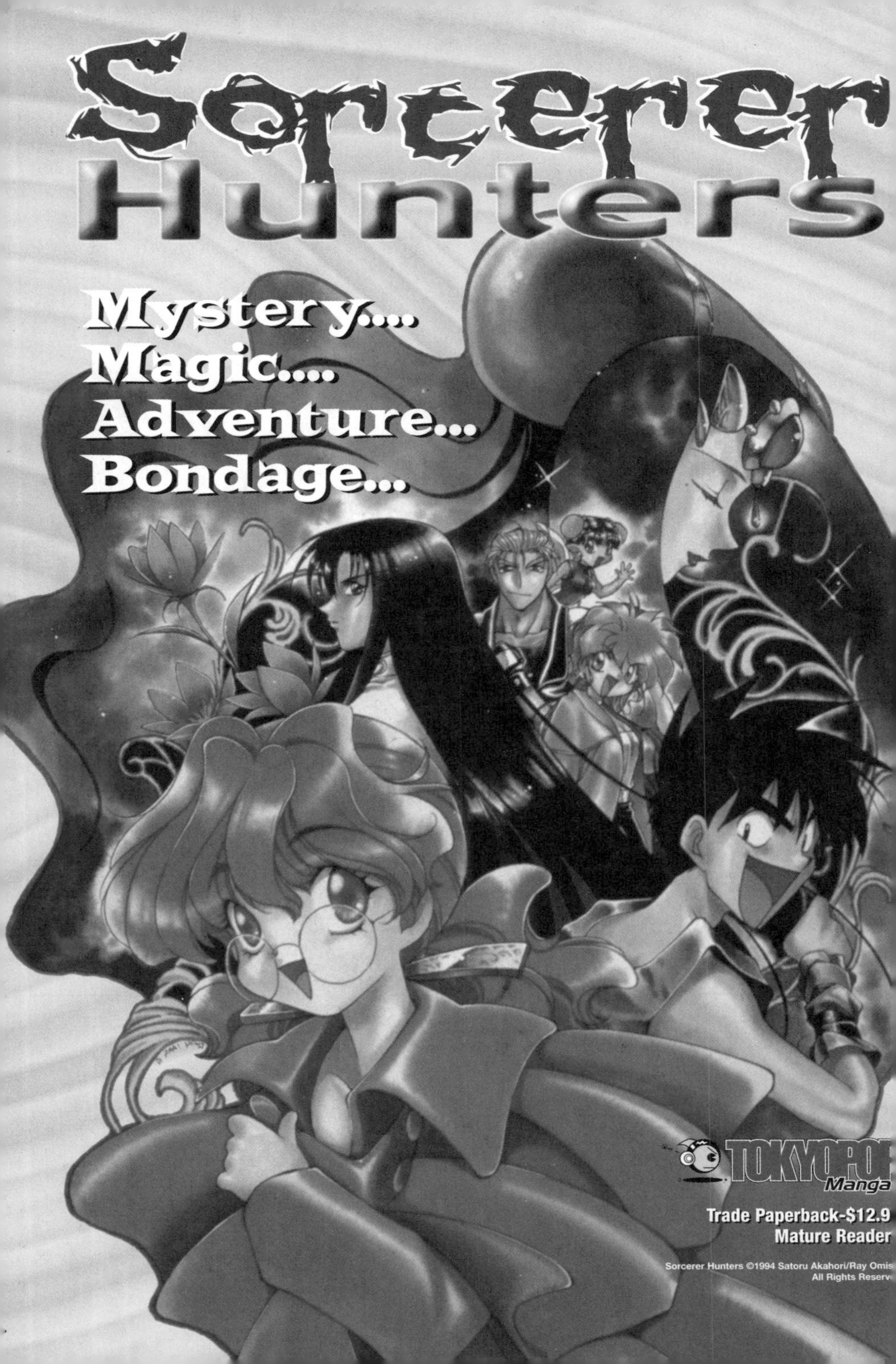

Sorcerer Hunters
Mystery....
Magic....
Adventure...
Bondage...
TOKYOPOP
Manga
Trade Paperback-$12.9
Mature Reader
Sorcerer Hunters ©1994 Satoru Akahori/Ray Omis
All Rights Reserv